DEATH BY MIRACLE

Fowler Brown

The Lethe Archive: Book One

fowlerbrown.com

COPYRIGHT

Contents

For Meg, without whose patience and support the Conclave would never have been founded.

CHAPTER ONE

Two suspects had gone for their guns. One of them lay dead on the floor. The other howled and spat curses as the police disarmed him, his skin and clothes still smoking where a godborn officer had struck him with a lightning bolt.

Sophia scanned the room for threats as other officers cuffed the suspects who'd been wise enough to surrender. Her pulse was pounding, her vision narrowed. Her ears rang from the gunshots and crackling thaumaturgy, the fractal afterimage of the lightning still floating before her eyes.

But there weren't any threats left to find. "Clear!" an officer shouted, rounding the back of the van parked in the corner. Similar calls echoed from the other rooms.

Sophia let out a long breath as she holstered her gun. Slowly, the adrenaline began to fade, and she actually had a chance to take in the room. It was a garage, more industrial than the somber, customer-facing front of the embalmer's office. Instead of bodies, though, the company van was loaded with weaponry, with more waiting on tables and in crates nearby. This place had been built for the cold business of death, but somehow, she doubted gun trafficking was what its designers had had in mind.

"All right, people, you know the drill!" Sophia called out. "Get that man to an ambulance. Secure the other suspects, cordon off the building, and touch nothing you don't have to. Hashet, I swear to all the gods, if you walk through that blood spatter, this will be your last crime scene." She headed for the van in the back corner and the crates stacked around it.

Let's see what we've got, she thought to herself.

The raid had gone by the book. Their entry had been quick and stunning, turning what could have been a deadly firefight into a few seconds of violence. No officers had been hurt, and they'd found more evidence than expected. The captain would tell her that she should be proud.

But as she crossed the room, all she felt was disgust. A row of wheeled stretchers stood along the wall, holding reminders that she hadn't gotten there in time: a horned man whose chest was a ragged mess of bullet holes. A woman with deep blue skin, probably part frost giant, with a precise slash across her throat. Two humans who'd gotten the business end of a shotgun. One had been partially prepared for mummification, but the thick odor of embalming fluid wasn't strong enough to completely cover the stench of death.

Sophia paused by the stretchers. No surprise finding corpses at an embalmer's, but normally they hadn't been killed by the employees. Were they the bodies of rivals? Victims of a deal gone bad? Hapless civilians who'd been in the wrong place at the wrong time? Hopefully forensics would give them some answers.

"Looks like they were doing more than just running guns." Her partner's voice brought her to a halt, and she waited for him to catch up. He stopped next to her and took in the bodies. "Damn shame."

Kofi Asena's gun, sword, and detective's badge were twins to her own, and his skin was just as dark as Sophia's, but that was where their similarities ended. His features were uncannily perfect, as if sculpted from pure imagination instead of crude matter, and neither the heat nor the raid had left a single hair out of place.

He liked to say that his looks were the only thing his grandmother, a nymph, had ever given him, but even the most distant divine ancestry would have been enough to make him a godborn, with the ability to work his inborn divine power into miracles.

"We should have thought of this sooner," Sophia said. "An embalmer's office was a great cover. And it gave them the perfect way to get rid of their enemies."

Kofi massaged his upper arm, the site of an old bullet wound, the way he always did when he was contemplating mortality. "We moved as soon as your informant tipped us off. Don't beat yourself up over a win."

A win. There were no pure, perfect victories, but looking at the bodies of the people she'd been too late to save, it was hard to feel triumphant. With the last of the adrenaline draining out of her, mostly she just felt exhausted.

Kofi clapped her on the shoulder and jerked his head toward the loading dock at the back of the garage. "Let's check out our haul."

They'd caught the suspects with enough equipment to outfit a small army. Pistols covered a table in the far corner of the room. Rifles and shotguns rested against the wall nearby, or leaned against crates packed with ammunition. The van parked in their midst had *Royal Funeral Services* printed on the doors in somber hieroglyphs, but it held no bodies. Just the real prize: a small collection of blades that shimmered with energy. Human criminals paid a premium for power they couldn't wield naturally, and with deadly miracles woven into the steel by godborn weaponsmiths, these blades were worth more than all the rest combined.

"'Service fit for a Pharaoh' indeed," Kofi said, chuckling at the slogan on the side of the van.

Sophia rubbed at her forehead. "How long have we been doing this, Kofi?"

He glanced at her, thoughtful. "We kept a lot of guns off the street. Caught the assholes who killed those people on the stretchers. Kept them from killing more."

That was true, but Sophia found her gaze drifting past him, across the guns. They'd stopped these, but more weapons would find their way into Memphis. More killers would take the place of the ones they'd caught. More bodies would be fished out of the Nile.

The gang war on the south side of the city was older than she was, and one raid wasn't going to stop it.

Kofi knew her too well for her look of professional detachment to fool him. "We're finally making a dent," he said. "It's hard for them to keep murdering each other if we've cut off the supply of weapons."

"It's one garage full of guns."

He grinned. "Actually, it's more than that. Follow me."

He led her back across the room, to where uniformed officers were securing the last of the suspects. "Him," Kofi said, nodding toward a weaselly man cringing against the wall. "Allow me to introduce my new friend, Amarat Benesu."

Amarat's clothes were soaked with sweat, like he'd just come from a jog in the sun, and he was chewing his nails ferociously. He held out his cuffed hands as he saw them approaching. "Please, you have to get me out of here! These people… You don't know what they've done!"

"We've got a pretty good idea," Sophia said dryly.

Kofi gestured at Sophia with an amicable smile on his face. "This is Detective Akerele, my partner. Why don't you tell her what you told me?"

"You don't understand, I can't—"

Sophia leaned in close and plucked at Amarat's shirt, making him flinch. The sweat-stained fabric was stamped with the logo of the Centurions, the Roman mortal-league pitz team. Originally Maya, pitz had been the most popular sport in the world for more than a century and a half. The Romans hadn't fielded a successful team in all that time.

"I can see you have a history of picking the losing side," Sophia said. "Now's your chance to correct that mistake."

Amarat's eyes darted to the other men and women cuffed nearby, and she could see the fight drain out of him. He lowered his voice to a whisper. "I can tell you whatever you want to know. Details. Plans. Who's supplying the guns. Just promise you'll keep me safe!"

Sophia traded a look with Kofi, eyebrows raised. He smiled.

She patted Amarat on the shoulder. "You'll be just fine. Give us a minute." She pulled Kofi away. "This is either a trap, or it's bullshit."

He shrugged, smile never wavering. "You should have heard what he was saying when I grabbed him. This could be the break we've been looking for."

Sophia narrowed her eyes at him. "Did he admit to taking money from the Celts?" *That* would be a major coup for the police department, something more impactful than a simple bust. The Celtic government funneled money and resources to criminals throughout the Conclave—anything to undermine their enemies—but their agents were rarely caught at it.

"No. Think closer to home."

Sophia sighed. "I'm really not in the mood for your…" She trailed off, frowning. "Setesh?"

Kofi grinned. "Like I said. This could be huge."

Sophia scoffed. "You can't be serious."

"Why not? Just because there aren't desert spirits running this place? You *know* he's behind this."

"Sure. This and every other arms deal and drug sale in Memphis. But that's not the same as proving it. He's been at this for centuries. Styx, we'd have a better chance nailing down the Celts."

"What if this is the break we need?"

Sophia could see the eagerness in his eyes, the dream of being the one to finally tear the facade of legitimacy from the Egyptian god of the desert. It would be the Furies making the actual arrest, of course—no one would send simple police after a god—but the officers who cracked the case would never be forgotten.

She remembered what that righteous zeal felt like. It was a mystery to her how Kofi kept his optimism alive, when he'd been in the force as long as she had. She wasn't sure whether to feel jealous or sorry for him.

And yet, despite years of experience warning her off, she couldn't help but feel a tiny spark of possibility ignite inside her. So little of what they did made a difference. But this...

A smile found its way onto her face. "Okay. You could be right. Just don't get overconfident. Take this slow, do it right, and we'll see where it leads us. We can— Hang on." Her phone was buzzing in her pocket. She slipped it out, expecting the station.

A torrent of emotion washed through her before she'd fully registered the name displayed on the screen. Fear and worry came first, followed by an undercurrent of rage. Kofi backed off, eyebrows raised. "I'll give you a minute," he said. Sophia realized her jaw was aching, and she forced herself to unclench it.

She answered the call. "Gahiji. What's wrong?" He wouldn't call without a reason. Her heart thundered in her ears as her imagination spun possibility after awful possibility.

There was a nervous chuckle on the other end of the line. "Am I not allowed to call my sister unless something's wrong?"

Fear boiled away before the heat of her anger. Even Gahiji wouldn't be flippant in a real emergency. "As if you've ever cared what's allowed."

He scoffed, and she knew exactly the face he wore, all hurt indignation, as if nothing was his fault. "Excuse me for reaching out. I'm trying to mend fences, and somehow *I'm* the bad guy?"

A uniformed officer Sophia knew gave her a worried look and mouthed, "Everything all right?"

Sophia managed a tight smile and a nod before leaving the garage and heading for the front of the building, where she wouldn't be underfoot or overheard.

"You're the bad guy because you're a *criminal*, Gahiji!" she hissed, keeping her voice low. "Styx, what kind of example are you setting for your daughter?"

Gahiji just sighed into the phone. She could picture him, all false innocence and pleading eyes as he tried to pick the right lie. He was probably getting ready whine again that all the good jobs were going to godborn.

The front office of the embalmer's was hot, dirty, and unwelcoming.

6

Probably to encourage law-abiding customers to find another place to handle their dead. It didn't help that the front doors were swinging open every few seconds, admitting gusts of summer heat as officers and EMTs went in and out. There was a radio on the front desk, ignored during the raid, with a news show still chattering away about Poseidon and Mazu's joint campaign against ocean pollution. Sophia shut it off and parked herself in a corner, by a window that looked out on the street.

"I'm clean, Sophia," Gahiji said finally. "On the straight and narrow."

"Oh really? So you weren't caught with stolen property a month ago? You aren't redoing your garage with money you make as a *fence*?" He tried to talk, but she kept going, speaking right over him. "Maybe I'm just imagining the phone calls I get from Teshan asking where you are some nights."

She heard Gahiji swallow. "She misses you."

Guilt took root in her heart, just as he intended, but Sophia forced it away with a growl. "Don't play that card. Sometimes I think I talk to your daughter more than you do."

"Let me put her on, then. If—"

"Oh no, you don't get out of this that easily. *You* called me for a reason. What is it?"

Another sigh. "I wanted to invite you over. Dinner tomorrow night, with me and Teshan. Meret too, if she's not busy at the shelter. I want to show you how things have changed. I'm trying to be a better father."

"Yeah? Is that you talking, or did Meret write you a script?"

Gahiji chuckled. "Why don't you ask Teshan?"

"Hey, no—" But he was already gone, shouting for his daughter.

Sophia's breath hissed out through her teeth, and she glared out the window. The sunset painted Memphis in shades of brilliant orange. In the distance, she could just make out the tops of the government center's ancient monuments basking in the light, framed by the massive skyscrapers of the last century. A handful of winged godborn soared through the sun-soaked air, the envy of the earthbound commuters trapped in rush-hour traffic below. Godborn and airplanes alike gave wide berth to the weather control towers that had been built around the circumference of the city in the last few years. Inside, crews of everyday humans without a trace of divine power could alter the weather with a few keystrokes. Just the latest marvel of modern thaumatechnology.

But the neighborhood around Sophia lacked both ancient grandeur and modern wealth. She had grown up in the Boneyard, and thirty years had changed exactly nothing. The streets outside were still cracked and dirty, and a familiar eye could pick out knotted black scars, built over but never truly repaired, from the dragonfire that had begun the district's rapid decline. The lights from the squad cars danced across graffiti and sun-bleached ads for cheap divorces and cheaper beer. A handful of people gawked, but most hurried past the crime scene with their heads down, barely risking nervous glances. The liveliest business in sight was the convenience store on the corner.

"Aunt Sophia?"

Just hearing Teshan's voice was enough to warm Sophia's heart. And to send a tendril of guilt coiling through her. Her free hand found the multicolored cloth bracelet Teshan had woven for her years ago and began slowly turning it around her wrist.

"Hey Whirlwind. How's it going?"

The old nickname would normally earn her an eye roll, but she could hear the smile on Teshan's face when she responded. "Okay. You coming to dad's dinner thing?"

"I don't know yet."

"You can bring your boyfriend if you want backup," Teshan said hopefully.

"Yeah... We broke up. Just weren't right for each other, I guess."

"That's what you said about the woman before him."

Sophia winced. This relationship had been as short lived as the rest. He'd accused her of losing interest as soon as the mystery faded. It was a familiar, tired refrain.

She cleared her throat. "Seriously, though, backup aside, there's a lot going on at work..."

Teshan snorted. "You don't have to lie to me. I've known how you and dad feel about each other since I was like eight."

"No lie. The job's crazy right now. Lots of big cases, not enough leads."

"Whatever. It doesn't matter. It's just dinner."

The hurt in her voice made Sophia cringe. "You know what? I'll be there."

"Yeah, okay." She'd sunk back into sullen teenager mode.

"I'm serious, Teshan. I'd love to see you."

"Uh huh. Hope you solve your case or whatever."

"Teshan—"

She'd already hung up. Sophia ran a hand through her hair. Outside, someone hitched their gryphon between two cars and headed into the corner store. Unusual, in a neighborhood like this. Then again, car thieves just had to deal with locked doors and alarms. Anyone who wanted to steal a gryphon had a razor-sharp beak and a nasty set of claws to deal with.

The gryphon folded its wings. Then it twisted its eagle's head to inspect the cramped parking space, scratched at its neck with a lion paw, and let out a frustrated cry.

"I know what you mean," Sophia grumbled.

Gahiji fought dirty, like always. Maybe if he worried more about being a good father to Teshan and less about how to use her to guilt trip Sophia… She realized she had a death grip on her phone. Shoving it into her pocket, she turned away from the window and glared through the dusty collection of pamphlets on the front desk. Most featured picturesque scenes from the Duat and the Field of Reeds, but there were a scattering of advertisements for other afterlives, from Hades to Irkalla.

Sophia barely saw them. She was tired of this case, tired of fighting with her brother, tired of working herself to the bone just to see more killers pop up like hydra heads to take the places of the ones she put away. She just wanted to go home and spend some time with a cold beer and her sketchbook.

But it wasn't fair to take all of that out on Teshan. Sullen teenager or not, the girl was right. However busy she was, however she felt about Gahiji, Sophia should be there for *her*. If she wrapped this scene up quickly, she might have time to run to the store and make Teshan's favorite pie before tomorrow night. It was the best peace offering she could think of.

She turned and headed back into the garage.

The last few suspects were being marched toward the doors. Forensics had arrived to process the scene, and they had opened the garage door in the back so they could get at all sides of the van. Kofi still stood by the wall, talking quietly to Amarat.

Sophia stepped around Kofi, seized Amarat by the shirt, and pressed him against the wall. "Setesh. Talk. Now."

He winced, sputtering. "I don't know—"

"You were happy to talk to my partner here. As long as we kept you safe, right? Well, you're safe. Most of your friends are cuffed. The rest..." She glanced at the bloodstains left behind by the suspect who'd been shot. "Well, let's hope that he picked an afterlife already, or he's got a lot of paperwork ahead of him."

Amarat held up his hands pleadingly. "You don't understand! It's not them I'm worried about."

"Good. You *should* be worried about buying yourself some leniency. Because the way things stand, it's not looking good for you. I count four victims and a *lot* of guns over there, and those are just the ones in this room."

He gave her a plaintive look, the same one Gahiji wore when he was begging for a favor. It made her blood boil. "Please, I'm not one of them!" Amarat said. "A friend brought me on for this one job, okay? Thought I could make some quick money!"

"I'm not hearing anything that will put Setesh behind bars. Are you?" she asked Kofi.

Amarat shivered. "Don't you get it? The way these guys talked about the boss, it was like—"

Amarat jerked back against the wall, almost tearing free from Sophia's grip. The front of his head exploded, spraying her and Kofi with gore.

Only then, an instant later, did the deafening *crack* of a gunshot register in her ears.

CHAPTER TWO

Amarat crumpled to the ground, twitching. Sophia whirled and went for her gun. Her eyes swept past the forensic techs diving for cover. Past the weapon-laden van, to the open garage door.

A figure stood silhouetted against the twilight, holding a pistol.

He turned, crouched low, and leapt straight onto the roof of the building.

Shouts filled the garage, echoing off bare walls.

"Godborn!"

"Shots fired!"

"Suspect is on the roof! Where's he going?"

"North! Still on the rooftops!"

"How'd he get past the police line?"

Kofi sprinted for the garage door. He couldn't vault onto the roof in a single bound, but his divine blood made him fast. He might be able to catch up. Maybe.

The other godborn officers ran after Kofi. They had strength and miracles of their own, hopefully a match for the killer's. But the suspect already had a head start.

Sophia looked around, mind racing. Her gun would barely scratch a godborn, and she wasn't confident she could get close enough to use her standard-issue miracled sword... There! She holstered her pistol and snatched up an energy-wreathed javelin from the pile of weapons they'd confiscated.

Then she turned her back on the garage door and ran for the front of the building. She had a weapon; now she needed a way to close the gap. She wouldn't be able to outrun a godborn who could leap ten feet in the air, not in a flat-out chase. There had to be another option.

She exploded out of the front doors of the embalmer's, nearly bowling over another officer who was shouting into his radio. She spun past him and was off again as soon as she got her bearings. North, toward downtown. In the distance, she saw a figure vault the gap between two buildings. Kofi and the other godborn officers were still on the roof of the embalmer's office, running with blades drawn. They were going to lose him.

An insane idea floated through Sophia's head, and she seized it before she could have second thoughts. She couldn't outrun a godborn, and she couldn't leap onto rooftops from the street.

But with some help, she might be able to fly.

Tearing after the suspect, feet pounding across the crooked sidewalk, she crossed the street before she'd left the bounds of the crime scene. A parked squad car blocked her path, and she slid across the hood and ducked under the caution tape, barely slowing.

"Memphis police! Out of the way!"

A middle-aged couple staggered back through their front door as she raced past. A teenager with headphones, oblivious to Sophia's shouting, got shoved aside as gently as she could manage. "Hey! Bitch!" Sophia kept running without a backward glance.

The street ended in a T intersection up ahead. And in the parking lot of the convenience store on the corner, the gryphon she'd seen earlier still waited, pawing at the asphalt between two of the cars.

Above and ahead of her, the godborn murderer hurled himself over four lanes of traffic. The officers running after him slowed, dismayed.

Sophia didn't. She raced into the parking lot, dodging a car that was just pulling out. The scent of something fried ages ago and endlessly reheated joined the smell of motor oil and sun-baked pavement. The gryphon twisted around and looked at her with piercing eyes. A predator's eyes.

Sophia's heart leapt into her throat, but with the adrenaline already singing through her veins, it only took a moment to wrestle the terrified primate part of her brain under control. She slowed to a jog, holding up the hand without the javelin. "Easy, girl. Easy. I need your help."

The gryphon let out a piercing cry. She could hear its breath gusting through its nostrils, and she winced, remembering that she was facing a divine-powered carnivore while covered in another man's blood. "Steady, girl. Don't worry about the blood. Maybe with your help we can catch the asshole who did this…"

The gryphon's claws tore deep furrows into the asphalt, but it didn't snap at her as she approached.

That was good enough for Sophia. She unhitched the beast in a hurry, found the stirrup with her foot, and threw her leg over the gryphon's back.

A man came running out of the convenience store, bell jangling in his wake. "Hey!" he cried. "What the—"

"Memphis police!" Sophia roared back, brandishing the javelin. "I'm commandeering your gryphon for the duration of an emergency!"

She yanked on the reins, and the gryphon twisted away from the store, breaking into a trot as she dug in her heels. "Hyah! Fly!" Gods grant that the owner hadn't trained the damn thing to only respond to commands in Latin or something…

The gryphon hurled itself into the air. The ground dropped away, and all of Sophia's instincts screamed that she was about to die.

She'd ridden an old, placid camel exactly once. This was nothing like that. The gryphon tossed its head, fighting with the reins as if it could sense that she was just mimicking the motions of riders she'd seen on TV. Each beat of its huge wings sent her stomach lurching, and every now and then it bucked and twisted, trying to throw her off.

But *Styx*, it was every bit as fast as it was unruly. She swallowed her fear and focused on keeping the gryphon pointed at the suspect's shrinking form, and the gryphon surged forward, driven by incredible musculature and natural divine power. Sophia's knuckles ached as she clutched the javelin. Each wingbeat brought her closer to the murderer. Her pulse pounded through her, warring with the deafening rush of the wind in her ears.

The gryphon swung to the left, and she almost fell out of the saddle. She yanked on the reins, turning the gryphon back on course, cursing under her breath. "Almost there, girl. Just bear with me a little longer." Gods help the suspect when she descended on him from the sky along with 1500 pounds of lion and eagle.

Kofi had been right, for once. The suspect he'd picked up must have had good intel, or there wouldn't have been any reason to kill him. The right tip about Setesh would have done more to clean up the city than the entire police department had managed in the last century.

And all of that potential had been snatched away with the single pull of a trigger. Spattering what was left of the thin, guttering dreams that had driven Sophia to join the police force all over the front of her shirt. She snarled through clenched teeth.

An airplane roared overhead, and the gryphon screeched, twisting in midair. "Easy!" Sophia patted its neck, where huge eagle feathers met lion fur. "Calm dow—"

It bucked again, and her feet came out of the stirrups.

For an instant of pure, absolute terror, the hand clutching the reins was the only contact she had with the gryphon. Dusty tenements and rattling cars loomed up at her, and she had a vision of herself splattered across the pavement as the suspect fled into the night, laughing.

Then the gryphon's nervous flapping brought the saddle slamming up into her midsection.

The air was blasted from her lungs, cutting off a scream she hadn't even realized she'd been making. She scrambled for a handhold and caught the far side of the saddle with a couple fingers, risking a dizzying glance toward the ground. Despite the gryphon's determination to throw her off, she was catching up. "Down!" she wheezed, gasping for breath.

"Descend!"

The gryphon dove. Sophia dragged herself back into the saddle. She caught a split-second glimpse of the suspect racing across the rooftop just below her. Then the gryphon spread its wings.

She barely had a moment to register the imminent landing when the gryphon's paws slammed against tile. Her mutinous mount bucked at precisely the right moment to send Sophia hurtling from its back, and then it beat its wings and threw itself back into the air with a resentful screech.

Sophia slammed into the roof, taking the hit on her back and sliding with her arm outstretched so she wouldn't impale herself with the javelin. She pulled herself to her feet, head spinning.

For the first time, she had a chance to take a good look at the suspect. He was tall, with olive skin and dirty, sweat-stained clothes. Tiny flames curled from his eyes, nose, and mouth. He shot a look, wide-eyed, at the woman who'd just fallen from the sky, but he didn't slow. He had to keep running to stay ahead of Kofi and the other godborn officers, and there was only one good way off this roof.

"Memphis police!" Sophia shouted, more breathlessly than she would have liked. She raised the javelin, and the miracle coiling around the steel tip hummed.

The suspect snarled, but he wasn't looking at her. Three construction workers crouched in his path. "Out of the way!" the suspect roared. The workers didn't move, frozen in terror amidst a scattering of their tools, right at the spot where the godborn would want to make the jump to the next rooftop. One of the workers was painfully young, not more than twenty. Barely a handful of years older than Teshan.

Sophia saw the moment when the suspect made his decision. She saw the shift in his eyes, the same careful attention she might devote to maneuvering a full cup of coffee.

Fire flared to life and pooled in his palm as he called upon his divine heritage.

She was moving before she had a chance for any conscious thought.

The suspect lifted his hand, flames rising to blast the three men out of his way. Sophia planted her foot and launched herself between the godborn and the civilians.

The two of them threw at the same time.

Her javelin buried itself in the murderer's leg, and he let out a piercing scream.

A ball of fire blasted into Sophia's torso. For an instant, there was only pain. Then the rest of her consciousness caught up, and she was tumbling wildly as she hurtled through the air. She flew over the crouching workers, past the edge of the building, and into the wall of the next one over.

She plummeted toward the ground, two stories below.

The hungry flames of the godborn's miracle chewed at her flesh. Through the agony, she could see the pavement rising up to meet her. She knew there was no way she'd survive the fall.

I'm sorry, Teshan.

CHAPTER THREE

Eight Years Earlier

Teshan flung her arms around Sophia's neck and sobbed into her shoulder. Sophia held her and let her cry. Gahiji stood awkwardly in the hall, giving his daughter an agonized look and running a hand across his shaved head.

Sophia silently gestured for him to go away. She saw the guilt in his eyes. He wanted to help, but mostly, he wanted to make up for the things he'd said. He'd make the conversation about him, and that wasn't what Teshan needed.

Mercifully, Gahiji backed out of the hall and out of sight.

"Marcus was my friend!" Teshan cried, her voice muffled by Sophia's uniform.

Sophia held her closer. "I know."

"It's not fair!"

"It's not. I'm sorry."

Sophia remembered feeling exactly the way Teshan felt, when she'd been a kid. Hugging her dad and weeping, devastated by the death of a friend. The Boneyard was the longtime battleground between Memphis's largest gangs, and it was a dangerous place to grow up. School buses usually provided some amount of safety—no one wanted to bring the police down on their heads by killing a bunch of kids—but stray bullets and errant miracles didn't discriminate.

"I hate them." Teshan's whole body shuddered with the rancor in her voice. "I hope someone—"

Sophia squeezed her niece, grimacing sadly. A child shouldn't have to know that kind of hate, but the Boneyard didn't give its children much choice.

"We're trying," Sophia said. "Me, and every other officer in the city. It's a slow, tough battle, but for people like you? Like Marcus? It's the most important thing we can do." It was conversations like this that had driven her to the police force. It was never easy, but the right thing never was.

Teshan sniffled, no longer sobbing, and Sophia felt a change ripple through the girl's body. "I want to do what you do. I want to be a police officer, so I can stop bad people."

Sophia smiled. Proud, and sad. "Maybe someday." *If your dad doesn't kill me for putting this idea in your head.*

Teshan pulled back, anger burning in her eyes. "That's what everyone says. 'You're just a kid.'"

Sophia winced and hugged her again, and Teshan didn't resist. "I know, I'm sorry. I just—"

A car door slammed shut, and Sophia twisted to glance out the window without letting go. Sure enough, Meret's car was on the street out front.

Thank all the gods.

"Your mom's here." Inspiration struck, and Sophia met Teshan's eye, frowning thoughtfully. "Why do you want to become a police officer?"

"To make things better." Tears still glistened on Teshan's cheeks, but her eyes were strong, unflinching.

Sophia squeezed her arms, proud despite herself. She remembered feeling that same pure idealism shining from Teshan's face, but these days... At its worst, her job made her feel like she was wandering through a sandstorm, unable to even see whether she was making any progress. Was that something she could wish on her niece?

Once I get my detective's badge, things will be different.

"Being a police officer isn't the only way to help people," Sophia said after a moment. "We'd have to talk to your parents, but what about volunteering at your mom's shelter?"

She watched, heart swelling, as hope swept the anger from Teshan's face. "You think I could?"

"Only one way to find out. Want me to talk to her?"

Teshan threw herself at Sophia and squeezed. "Thank you, Aunt Sophia."

"For you, Whirlwind? Any time. Give me a second to talk to your mom?"

Sophia was waiting in the hall when Meret got the door open. "Where is she?" Meret demanded. "Is she okay?"

"She wasn't hurt. Her friend Marcus..." Sophia shook her head.

Meret was short, with light brown skin and a loose puff of curly black hair. Her cheeks were streaked with tears, and her slacks had a spattering of blood across one leg. Not a good day for her, either.

Pain, anger, and guilt flashed across Meret's face before she composed herself. She offered Sophia a sad, tight smile. "Thank you for being here for her. I'm sorry I couldn't get back faster."

"You've got nothing to apologize for." Meret spent so much time at the shelter, working to make the Boneyard a little safer, a little more hopeful, that she slept there more often than she slept in her own bed. Sophia shook her head. "She's a tough kid." She glanced over her shoulder. Teshan was nowhere in sight, but that didn't mean she wasn't eavesdropping. Sophia lowered her voice. "She's a tough kid, but seeing a friend take a bullet, right in front of you..."

Meret rubbed at her face. "Gods, this city... I know a couple therapists who work with kids."

"That's a good idea. But honestly? She's feeling helpless, Meret."

A muscle twitched in Meret's face. Her fingers found the thin silver bracelet around her wrist and started to fiddle with it absently. "Every day, when I came home from school—when I couldn't find a reason to

20

be somewhere else—I walked up to that door wondering whether my father had already started throwing things. I wanted better, for Teshan."

Sophia put a hand on Meret's arm. "And you've given it to her. For all my brother's flaws, that's one thing Teshan's never had to worry about." She shook her head. "To be honest, I think it would be good for her to feel like she was *doing* something. Like volunteering at the shelter?"

Meret bristled. "It's right in the center of the Boneyard! The next block over changes hands two or three times a week! This morning part of the building caught fire because some idiot godborn couldn't aim his miracles!"

"And fucked up as it is, that's how things are *here*, too. At *home*. At least the shelter's neutral ground." Meret flinched. "Think about it? Maybe she could help in the kitchen, or sort donations. It would keep her out of trouble. Gods know Gahiji could have used something like that when we were kids."

Meret closed her eyes for a moment, taking a deep breath. "You're right. I'm sorry. Just feeling overwhelmed." She hesitated, and then pulled Sophia into a hug. "I appreciate it. Everything you do to keep Teshan safe."

Sophia chuckled. "And I'm just glad she's got *one* responsible parent."

Meret's eyes were distant when she drew back. "Gahiji's trying."

Sophia snorted. How many times had she heard that? "I have no idea what you see in him."

"I know monsters, Sophia. Your brother isn't one."

Sophia grunted.

Meret started past her. "I'm going to find Teshan. Are you staying for dinner?"

"Can't." Sophia sighed. "I need to get back."

"Making Memphis safer?"

Sophia gave her a weary smile. "Let's hope."

CHAPTER FOUR

Sophia jolted, gasping for breath. Her arm slammed into something hard, and she hissed and rubbed at her elbow. "What the Styx…"

She was sitting in a chair next to a window. Another chair, empty, faced her from a few feet away. Outside, twining bands of mist drifted past with languorous ease. Through the haze, she could just make out the tips of tall evergreen trees and the harsher lines of scattered buildings.

She blinked. Trees? Mist?

Some of the clouds lifted from her mind. She remembered the mad chase across Memphis, her brief stint as a gryphon rider… She remembered hitting the murderous godborn with the javelin, and taking a miracle to the chest in return.

Ice crept across her heart, stealing the breath from her lungs.

Her reflection, staring back at her from the window pane, looked the same as ever. Dark skin. Black hair, hanging in short twists. A thin jacket, over a button-down shirt.

She realized with a jolt of alarm that the woven bracelet Teshan had made her was missing. So was her gun. Still, she didn't look like a woman who'd been set on fire and thrown off a building.

"You're dead."

Sophia jumped. There was a woman standing in the shadowed corner, leaning against the wall with her arms folded and a resigned look on her face. She took in Sophia's expression and rolled her eyes. "Here it comes. 'I can't be dead! I don't *feel* dead! Where am I?' Seriously, the valkyries have offices in every city in the Conclave. Am I the only one who read the pamphlets?"

Sophia's jaw clenched. She knew where she was now. The two chairs and a bare, lonely table were the only furnishings in the small room. The walls were blank, the single door unmarked.

But the view through the window was unmistakable: she was in the Valkyries' Tower, the hub at the heart of the many realms of the dead. She *had* read the pamphlets, just as carefully as she'd filled out the paperwork to select an afterlife. After all, she was in a high-risk profession.

No. *Had been* in a high-risk profession.

There were no breathless questions bubbling to the surface. Just a moment of vertigo, as she half expected to plunge through the floor, before she could convince herself that she wasn't an insubstantial ghost. At least, not here. She kept herself steady by studying her new companion.

The other woman had tan skin, dark eyes, and short-cropped black hair. She wore forest camo pants, combat boots, and a black sleeveless jacket that went down to her knees, displaying her lean muscularity and an SPQR-and-anchor tattoo on the biceps of her right arm. Roman Navy? Sophia wondered how she'd come by the ragged scars criss-crossing her face.

"Well? Learn anything useful by staring at me, *detective*?" the woman asked with a tired sigh.

Sophia narrowed her eyes. She'd dealt with more than her share of scorn before. Scorn just helped her focus. "Is every valkyrie as rude as you are?"

That earned her a derisive laugh. "Oh, I'm not a valkyrie. My name is Caelistra Horatia. I'm a Fury."

Something hot and electric jolted through Sophia's heart. Eagerness? Anticipation? The last spark of a hope she'd put behind her long ago?

She could only think of one reason she'd be greeted by a Fury instead of a valkyrie after her death.

"You think I'm Fury material?"

"No."

Caelistra pulled a cigarette from a pack she kept in her pocket and started tapping the damn thing against her arm. "But someone higher up thinks that the ridiculous way you got yourself killed counts as 'heroism,' and I was due to take a recruit. So here we are. Partners. Assuming you don't back out before we start." She gave Sophia a hopeful look.

Sophia barely heard the derision. *Someone* in the Furies thought she was worthy of joining their elite ranks? *Her?* She tried to imagine herself hunting a chimera or capturing a rogue god, and her imagination failed her. The most she'd ever dared hope for was to sniff out some lead that would bring down a major player, someone like Setesh, and she'd even put *that* dream to rest in recent years. She'd always known it would be someone else who made the actual arrest. Someone from the Furies, the ones actually responsible for fulfilling the Conclave's promise that gods and humans would be held to the same laws.

"I'm in," Sophia said. She didn't have to think about it. The chance to join her grandparents in the afterlife they'd chosen, to relax on the pristine beaches of Osiris's kingdom, the chance to lay down her troubles and finally *rest*... All of that was in and out of her head in an instant, overwhelmed by an old hope she'd thought she'd abandoned. "Where do I sign up?"

Caelistra sighed and pushed herself off the wall. "Follow me."

They left the room and emerged into a massive open space at the center of the tower. The diameter was large enough to surround any skyscraper in Memphis with room to spare. At the center of the chamber was a bank of elevators, flanked by four huge stairways that stretched down into the floor and up into the ceiling. The dim felt somber rather than eerie despite playing tricks on the eyes, and Sophia had to strain to make out doors all around the circumference, similar to the one they'd come through.

Other pairs stepped out of them now and then, all cut from the same cloth: one person wearing formal attire and a comforting smile, and one person who looked as turned around as Sophia felt. Valkyries and their befuddled charges.

Caelistra pulled out a lighter and lit her cigarette, earning disgusted looks from some passing valkyries. "Got something to say?" Caelistra asked with a long, pointed pull from the cigarette. "None of us can get cancer anymore, you know." She led Sophia toward the stairs.

They joined the throng of souls making their way down, Sophia trying her best to avoid breathing cigarette fumes. "What's up there?" she asked, pointing toward the ceiling.

"Do I look like a tour guide?"

"Not really. You look like someone who'd prefer her recruit well informed."

Caelistra scoffed. "I don't want to *have* a recruit." She took another drag from her cigarette, glanced at Sophia, and sighed. "Upstairs are the Deathgates. One for every major city in the Conclave, and a few other places besides. Since we can get back here at will, they're the easiest way for Furies to get around. You'll be taking them all over the place. If you last that long."

Light spilled across the stairs as they descended into the next chamber, in contrast to the gloom they'd just left behind. The first thing that Sophia noticed was a large desk off to one side, staffed by teams of valkyries answering questions from anyone who approached. A huge map of the Earth stood behind the desk, flanked by smaller maps representing other realms of existence. Points of light stood out from the maps, varying wildly in brightness and density. Brilliant clusters stood out around the Conclave's largest cities: Kumasi, Èkó, and Memphis burned like spotlights on Africa's surface, rivaled by Athens, Rome, and Oslo to the north and Mumbai, Kyoto and Xi'an to the east. Babylon blazed like the sun, proud and unequaled, while Atlantis shone strong from the depths of the sea. Smaller lights speckled the Conclave like stars.

Regions outside Conclave jurisdiction were far dimmer, but none approached the swath of darkness that was the Celtic Union clawing its way through northwestern Europe. Or, across the Atlantic in Amazonia, the brutal dominion of the Aztec League, poised on the map like the maw of a great beast. Faintly lit independent nations formed a broad belt between the Aztecs and the bright spots of Lakota cities, which stood proud despite their isolation as the only Conclave territory anywhere in the continent.

Above the map, a digital readout said, "Proudly serving 4,953,282,647 souls and counting since 2663 AUC." Sophia's eyes saw the words in familiar hieroglyphs, but if people from all over the world were reading it, the sign had to be printed in Immortal. *Gods, that many have lived and died since the founding of the Conclave?* Sophia thought. The number ticked upward as she watched, one or two per second.

Another display, slightly smaller, showed the current time, Babylon Standard, and the date: July 14th, 2772 *ab urbe condita.* Another time, with different company, Sophia might have made the standard joke about how ridiculous it was for the Conclave to number their years from the founding of Rome, the alliance's smallest member-nation.

Instead, surprise brought her up short in the middle of the stairs as she took in the date. "I've been dead for a *month?*"

"It takes time for the soul to find its way here." Caelistra seemed content to stand in the way, ignoring the people who shot her irritated looks as they maneuvered around her.

All the pieces of Sophia's situation that she'd been desperately avoided came crashing down on her. A month. Kofi and the rest of the station would have held a memorial. Her family would have held another. Teshan would have mourned her. Her father would be heartbroken, fifteen years of recrimination notwithstanding. Gahiji had probably packed up her things.

Caelistra glanced at her expectantly, and a small, satisfied smile tugged at her lips. It was that smile that got Sophia moving. She wasn't about to give Caelistra the satisfaction of seeing her falter.

This floor had no rooms between the stairs and the tower walls. Just floor-to-ceiling windows encircling the chamber, offering a tremendous view of the twining mists.

And beyond, the hints of distant, diverse landscapes.

Caelistra must have seen the curiosity furrowing Sophia's brow as they reached the landing, because she nodded toward the window. "Go on. Take a look."

It was easy enough to stay with the crowd as countless other dead souls flooded toward the edges of the room. Sophia found herself staring at the otherworldly vista, and it took her some time to realize that she wasn't breathing. Of course. Breathing was optional, now.

Some distance below, she could make out a great stone bridge as wide as a city highway, lined with towering statues in a familiar style. She'd chosen a direction at random, but beyond the bridge, she could see hints of glittering oases, sandstone buildings, and intricately carved obelisks when the mist parted just right.

The Duat. The gateway to the ancestral afterlife of the Egyptian side of her family.

"Tempting, right?" Caelistra was by her side, leaning against the window with the cigarette smoldering between her lips. "Osiris has been making improvements for the last three thousand years, at least. He's never satisfied. Not a bad place to retire."

Sophia swallowed, looking to either side, and Caelistra misread her hesitation. "Lots of other choices, to suit any style," she continued. "You'd have to do a bunch of paperwork to switch afterlives now, but it might be worth it. Irkalla's popular, obviously. Yomi is wonderful if you like the ocean. There's the Reincarnation Office, of course. Asgard has an application process, but you did die in combat, technically, so Odin might take you..."

She pointed out option after option, each joined to the Tower by a stone bridge. Sophia quickly stopped listening. She could admire Yomi's grand mountains and sun-swathed beaches, or the hints of Valhalla's golden roof peeking through the mists in Asgard, but they held no more temptation than the Duat.

There was a longing in Sophia's heart, but it wasn't for the afterlife.

She realized that Caelistra had stopped and was looking at her expectantly. Sophia shook her head. "You're not getting rid of me that easily."

Caelistra sighed and looked disappointed. "Oh well. Worth a try." She pushed through the dead and headed back to the stairs. "Just two floors down, then. Fury HQ is in Hades."

The bridge to the Greco-Roman underworld was lined with sculptures: gods and ancient heroes that Sophia recognized from the history books, mostly, but also some famous mortal artists and politicians from more recent times. Curious, she leaned over the edge and looked down. Beside the vague suggestions of other, lower bridges, all she saw was swirling mist and the looming bulk of the Valkyries' Tower. Here in this otherworldly realm, she wouldn't have been surprised if both went on forever.

Caelistra sighed impatiently. "Come on. The sooner we get you geared up, the sooner we can be done with each other."

Sophia coughed as a cloud of tobacco smoke washed over her. "Can't wait." Caelistra smiled mirthlessly and led her over the bridge.

A chime sounded when they were halfway across, and a placid voice said, "You are now entering Hades. This realm is open only to the dead and to living individuals who have received a special exemption from Persephone or Hades directly. Newly arrived residents, please follow the directions of your assigned valkyrie. Visitors from other afterlives are required to stop by the admissions desk for processing."

Sophia started toward a line that was forming to one side, but Caelistra shook her head. "Nope. This way. Unless you want to spend a few hours waiting for the ferry."

The mists parted as they stepped off the bridge, revealing an overgrown cave mouth. A large desk sat beside the entrance, where valkyries stamped paperwork and ushered the dead inside. The valkyries were from all over the Conclave, but the people in line looked almost exclusively Greek. The last time Sophia had seen so many Owls jerseys, she'd been at a pitz game, cheering as Egypt kicked their asses.

Caelistra ignored the cave completely and headed for a door off to one side. Above it, a sign read, "FURIES ONLY."

Caelistra pulled something from her belt and held it up to a small scanner. There was a beep, and the doors slid open, revealing a tunnel of rough stone. She dropped the stub of her cigarette and crushed it beneath her boot before starting inside. Sophia let out a sigh of relief. Caelistra looked at her and lit another.

A heavy silence swallowed them as the doors swung shut. Caelistra shoved her hands into the pockets of her coat and started down the tunnel, following a string of faint lights without checking to see whether Sophia was with her.

"So how does this work?" Sophia asked.

Caelistra just sighed.

"You said we'd be partners, right? Do you want a partner you can rely on, or are you just going to keep me in the dark?"

"Look," Caelistra said. "Just because you were a homicide detective doesn't mean you're ready for this. You've chased down a couple godborn criminals. You've probably seen a couple news stories about the Furies arresting some demigod, or stopping monsters from snacking on some town. That doesn't mean you have the first idea what you're in for."

"Seems like I'd be more prepared if you told me what we're doing," Sophia said. Caelistra reminded her of her first captain. He'd also been quick to predict that she'd fail. She'd found that the best revenge was to do her job with exacting professionalism.

Caelistra grunted, shifting her cigarette to the other side of her mouth. "First we go to HQ and get your contract signed. Then we get you geared up and invested with a bit of divine power, courtesy of whichever Director is least busy. After that, we get our first case. A milk run, since you're a recruit. You'll probably screw something up and get killed. I'll say some nice words at your memorial, I'll have a few days of peace, and then I'll probably get saddled with some other greenhorn." She shrugged. "Or maybe I'll get lucky, and I can get back to doing something that actually matters."

Something that actually matters. Caelistra had no idea how desperate she was for that.

"How about we assume I don't screw it up. What then?"

"Then I'm pleasantly surprised, and you get to spend the next few months undergoing the most exacting training regimen in the Conclave. There's a little ceremony, you get the full amount of divine power, Hephaestus makes you some adamant gear, and congratulations, you're a Fury. And also someone else's problem, so I guess I win either way. Hurray."

She sped up, clearly done with the conversation.

Sophia wasn't. "There's no job interview or anything?"

"Consider this first assignment your interview. You're here because of your record. And because you're a dead human without a trace of divine blood."

"Why's that important?"

"Because of the small infusion of divine power you're going to get. Think of it like a blood transfusion. A godborn's soul would reject the divine power, since it's different from their own. A living human's body would be destroyed by the process. That just leaves the dead."

"Lucky me."

Caelistra shook the ash from her cigarette. "I mean it when I say it's a *small* infusion. You need a body to interact with the living, and it'll give you that. And any amount of divine power lets you speak Immortal, which is important when a single case could take us all over the Conclave. But don't let the power go to your head." Caelistra shot her a look that managed to convey her complete lack of confidence. "You'll be stronger and faster, but no more than a minor godborn."

Caelistra misunderstood. It wasn't strength or power that set Sophia's heart racing. She'd always been most envious of a godborn's ability to speak Immortal. To never have to worry about language barriers again—to simply understand any language, and to have her own words heard in the listener's native tongue. "I'll keep that in mind."

"I doubt it."

Sophia studied her, frowning. "Why? You don't know me."

"I know your type," Caelistra said with a snort. She slipped a small disc of white plastic from her pocket and tossed it to Sophia. "Hold this."

"Why?"

"Because you don't have your badge yet, and it will stop Cerberus from eating you."

They emerged into a cavern. To their right, a line of dead souls shuffled out of another tunnel, guided by their valkyries toward the single opening in the opposite wall. To their left lay a titanic, three-headed dog.

One of Cerberus's massive eyes opened lazily and fixed on her. Sophia immediately clamped down on the instinct to turn and run.

Massive, corded muscles shifted beneath fur as Cerberus rose to his full, four-story height. His black fur blended with the shadows, but all six of his eyes shone like lanterns. His footsteps shook the ground as he padded over. All three heads, each as large as a truck, pressed in around them. It took every bit of Sophia's willpower not to tremble.

Cerberus sniffed, and the pressure almost pulled her off her feet.

Then he gave a single wag of his tail and went back to his side of the chamber, seemingly satisfied. Sophia watched incredulously as he walked in a quick circle and then lowered himself into what she now saw was an appropriately gigantic doggy bed.

"Hades must go through an incredible amount of kibble," Sophia said. She was proud that her voice didn't crack.

Caelistra rolled her eyes. "This way." Sophia let her take the lead and then surreptitiously wiped her hands on her pants.

Caelistra took the token back as soon as they were out of Cerberus's den. They reached a busy checkpoint, where the ponderous apparatus

31

of bureaucracy sorted souls into three different tunnels. Caelistra led them down the leftmost tunnel, into which the fewest—and most despondent—souls were being sorted.

They rounded a corner and emerged into a massive cavern.

In front of them loomed a huge stone statue of one of the most famous scenes in history: Zeus, Poseidon, and Hades sealing away the Titans. Behind that… Vertigo crashed over Sophia as she struggled with the scale of what she was seeing. She knew, intellectually, where the Furies were headquartered, but standing there in person was another thing entirely.

A forest of stalactites and stalagmites jutted into the air, most of them with gleaming windows cut into the sides. Thin bridges wound throughout the cavern, carrying people among the buildings, and cable cars twisted among the stalactites on the ceiling. Sophia glanced over the edge of their platform and immediately regretted it. Beneath them was a massive lake of magma, lighting the cavern from below and heating the air like the worst days of an Egyptian summer.

The city stretched as far as she could see in every direction, carved from the cavern itself. The entire thing looked uncomfortably like the glowing maw of some massive beast, ready to clamp shut and swallow them. Strange, many-winged creatures fluttered furtively from building to building as she watched. She didn't see any tormented prisoners or screaming victims—torture and any kind of eternal punishment had been abolished by Conclave law—but that did little to ease her mind. They were in Tartarus, prison city of Hades and unwilling home to many more loathsome creatures than just the Titans.

"Gods," Sophia breathed.

"You can play tourist later," Caelistra called. She was already walking, surefooted, across a thin stone bridge with only magma beneath. "Headquarters is this way."

Sophia followed. She was so focused on navigating the winding bridges that she barely realized when they reached their destination.

A stalactite as tall as Khufu's Pyramid stabbed down from the roof of the cavern, belted by a wide platform and joined to its neighbors by a series of bridges. They approached the main entrance, a large set of doors beneath the Furies' seal: a shield stamped with three feathers in a triangle around a broken sword, over the word *Unrelenting* in Immortal.

Three feathers, for the Furies. A broken sword for the peace they'd built for the Conclave, and for the fate of their enemies. Sophia was acutely aware of the tension between the two ideas.

The doors opened for Caelistra's badge. Inside, there was a large lobby of beautifully carved stone. There were a handful of other Furies inside, and except for the one behind the desk at the back, they were all hurrying about business of their own.

Caelistra waved lazily at the man behind the desk. "Got a recruit here. Need a contract and a bit of a Director's time."

"Room forty-seven," he said, without looking up from his computer. "And put that out."

Caelistra walked past with her hands in her pockets. The cigarette remained defiantly where it was.

"Thanks," Sophia said. He raised a hand in her direction and then went right back to typing.

Caelistra pushed open a door and then led her through a dizzying series of turns. She stopped outside their destination and knocked.

"Send her in," a woman's voice called.

Caelistra stepped aside and gestured with an exaggerated flourish.

Sophia gave her a wide smile. "I look forward to working with you." She opened the door and went inside before Caelistra could retort.

A bulky machine took up most of the room, stretching from beneath the floor up into the ceiling. It was all cold metal and faint, blinking lights, except where two handles extended from either side. A handful of cables were visible behind a pane of glass, surrounded by the telltale shimmer of the miracles they conducted.

On the far side of the machine stood a woman that Sophia recognized from the news. She had olive skin and short black hair. She was a head shorter than Sophia, but just as muscular.

She smiled, and a deep, primitive part of Sophia's brain quailed, transfixed by a predator's gaze. "Hello. I'm Director Tisiphone," the woman said, extending her hand.

Tisiphone's charcoal trousers and white blouse wouldn't have been out of place in a courthouse or boardroom, but the way every shadow in the room bent slightly toward her made it impossible to forget that she was a vengeance goddess as old as the world. One of the three original Furies, from back when the Furies were nothing more than three women doing what they could to punish the guilty.

If habit hadn't driven Sophia to shake Tisiphone's hand, she might have stood there blankly for the rest of time. "I'm Sophia Akerele," Sophia managed, a bit belatedly. "It's an honor to meet you."

"I'd say that my sisters and I make a point of meeting all the new recruits, but since the divine power transfer requires it, I'm afraid that wouldn't mean very much. We've been doing this for a long time, and it's developed into a bit of a ritual. Are you ready?"

Sophia nodded.

Tisiphone's expression grew solemn. "You will only receive enough power today to work the most basic of miracles, and even those will only come with training, but the divine investment process will still change the very core of what you are. Before, you were a mortal, without a trace of divinity. Now, you are a soul, bereft of matter, unable to interact with the living. After we are through with the Investiture, you will be a creature of blood and shadow, sworn to defend and uphold the Babylon Conclave and its people. Is this a responsibility you can accept?"

Sophia's heart thundered against her ribs. This was it. She'd left the Boneyard dreaming of becoming a police officer. Dreaming of fixing the neighborhood where she'd grown up. Since then, over long years as a uniformed officer and then as a detective, she'd learned the danger of having dreams. But if anyone had the opportunity to change things, it was the Furies.

"It is," she said.

There was genuine warmth in Tisiphone's smile. "Good. I owe you a final word of warning before you sign the contract and make this official. A mundane blade or bullet will do little harm to a creature of divine power, but thaumaturgy or a miracle-forged weapon will be beyond your capacity to quickly regenerate, and unlike the living, your soul is no longer separable from your body. Should you be killed, there will be no afterlife. No second chance. Just oblivion. Do you understand the risk you are accepting?"

"I do."

"Very well. In that case, you will find the standard equipment package on the table behind you. Thaumatech phone, capable of making calls across realms, thaumatech gun, miracle-forged sword… All top of the line. And your badge, of course. The dead don't need sleep, but most Furies rent rooms somewhere in Tartarus, for convenience and privacy. Your partner will teach you the basics of working miracles and anything else you need to do the job, and she should be able to help you out with anything else you might need."

Sophia bit back a skeptical reply. Caelistra, helpful?

Tisiphone held out a heavily-laden clipboard. "Your employment contract. Please sign it."

It took some time for Sophia read it; she kept finding herself going over the same paragraph again and again without registering what it meant. Finally, some time later, she signed on the highlighted lines.

Tisiphone smiled as she took the contract back and set it aside. "Excellent. Now, as you may know, every godborn has an affinity for certain types of power. We Furies have dominion over shadow, over our own lifeblood and that of our enemies. It is a piece of that essence, a piece of *my* essence, that you will be accepting into yourself. If you don't mind, please grasp the handles."

This was it. The last step before she took her first case not as a police officer, but as a Fury.

Sophia wrapped her fingers around the handles on her side of the machine, and Tisiphone smiled apologetically.

"Creating a physical body for your soul out of pure divine power is not an easy process. I'm afraid this is going to hurt."

Darkness rose from Tisiphone's skin, licking at the air like flame.

Then the entire room went black, and Sophia screamed as a million tiny needles stabbed into her palms.

CHAPTER FIVE

A few hours later, Sophia stood before a Deathgate, staring at the label printed on the stone above, sure there had been some kind of mistake.

"You didn't tell me we were headed back to Memphis."

Caelistra tapped her cigarette, idly releasing a small flurry of ash. "I thought you might appreciate the chance to show off your local expertise. I didn't know I'd need to tell you things plainly spelled out in the case file."

As if there had been any time to read it. Sophia had blacked out—to her relief—for the actual infusion of divine power, but the instant she'd awoken, Caelistra had slapped the file into her hands and started off toward the Valkyries' Tower.

Sophia took a deep breath. The Deathgate looked like a curtain of grey smoke, thin tendrils curling across the floor. Eerie, but it was the prospect of returning to the city that had been her home that filled her with dread. Not that she would let it show while Caelistra's eyes were on her.

"How does this work?"

"It's a gate. You walk through. It's really not complicated, unless you're trying to bring a living person with you or something."

"Wonderful. Shall we?"

Sophia steeled herself and strode into the smoke.

She stepped out of a hillside in Hathor's Park, smack in the center of downtown Memphis. After the placid, neutral temperature of the Tower, the Egyptian heat felt like a wave of fire. Honking horns rose over the laughter of a trio of old men playing cards at a table nearby. The clear, fresh smell of water lilies mingled with the pervasive exhaust of downtown traffic.

Home.

Caelistra emerged while Sophia was still marveling at the realization that she'd just moved between realms like it was nothing. It was disorienting, watching her step out of what looked like solid ground; on this side, miracles hid the Deathgate from sight.

"Feel that tug in the back of your mind?" Caelistra said. "That's your tie to Death. Your soul knows where it's supposed to be. Focus on that feeling, and you can get back to the Tower in a few seconds, as long as you're close enough to a Deathgate. Leave the city and you might have to hoof it back." She held up a set of car keys she'd signed out from Fury HQ, and a car at the edge of the park gave an answering beep. "That's our ride."

The car had been baking in the sun, but Caelistra didn't seem to notice the heat. She stubbed out her cigarette, climbed behind the wheel, and flipped on the lights and sirens. She was off before Sophia had finished buckling her seatbelt.

Sitting still made it difficult to focus. She knew that Tisiphone had only infused her with a scrap of divine power, but it felt like so much more. She *surged* with energy, like she could run the length of the Nile, vault to the tops of the skyscrapers around them, punch through a car door. With the power thrilling through her veins, it was a constant struggle not to *try*, just to see what she could manage.

What she could manage…

Tentatively, Sophia opened one of her hands and tried to concentrate. She could feel the divine power churning at her core, a well of black and crimson that roiled like a storm cloud. In theory, working a miracle was as simple as focusing her will on what she wanted the power to do. Plenty of godborn children did it by instinct.

She focused.

Nothing happened.

Caelistra chuckled dryly. "Looks like you're going to need some practice."

Sophia turned a challenging look on her, fighting down embarrassment. "So teach me."

She got a snide laugh in response. "Trust me, that's the last thing you want," Caelistra said. "You'll get all the training you could ever ask for—and more—once we're done with this case. And it'll be from someone who's actually good at teaching. Until then, it's my job to make sure you're never put in a position where you need to work a miracle."

Sophia knew the sour look on Caelistra's face. She wasn't going to budge.

Well, if she wasn't going to provide any actual guidance, that left only one option: to do the job, and do it well, in spite of her.

Sophia flipped open the case file in her lap. Studying it helped keep her from trying, and failing, to work more miracles. More importantly, it helped keep her eyes off the city streaming by outside. There were too many memories out there, and death had turned all of them painful.

When they arrived, though, the sight of the actual crime scene was enough to consume her attention. The media frenzy around the Memphis Convention Center was more than she was used to, but the red police tape and the flashing lights on the squad cars were familiar. Comfortable, like an old pair of shoes.

A crime scene, comfortable? Kofi would have made a snide remark about her spending too much time on the job. Gods, she hoped he was okay.

Caelistra shut off the engine and the sirens as soon as she'd pulled up to the curb. They both climbed out of the car.

Then Caelistra put a cigarette in her mouth, lit it, and tipped her head back with her eyes closed.

Sophia crossed her arms and cleared her throat. "Don't we have a job to do?"

Caelistra opened one eye. "Wrong. *You've* got a job to do. You were a homicide detective before, right? This can't be that much more complicated than a standard death by miracle. So go solve it. I'll be right behind you, just in case you royally screw up and someone starts shooting."

So that was how it was going to be. Well, at least they'd be doing things Sophia's way. "Sure. Right this way, *partner*."

If Caelistra was waiting for her to balk at the challenge, she was going to be disappointed. Sophia slipped the badge off her belt and held it up as she waded into the crowd of chattering reporters. "Conclave Furies! Move aside!"

It was like slogging through river mud, but at least they moved. A few journalists had the presence of mind to press microphones in her face and shout questions. Sophia just pushed past them, Caelistra trailing in her wake. "All questions should be referred to the Fury press office. Move aside!" It was a relief to finally duck under the police tape and leave the reporters behind, doubly so because Caelistra snuffed out her cigarette before entering the crime scene. The convention center rose ahead of them, swarming with police.

A harried-looking man with rolled-up sleeves and a completely shaved head pushed between a pair of uniformed officers to meet them. "Furies? I'm Sabu Inheru, the detective in charge."

Sophia shook his hand. "Sophia Akerele. This is my partner, Caelistra Horatia. The file we received was basically just a when and a where. You want to fill us in on what actually happened here?"

Sabu swallowed and glanced over his shoulder. "It's easier if I just show you. I've got to say, this is one crime scene I'm happy to hand over."

Sophia grimaced. That never boded well.

Caelistra fell in beside her as they climbed the stairs. "Worried about being recognized?" she asked coolly, but at least she kept her voice down.

Sophia snorted. "Downtown? Memphis has more than thirty thousand police officers, and this is nowhere near my old precinct." At least that was one thing she could worry about later.

The front doors of the convention center had seen better days. One was hanging completely off its hinges. The glass from the other was a shattered mess across the floor, mingled here and there with blood. Above the doors, a banner proudly welcomed attendees to the 20th Annual Memphis Thaumatechnology Convention in gold hieroglyphs.

Since before the Great War, industrialization had been bringing miracles to the masses, miracles that had once been the domains of jealous gods. Now, mortal and godborn innovators were working together to revolutionize agriculture, weather control, construction, manufacturing, medicine, communication… Not to mention personal gadgets and entertainment, of course.

The convention center was an enthusiastic glimpse of a bright future that had been turned into a nightmare.

Sabu led them past the debris, down a hallway that was strikingly untouched, and into the security office. "Sorry, it's a bit cramped," he said as they squeezed inside. A solemn police officer sat at the main computer alongside a nervous woman from building security. Sabu nodded to them. "Play the tape."

The video was silent, but the picture was clear. It showed one of the major exhibition halls, packed with posters, tech displays, and people. Seconds into the tape, gunmen kicked in the doors. The security guard by the entrance was gunned down before he could go for his radio. One of the perps fired into the ceiling and shouted a command. Presenters and guests scrambled over each other to get on the ground.

The killers swarmed through the room. They were disorganized, unprofessional, but they were coordinated enough that people died in their path. A woman who'd been too brave for her own good. A green-skinned godborn man who hadn't answered their questions fast enough. And three of the caterers, gods only knew why.

They didn't stop until they found what they were looking for: a terrified Indian man in a threadbare dhoti, and the glass and metal device, about the size of a pineapple, that he was clutching to his chest.

41

Sophia frowned at the video, worried. This was terrible, but there was nothing so far that the police couldn't handle. Nothing that would make this Fury business.

"There," Sabu said, leaning in close and pointing at the captive. "Watch him." The poor man trembled as he was marched to the doors, his device held tight in his arms. One of the gunmen glanced at his phone and spat what had to be a curse before gesticulating wildly with his weapon and barking an order at the hostage. The poor man protested, and took a punch to the gut for his trouble. Then, with a gun in his face, he did something to the contraption he carried and scrambled back, arms held high.

There was a flash of white, and the video turned to static.

Sabu swallowed. "Come with me and I'll show you… whatever it is. Maybe the forensics people have figured it out by now." He didn't sound confident.

He led them to the exhibition hall turned crime scene. Along the way, police officers spoke quietly to survivors. There were people from all over the Conclave among them: humans of all sorts, a handful of unfamiliar godborn, even a few merfolk who probably wished they'd stayed in Atlantis. One woman with thin silver lines glowing across her skin was arguing intently with an officer, but most of the others just sat and stared, or wept quietly.

The Furies had gotten the call while Sophia was receiving her divine investment, and the pain and shock on the faces they passed were fresh, raw. The conference had barely begun for the morning before the attack interrupted.

"It was the Dockyard Hounds," Sophia said. "They all had the snarling dog tattoos on their necks."

Sabu nodded grimly. Caelistra scratched absently at one of the scars twisting across her chin. "Some local thing?"

"The Hounds are one of the two major gangs in Memphis. Almost all humans. They've been at war with the Silver Court—smaller, but all godborn—since before I was born. This is a little outside their usual reach, though…"

Normally they just fought over the Boneyard, ruining and ending lives as they squabbled over territory. Whatever they'd taken—whoever they'd kidnapped—must have been quite the prize to be worth the risk.

"Through here," Sabu said, taking a turn. "Can't go through the main entrance." He wiped his hands on his pants. "You'll see why."

The exhibition hall was thoroughly destroyed. Blood decorated the tiled floor, human and godborn alike. Tables were smashed or overturned, and more than one piece of novel thaumatechnology leaked its miracles onto the floor, sparking erratically or freezing the air into solid ice as the police worked to contain them.

But it was the front of the room that drew Sophia's attention. One look, and she immediately understood why the Furies had been called.

The exhibition hall's main entrance was gone, a perfect sphere of floor, walls, and ceiling simply scooped away. At the edge of the sphere, tile, stone, and steel alike had been transformed into something like glass, all meandering cracks and jagged edges. Sparks of strange orange lightning crackled from point to point, and a faint shimmer, like a heat mirage, rippled slowly through the air around the sphere's circumference.

And slowly, inexorably, with a squeaky grinding noise like splitting ice, the corruption was spreading. The tiles at the edge of the radius were warping, transforming into that same glass-like material and splintering into jagged shards under the weight of the miracle.

It looked like an infection in reality itself.

"What *is* it?" Sophia breathed. Just watching it, breathing in the ozone-and-rotting-wood reek, sent a sickening dread coiling through her gut.

Sabu had paused to consult with his forensic techs, and he grimaced as he rejoined them. "In the video, the man they kidnapped had a device with him, right? Well, as best we can tell, it was a thaumatech bomb, of some kind. Or they used it as one, at least."

Sophia sighed and rubbed her forehead. "Well, at least they only had the one."

"Don't celebrate yet. The bomb wasn't destroyed in the blast. See that?" Sabu pointed to a pile of crimson-stained clothes near the blast radius, surrounded by a tremendous amount of gore and a scattering of dust. "According to the surviving witnesses, after the Hounds activated the bomb to cover their escape, they made one of the other hostages go into the blast zone and retrieve it. He made it out with the bomb." He swallowed. "And then his skin turned to sand."

"Ra's burning beak," Sophia cursed softly, eyeing the poor hostage's remains.

"As soon as the suspects had the bomb in hand, they left. Had a getaway van parked behind the building."

If the Hounds followed their usual protocol, the van would be scrap in a matter of hours. They needed to hurry. "Anything else?" Sophia asked.

"As for the blast itself..." Sabu shifted uncomfortably. "Our techs' thaumascanners are having trouble making heads or tails of it. There's definitely some kind of storm miracle involved, judging by the lightning. The contagious, spreading transformation is more complicated, but there are godborn who have the ability to alter the properties of materials that they touch, so..."

Behind Sophia, someone cleared their throat. "Excuse me? Sorry, no offense, but he has no idea what he's talking about."

It was the godborn Sophia had noted in the hall earlier. She had light brown skin, shining with a wild, irregular, almost organic tracery of spiraling silver lines. Her hair was short and black, buzzed along the sides of her head. She wore grey dress pants, a loose white blouse, and a necklace dangling with charms, all depicting phases of the moon.

Sophia narrowed her eyes. "And who are you?"

"Dr. Ixtele Tinaalto." She pointed to the name tag on her chest, where she'd hand-written a pronunciation guide in Immortal: "Eesh-tay-lay. It's Mayan."

A police officer jogged after Ixtele and flinched when he saw who she was talking to. "I'm *so* sorry, Furies. Ma'am, *please*, you can't be in here—"

Sophia held up a hand. "It's okay. We'll keep an eye on her." Sabu nodded to the officer, who hurried off, looking relieved. Sophia tapped her pen against her notepad, looking at Ixtele. "You were here for the conference?"

"Yeah. One of the presenters. I'm a professor of thaumaturgy at the University of Attica, Athens, and I specialize in affinity analysis. It's funny, I was looking forward to being back in Memphis before all this insanity started. I was here at the beginning of grad school, taking samples for a paper on the thaumaturgical variance in the waters of the Nile, and—"

"Kind of pressed for time, here," Sophia interrupted. "Is this relevant to the explosion?"

"The explosion? Right. No. Maybe? Have you ever seen Zeus's Grave?"

The rapid pivot caught Sophia off guard. "Um… No?" She knew about it, though. Zeus's death had left a city-sized circle of eastern Europe a blasted, uninhabitable wasteland for the last two thousand years. The only thing worse had been the notorious string of rapes and murders left in Zeus's wake *before* his death. Famously, Jupiter had sworn a single vow upon being chosen to ascend to Olympus as Juno's co-ruler: to never allow a repetition of Zeus's crimes.

"I've seen it," Caelistra said softly. For the first time, she actually looked like she was paying attention to the conversation.

"Are you saying a god died here?" Sophia couldn't keep the incredulity completely off her face.

Ixtele guffawed, drawing looks from all over the room. If she noticed, she didn't seem to care. "That's an interesting idea, actually. I would assume that the radius of the explosion would be proportional to the power of the god in question, but we don't have a lot of data points, do we? Maybe if it was a really tiny, weak god? I wonder… Oh. You just want the boring facts, don't you?"

"If you don't mind," Sophia said, amused.

45

Ixtele shrugged, looking disappointed rather than embarrassed. "Suit yourself. I can be boring if you want."

Sophia wasn't convinced of that, but she didn't interrupt.

Ixtele studied the blast area, drumming her fingers against her arm. "I'm very sure a god didn't die here. Well, mostly sure. Ninety nine percent sure. But the principle's basically the same, and the effects are definitely similar. So that's good news."

"I'm fairly sure it's not."

Ixtele shrugged. "I don't know. At least you should be able to contain a blast like this in your badges. You know, if the guys with the bomb try to blow it up again. You *would* have to be really close, though. So that's the bad news, I guess."

Without a word, Caelistra turned on her heel and walked toward the destruction. "Is she…" Caelistra unclipped the badge from her belt, and Ixtele's grin widened. "Ooh, would you mind if I—" She tried to scurry forward. Sabu looked alarmed, but Sophia reacted first, putting a hand firmly on her shoulder to stop her.

"Stay here, please. I don't want to have to explain to my bosses how a civilian got herself disintegrated in what was supposed to be a secure crime scene."

For just a moment, as she tried to keep Ixtele back, Sophia could feel the surging energy pressing against her fingers. Ixtele's build was more slender than Sophia's, but it wasn't muscle that Sophia felt; it was divine power, electric, *alive*. Ixtele turned a frustrated glare on her, and unless Sophia imagined it, the threads of silver across her skin flared brighter.

Sophia refused to back down. Ixtele looked surprised, then intrigued. She took a step back. "Right. Okay. I wouldn't want to get you in trouble with your bosses."

Still keeping an eye on her, Sophia glanced toward the blast zone.

Caelistra's badge, held high, had begun to attract thin arcs of orange lightning from the eerie glass.

Sophia had thought her badge was just a simple piece of metal stamped with the Furies' seal. It certainly *looked* unremarkable enough, shaped like a shield with the Furies' broken sword and feathers stamped on the middle. "Intercontinental Treaty Coalition" was engraved across the top, with "FURIES" just below and their motto, "Unrelenting," at the very bottom. But as she watched Caelistra, it suddenly felt a good deal heavier on her belt.

Zeus's Grave had driven home the need for technology to contain the blast of divine power that followed a god's death. The Furies had to be a credible threat to the gods, if they were supposed to uphold the central promise of the Conclave: legal equality, with the same laws for gods and mortals alike. But knowing that the world-changing thaumatechnology existed and realizing that she was carrying it on her belt were wildly different things.

"How do you know all these things?" she asked Ixtele.

Ixtele was craning her neck to watch Caelistra with the intensity of a starving predator. "Because it's my job?" she said distractedly. "I wrote a paper on Zeus's Grave."

It occurred to Sophia, for the first time, that she wasn't picking up any of the faint, mental echo that came when the brain translated Immortal into her own tongue. Ixtele was speaking Egyptian. Strange, for a godborn.

There was a flash of light from Caelistra, and for a bizarre instant, everything was cast in shades of grey. Sophia blinked, and the world returned to normal as Caelistra rejoined them.

"The professor's right. I soaked up some of the energy. It's not expanding anymore."

"Thank all the gods," Sabu muttered.

"Actually, it *is* still expanding," Ixtele said. "Sort of. At least, I expect it'll start up again in a few days. Your badges could have caught the initial blast, and they can siphon off the excess here, but the actual infection is worked too deeply into reality. Someone's going to have to keep doing that periodically, or it'll keep growing." Her eyes lit up with curiosity, and she tapped a finger against her lips. "Can I see your badge? With this much power soaked into it…"

Caelistra looked at her coolly. Her badge's faint orange glow was fading by the moment as she clipped it back onto her belt. "No."

"Please, Professor, is there something to contain it permanently?" Sabu said.

"What?" Ixtele pulled her eyes off Caelistra's badge before frowning at the detective. "Oh. You don't understand. When divine power's condensed beyond a certain point, it changes state in a fundamental way. That's why gods don't just have *more* divine power than the rest of us; their power is *different*. I'm a demigoddess, and thaumaturgically speaking, I have more in common with a satyr or a gryphon than I do with my mother."

Sophia raised an eyebrow ever so slightly. "Didn't the Maya gods all swear never to reproduce?"

A mischievous grin appeared on Ixtele's face for a moment. "They did."

"Hmm." Caelistra gave the room a lazy scan, hands in her pockets. "If you're a demigoddess, where were you during all this? You could have taken a few gunmen, right?"

Sophia saw the surprise on Ixtele's face, and she had an uncomfortable feeling she knew what was coming next. *Shit. Provoking a cooperative witness? So much for letting me take the lead.* "Caelistra—" she began.

But Ixtele was already responding herself. "I was at a presentation on the other side of the building. It ran late, or I might have been here. I don't know whether you're implying that I'm a coward or that I was working with the bombers, but it's funny either way."

Sophia was caught completely off guard. Ixtele was actually smiling, without a trace of affront or embarrassment. It took Caelistra opening her mouth again for Sophia to recover. "The Hounds are more likely to kill a godborn than work with them anyway," she cut in. "Doctor Tinaalto, you were telling us about the bomb?"

"Right. The point is, I would bet good money that this explosion looks like Zeus's Grave because the power inside that bomb went through the same kind of compression. Until someone develops a way to clean it up, this spot's going to stay like this *forever*."

Sophia grimaced at the idea of the awful, spreading madness consuming all of Memphis. "At least it's contained for now. Our top priority has to be retrieving the bomb. If the Hounds think this will turn the tide in their war with the Silver Court, they won't hesitate to use it again." She turned to Sabu. "I'm going to need every file the police have on the Hounds, plus everything related to this attack. Oh, and do we know the name of the man they kidnapped?"

"Rashmi Baghvara. According to the conference roster, he wasn't a speaker or anything. Just signed up for a space in here during the poster session. Actually—"

Ixtele interrupted before he could continue. "Everyone here knows him. He's... Well, he's complicated. Five years ago, I would have said he was a genius. He had a job with Crucible Thaumatechnology here in Memphis, doing really cutting-edge work."

"And then?" she asked.

"And then he got obsessed with this crazy idea. He would corner anyone who'd listen and talk your ear off, so I've heard the details a thousand times." A sad look crossed her face. "He thought he'd figured out how to make a battery for divine power."

Sophia cleared her throat. "So..."

"So, the Second Law of Thaumadynamics has some pretty serious things to say on the subject," Ixtele said with a sigh. "Divine power doesn't like to be stored. Even back in Maya, where divine power is as abundant as electricity is here, they have to generate and distribute it constantly."

"How can it be put into a sword or a cell phone, then?" Sophia asked.

"That's a different thing. In your sword, the power's been worked into a miracle. It performs that miracle, and only that miracle—strengthening the blade, honing the edge, or whatever it was made to do. It can't be drawn out and used for something else. It's kind of like pouring concrete: you can cast it into a shape, but you can't use it for something else without completely breaking it down and starting over. With thaumaturgy, if you try, it will explode as soon as it's released. We call it the Containment-Feedback Paradox." She sighed. "Rashmi should have known that."

Sophia still felt like she wasn't seeing the whole picture. "You sound like you feel sorry for him."

Ixtele looked at her in surprise. "I do, actually. Even before he got kidnapped, I mean. He had all these grand dreams: an end to disease, an end to war, the ability to easily settle other planets... But that's all they were. Dreams. At best, all he was ever going to make was a bomb." She shook her head. "We all tried to tell him that, but he wouldn't listen."

Caelistra snorted. "And why did the conference let him bring a *bomb* into the building?"

"I assume they didn't," Ixtele said. "He was signed up for a poster session, just like last year. He wouldn't have had permission to bring an invention. The poor guy probably snuck it in so he could prove to everyone that his idea was finally going somewhere." She sighed, eyeing the hole that had been blasted out of the room. "We can all see how well that turned out."

There was one more question gnawing at Sophia's insides. "Can he build more of them?"

Ixtele shrugged. "Of course. The materials would be rare and expensive, though."

At least that makes our priorities clear.

Sophia gave her a sharp nod. "Doctor Tinaalto, thank you for your help. One of these police officers should be along to take your statement and get your contact information soon, if they haven't already."

Ixtele gave her an offended look. "What? That's it?"

"Unless you have more to share, we've got kidnappers to find."

"Sure, but the bomb... If I could just get a closer look at it..." She rubbed her hands together eagerly.

"Your expertise has been invaluable, but it's time for legwork now, and you're a civilian," Sophia said firmly. "I'm sure you didn't come to

Memphis to follow around a couple of Furies."

Ixtele crossed her arms defiantly. "Yeah. I came here for the conference, which is pretty much shot at this point, and to go out into the desert and see whether the rumors of a phoenix sighting were true. Not great odds. On the other hand, I could have a chance to see Fury thaumaturgy for the first time…"

Unbelievable.

"This is a criminal investigation, not a sightseeing opportunity. Thank you again. We will contact you if we need your help."

"Suit yourself." Ixtele headed reluctantly for the door. She shot one last glance over her shoulder, sighed, and then left.

"What's next?" Caelistra said.

"We track down the Hounds. Luckily, I know where to look. Sabu, you've been a big help, but we need one more thing from you. Can you get us access to the Memphis police network? Preferably portable?"

"Right away." He jogged to the corner and called over two other officers.

Sophia ran a hand through her hair, shooting a sidelong glance Caelistra's way. "This is a milk run?"

Caelistra yawned. "Would you rather be hunting the sea serpent that's been wrecking ships in the Mediterranean?"

CHAPTER SIX

"Traffic cameras and your 'personal experience?'" Caelistra said flatly. "That's what we're going on?"

"I thought you wanted my local expertise," Sophia said. "Just keep your eyes on the road. I'll find them."

A tablet provided by Detective Inheru rested on Sophia's knees, and she was scrolling through the Memphis PD traffic camera database. There weren't cameras on every corner—Egypt wasn't some Aztec-style police state—but they dotted the city, keeping an eye on large highways, major tunnels, and traffic hotspots. Caelistra was taking them in the general direction of the docks, but they needed more specifics.

In any other city, Sophia would have turned the task over to police techs, but in Memphis, she didn't need any help. She quickly isolated the streets that the Dockyard Hounds could have taken from the convention center. The major thoroughfares required only a brief scan. She wasn't surprised when she found no sign of the kidnappers' van. If they were smart, they would have tried to stay out of sight until they could trade it out.

She turned her attention to the remaining options: routes that would take them in unexpected directions, side streets the locals favored when traffic was bad…

"Gotcha."

It was the same van that had been caught on the convention center's cameras. Darkened windows, blank sides, a dull green paint job.

She advanced the image, frame by frame, until she had a view of the license plate.

All she had to do then was dump the number into the police algorithm, and it would do the rest of the work for her.

She tapped the START button and sat back in her seat.

"Looking awfully proud of yourself."

Sophia snorted, crossing her arms. "Would you rather they get away?"

Caelistra gave her a sidelong glance. "Assuming you find them, I want you to stay in the car. I'll handle it."

Sophia didn't even try to keep the incredulity from her face. "You've got to be kidding."

Caelistra shrugged, her eyes back on the road. "You're a recruit. You've got, what, a little bit of training with the police and a couple of firefights under your belt? If you last long enough to become a Fury, feel free to run off and try to hunt down the Midgard Serpent by yourself. Until then, it's my job to keep you safe. And that means you stay in the car."

"And let you go in without backup?" Recruit or not, that went against everything Sophia had ever been taught.

"Yes. You want to live long enough to be a Fury? This is how." She chuckled. "Besides, even if they're all deadeyes and expert duelists, they would need miracled weapons to even do me any lasting harm."

"Which they have," Sophia insisted, but Caelistra just shrugged. "Mundane bullets won't kill me either, you know. What happened to this being my case?"

"You're welcome to take the lead when we're talking to witnesses. But I've read your file. You'll have plenty of time for acts of stupid heroism later, when you're someone else's problem."

The tablet in Sophia's lap chimed. She felt a fierce, resentful triumph as she scanned through the results. "Here we go. They traded out the van, but they were in a hurry. I've got their new ride leaving the same garage where they stashed the old one." She tapped at the screen, selecting a dark blue SUV. She studied the screen for a second. "Take a left up here. It looks like they're heading for the north part of the docks."

They passed through the very edge of the government center, where classical architecture still abounded. Sophia had always thought that it was strange for a democracy to proudly celebrate the days when pharaohs had ruled with iron fists and gods had demanded worship, but maybe it was natural to look on the past with a nostalgic eye. Temples had been converted into art museums, palaces into hives of bureaucracy, but the architecture remained undeniably grand.

Caelistra glanced over as she pulled up to a stoplight. "Find our destination?"

A slow smile spread across Sophia's face, and she tapped twice on one of the thumbnails, blowing it up to fill the screen. "Yes."

"Care to share it with the class?"

"Head to the river and go south along the waterfront. I can't tell which building they're in exactly, but I can narrow it down to a single wharf."

"You're the local expert. What are the odds that the Hounds surrender peacefully?"

"Next to zero."

"Figures." Caelistra popped her neck from side to side. "Everyone's got to make my life more difficult."

Sophia's heart swelled as they rounded a corner and the Nile came into view. The river glittered in the midmorning sun, as busy a thoroughfare as Memphis's largest highways. Its banks were rich with greenery, left to flourish despite the metropolis rising around it. She loved Memphis's proud skyscrapers, its ornate, ancient tombs, its people, but it was the sight of the Nile that always made her feel like she was at home.

Caelistra drove them into the docks, and they were quickly swallowed by swarming industry. Laborers used cranes and forklifts to load cargo onto ships. Grain barges delivered the river's bounty from farms upstream. Food trucks visited worksites, offering late breakfasts or early lunches to workers on break and filling the air with the scents of griddle-cooked flatbread, garlic, and spiced chicken. There were people everywhere, all hard at work keeping the city afloat.

And any of them could be sentries for the Dockyard Hounds.

"No sirens," Sophia advised. "The Hounds don't own the whole dock, but they're working on it. We—" She paused, wincing, and cleared her throat. "The Memphis police have been trying to uproot them for years, but it's an uphill battle."

"Just point the way." Caelistra glanced around and chuckled grimly. "Sure feels like we're getting closer."

The dockyards were industrial, utilitarian, the steel foundation beneath the city's proud monuments and upscale commercial districts. But as they drove farther south, the buildings around them became more and more rundown. More than one had broken windows, fire-blackened sides, and graffiti. Sophia knew enough to recognize some of the spray-painted images as Hounds territory markers.

"Three more blocks," she said, consulting the tablet.

"How confident are you that you actually found the right place?" Caelistra asked

"Very. See that block of warehouses? It has to be one of those."

Caelistra chuckled. "Sounds like you're trying to convince yourself."

They were barely half a block away when the second-floor windows of the nearest warehouse exploded.

CHAPTER SEVEN

Gouts of flame and smoke erupted into the open air, and a man toppled from one of the warehouse windows, screaming until he struck the ground. The rattle of gunfire joined the industrial noise of the docks, and everyone in sight fled.

Caelistra slammed on the accelerator.

"Still think we're going to the wrong place?" Sophia had her phone in her hand, the Furies' direct number for Memphis PD dialed in. "This is Sophia Akerele, with the Furies. We're at 782 River Way, in the docks. We've got an explosion, shots fired, and the suspects may have the same thaumatech bomb that was used at the convention center. Send teams to secure the area." She hung up a moment later. "Police are on the way."

"Good." Caelistra sent the car screeching to a stop in front of the warehouse. She shut off the engine, yanked out the keys, and tossed them to Sophia. "Stay here and try not to get into trouble."

Sophia ground her teeth, but Caelistra climbed out of the car before she could argue, stalking toward the warehouse with the hem of her coat flapping behind her. She held out her hands, and the car's shadow bent toward her, crawled up her legs like clouds of smoke, and pooled in her palms, tiny wisps curling away from her skin. The darkness rippled outward, taking shape. When it retreated, Caelistra held an ax with a wide, curved head and a heavy shield, both made of the same gleaming, dark grey metal: adamant, forged by Hephaestus himself.

More shadows gathered at her command, twisting into a huge claw that tore the nearest door from the warehouse. Caelistra vanished inside, shouting, "Conclave Furies! Drop your weapons!"

Try not to get into trouble. Sophia snarled softly. She wasn't a child. She'd spent her entire career in parts of the city just as dangerous as this one. She drew her pistol, just in case trouble found her, and glared after Caelistra, listening to the distant sound of gunfire.

Even for a Fury, going in alone, without backup, was a stupid idea. But Caelistra's orders had been abundantly clear. If she thought she had the situation under control, Sophia certainly wasn't about to jeopardize her future with the Furies by disobeying.

So she sat there, sweating as the sun slowly turned the car into an oven. She refused to turn it back on and use the AC. That felt like admitting that she was going to be there a while. Instead, she leaned on the glove compartment and kept watch.

The streets were empty. Everyone not involved in the firefight had wisely chosen to run away. Smoke still poured from the second floor of the warehouse, though only through that one window. The flames hadn't spread, yet. The gunshots were growing further and further apart. She wasn't sure whether that was a good sign or bad.

She was still watching when, moments later, a side door crashed open. A man staggered out, favoring one leg and clutching his side. Blood stained his clothes, and more trickled from a deep slash across his scalp. He had a pistol in one hand, and when he turned to scan the street, his eyes passing right over Sophia's car, she saw that there was a dog tattooed on his throat.

He turned away from the street, limping along the edge of the wharf toward a moored motorboat, and Sophia's eyes caught on the backpack slung over his shoulder. It bulged irregularly, and he carried it as though it was heavy.

It was exactly the right size to hold Rashmi's bomb.

Sophia was out of the car and on the run with hardly a moment's thought. Caelistra's orders be damned, it was better to risk her future than to risk losing the bomb.

She pounded down the wharf, moving faster than she'd ever run in life, while the Hound was busy climbing into the boat. He set the pack down with a pained grunt and turned toward the motor.

He saw Sophia charging toward him, and his eyes went wide. He started to raise his gun.

Sophia jumped.

She crashed into him before he could get off a shot. Her shoulder struck his jaw, and he collapsed against the side of the boat. His weapon went spinning out of his hand and splashed into the water.

He blinked up at her, groaning through gritted, bloody teeth. "Conclave Furies. Don't move," she ordered, keeping her gun trained on him. The boat was rocking wildly from the scuffle, but she kept herself steady.

The Hound slumped against the side of the boat with a defeated sigh. She could see blood pumping between the fingers of the hand he clutched to his abdomen. "Better hurry," he groaned.

Shit. Heart pounding, she seized the backpack with her free hand and unzipped the top, all without taking her eyes off the suspect. She expected the pulsing glow of the thaumatech bomb, charged and ready for use.

Instead, she found cash. Stacks of Roman bills, standard throughout the Conclave, bound with rubber bands. A few were smeared with blood. She raked a hand through, just to be sure, but there was no bomb. Just money.

Caelistra was going to be pissed, but it was too late to do anything about that. "Who attacked you?" Sophia asked.

"Don't know. Godborn. Six of them"

Sophia's eyes narrowed. "The Silver Court?"

He shook his head, grimacing. "No. Not water spirits. Something else." His eyes met hers with a desperate, pleading look.

"Don't worry. There's ambulances on the way. I'll get you—"

"No!" He coughed, each spasm clearly racking him with pain.

"They're after the inventor, and his bomb. Please… Please, you have to stop them."

The last word was barely a gasp. The moment it left his lips, he fell back, his head knocking against the lip of the boat. Sophia saw the life leave his eyes.

"Shit," she said aloud. She clambered back onto the dock. Then she hesitated.

She'd assumed from the start that this was no coincidence. Whoever had been inside the warehouse when they'd arrived, setting off explosions and shooting up the Hounds, had to be after the bomb. But these godborn… if they weren't the Hounds' age-old enemies, who were they?

All of her instincts said that she should follow Caelistra inside and offer what backup she could. But her orders…

An idea hit her like a gunshot: what if this was a test, but not in the way she'd thought? Surely the Furies would care more about whether she'd helped recover the bomb than about whether she followed orders. It was easy enough to imagine Caelistra's scornful look. "Wow," she would say. "You stayed in the car for the whole gunfight, just like you were told. Too bad obedience isn't what makes a good Fury."

That decided it. The door the dead Hound had used was still open. She headed for the entrance instead of back toward the car. After a quick glance inside, she ducked through the doorway, her gun at the ready.

The smell of carnage and gun smoke rolled over her as soon as she was inside. The warehouse was dimly lit, many of the lights shattered by the explosion, but one perk of a Fury's affinity for shadow was the ability to see in the dark with perfect clarity. Tall shelving units, packed with crates, made the ground floor into a maze. By design, Sophia suspected. Cinders drifted down from the catwalk above, which was twisted out of shape by the same explosion that had shattered the windows.

Shots echoed from the back of the building, punctuated by an occasional scream. Moving as fast as she dared while still scanning for threats, Sophia followed the sounds.

She found the first of the dead as soon as she rounded the nearest shelves. Men and women torn by bullets, or caught beneath toppled shipping containers, or shredded by deadly miracles as if they'd been caught in a hurricane. Only a few had weapons in their hands. One man, nearest the door, was curled around a bag of felafel, his blood staining the spilled food.

Sophia clambered over a shipping crate that looked like it had been ripped apart by a dragon. She picked her way through a scattering of bullets spilled from an open box. She followed a smear of blood deeper into the warehouse.

A cry of pain echoed from somewhere up ahead, followed by Caelistra's voice. "Conclave Furies! Put down your weapons!" Gunfire was the only answer.

Heart thundering in her chest, adrenaline sending her eyes darting from shadow to shadow, Sophia ducked under a fallen shelving unit and caught her first glimpse of the battle.

At the far end of the warehouse, a bedraggled group of Dockyard Hounds made their last stand. They were scattered among pieces of cover, firing wildly as they yelled to one another, their words lost in the din. One woman at the very back stood over Rashmi Bhagvara, holding a gun to the inventor's head while he fiddled frantically with a contraption of glass and steel.

The bomb. Less than a foot in any dimension, but still the most dangerous thing in the room.

Six black-clad figures with automatic rifles advanced on the gangsters, hardly slowed by the hail of lead. Sophia felt the air around her shift as a one of the figures took a hand off his gun to conjure a tiny cyclone in his palm.

A flicker of movement overhead seized her attention, and she looked up, ready to fire. She found Caelistra striding across the catwalk toward the back of the building, catching bullets on her shield as three desperate Hounds tried to gun her down. Sophia took aim at one of them.

Something huge crashed into her from the side. She slammed into the floor, the air blasting from her lungs. She heard something sharp scrape across the concrete as she tried to twist around. A fist smashed into her ribs, sending a wave of pain through her, but she'd felt worse. She lashed out with her elbow, fighting blind, and felt something crunch.

She rolled onto her back, scrambling to get free. A gigantic man with a snarling dog tattoo at his neck loomed over her, pinning her to the ground. His fist caught her across the jaw, and she felt her lip split. She saw the glint of metal in his hand an instant before his knife stabbed toward her.

She deflected the strike, but not quite enough. The blade sliced into her biceps, and agony flared through her right arm. The man might be a mortal, but this was no mundane knife. She could *feel* the weapon's miracle warring with her own divine power as her body tried to heal the wound, and it was like having burning oil poured into the gash.

Her fingers were numb on the grip of her gun, and she barely managed to keep hold of it. She seized his wrist with her other hand before he could stab her again. She felt something pop in his hand as she wrenched it away, and he let out a howl, rearing back. She bucked her hips and twisted to one side, throwing him off.

He scrambled after the knife, and she kicked him in the side of the head. He crumpled and didn't get back up.

"Asshole," she muttered.

Sucking the blood from her lip, she inspected the gash on her arm. Deep, still painful, but she could still use her right hand. The wound could wait. She turned back toward the rear of the warehouse.

She saw the last Hound foot soldier fall, riddled with bullets. The woman holding Rashmi broke and ran, leaving Rashmi to cower on the floor as she fired blindly behind her. At a gesture from one of her assailants, a rush of wind slammed her sideways into a shelving unit. She crashed to the ground, and he shot her in the back.

Sophia ran toward them, but she could tell she wasn't going to make it in time.

Caelistra leapt off the catwalk at the top of the warehouse and landed among the godborn killers like a diving falcon. A blow from her shield sent one of the gunmen flying into a row of shelves with enough force to bend metal and splinter wood. Another turned a rifle on her, and Caelistra smashed her ax into the weapon, tearing it from his hands. Ribbons of shadow coiled around her as she prepared a miracle.

"Hold them off!" one of the godborn shouted. As the rest turned to fend off Caelistra, he seized the bomb by one of its handles and tore it from Rashmi's hands before pointing his gun at the inventor. "You're coming with us," he snarled. Abject terror spread across Rashmi's face, and rage boiled through Sophia.

She leaned out and shot the godborn holding Rashmi's device in the back.

He fell to one knee, howling in rage, spinning to face her. The wind whipped at his surroundings as he gathered his power, but she kept firing, driving him into cover.

Behind him, she saw Rashmi's eyes lock onto her. He wasn't a young man, but the day's events had left him looking practically haggard, his thick black hair as disheveled as his blood-spattered dhoti, his face a mask of shock and terror. *Go!* she urged him. She was relieved when he turned and scrambled toward the door.

Relieved, at least, until a woman ducked through the doorway before Rashmi could reach it. She was short and slender, her features obscured by a hooded jacket, a face mask, and dark sunglasses. That was all Sophia had time to see before the newcomer seized Rashmi by the arm and dragged him toward the door. Rashmi kicked and fought, until the woman holding him leaned in close and snarled something in his face.

The leader of the gunmen turned, and Sophia watched him tense with rage as he saw his prize escaping. He unleashed the miracle he'd been preparing, and the air spun itself into blades of cutting wind.

Rashmi's captor threw him out of the way and placed herself between the inventor and any danger. There was a flash, and the hissing blades disintegrated harmlessly. Without pausing, she seized Rashmi's arm again and dragged him back toward the door.

No! She had no idea who this new threat was—certainly no friend to the six godborn who'd been slaughtering the Hounds—but she'd be damned if she let the woman take Rashmi. Sophia raced closer to get a clear shot, but a torrent of gunfire drove her back into cover. She looked toward Caelistra, who, incredibly, was holding her own in close combat with three suspects, but even her skills weren't enough to buy her an opening.

Sophia watched helplessly as Rashmi and the masked woman vanished through the door.

The leader of the godborn hit squad let out a frustrated cry. He started after them, but he stopped when he saw Sophia. There was no cover on the way. She'd have a clear shot.

He raised his hand toward the wall beside him instead. There was a *whump* like a grenade exploding, and a wave of force tore a ragged hole in the concrete. "Fall back!" he called. "Forget the Furies."

His people made an orderly, professional retreat. Sophia watched helplessly, pinned down by covering fire, as one by one they slipped out of the building, forcing even Caelistra back as they withdrew.

Sophia rose from cover, her heart pounding as she ran to Caelistra's side. "They have the bomb," she called. "We have to go after them!"

Caelistra shot her a look, her eyes narrowed. *Guess she really did want me to stay in the car.* But after a moment, Caelistra led the way through the hole in the wall, her shield raised before her.

No bullets struck. No miracles assailed them. Sophia followed, shoulders tense, expecting an attack at any second.

Instead, she saw the six suspects at the very edge of the wharf, barely twenty feet away. Behind them, police speedboats were closing in, their sirens wailing. "Give it up!" Sophia shouted. "There's nowhere to go!"

The leader thrust the bomb into a heavy, plastic-lined bag and sealed it shut.

Then all six of them stepped back and dropped into the water.

"Damn it!" They raced to the water's edge. Faint trails of bubbles led off in six different directions before vanishing entirely.

The first boat pulled up, and Sophia shouted to the officers inside, "They went into the water! Set up a search grid, and close off the shores! We have to catch them!"

Caelistra turned away as the boat sped off. "They won't find anything." For the first time since Sophia had met her, she sounded angry.

Sophia swore under her breath. The hit squad escaping was one thing, but escaping with the bomb… *Gods damn it, we were so close.*

"I told you to stay in the car," Caelistra remarked coolly. "Why am I not surprised…"

Sophia turned without a word and stalked back toward the warehouse. She could explain herself later. Right now, there were more important things to worry about.

She checked around the back of the building, but Rashmi was gone without a trace. As the first police cars pulled up, she ordered them to set up a cordon, but she didn't have high hopes. Then she went back into the building.

There had to be something. Some clue about who the attackers were, or where they'd gone with the bomb. Some hint about whoever had taken Rashmi. Even the most careful criminals always slipped up somehow, and there'd been no time for care in the firefight.

She heard Caelistra follow her back inside. "The woman who took Rashmi had a face mask and sunglasses. Did you see anything else?" Sophia asked.

"Nope. Too busy fighting."

Sophia squashed the frustration building inside her. "I've never seen someone hold their own against that many godborn," she said. "You made it look easy."

Which was part of the problem. Caelistra would be so much easier to ignore if she were just full of herself, like so many of the condescending assholes Sophia had worked with throughout her career. But it was the best olive branch she could muster, and all of this would go smoother if they could work the scene together.

Caelistra stopped studying the room long enough to give the stinging gash on Sophia's arm a pointed look. "And you fight like a brawler, just hurling yourself at your enemy until one of you is out of the fight. You should have been in the car, out of harm's way. Flattery isn't going to make me forget that." She gestured at the spattered blood and fallen weapons before Sophia could reply. "Let's focus on something you're supposed to be good at. What do you see, *detective?*"

Sophia swallowed the retort on her lips, refusing the bait. Irritatingly, Caelistra was right: now was the time to be analytical, while the evidence was still fresh. "We've got new players. The godborn hitmen, and the woman who took Rashmi. This isn't just a gang war."

"Lovely city you've got here," Caelistra remarked.

A ragged cough from the rear of the room snatched their attention. Caelistra hefted her ax, gesturing silently. They circled around, approaching from two sides with their weapons ready.

They needn't have bothered.

It was the Hound woman who'd been holding Rashmi at gunpoint. She was crawling toward the back door, but with the gunshot wound in her back, she hadn't made it far.

Caelistra kicked away her gun.

Sophia crouched at the woman's side and put a hand on her arm. "You're going to be all right. Help's on its way."

The Hound smiled a bloody-toothed grin, matching the snapping dog tattooed around her neck. "Liar," she wheezed. She shook her head, grimacing in pain. "We had to do it. We had to."

"Do what?"

"Take him. Take the bomb. Otherwise..." A fit of wet coughs interrupted her. "Otherwise, someone else would have. Someone worse."

Caelistra laughed bitterly. "Says the woman who detonated the thing in the middle of the city."

Sophia ignored her. She leaned in, a sympathetic frown on her face.

65

"Who?"

"You know who. *We're* all human. Can't even charge the damn thing ourselves. But the Silver Court… They would have turned the docks into a wasteland. Our families would never have been… safe…"

The last word rattled out of her, and she didn't take another breath. Sophia slowly lowered her back to the ground.

"Wonderful," Caelistra remarked. As she looked around, her ax and shield broke apart into shadows and dispersed into the air. "This seems like a job for forensics."

She was right, but that didn't mean they were done. Sophia stood up and walked back toward the car. "I've got an idea."

"Does it involve disobeying orders again?"

Sophia rounded on her. "I saw a Hound heading for a boat with what could have been the bomb. Are you going to throw me out of the Furies for taking the initiative?"

Caelistra glanced at her casually and then busied herself cleaning off some blood and grime that had crusted over the SPQR tattoo on her arm. "Not today."

"Good. In that case, there's one last place I want to go before nightfall. Somewhere we might be able to get information."

"And where's that?"

"Neutral ground."

And gods help me figure out what I'm going to say to Meret.

CHAPTER EIGHT

Rashmi Bhagvara pressed himself against the car door, his eyes squeezed shut. He couldn't stop his hands from shaking. It was just an autonomic response to terror and adrenaline, as natural as sweating in the heat. The danger had passed, but his body didn't know that yet. It was still telling him to panic, and by all the gods, it was hard not to listen.

"We're almost there, Rashmi. Don't worry. You're safe now." The words were comforting, but his rescuer's voice was not. It was a soft, rasping hiss, full of mocking condescension. Scorn, however, he could handle. Ever since he'd begun work on his magnum opus, he'd been laughed at by his peers.

What he couldn't handle was being threatened at gunpoint by gangsters. Or seeing people torn to ribbons, their blood spattering his skin. Or watching them gasp out their last moments, staring at him with blame in their eyes.

He leaned to the side and retched, but there was nothing left in his stomach, not after the first two times. His rescuer scoffed. "You've got blood on your cheek," she said.

Rashmi didn't move, not trusting his stomach if he touched the blood. This was only the fourth time he'd interacted with her, but he'd known from the start that she could be cruel. He used to wonder why his patron kept a woman like this around, but he didn't have to wonder any longer. He'd seen the speed with which she moved, the power of the miracle she'd deflected like it was nothing.

What he didn't know was her name. Until today, he'd thought that perhaps she was just eccentric or private, like her employer: the wealthy, anonymous patron who'd funded Rashmi's work. Now, he was too afraid to ask.

He felt the car lurch to a halt. "We're here." He took a deep breath, sat up straight, and opened his eyes.

A frown crept across his face. He didn't recognize the building they'd stopped at. Styx, he didn't recognize this part of the city at all.

But his rescuer was already climbing out of the car, so he had no choice but to follow. He swallowed as he looked around, trying to work some moisture back into his painfully dry mouth. "This isn't my workshop."

She laughed at this, circling around the car toward him. "It is now. Unless you want the Hounds to find you again. Or the people who slaughtered them to get to you."

Rashmi shivered and quickly shook his head. He let her usher him inside, barely taking in the street or the buildings. There was no one else in sight, but he kept his head down, his shoulders hunched. He could still feel the gunshots in his bones, still smell the awful stench of blood and shit as people died around him.

Why was this happening to him? He was just a thaumatechnician.

But he knew the answer to that, as much as he didn't want to admit it. He wanted to change the world for the better, but those gangsters who had kidnapped him... They looked at him, and all they saw was a source of deadly bombs.

At least his patron believed in him. That was the thought that kept him going. If he could just finish his work, so many of the world's problems would be solved.

"Out of the way." His rescuer swept past him as they reached the door, and Rashmi's gaze dropped toward his feet at the violence in her voice. He listened as keys scraped against lock after lock after lock. They were taking no chances with security, this time.

The instant the door was open, she bundled him through it.

And into a dingy, cramped room. Rashmi had a few seconds to take in the shuttered windows, the tiny workbench, and the haphazard collection of tools before she caught him by the shoulder and slammed him into the wall with enough force to rattle his teeth. A hand closed around his throat.

His rescuer loomed over him, little more than an ominous, hooded shadow in the dim light. "While you were the Hounds' prisoner," she rasped, "what did you tell them?"

Rashmi's voice failed him, until she tightened her fingers around his neck. "Tell them? Styx, they didn't have time to ask me any questions!"

"And if they had? What would you have said?"

"Nothing!"

She produced a curved, bronze knife with her free hand and raised it toward his face. He could hear the leather of her gloves creaking, her grip on the hilt was so tight. It was an archaic weapon, the sort of thing that belonged in a museum, but the edge looked deadly sharp. "And if they'd tortured you?" She lowered her voice until it was barely a whisper. "If they'd broken your fingers? Peeled off your skin? Plucked out your eyes?"

Rashmi cringed, pressing himself against the wall as if he could escape through it. He wanted desperately to squeeze his eyes shut, but somehow he couldn't take them off the wicked point of that knife. He said the first thing that came into his head. "Even if they'd tortured me, they wouldn't have gotten anything useful. The data show that torture subjects say anything to make the pain stop."

When she tipped back her head and laughed, the sound was somehow more terrifying than the sight of the knife. "Strange. That certainly hasn't been my experience." She waggled the knife in front of his eyes. "You didn't share any details about our employer?"

He blinked at her. "I don't *know* any details."

There was a long silence. The blade hovered in front of him, unwavering. He tried to avoid looking at her face, but out of the corner of his eye, he could see himself trembling in her sunglasses. During the shootout in the warehouse, he'd felt helpless, one stray bullet away from a random death. This was different. This was worse. He knew with a harsh certainty that if he said the wrong thing, he was never leaving this room alive.

Swallowing, working up every ounce of courage he could muster, he forced himself to look at her face. At her glasses, at least. "My patron—your employer—believes in my work. That's why we're here, isn't it?"

She let out a soft chuckle. "So you have a bit of a spine after all." The knife disappeared. It took him a moment to realize that her hand wasn't coiled around his neck, that it was his own fear pressing him against the wall now.

Turning her back on him, she started to pace slowly in the opposite direction. "How quickly can you build another device?"

Rashmi winced, his eyes going to the workbench by the far wall. The setup was… Disappointing would be too harsh a term. He'd known that he was leaving behind the comforting sterility and cutting-edge equipment of his old lab at Crucible Thaumatechnologies when he'd handed Thoth his letter of resignation and chosen to pursue his dreams. Still, this was a sizable step down even from his last workshop.

"Not quickly."

He saw her pause, her hood twitching ever so slightly toward him, the knife spinning deftly between her fingers. "Even if you were… properly motivated?"

Merciful gods… There was no way his patron knew about this. His harsh treatment, these threats… Or was there? It terrified him that he was no longer sure.

But the knife demanded a response, and he only had one response to give.

"The process is delicate, and some of the steps require substantially altering commercially available materials. That takes *time*. Besides… I appreciate the new workshop here, but frankly, these tools won't be enough."

His rescuer… No. That was accurate, but not the most relevant label, at the moment. He could see, now, that the locks on the door required a key even from the inside. He could see the chains fastening the tools to the workbench.

She *was* his rescuer, but she was also his new *captor*.

"The boss will not be pleased," she growled.

Clenching his jaw, balling his hands into fists, Rashmi forced himself to raise his eyes from the floor. He got to the level of her neck before his resolve failed him. As firmly as he could manage, he said, "I cannot do the impossible. Physical laws are physical laws. Making another device will take at least a week, just like last time, and that's *if* I have all the parts. Knowing more about what I'm doing doesn't speed up chemical reactions. If you had recovered the device at the warehouse—"

He knew immediately that he'd gone too far. She crossed the room in a flash, tearing him from his feet and slamming his face into the workbench. He flailed, hands reaching for something, anything. He felt his fingers closer around a wrench just before his captor stabbed the bronze knife into the wood a fraction of an inch from his hand.

She leaned in close, and he cringed away, eyes squeezing shut out of sheer terror. "Are you criticizing me, mayfly?"

Rashmi could feel his body trembling, his heart thundering. Natural reactions to the presence of a killer. Nothing to be ashamed of.

"No." His voice cracked, and he had to swallow before he could continue. "I just mean that I can't rush the timetable."

"You will have the materials you need. They will be brought to you, of course. For your own safety, it is important that you don't leave."

For his own safety. Of course.

Back in the warehouse, just before he'd been dragged out the door, he'd caught a glimpse of one of the people fighting their way through the gangsters to reach him. Not one of the godborn killers—one of the Furies. He remembered the look of burning determination in her eyes, the courage with which she'd strode into gunfire, putting herself into harm's way for him. Now, more than ever, those were qualities he wished that he possessed. Would things be different now, if the Furies had rescued him instead?

But they hadn't. He had to deal with the reality of his situation.

"With the right materials, I can build another device, but it's going to take at least a week. And if you need it done before then—"

A low, dangerous chuckle crept out from behind his captor's balaclava. "I'll just have to recover the first one."

Rashmi stared at her. "From those killers who attacked the wharf? Are you... I mean..."

She laughed. Slowly, gently, she reached a hand up to cup his cheek. Even with the glove between her skin and his, Rashmi had to fight the urge to tear himself away.

"Don't worry about me, mayfly. Just focus on getting this place ready; there's a great deal of work still ahead. I will bring back your precious invention."

CHAPTER NINE

"*This* is where you go for vital information about the city?" Caelistra said, skepticism plain on her face. "The Riverside Shelter? It sounds like a nursing home."

Thanks to traffic and time spent wrapping up the crime scene at the docks with the police, it was late afternoon by the time they arrived at the shelter. Sophia had hoped to find some clue in the bloodstained warehouses, but they'd found nothing they didn't already know.

"You've been a Fury for what, twenty years? And you've never been to a place like this for information?"

"Forty-five years, actually. Longer than you were alive. And I'll follow a lead anywhere. Assuming, you know, I actually *have* one."

Sophia ignored the jab and offered Caelistra a bright smile instead. "Pay attention, then. You might learn something, partner."

Seeing the shelter drove everything else from her head. This was everything she'd been trying to avoid since returning to Memphis. She almost would have preferred another fight. *Gods, if there's another way...* No sudden inspiration struck.

As Caelistra found a place to park, Sophia lowered the sun visor and checked herself in the mirror. She didn't look like a woman who'd had her head bashed into a concrete floor. Her face had repaired itself moments after the injury, and there wasn't a trace of bruising or pain.

Her arm, where she'd been slashed by the miracle-edged knife, though, bore an angry scar, only just healed, and her sleeve was torn. There was no blood, though; separated from her body, it had shimmered away into nothing.

Being a Fury recruit was strange.

A wave of cigarette smoke drew Sophia out of her thoughts with a disgusted cough. She found Caelistra regarding her with her usual expression of cool disdain. "You're stalling," Caelistra said. She tapped ash out the window. "I wonder what you're afraid of."

"Ugh. Come on. And put that thing out. You can't smoke inside."

Sophia grimaced as she got out of the car. Sand spiraled past on a breath of burning wind as if to remind her that the desert was never far away. Even with the sun setting, the heat was merciless, a crushing fist that was only just beginning to loosen its hold. This deep into summer, even night would barely bring any relief. At any other time, it might have driven her to hurry inside.

The shelter was the heart of the Boneyard, in more ways than one. The buildings all around bore neglect and desperation like a crushing layer of sand, but the shelter stood strong. Its windows were intact, its sides unscarred by bullets or graffiti. It was an oasis, deep in the desert. The Dockyard Hounds and the Silver Court fought over everything else, but never this. Not when both gangs had family inside.

This was where people went to be safe.

Sophia felt anything but safe as she and Caelistra headed for the doors. Her job had brought her here more than once, but it wasn't because of police work that she knew the Riverside Shelter. No, the shelter had been built, almost single handedly, by Meret. Gahiji's lover. Teshan's mother.

Meret had always been the best thing in Gahiji's life, but the possibility of running into her now sent dread curling through Sophia's veins like poison. Seeing someone she'd known before, someone who'd attended her *funeral*, would open herself up to all the pain she'd been trying to hide from. Not to mention that it might be a technical violation of Fury regulations, which prohibited contact with people from one's

74

life.

But with the bomb missing, she didn't have the luxury of passing up a chance at information.

The two of them got a few looks as they entered, but everyone inside had bigger things to worry about. The main room was a crowded mess of mismatched furniture and bedraggled people. Many of them were huddled under blankets despite the heat outside and the straining air conditioning. Others devoured the scraps of food with their backs to walls, eyeing anyone who came near with naked suspicion. There were a heartbreaking number of children among them. Families with ties to one gang or another glared daggers at each other, but everyone respected the shelter's neutrality. Volunteers wove through the crowd, distributing food, clothing, a comforting word… whatever they could offer that might help.

To one side, a space had been cleared for a small, makeshift hospital. People lay on rows of cots, and Sophia could make out gunshots and miracle-inflicted wounds among them. An exhausted-looking godborn with metallic copper skin was moving from patient to patient, doing what he could to mend injuries with his miracles. Perhaps some distant descendent of Asklepios, Serqet, or another famed healer.

Sophia finished looking over the room, and a heavy tension released in her back. Teshan wasn't among the volunteers, today. Meret was one thing, but seeing her niece would be too much to bear.

A man Sophia didn't know approached the two of them with a gentle smile on his face. "Welcome to Riverside. What can we do to help?"

Sophia nodded toward the healer and his patients. "What happened?"

The volunteer grimaced, but some of the nervous tension left him when he saw their badges. "Gang violence is at an all-time high today. Something about the bombing at the convention center, is the rumor. There was a shootout on Sixty-Sixth. Bunch of people caught in the crossfire."

"They should be at a hospital," Caelistra muttered.

"Some of them wouldn't have made it to a hospital," the volunteer said. "And with respect, Fury, not all of them trust doctors."

Sophia spoke up before Caelistra could make a fool of herself. "I was actually looking for…"

The words caught in her throat as she glimpsed Meret from across the room. Meret's sleeves were rolled up, sweat streaking her face as she helped one of her volunteers move a box of donations. She looked up as they set it down, and her eyes met Sophia's.

Her mouth fell open. Then she murmured an apology and wound through the room, looking dazed.

"Sophia?"

Sophia smiled, blinking back tears. "Meret."

Meret reached out a hand toward Sophia's arm, hesitant. She looked surprised when her fingers met resistance. Sophia pulled her into a hug.

"My gods," Meret murmured. Sophia felt her swallow heavily. "Are you… Did you…"

"Don't worry, I actually died. No money wasted on the funeral."

It was a horrible joke, but Meret barely seemed to hear it. "But, how?"

Sophia disentangled herself and stepped back, tapping the badge on her belt. "Apparently the Furies didn't think I'd earned a vacation just yet."

Meret stared at her in surprise before breaking into a tearful smile. "The Furies. Of course they'd want you. You're here on business, then?"

"What are the chances, right? Of all the places in the Conclave…" Sophia shook her head. "Can we talk privately?"

Meret led them to her office. A few people tried to interrupt her on the way, and she kindly but firmly asked them to wait. Even knowing her for as long as she had, Sophia marveled at her gentle manner and easy compassion. Growing up in the Boneyard had hardened Sophia and her brother, though in wildly different ways. Meret, though, took all the suffering and violence and returned it as kindness.

The office was small and humble, located on the first floor, at the very back of the main room, giving it the best view possible without looking down on anyone. The most prominent feature was the huge paper calendar that hung on the wall behind her desk. Color-coded notes were crammed onto its surface, marking everything from career development sessions, to after-school activities, to addiction counseling. With all of her responsibilities, scheduled and unscheduled, it was no wonder that Meret slept in her office more often than not.

One slot, exactly two days away, was empty except for a note in different, flowery handwriting that said, "Teshan's birthday!" It was like a knife in Sophia's heart.

Business. Focus on business. "This is my partner, Caelistra Horatia. Caelistra, this is Meret Tanu. She runs the shelter. She also happens to be the mother of my niece."

Caelistra slowly turned toward Sophia. "Oh really?" She wore an amused smirk, like a dragon that had woken up to find a bus full of tourists an inch from its face.

"But that's not why we're here," Sophia continued quickly. "Meret, did you hear about the convention center bombing?"

"Of course. Are you working that case?"

"Yes. I can't say much, but it's looking more and more like it's connected to the gang war. I know people tell you things. If there's anything that might help us…"

Meret sighed, wiping the sweat from her forehead and teasing some stray hair back into place. "Well… The Silver Court's been hitting the docks hard over the last few days, but nothing like today."

"Any idea why?"

"Money or turf, I assume? The usual reasons."

Sophia nodded, but she had her doubts. The godborn who'd taken the bomb didn't feel like Silver Court to her. They were too precise, too professional, without the boisterous swagger she was used to seeing from gangsters. Not to mention that the Silver Court was all water spirits, and while they'd escaped into the river, all the miracles she'd seen from the killers at the docks had called on the wind.

"The Hounds are hitting back, of course," Meret continued. "Which means the Boneyard's caught in the middle, like always. The police are outmatched, or too corrupt to help…" She trailed off, massaging her temples. "Ugh, listen to me. You know this city as well as I do, and I'm just rehashing old complaints."

"Don't worry about it. You're sure you haven't heard anything out of the ordinary?"

"Sorry. I'll give you a call if I do?"

Sophia gave Meret her new number. The number for her *thaumatech* cell phone, that worked even across realms. It was still a bizarre thought, suddenly carrying around something that would have cost six months of her old detective's salary.

"I wish I could be more help. Still… It was good to see you, Sophia. And nice to meet you, Caelistra."

"Likewise," Caelistra said, heading for the door.

Sophia hesitated. She moved around Meret's desk and lowered her voice. "Meret… I really hate to ask you this, but please… Will you not tell my brother that I'm a Fury? Or Teshan?"

Meret looked flabbergasted. "But you're *back*! You're—"

"I'm not." Seeing Meret's face—seeing *Teshan's* features in her face—was agonizing. "I'm still dead, and technically I'm not supposed to reach out to family." The words came, but she had to tear them out of her chest to get them out.

Meret hesitated.

"Please. I don't know if Gahiji really cares—"

"He does care. You should have seen him at your funeral. He may still blame you for leaving the Boneyard, but he cares."

Sophia felt the hot, familiar anger curling her lip and tried to fight it down. "I joined the police to *help*. Something *he*…" She shook her head, taking a deep breath. "That's not the point. If Teshan thought I was back and didn't come see her…"

Meret embraced her. "I won't say anything."

"Thank you. Take care of them, will you?"

There was steely ferocity in Meret's eyes as she met Sophia's gaze. "Always."

Sophia turned away, blinking back tears.

Caelistra was waiting for her outside the office, her arms crossed and a smirk on her face. "You surprised me. I didn't think that was possible."

"Yeah?"

"You went to someone you knew. Someone from your life. You *did* read your contract, right?"

"I read it. But you're the one who took a case in Memphis." Sophia put her hands on her hips, fighting the anxiety welling up in her chest. She thought she had Caelistra's measure. If she was wrong… "You've been waiting for me to give up or get myself into trouble. Going to turn me in?"

Caelistra was still studying her, her face inscrutable. "Probably. Assuming you really wasted my time just to visit an old friend who didn't know anything."

Sophia chuckled as relief poured through her. "Then I'm glad I wasn't wasting our time."

"She told us nothing we didn't already know."

"Sure. But we weren't here to talk to her."

Caelistra frowned. "What?"

Sophia nodded toward a man hunched over a card table in the corner of the room, the hood of a sweatshirt pulled up around his face.

"We're here to talk to *him*."

CHAPTER TEN

Bekenre Djemi was a drug dealer and a thief. He was a godborn of some variety, though Sophia had never actually seen him use any divine power. He was skittish, resentful, and an asshole in just about every way a person could be.

Unfortunately, he was also a useful informant.

"Stay here," Sophia said. "A new face will just make him nervous."

"He looks nervous already," Caelistra remarked skeptically.

Bekenre was busy playing cards with two other men, and by the looks of things, he was losing badly. Which wasn't surprising, given that Sophia could tell from across the room that one of the others was cheating outrageously, and Bekenre didn't seem to realize it. He kept darting looks over his shoulder, as if he expected a mortal enemy to come sneaking down the stairs.

"He'll talk to me," Sophia said.

Caelistra was watching the card game without seeming to pay any attention. "He dangerous?"

Sophia snorted. "Bekenre? He's a pushover. Plus, he wouldn't try anything here. Hurt someone in Meret's shelter, and half the city would come after you."

"Great." Caelistra pulled out a cigarette. "I'll be outside."

Sophia wound her way across the room with her hands in her pockets. Bekenre wouldn't be pleased about her approaching him in public, but she didn't have time to stage an excuse for a more private conversation. Besides, she wasn't Memphis PD anymore. This was a bridge she could afford to burn.

She kept a tight lid on her emotions as she crossed the shelter. Talking to Meret again was like seeing Teshan without actually being able to speak to her. And making Meret promise not to tell anyone she was alive—in a sense—only made her feel worse. She knew it was the right choice, the only way to avoid causing them pain, but *gods* did it hurt.

Styx, she hoped that Bekenre had something useful for her. She wasn't sure how much longer she could tolerate being in this city.

Ahead, Bekenre leaned back with a disgusted sigh and threw his cards down on the table. He stretched, looking around, and saw Sophia walking toward him.

She smirked.

Eyes wide, he leapt to his feet, flipped over the card table, and bolted for the stairs in the corner.

"Gods damn it... Caelistra, circle around and cut him off!"

Caelistra finished lighting her cigarette on her way out the door, giving no sign that she'd heard.

Muttering curses under her breath, Sophia tore after Bekenre. People scrambled out of her way, toppling more furniture. A few shouted complaints at her, but she was too intent on her target to hear.

There was only one reason she could think of for him to run: he knew something about what was going on in the city, and it had him terrified. She had to catch him.

She was gaining on him as he raced up the stairs, taking them two at a time. He shot a scared look over his shoulder and ran headlong into a pair of children who were rounding the corner at the top. Both kids toppled, and the younger one burst into tears.

Without stopping, Bekenre turned toward the back of the building. Sophia slipped past the kids—"Coming through! Sorry!"—and raced after him.

She vaulted over wheeled carts and overturned chairs, stacks of books and mounds of clothes. When Bekenre looked back, she was surprised at the sheer terror in his eyes. He ducked into the kitchen, and Sophia followed, shouting, "Out of the way!" People pressed themselves to the walls, and Bekenre barreled past. He seized pots and pans, overturning them behind him and sending boiling water and hot metal into Sophia's path. She made a running leap over the debris instead of slowing. Bekenre shouldered his way through the back door and into the rearmost hallway.

"There's nowhere to go!" she shouted after him. "Give it up!"

He covered his head with his hands and jumped through a window. Glass shattered, and he plummeted out of sight.

Sophia reached the window a moment later. Down below, Bekenre raced across the pavement, apparently unhurt.

Two could play at that game.

She sprang through the broken window after him before she could think about it.

For a long, terrible moment, she was falling, her chest on fire, helpless as she watched her death approach. But that was behind her, done with. She seized her fear and wrestled it into submission just before she slammed into the ground.

A dangerous fall for a mortal was barely a heavy impact for her, now. She was up and running in an instant, parallel to the shelter's back wall, barely fifteen feet behind Bekenre. He glanced back, panicked, and frigid mist began to pour from his hands.

"Don't do it!" Sophia almost reached for her gun, but if she wanted answers, shooting him wasn't an option. She winced, expecting a miracle to the chest.

Instead, mist poured from his hands and solidified into a block of solid ice. He leapt onto it, and another, taller block formed in front of him, and another after that.

Stairs. He was making stairs to the roof.

The first block splintered and crumbled before Sophia was even close.

She was running out of options. If he made it to the roof, he was gone. There were no gryphons in sight, and she wasn't eager to try that again anyway. She could try shooting the ice out from under him, but she wasn't confident that would work, and she didn't want to risk hitting someone in the building.

Sobek's fangs, it's too bad Caelistra *couldn't be bothered to cut him off!*

She looked around as she ran, desperate.

And a grin spread across her face. Instead of chasing after him, she veered to the right.

Toward the hose coiled at the back of the shelter.

Bekenre paused, panting, struggling to gather more power. Each miracle was clearly taking a lot out of him. Whatever he was—part frost giant? A descendent of some northern god?—he clearly had enough humans between him and his divine ancestor that this was slowing him down. Not that the sweltering heat was doing him any favors.

Finally ready, frost poured from his fingers, and he leapt before the last platform between him and the building was completely finished.

Sophia opened the spigot and turned the hose on him.

Water sprayed over him, freezing the instant it touched the miraculous frost gushing from his hands. His momentum tried to carry him forward, but the ice held him back. He stumbled, smacking into the next block. Reeling, disoriented, he was still standing on the pillar when it split apart beneath him and sent him crashing to the ground.

When he tried to right himself, dazed, bleary-eyed, and surrounded by rapidly melting ice, Sophia was waiting.

She hauled him to his feet and slammed him into the wall of the building, pressing her forearm into his collarbone. "Conclave Furies," she growled. "Don't try anything stupid."

If anything, the terror on his face deepened. "Furies? Gods above, Sophia, I heard you died, but I didn't know—"

Sophia's heart was still hammering in her chest, more from adrenaline than actual exertion, but she gave him a menacing look.

He quailed, pressing himself against the wall to get away from her.

"What do you want?"

"Answers."

"I don't know anything! I swear! Let me go!"

"You always know something."

He managed a weak smile. "You seem angry, but whatever happened, I swear I had nothing to do with it. No need to take out your bad day on harmless old Bekenre, right?"

Angry? Why would I be angry, when I just made sure that I'd never see the people I love ever again?

Sophia heard footsteps. She looked up and found Caelistra sauntering toward her, cigarette dangling, hands in her pockets. "You caught him."

No thanks to you.

When she looked back at Bekenre, her expression was enough to make him flinch. "Look, it's *not* a good time to be talking to the law!"

Sophia leaned in closer. "Then maybe you should talk quickly, before someone sees us."

She watched the fight drain out of him. "Look, what do you want to know?" he whined. "I'm small time, right? I'm not involved in anything even close to Fury business."

"But you know who is."

"Are you kidding? Anyone who's not with the Dockyard Hounds or Silver Court is just keeping their head down, if they're smart."

"When have you ever been smart, Bekenre?"

"I'm smart enough to stay out of this shit. The war's always been bad, but you could usually avoid it if you were careful. The last few days? It's like the whole fucking city's gone crazy. Shootouts in the docks, Silver Court murdering people in the streets. Gods grant that all this bullshit blows over after the auction."

Sophia narrowed her eyes. "Auction?"

Bekenre swallowed. "I, uh, I don't—"

"Spill it. Everything you know, right now. You cooperate, and I make sure the whole shelter knows you got away. You don't, and I tell everyone how helpful you were."

His shoulders slumped. "I can only tell you what I know, all right? It's not a lot."

"You'd better hope it's enough, then."

"Okay. Look. You know Setesh? God of the desert?"

Sophia groaned softly. "Yes."

"Word is he's holding an auction under the Sandstorm Club tomorrow night. Very high class. Very exclusive."

"And incredibly illegal?"

"You get it. Whatever he's selling, it's big. Big enough that some really shady players from *outside* Memphis are going to be in town. That's the word on the streets this afternoon, at least." He was doused with sweat, barely whispering by the end.

This afternoon. Which means things changed after the bomb was stolen from the Hounds?

"Who?" she asked.

"I don't know, okay? Foreigners, I guess?"

"And what are they buying?"

"How should I know?" His gaze darted from side to side. "Look, I've told you everything I know. Please, just let me go."

She leaned in close, until her nose was almost touching his. "Bekenre?" He nodded. "If I find out you were lying or hiding something from me, I will be back. And I will not be happy. Do you understand?"

Sophia released him. He straightened his sodden sweatshirt, shot one last look around, and then scampered off.

Caelistra was surveying her coolly. Somehow, Sophia suspected she wasn't about to praise her for her quick thinking with the hose.

"Setesh," Caelistra said, her tone thoughtful.

Sophia shook her head. "Memphis PD has spent decades trying to get something on the bastard. But he's always a step ahead. Always completely clean, no matter what's going on around him." She bared her teeth. "Maybe this time…"

85

"Don't get your hopes up. We're not here for Setesh."

"Oh really? Even if he's the one who has the bomb? The people who took it weren't gangsters, Caelistra. They were too professional. That's more Setesh's style."

"Maybe." She took a long draw from her cigarette before crushing what was left of it under her heel. "I'm going back to Tartarus. I think I know a way to get us into that auction."

Sophia gave her an incredulous look. "Decided to help, all of a sudden?"

Caelistra scoffed, exhaling a cloud of smoke through her nose. "Please. If I left you in charge of this, you'd probably walk up to the front door of his club and kick it down. You'll forgive me if I prefer subtlety, going up against a god."

"Is that what you were doing while I ran Bekenre down?" Sophia asked dryly. "Subtlety?"

Ignoring her, Caelistra dipped a hand into her pocket and tossed Sophia the car keys. "Take the car back to the spot where we found it. Don't want some other Fury popping through the Deathgate and ending up without a ride. After that, do whatever you want. If the auction's not till tomorrow night, we've got plenty of time to prepare." She shut her eyes, and darkness gathered around her until she was hidden from sight. When it faded, she was gone, back in the underworld.

Sophia snarled at the empty air. Irritating as Caelistra was, the right thing to do was probably to return the car and then insist on helping her find a way inside the Sandstorm Club, whether she wanted the help or not. At the very least she would seem diligent.

And maybe she would, in a couple of hours, but there was something she needed to do in Memphis first.

CHAPTER ELEVEN

Sophia drove the car back to its spot first. Not because Caelistra had told her to, but because it was entirely possible that the Furies tracked the cars, and she didn't want anyone knowing where she was going next.

She had to change buses three times to get from downtown back to the Boneyard. It was a trip she remembered well from her childhood, even if she'd only made it rarely. Her dad was big on culture, and the only culture in the Boneyard tended to involve drugs and gunfights. Whenever he could afford it, he'd taken her and Gahiji downtown: to museums full of ancient Egyptian art and artifacts; to Memorial Square, the first place their great grandmother, Sophia's namesake, had gone when she'd emigrated from Greece; or to the Yoruba embassy, where their grandfather had worked.

Gahiji had always complained about those trips, but Sophia had devoured every last piece of information she could find. Every scrap of culture, past and present, near and far. Every way of life. Every hint that things could be different. That they could be *better*.

She'd been naive, then, dreaming of a better life. It wasn't some characteristic flaw of Egyptian culture that kept the Boneyard poor and violent, something that could be turned around if they just adopted another way of life. It was an overwhelmed and underfunded police force, entrenched criminal elements, insufficient social services, and a thousand other problems that went away only a few blocks north.

Sophia had spent her entire career trying to help the Boneyard, and when her superiors finally let her, it was like trying to fight a hurricane.

Maybe a Fury with the right lead could do what a mortal couldn't.

She watched the city stream past. Skyscrapers gave way to smaller offices and apartments, which gave way to crumbling malls and tenements. Each time the bus stopped, the people outside were a little poorer, a little more desperate. When she got off, only two blocks from Gahiji's house, she was in the same city, just the part of it that had been left behind.

She had to swallow a painful lump in her throat as she focused on her goal. It would be torture to see Gahiji and Teshan and not say anything, but there was something she wanted back. A reminder of her old life and the people in it, all the more important if she couldn't reconnect.

Walking those two blocks felt like it took hours. She'd taken this street home from school every day, and it was alive with memories, good and bad. A fight behind that convenience store, after another kid had picked on her brother. Awkward high school dates at the now-shuttered movie theater. Hiding on the floor of the drug store as the Dockyard Hounds and the Silver Court murdered each other in the street outside.

She'd grown up alongside plenty of godborn, but there wasn't a single one in sight anymore, at least none that couldn't pass as human. They'd all left, or been killed by the Hounds.

She stopped outside a tiny restaurant called Kehinde's, home of the best Yoruba food in the city, and breathed in the best parts of her childhood. She had a few denarii in her wallet, an advance on her first paycheck, and she was sorely tempted to go in and order something, even if food was optional for the dead. But the owner was a friend of her dad's, and the neighborhood had enough shit going on without spreading rumors of dead women coming back for a bite to eat.

She kept her head down and hurried down the street, wondering whether coming back here was a terrible idea.

Gahiji's house stood out from the packed apartments and

abandoned lots that filled the rest of the block. It was a standalone unit, showing its age but still too nice for the area. It had been their dad's, and he'd held onto it even as the neighborhood had disintegrated around them. Out of stubbornness, perhaps. Or maybe he'd just been unable to part with the last place he'd lived with his wife.

Now their dad was in a retirement home, and Gahiji had the house. Because *of course* he did. So what if he'd rarely had legitimate work capable of keeping the lights on? Last she'd heard, he'd finally taken a job at the shelter, like she'd been urging him to for years, but whether that would last...

As she gazed at the house, the bitter sister in Sophia picked out all the signs of neglect—withered plants, chipped paint, bullet holes in the front stairs—but she tried to ignore them and force herself to move. The sooner she was out of here, the better.

Just like she remembered, the window to her old room didn't latch right. She slid it up, as silently as she could, and listened. Two voices, Gahiji and Teshan. Even with senses sharpened by divine power, she couldn't hear what they were saying, but she could tell Teshan was upset.

Sophia fought down the urge to go to her. Instead, she lifted the screen aside and climbed through the window, each movement sure and careful.

The room was Teshan's now, the last traces of familiarity swallowed by teenage sensibilities. The wall over the desk was plastered with posters. Bad Horn Joke, a band of horned godborn from across the Conclave. Caution Tape, a band Sophia had liked growing up, now billing itself as "classic" for their reunion tour. Apollo himself, shirtless and stunning and timeless as ever, advertising a concert in Waset.

There were still comic books on the shelves, but the old standbys were outnumbered by campy science fiction, with angsty teenaged godborn traveling the stars with outlandish hair and more divine power and laser guns than common sense.

A few of Teshan's best drawings hung above the comics. The subjects were varied, from sketches of fashionable gods to portraits of family members, but for a sixteen-year-old, the quality was impressive. Sophia's heart ached to see how far she'd come. It was hard to pull herself away.

She crept to the open door and waited, ears straining. A crowbar leaned against the door frame, a sad admission of the neighborhood's dangers.

"It's okay. It's going to be okay." Gahiji's voice.

She grimaced and eased her head around the corner. There was a light on in the kitchen, but that wasn't where she was going. She turned the other way, keeping her steps as light as possible. The smell of the place made her heart ache. The house had been Gahiji's for years now, but the scents of leather and old wood still reminded her of her childhood.

She found her belongings piled in the front hall. Everything was packed into boxes, but they were all open, as if Gahiji, in characteristic fashion, had begun going through her things and given up partway. Frozen in place, Sophia stared at the bits of her life peeking out at her through the cardboard. This was everything? A few piles, all left to Teshan? Almost thirty years, distilled into this?

A plaintive *meow* made her jump, heart hammering against her ribs, but it was just her cat, Imhotep. He brushed against her ankles, looking up at her with accusatory eyes. Any doubts that he recognized her vanished in an instant. He *meowed* again.

Sophia bent down to pet him. She was relieved when the conversation in the other room continued. No one had heard.

"Hey Im," she breathed. She scratched behind his ears, and he purred up at her. "I'm sorry, I'm not here to take you back. You probably don't want to live in Tartarus anyway."

She stood up, wiping a tear from her cheek. Imhotep wound around her leg again, a warm bundle of stripes and demands for attention. When she ignored him, he *meowed* at her and walked down the hall, tail bouncing.

Thank you, Gahiji, for doing this one good thing.

Sophia bent over the nearest boxes. She had to get through this before she broke down completely.

The first box was filled with clothes. She dug through it and then set it aside. The next was desk supplies, a couple of books. The last box in the stack held some of her meager kitchen gear.

A thought struck her, and despair rippled through her in its wake. *What if it's not here? What if it's in an evidence locker, with everything else I was wearing when I died?*

She had to keep looking. She rebuilt the stack, putting everything back where it had started, and dug into the next one.

More clothes. Mugs. Books.

Every little thing was painful. Even random clutter that she wouldn't have given a second thought to while she'd been alive was a harsh reminder now. But she picked through it all anyway, setting box after box aside. None of it was what she was looking for.

She found a set of old comic books. A pair of old hiking boots with a box all to themselves.

Her sketchbook.

Longing stole the breath from her lungs. She'd barely had a quiet moment to herself, but one would come eventually, and when it did, it would be a tremendous comfort to draw. That book held so much of the last few years, drawings from moments of triumph and moments of despair.

It took all of her willpower to leave it behind. Gahiji would notice. Besides, it would be better to make a clean break and just get a new sketchbook.

She forced herself to close the box and put the stack back together. Her breath stung her throat as she started in on the next.

As soon as she opened it, she was confronted by a pair of drawings Teshan had done when she was seven. "Aunt Sophia fighting bad guys" was Sophia's favorite. It showed her punching a monster—maybe a manticore, though it was hard to tell—in the face.

She had to take a deep breath and force her hands to stop shaking before she moved them aside.

Underneath was a dark blue bag, cinched shut, with Memphis Police Department written on it in gold hieroglyphs.

Jackpot.

Sophia pulled the bag open. Inside were a handful of personal items. Her watch, a necklace, her phone.

And, nestled at the bottom, the reason she was here: the bracelet of colorful, woven string that Teshan had made her years ago. The bracelet she'd been wearing when she died.

She was dead. Guilt, and anger, and abject terror welled up inside her, along with a thousand other emotions she hadn't let herself feel since she'd woken up in the Valkyries' Tower. Kofi would never rib her about her latest horrible date. She would never have another fight with her father, or share another drink in one of the rare moments they got along. Styx, she'd never fight with Gahiji or hold Teshan when she was scared. They were her life, and her life was behind her. Career with the Furies or traditional afterlife, there was no way around that, not without hurting the people she cared about.

But she still had a job to do.

Sophia untied the bracelet and, holding one end with her teeth, tied it back around her wrist. She hesitated as she closed the knot. Was this a terrible idea? Was this just going to make her miserable, tethering herself to a life she was supposed to have left behind?

"You're such a hypocrite!"

Teshan's shout brought Sophia back to the present. She cinched the bag up in a hurry, leaving the rest behind. The bracelet Teshan had made was the only thing that mattered. She hurriedly stacked the boxes back the way they'd been.

"Teshan, I know you're mad—"

"And why aren't *you*? Anhur's *hairballs*, she's—"

"Language, Teshan!"

"Funny how you only care about that when there's something you'd rather not talk about."

Everything was back in place. No one would notice that the bracelet was gone. Or, if they did, they'd just think it had gotten lost in the move. Sophia risked a glance back into the hall.

Teshan was framed in the doorway to the kitchen, her back to Sophia. Her arms were crossed, her hair wild.

Sophia had been here for fights like this—Styx, she'd been a part of more than a few—and she knew how this was going to end. She had to get out before Teshan stormed into her room.

Sophia darted into the hall, her heart pounding. In the kitchen, Gahiji was still arguing himself into a hole. "I'm just trying to do what's best for you. I know how you feel."

"Do you?"

"Of course I do! She was my sister! I loved Sophia too!"

Sophia's heart leapt into her throat. *She* was *my sister. I'm in the past tense now.* She stumbled and her foot caught the edge of the doorjamb.

"Hang on, did you hear that?"

Shit. Sophia forced herself back into motion, racing across the room and sliding the window open. She leapt through, spun the instant she was on the ground, and slipped the screen back into place.

She had just closed the window and ducked out of sight when the light turned on inside. She cast about for a place to hide and vanished behind a neglected desert shrub.

Teshan's face appeared in the window, tear-streaked and angry.

Sophia stayed perfectly still. The Furies were right to prohibit contact with friends and family from life, and not just to keep the death gods happy. However great the temptation, getting back in touch would destroy Teshan. She didn't need that emotional rollercoaster.

But knowing that didn't help soothe the Sophia's heart.

Teshan gave up and turned back around. Sophia heard her shout one last parting shot at Gahiji before the door slammed.

She had what she came for. She gazed at the bracelet around her wrist and finished cinching it into place. It wasn't a tether to her life, dragging her back: it was a token of what mattered most. Even if she never saw Teshan again, her niece would be with her, a reminder that there were still innocents worth fighting for.

Sophia closed her eyes and focused on the Deathgate at the center of Memphis, drawing on her connection to Death. She needed to draw something, to clear her head. Maybe the thaumaturgy professor from the convention center... Ixtele? The lines on her skin would make for an interesting portrait.

But as soon as she could think straight again, she needed to get back to work.

They had a black market auction to infiltrate.

CHAPTER TWELVE

Nine Years Earlier

"Aunt Sophia? I made you something."

Sophia swallowed the insult she'd been about to throw at her brother before it could reach impressionable seven-year-old ears. She shot Gahiji a warning glance before facing Teshan.

Her heart almost broke when she saw Teshan's face, the girl's eyes moving from her dad to Sophia and back again. "What's wrong?"

Sophia smiled as convincingly as she could. "Nothing's wrong. You want to show me what you made?"

Teshan beamed at her, but Sophia couldn't tell whether her niece was fooled or just trying to make her feel better. She held up the bracelet she'd made as if it were a priceless treasure.

"Wow, is this for me?" Sophia crouched in front of her.

"Uh huh! We learned how to make them in school. I made Dad one already, but I didn't want you to be jealous."

Teshan's innocent cheer made it impossible to stay mad, even at Gahiji. Sophia wrapped her arms around the girl. "Thanks."

Teshan tried to wriggle out of her grip. "Put it on! Put it on!" Chuckling, Sophia let her niece put the bracelet around her wrist and then helped her tie it. Teshan pointed out each of the individual strands. "We were learning about the Conclave's colors, see? Gold for prosperity, green for fertility, blue for trade, and white for peace!" She looked thrilled that she'd remembered them all.

Sophia hugged her again, wishing she never had to let go. Teshan's effervescent joy was a light at the heart of the Boneyard, a light Sophia would do anything to protect. "It's wonderful. Thank you so much."

"You're welcome!" Teshan tilted her head back and did her best impression of puppy-dog eyes. "Will you come do art with me?"

Sophia scrubbed a stray bit of dinner from Teshan's cheek, smiling down at her. She was dangerously behind on paperwork, and she'd promised her arthritic neighbor she'd take a look at his leaky sink, but she couldn't say no to that face. "Sure. Grab your stuff and I'll meet you in your room. Sharpen me a pencil?"

Chortling, Teshan swept across the kitchen toward the table where she'd been drawing earlier. She snatched up paper and pencils, hugged her dad's leg on the way past, and grabbed a bottle of juice from the fridge before tearing down the hall and back to her room. Leftover paper fluttered to the floor, and the fridge swung open in her wake.

"Slow down, Whirlwind!" Sophia called. She picked up the paper while Gahiji shut the fridge.

As soon as Teshan's door closed, Sophia said softly, "She knows we're fighting." Inevitable, maybe, but it was something she'd been dreading more and more as Teshan got older.

"I'm happy to stop any time," Gahiji replied.

Sophia rounded on him. "Really? This is *my* fault? You promised me you were done. You *promised*. And then I find you with a bunch of stolen jewelry?"

He glared at her as if this were all her fault for coming over earlier than he'd expected. As if it were her fault for finding out what he'd done. "I didn't steal it," he said.

"I know that. You put your thieving days behind you, and now you're a fence. I feel so much better." She leaned on the counter, staring down at the floor. "What if you'd gotten caught?"

"I wasn't going to get caught."

"Really?" Sophia lowered her voice even further. "I've bailed you out of jail three times since Teshan was born. *Three times.* What was I supposed to tell her this time?"

Gahiji didn't get mad. He never did. He just leaned back against the fridge, rubbing his forehead with one hand. "You don't know what it's like, Soph. You got out."

She had to fight the urge to throw something at him before she could manage intelligible speech again. "I didn't *run away* from the Boneyard, Gahiji. I joined the police to try to clean it up."

"How's that going for you?"

"It would be going better if my own brother weren't part of the gods-damned problem!"

Gahiji sighed, shaking his head. He retrieved a cutting board and a bread knife and laid them on the counter. "Want anything?"

"No, *Gahiji*, I don't want any food. What I want is for you to get your shit together for your *daughter!*"

Gahiji cut himself a slice of bread and began spreading fig jam on it. Sophia watched him, fuming. He took a bite, eyeing her. Finally, he said, "I talked to Dad yesterday."

"Don't change the subject."

"It would mean a lot to him if you went to see him."

Sophia looked away, jaw clenched. *There's no reason to feel guilty. I have nothing to feel guilty about.* "I brought him his groceries and a couple of new puzzles," she said. "And I made sure the retirement home knew about the termites."

"Sure. All without going inside to actually talk to him."

"I thought I'd spare us both the shouting match."

Gahiji sighed. "He loves you. He really does. He just…"

"He just thinks that if he keeps supporting you, keeps giving you everything you could ever want, maybe someday you'll turn away from your life of crime," Sophia said, years of bitterness leeching into her voice despite her best efforts.

Gahiji gave her a sad look. "He loves both of us, unconditionally.

Isn't that a parent's job?"

Sophia scoffed. "A parent's job is to do what's best for their kid."

"Because you're an expert?"

Sophia looked him straight in the eye. "I don't have to have a kid of my own to know that Teshan's going to be devastated if you end up in prison for the rest of her childhood." He gave her a hurt look, and she let out a frustrated sigh. "Gods, Gahiji… I know what it's like, living in the Boneyard. Half the people I arrest aren't bad people. They're just out of good options. But you're not. I know Meret's offered you a job at the shelter. An, honest, paying job. Why don't you take it?"

It was a while before Gahiji responded. He took another bite, chewing without meeting her eye. "I'm thinking about it."

"I don't see what there is to think about."

"No. You don't."

Sophia threw up her hands. "Incredible." She stormed out of the kitchen.

She was a few steps into the hall, car keys already in hand, when she remembered that Teshan was waiting for her. *Do art with me.* Teshan had always been overawed by Sophia's sketchbook, and with every wild drawing she improved on the last, eager to impress.

"Heading home?"

Sophia blinked, eyes focusing again. To her right, the door to the master bedroom was open, and Meret was inside, probably finishing up her own paperwork for the day. She gave Sophia an exhausted smile as she pulled out one of her earbuds.

"What do you see in him, Meret?" The question forced itself out of Sophia before she could stop it.

Meret's gaze drifted toward the kitchen for a moment, her eyes losing focus. "Loyalty."

Sophia scoffed. "To himself, maybe."

Frowning, Meret took out the other earbud and set her laptop aside. "Loyalty's never simple, in my experience. If it were obvious, we wouldn't spend so much time and energy trying to find it in the people around us."

Sophia leaned against the doorjamb, crossing her arms. "You think Gahiji's a better man than I give him credit for?"

Meret drummed her fingers against her knee, regarding Sophia thoughtfully. "My father talked constantly about loyalty. 'Family is everything. Be loyal to them, always,' he would say. And then, if he thought we weren't listening to him—which he thought most of the time—he would beat us."

"Alcohol?" Sophia asked with a grimace. It was a guess. She'd always wanted to know Meret better, but they were both too busy, each fighting to save the Boneyard in their own way.

Meret laughed bitterly, absently rubbing at a white scar above her collarbone. "Oh no. He was a violent, monstrous man, but in the eighteen years he lived with us, the only thing he ever let cloud his judgment was anger. When I was ten, he dragged one of the dogs inside and caved in its skull in with a tire iron to teach us a lesson about obedience, but at least he was *sober*."

Sophia had to fight back a surge of bile. "Fuck… Meret, I'm so sorry. I didn't know."

"No need to apologize." Meret's eyes refocused as she visibly dragged herself out of her horrible past. "My father said he valued loyalty, but he never knew the real thing. What he really meant was fear. Obedience. I've spent my whole life trying to be the furthest kind of person from him, and I was lucky to find Gahiji along the way. He isn't perfect, but for all his faults, he cares about his family."

"I wish he had a better way of showing it," Sophia grumbled.

Down the hall, Teshan yanked her door open and poked her head through. "I'm ready!"

Sophia and Meret shared a smile. "Coming!" Sophia called back. As soon as Teshan withdrew, she said softly, "You really think I'm too hard on him?"

"He's doing his best."

Sophia sighed heavily, shaking her head and pocketing her keys as she went back into the hall. "That's what I'm afraid of."

CHAPTER THIRTEEN

Sophia met Caelistra at the Deathgate the next evening at exactly 9:30pm, Memphis time. She'd eventually tracked Caelistra down to help strategize, only to find the work already done. The next ten hours had been spent preparing.

"Cutting it a little close," Caelistra said, without turning away from the curling fog that marked the transition back to the world of the living.

"Not like I had a closet full of clothes to pick from. I'm glad the Furies were paying, or this outfit would have cost most of my first paycheck. Is this really what people wear clubbing?" The tailor Caelistra had recommended was a dead, enthusiastic cyclops with a shop in Tartarus—gods only knew who her customers were, besides Furies. She'd insisted on outfitting Sophia in the latest fashion, and this had been the best of the three options.

Sophia wore closely fitted charcoal pants, a button-up shirt open at the collar, and a matching vest. Her unfamiliar shoes pinched her feet, and she kept shrugging her shoulders, unused to the fit. It was the sort of thing she *might* have felt comfortable wearing on a date, except that the fabric was all wildly expensive. At least there were pockets. After spending some time on makeup, she'd barely recognized herself in the mirror.

Caelistra looked her up and down. "I have no idea. The last time I went to a club, it was in Rome, in 2722. I suspect things have changed in the last fifty years." She glanced coolly at the bracelet around Sophia's wrist and then looked her in the eye. "Get that from the tailor too?"

Sophia replied with the most casual shrug she could muster. "Thought it spiced up the outfit."

Caelistra's outfit was even more startling. She wore a black dress that barely went down to mid-thigh, showing off a trim physique that was all corded muscle. Anywhere but a nightclub, the dress could have passed as lingerie, which made it just about the last thing Sophia could have imagined her partner wearing. Caelistra had done something with makeup so the scars across her face looked like a rugged kind of fashion statement. The only things that hadn't changed were her hair and the SPQR-and-anchor tattoo on her arm. "Let's hope you don't have to fight in that," Sophia remarked.

Caelistra let out a weary sigh. "This is an *infiltration*. If you're planning on getting into a fight at all, please tell me now. You're welcome to go off and get yourself killed by an angry god, but you can do it on your own." She turned and strode through the Deathgate without another word. Sophia followed, curious why that had struck a nerve.

Now that the sun was down, it hardly took them any time at all to drive from downtown Memphis to the north edge of town. Caelistra let out a soft whistle as the buildings parted around them and the nightclub came into view. "I heard stories, but somehow, that is even more ridiculous than I was expecting."

The Sandstorm Club was a monument to Setesh's arrogance, not to mention the butt of a thousand "compensating for something?" jokes. The club sprawled across the top of a mountain, looming over the Great Pyramids and standing head and shoulders above the skyscrapers downtown. Massive spotlights stabbed into the sky from all around the club, a constant demand for attention.

"No joke," Sophia said. "Setesh apparently bought up all the land behind the pyramids in 2673? 74? Something like that; about ten years after the Conclave was founded. He did it all piecemeal, through third parties. Then, as soon as the land was his, he personally raised a mountain out of the desert and built the club on top. The other Egyptian gods were furious, since the whole thing looked like an insult to the pharaohs buried in the pyramids."

Caelistra chuckled knowingly. "But of course he wasn't doing anything precisely illegal, so they couldn't do anything about it."

"Setesh in a nutshell," Sophia grumbled. "People bring nuisance lawsuits against the club, and politicians try to rezone it out of existence, but it never works. He always finds a loophole. It's been almost a century, and the damn thing is still taller than any of the buildings in the city."

"Makes sense. He wants to show that the desert still hasn't been conquered by civilization."

They joined the line of cars snaking up the mountainside and waited a good twenty minutes before they reached a spot where a valet would take their car. Sophia scanned the crowd gathering outside, but all she saw were eager partygoers, held back by a wall of huge bouncers. Behind them, the club's doors, etched with a glittering, stylized sandstorm, had yet to open.

Caelistra paused at the curb to smoke one last cigarette while Sophia eyed the line that was already forming. "You sure your connection came through?"

"I'm sure," Caelistra said. "We're on the guest list."

"How *did* you manage that, exactly?" That was the one part of the planning Caelistra had taken care of while she was still in Memphis.

Caelistra shrugged. "I've got a friend who's dating Eris's daughter. Evidently Setesh has been a big fan of Eris ever since that farce with the apple caused the Trojan War."

"You have a friend?"

"Ha ha. Very clever." The club's doors began to grind open, and Caelistra breathed out a sigh of relief as she flicked away her cigarette. "And the gods save me from your witty banter. Perfect timing."

Throbbing bass rolled out into the night like the heartbeat of the mountain itself, the rest of the music impossible to hear from outside.

And all around the mountaintop, the sandstorm that gave the club its name roared to life.

Sand spiraled into the sky, forming a twisting column that encased the entire summit, and what had been a grand view of the pyramids and the glittering city below was rapidly shrouded from view. From within the club, spotlight after spotlight flared to life, casting hypnotic patterns across the wall of dust.

Caelistra raised an eyebrow. "He does this every night?"

"Just about. Works the miracle for the storm personally, from what I hear."

"Hmm."

Sophia headed for the shorter of the two lines trailing toward the doors, ignoring the envious glances from the people in the other. They didn't have to wait long. "Names?" asked a bouncer with a tablet in her hand. The woman's biceps were almost as big as her thighs.

Sophia gave the fake names she'd been provided with. Two other bouncers eyed them while the first consulted the list. "Go on. He has to search you before you can go in."

The search was quick but professional. Sophia felt naked, marching into Setesh's lair without a gun and a sword. He was a god, capable of sending her to oblivion with the flick of his wrist, but at least she would have felt better armed. It was a small consolation that Caelistra could summon her weapons and armor from nothing if it came to that.

The bouncer motioned them through. They were in.

Dance music wrapped them in its crushing grip the instant they were through the doors. The melody was lively and infectious, but it was the bass that roared in Sophia's ears, reverberated in her bones, urged her feet into motion. Just trying to walk across the floor, she caught herself swaying in time with the music.

Caelistra shot her a glance, and Sophia was startled to see her moving to the beat as well. Until she felt the tingling numbness of something interfering with her own divine power. "Thaumatech speakers!" she shouted to Caelistra. She'd never heard of them before, but it made sense.

Caelistra had to bend close to Sophia's ear just to be heard. "Don't fight it. Just blend in. Wait till I give the signal."

So they danced. Near each other; definitely not *with* each other.

People poured through the open doors, and the party surged to life around them. Sophia danced with a merfolk man who was unable to meet her eyes, his gills flapping nervously. With a gorgeous woman who had some kind of thaumatech hair dye that changed color in time with the music. With a centaur whose hooves clattered enthusiastically across the dance floor. All the while, she kept Caelistra in sight, waiting for the signal.

The club itself was a stunning display of light and thaumatechnology. It was composed of seven or eight large courtyards and overlooking balconies, all open to the night air and displaying the spiraling sandstorm to full effect. The patterns flashing across the storm shifted and writhed, hinting at the monstrous one moment and the sexual the next. Fine glass and elegant marble stretched in every direction. The amount of money that had gone into this dancefloor alone could probably have turned the Boneyard into a paradise.

But they were there on the job. Sophia pushed past the spectacle and scanned the place like a detective, noting entrances and exits, cameras and guards.

She was ready when Caelistra danced toward her and took her arm. "Let's get some *drinks!*" Caelistra roared. Even knowing what to look for, Sophia couldn't find a trace of the Fury she was used to beneath Caelistra's party-girl mask.

They crossed the dance floor toward the bar. Their path led them behind a set of huge speakers and, not coincidentally, beneath a pair of cameras. She squeezed Caelistra's arm, and Caelistra made a show of tripping over a cord. As she righted herself, she slid a tiny plastic device into an empty power socket.

And then they were off again, laughing together as they approached the bar. A bartender finished helping a young couple and greeted them with a smile. "Two house specials!" Sophia shouted to him. "No, no. Make it four! Human strength!" It was safer for her to do the talking if they were going to pass for human, since Caelistra didn't know Egyptian. It only took two people hearing the same conversation in different languages to piece things together.

Sophia paid the man with a fancy, unfamiliar card—tonight, the Furies were buying. They retreated from the bar with their drinks, and Caelistra clinked the glasses together. "Good health and long life!"

Sophia snorted and tossed back the drink. It was delicious, with a splash of raspberry masking the alcohol. It probably would have hit her like a ton of bricks, before her death. Now, the divine power at her core just burned through the alcohol like any other toxin.

It took a miracle to get a Fury drunk.

"Phew, I haven't had this much fun in ages!" Caelistra shouted.

"Just don't overdo it," Sophia called back. "I don't want to have to carry you home." They moved out of the crowd—at least, as much as that was possible—and Caelistra leaned against a pillar beneath one of the balconies. There was a service entrance right behind her, and a pair of bouncers watching the two of them from beside the door.

In all the time they'd been dancing, Sophia hadn't seen a single member of the staff go in or out of that door.

Which made it the most likely target.

They finished their drinks and set their glasses on an abandoned table nearby. "Ready to get back out there?" Caelistra asked. That was the signal.

Finally. "Let's do it," Sophia said.

Caelistra adjusted the straps of her dress and thumbed the remote trigger on the device she'd planted.

All the lights in the far corner of the room flared brighter for an instant. Then they flickered and cut out completely. The surrounding speakers warbled erratically, the miracle on the fritz along with the sound. Sophia felt compelled to turn in circles, to jump, to fight... Until the speakers shorted out completely in a shower of sparks.

The camera in the corner died in the same power surge.

"Woah there, looks like we've got some technical difficulties, everyone!" the DJ's voice rang out. She was chuckling as if nothing was wrong, but more than a few bouncers were leaving their posts and heading toward the disturbance.

Including one of the two by the door Sophia wanted to get through. She glanced toward his companion, urging him to move too, but he stayed where he was, arms crossed.

"Well, that half worked…" Caelistra said.

Sophia scanned the crowd around them instead of responding. As the lights flickered madly, she stuck her foot into someone's path.

Her target tripped and went smashing straight into a huge godborn with furred skin and a lion's head. The godborn grabbed the man by the shirt and lifted him into the air, and someone screamed.

The remaining bouncer hurried from his post to intervene.

Caelistra and Sophia were moving as soon as his back was turned. They ducked behind a pillar, out of sight of every camera but the one they'd disabled. Then they were through the door.

And inside a dimly lit stairwell. Caelistra's carefree grin vanished, her face all business once again. In the space of moments, she opened the purse she'd brought along for the evening, unfurled a long black dress, and pulled it on over her clothes.

Sophia held out her arm as soon as she was done. "Shall we attend an auction?"

Caelistra snorted, and they hurried down the stairs into the mountain. By the time the music started up behind them again, they were almost out of earshot.

CHAPTER FOURTEEN

The interior of the mountain was a twisting warren of stark, utilitarian tunnels. Sophia and Caelistra found a trickle of employees heading to the lower floors and followed them down, ducking out of sight whenever anyone hurried past in the other direction.

Before long, they could hear the low murmur of laughter and conversation ahead. The service corridor joined a large passageway decorated with carpet and flickering lamps, where guests who'd entered the mountain without the need for sabotage and misdirection filed toward the auction. There were guards here and there, but not enough to watch the whole corridor.

Sophia and Caelistra ducked out of sight, waited for the right moment, and slipped into the crowd without attracting any notice.

Ahead, a set of double doors stood partway open, their surfaces engraved with desert landscapes. Sophia rolled her neck from side to side, trying to loosen some of the tension in her shoulders. She'd blended into a high society party for a case, once. She could do it again.

As long as she didn't dwell on the fact that this party was full of the city's worst criminals and hosted by a god best known for dicing his brother into tiny pieces and scattering them across the world.

"Ready?" she asked softly.

Caelistra casually smoothed her dress as they pressed forward with the other guests. "If anyone gives us trouble, just look contemptuous and walk away. Best way to fit in." But the heavily armed guards in black and gold let them pass without a second glance, and the other guests were too busy nervously scanning for their enemies to pay them any mind.

The massive auction hall wouldn't have been out of place in a palace. Miracle-threaded tapestries covered two of the walls, their fibers in constant movement as soldiers and monsters and gods clashing across their woven battlefields. The wall opposite the curtained stage was transparent, even though no glass had been visible from the outside. They were below the sandstorm, and the window offered a stunning view of the pyramids and the gleaming lights of Memphis.

Above, glittering crystalline chandeliers cast a dim glow across the room. Instead of pillars, trickles of shimmering sand poured from slots in the roof into gilded basins that never seemed to fill. Even the floor tiles were a feat of frivolous thaumaturgy, with a fractal of stark white veins slowly branching across a background of black tiles before crumbling to nothing and reforming in a new pattern.

Sophia found their first destination with a quick scan of the room. "Over there," she said quietly, nodding toward a trio of employees who were handing out tablets to the guests.

Her heart pounded as they waited, but as far as anyone was concerned, they were just two more guests. "Your bidding interface, ma'am." She took it, and they retreated to one of the walls.

Caelistra studied the tablet for a minute before nodding to herself and punching in her account information. "Just like we thought. Anonymous and untraceable. Setesh wants return customers, after all."

"This was a good plan," Sophia admitted reluctantly. When Caelistra had proposed simply *buying* the bomb, she'd been skeptical, despite the number of decimal places in the account they'd been entrusted with. "I couldn't have put all this together so quickly—"

"I'm so glad I've won your approval," Caelistra interrupted, rolling her eyes. "I already knew you had a lot to learn. Don't expect me to be impressed if you've just realized it." She turned around before Sophia could reply. "It looks like they're getting ready to start. Let's join the crowd."

Sophia took a deep breath and made herself focus on something else instead of scowling at the back of Caelistra's head.

She studied the room as much as she could without drawing attention. There was no sign of merchandise, Rashmi's bomb or otherwise. Not surprising. She expected that everything for sale was concealed behind the curtain. Considering the nature of the crowd and the number of guards Setesh had posted around the room, making a grab for the bomb certainly wasn't an option.

The occupants of the auction hall represented every criminal faction in Memphis, and more beyond. A few wore masks, but most seemed unconcerned with anonymity. Three people with scarves around their necks stood in one corner, glaring daggers at everyone who got close. Dockyard Hounds who'd survived the attack on the wharf, probably. Two men in ostentatious togas, surrounded by a circle of bodyguards, were no doubt from the local arm of the Roman Mob. A woman with a crocodile head, probably some local power broker, was holding court near the center of the room. And across the way…

Sophia leaned closer to Caelistra without slowing down. "See the man in the vest?"

Utterly casual, Caelistra glanced in the man's direction. "Yes."

"That's the leader of the Silver Court, the Hounds' main rivals. He calls himself the 'Silver King.' The four people around him are his closest advisors."

"Looks like he doesn't trust Setesh's security. He's got more bodyguards than anyone in the room."

She was right. The Silver Court recruited disaffected young water spirits who dreamed of something more than a future in irrigation or water treatment. Then it twisted those dreams and convinced them that their inborn power and natural grandeur entitled them to the worship of fawning mortals just like their ancestors had experienced. Only the most powerful—and fanatical—among them would have earned a place at their boss's side, and it was surprising so many had made the cut.

Was the Silver Court expecting an attack? Planning to start something themselves? Or were they just trying to be prepared after all the violence in the last few days?

"Ah, my friends!" A deep, booming voice brought them both around in an instant.

Barely five feet behind them, Setesh himself had stepped through a curtain of sand to greet another group of guests. He shook a woman's hand, laughed at a joke told by one of the others, and then turned away.

Focusing directly on Sophia and Caelistra. "Welcome!" he said, his voice a low rumble. "I don't believe I've had the pleasure."

Panic wrapped its icy claws around Sophia's heart.

The god of the desert was a tall, powerfully built man with light brown skin. His clothing was eye catching in its simplicity, a classical skirt and shirt of unadorned white linen. He needed no finery to call attention to himself. He appeared human from the neck down, but his head was that of a long-extinct animal called a sha: it had black fur, triangular ears that were thinner at the base than at the top, and a long, curved snout, almost like an anteater's. At first, Sophia thought he had sand-colored irises, until she realized that his eyes contained shifting rings of actual sand, circling his pupils in slow, hypnotic halos. The very air around him shimmered like a heat mirage, the shapes suggested within as ephemeral as they were blood-chilling, and Sophia thought she could *feel* the heat against her skin.

Years of training and experience were all that saved her. She smiled and bowed her head, speaking automatically as she struggled to regain control. "Our host himself! I must say, we are delighted to be here. This is quite the event you've put together, your worship." It was the proper term of address, a holdover from the days when people had still worshipped the gods, but it still tasted sour on her tongue.

Setesh's eyes glittered with dark amusement. "I try to impress." Sophia felt like his gaze was boring into her soul, and she had to fight not to look away. Setesh tapped a finger against his chin, lowering his voice until only the three of them had even a chance of hearing. "I hope you enjoy the auction. I would be mad as a Fury on the hunt if any of my guests were less than pleased." His smile displayed long rows of finely pointed teeth, glittering with cunning malice.

Sophia froze for a split second before she seized the abject terror churning through her guts and wrestled it back under control. She turned to Caelistra, who was just recovering as well, and traded an empty smile before returning to Setesh. "Well, I can't speak for anyone else, but *we're* just here to enjoy ourselves and spend some money."

Setesh laughed softly. "I'm delighted to hear that. Please, if there's anything you need, just ask one of my employees. Now, if you'll excuse me, I'm afraid the guests of honor are nearly here."

He strode past them, still pausing to greet everyone he passed. He never shot a single glance back their way, but Sophia still felt like she wanted to vomit. It only helped a bit when he vanished through a door beneath one of the tapestries.

"He knows," Caelistra growled.

"How..."

"It doesn't matter how." Caelistra rounded on Sophia, a startling, uncharacteristic intensity in her eyes. "We have to go."

Sophia was still trying to piece her composure back together, but that brought her up short. "What?"

"You heard the same conversation I did. It's time to leave."

Sophia caught her by the shoulder. "No. We weren't lying. We're here to buy, not cause trouble. No heroics, remember?"

"You think Setesh is going to sell *us* the bomb?"

"Maybe." She glanced around. "He could have called his guards. Styx, he could have just killed us, and no one would have batted an eye."

Caelistra glanced around, glaring. "This is a terrible idea."

"It'll work," Sophia said firmly. Inside, though, every old doubt she'd ever felt was bubbling back to the surface. Setesh had barely spoken to her, and her knees still felt like jelly. The amount of raw power he gave off was like standing near a furnace, and he hadn't even been *doing* anything. What the Styx had she been thinking, signing up for a job where she might need to *fight* someone that strong?

But she'd be damned if she let Caelistra see the slightest uncertainty, and fear didn't alter the mission. "Nothing has changed," she said. "We wait for the bomb, and we try to win it. Barring that, we see who does. Besides, I'm curious about these guests of honor he…"

She trailed off as the main doors opened, and a group of people strode through.

Actually, *two* groups of people, staying as far apart as they could and glaring murder at each other. On the left was a procession of men and women wearing formal clothing but marching like soldiers. The godborn at the head of the column had patches of scales dotting his skin, and tiny white and teal feathers grew here and there from his scalp to mingle with his hair. From the look on his face, he could have been walking through a sewer.

Aztecs. They weren't in uniform, no doubt to ensure some level of deniability, but otherwise they were right out of a propaganda broadcast. The only thing missing was a smug god surrounded by "adoring" subjects and offering a better life to those who threw off the yoke of materialism and devoted themselves to the worship of true, deserving deities.

Never mind that some of their worshippers would have their hearts carved out in exchange.

The other group was smaller, but wilder. They had uncommonly pale skin, which some had decorated with whorls of blue body paint. Each one had faintly luminous eyes that kept them from passing as human.

Celts. The Aztecs' main rival for the coveted title of Most Dangerous International Pariah.

"Still feeling confident?" Caelistra asked dryly.

Setesh appeared on the balcony overlooking the room, something that could have been a smile twisting his snout in a toothy display. "Ah, welcome, welcome!" he called to the Aztecs and the Celts. "My friends, if you will join me, we can begin our business. Just through there, if you please." He pointed to the door he'd gone through earlier before turning to address the rest of the room. "As for the rest of you, I hope your accounts are well stocked, because it is nearly time for the bidding to begin!"

People parted before the menacing newcomers. Only a handful actually stared, but Sophia read bravado in the flagrant unconcern most of them tried to project.

"Clever," she said softly. "He's showing off. No one in this room wants to mess with the Celts or the Aztecs. And he's bringing them in at the same time to set them up as rivals." Her heart sank. "The bomb's not going up for auction. He's got it in there. A private showing, for the Conclave's worst enemies."

Caelistra grunted, her jaw clenched, as the Celts and Aztecs disappeared into the private room. Sophia knew how she felt. If the Celts got hold of a bomb like this, the Conclave would have more than border skirmishes to worry about. This could ignite a full-fledged invasion, on a scale they hadn't seen since the Great War.

The Aztecs, far off in Amazonia, didn't share any borders with the Conclave. Yet. But if they could bomb key areas—or, gods forbid, cities—into impassible wastelands, they might have the strength to conquer the whole continent, one nation at a time. The rest of the Conclave might be across the ocean, but the Lakota were far too close to the Aztecs for comfort.

"We need a new plan," Caelistra said grimly.

"Unless we go with our old backup plan. See who wins the bomb, follow them out, grab it later. We can probably call in backup, under the circumstances."

"Maybe." Caelistra ground her teeth, hesitating.

Sophia didn't know what she was thinking, but this was no time for indecision. "Let's get a closer look."

The curtain on the stage parted just as they began crossing the room, and a rail thin man stepped out, a microphone in his hand. His clothes were a wild array of patterns and colors, and he had a beard that could rival Jupiter's. "Honored guests! It is my pleasure to welcome you to Setesh's auction hall. But you are not here to listen to me gabble." He grinned widely. "If you would be so kind as to direct your attention right here to the stage… Without further ado, allow me to present the first item of the evening!"

A hush fell over the chamber as the announcer snapped his fingers. Sophia glanced at the stage as she squeezed past a pair of huge godborn. A thin pedestal emerged from the floor, a cloth-shrouded object resting upon it.

"This first little treasure is said to be the source of immortality itself. A tall tale, or none of you would be able to afford it." A few people chuckled. Most just leaned forward hungrily. "It will, however, revitalize the body, erasing disease and returning you to your prime. A potent miracle, for whoever is lucky enough to win it today. Not to mention a culinary delight, by all accounts. I give you… A single golden apple, guaranteed genuine!"

The auctioneer swept the cloth aside, and appreciative murmurs spread through the crowd.

"This apple comes not from the Isle of the Hesperides—they've upped security, since that incident with Heracles years ago—but rather from the most bountiful orchards of Asgard. Cultivated by the goddess Idunn herself, and so fiercely guarded that the enterprising scamp who plucked it from the branch only managed to pluck a single fruit. Bidding will begin at seven hundred and fifty thousand denarii."

"To the right," Sophia whispered, gently guiding Caelistra's arm. "Good view of the stage. Close to the door and the balcony."

The bids rose quickly, and tapered off just as fast. In less than a minute, the golden apple went to a tiny, hunched figure wearing an ornate silver mask for the tremendous sum of fifty million denarii. Sophia had to fight to keep her eyebrows from climbing off her face. She wouldn't have made that much in an entire lifetime at her old detective's salary. Even as a Fury, she would have to save for centuries. She'd thought the account they had access to for the auction had been staggeringly large, but even that would only afford them a single item at that cost.

I guess it's hard to put a price tag on youth.

"The lucky winner will receive a message with instructions on how to collect their item. Up next, we have a botanical item of a rather different variety: a single red lotus flower!"

Sophia's stomach churned. She'd heard of red lotus. An incredibly potent drug, apparently capable of producing ecstatic hallucinations, if properly prepared. And incredibly *fatal* hallucinations, if not.

Setesh was selling something stolen from the gods of Asgard and one of the most dangerous controlled substances in the world, and he wasn't worried that the two of them were attending his auction? Either item auctioned so far would be enough to send a team of Furies to kick down his door. What did he know that they didn't?

She took a drink from a passing waiter and used the exchange as an excuse to turn and give the door to Setesh's private room a quick look. There was no way they were fighting their way in. That would be suicide in more ways than one. Unlike the bouncers upstairs, the guards outside looked committed and professional. It would take a massive distraction to do the job. She scanned the room, searching for options.

On the stage, item after item sold for staggering sums: two stolen paintings by famous artists. A pair of shoes worn by a star player in the most famous pitz game of the century. An intact dragon heart, larger than a human torso, glistening within its refrigerated glass case.

Sophia took another sip of her drink. It tasted like… Like laughter. Genuine, easy laughter, shared with good friends.

She cleared her throat and lowered the glass. *So that's what miracled alcohol is like. Better slow down.*

As bidding escalated for the dragon heart—gods knew why anyone would want that—Caelistra leaned closer to Sophia and murmured, "Something is wrong."

Sophia glanced around at the crowd. They were in a room full of masked criminals, and Setesh was busy selling a bomb to either the

Aztecs or the Celts, but aside from that, she didn't see anything out of place. "Can you be more specific?"

Caelistra didn't answer.

The auctioneer raised his hands for silence. "The next item is a bit unusual, even for us. A specialty piece, for a collector? A guard, for one's most prized possession? An unusual conversation starter, perhaps? I give you…" He leaned forward conspiratorially, lowering his voice as he hissed into the microphone, "A live hydra, descended from the great Lernean beast itself."

Sophia stopped and stared at him as eager whispers spread through the crowd. He stepped back, and the entire stage split apart. An elevator rose up from below, revealing a basin of water as large as the stage itself.

And wallowing in the basin, the hydra.

It was a massive serpent, easily as long as two city buses from tip to tail. Two thirds of the way up, its body split into seven identical snake heads, each large enough to swallow a person whole. The hydra uncoiled slowly, its heads rising, regarding its audience with cold, slitted eyes.

And then it struck, sending water sloshing onto the floor. Mouths opened, displaying fangs as long as Sophia's arm, and those closest to the stage leapt back in terror.

Until chains clattered, pulling taut. The hydra jerked back, hissing ferociously, and Sophia noticed the thick metal collars around each of the beast's heads, all chained to a single loop at the center of the water. The hydra curled back resentfully, one of its heads turning to regard the chains while the rest watched the room. Eyeing its prey.

It took an effort to tear her eyes off the monster, but Sophia managed to glance around at the room. Every eye was fixed on the hydra, even the guards'. This was their chance. If they could get to the balcony…

On the other side of the stage, there was a flash of movement as a figure pushed past two other audience members. A porcelain-white mask covered her face, but Sophia recognized the way the figure moved.

It was the same woman who'd taken Rashmi at the wharf.

Before Sophia could act, before she could say anything, Rashmi's kidnapper leapt onto the side of the stage. Unperturbed by the hydra, she raised something in the air and crushed it in her hand. Golden power bloomed between her fingers. Bands of energy twisted outward, spiraled past the hydra's heads, and flowed into the locks on the collars.

Light flared. The locks melted, and the collars sprang open.

And with seven simultaneous, screeching hisses, the hydra was free.

CHAPTER FIFTEEN

The hydra exploded from the stage. It bit off a woman's head, savaged two of Setesh's braver guards, devoured anyone within reach. Two of the heads ripped a man apart and fought over his remains. Another snapped shut less than a yard from Sophia, shearing a man's torso from his legs. She backpedaled, casting about for something she could use as a weapon, and caught a flash of movement at the corner of her eye instead. A screaming, flailing man flew through the air and bowled her over.

Sensing easy prey, one of the hydra's heads slithered after her, hissing as it prepared to strike. The carrion stench of its last meal rolled out of the huge, dripping maw.

Desperate, her eyes fixed on the arm-length fangs, Sophia scrambled back. Her hand found the grip of a gun. She snatched it up and squeezed the trigger.

Mundane bullets would have barely stung the hydra, but the only guns in the room belonged to Setesh's guards, and they didn't skimp on weaponry. The bullets tore into the roof of the serpent's mouth, and the head reared back, sheltering behind the necks of its brethren.

Sophia threw herself to her feet before another head could decide to eat her. She looked all around, but she couldn't find Caelistra anywhere. It wasn't just panic throwing the room into madness. Everywhere she turned, people ran for the exits, but many others took advantage of the chaos to settle old grudges. Men and women tore into each other with scavenged firearms, with thaumaturgy, with bare hands. Whether they were killing for old blood feuds or to clear an escape route, each gunshot or coruscating miracle added to the mayhem.

Sophia picked out the door to the private room where Setesh had been entertaining his foreign guests. She was there for Rashmi's bomb, and if Setesh wasn't going to offer a chance to buy it, maybe she could use the chaos to *take* it instead. She could imagine Caelistra's objection, that they weren't there to take risks, but Caelistra was lost in the melee somewhere, and she could take care of herself.

Bullets hissed through the air, and Sophia hunched over, keeping as low as she could while she ran. A severed hydra head slammed into the ground just ahead of her, cracking the tiles. Sophia skirted the head, which thrashed and sprayed blood across the floor as it died. *Idiots*. Someone was about to find two new, very angry heads intent on eating them alive.

Ahead of her, the surviving Dockyard Hounds advanced on the Silver Court from all sides, firing guns torn from Setesh's guards. Sophia watched one of the Hounds get cut in half by a jet of pressurized water, saw another boiled alive in a cloud of steam, but it wasn't enough. The Silver King and his advisors fell, riddled with bullets.

Styx, it's going to be a chaotic day in the Boneyard tomorrow.

But that was a worry for later. To her right, a group of terrified waiters had taken cover behind the half-shattered remains of an overturned table. Sophia ducked behind them, happy to take any chance to avoid notice.

Her heart thundered in her ears as she closed in on her target. She fought to stay focused, to ignore the screams of the dying and the awful, spreading carnage around the rampaging hydra. She had a job to do.

But she wasn't the only one. The auction guards—those who remained—had done their best to fortify the area around Setesh's private room, but masked figures crackling with thaumaturgy were overwhelming them one by one. As Sophia edged closer, a familiar figure, slender and hooded with a bone-white mask, slipped past the guards, tore open the door, and ducked inside.

Rashmi's kidnapper was going to beat her to the bomb.

Shit. Sophia considered going after her, but all she had was the gun in her hand and—she checked the magazine—six more shots. Watching the godborn cut their way through Setesh's guards and take up positions around the door, she knew that wasn't going to be enough.

Gods damn it, where is Caelistra? She turned to look around.

With a roar like a thunderclap, something exploded on the balcony above.

Sophia ducked instinctively. A man plummeted off the balcony, flames trailing from his clothes, his hair. He landed in the hydra's pool with a splash and a hiss of steam. He rose, snarling, and shattered the side of the pool with a gesture before striding out onto the floor. It was the leader of the Aztec delegation. His scales were blackened here and there, some of his feathers scorched, but he looked more enraged than wounded.

Another man followed him over the edge of the balcony a moment later. Blood streamed from his scalp, but he had a wild grin on his face and a sword of golden light clutched in his hand. One of the Celts. Amidst all the chaos, despite the hydra still slithering across the floor and snapping up everyone in its path, he howled a battle cry and charged at the Aztec.

Evidently the bidding for the bomb hadn't gone well.

Their miracles met with a burst of light and an explosive roar, and Sophia scrambled away, shielding her eyes. She took cover behind an overturned table. Let the Celts and the Aztecs fight; she just needed to find…

There. Thank the gods.

Caelistra fought with her usual brutal competence and a look of grim determination on her face. She kicked a godborn in the chest, sending her sprawling, took a blow to the side, and punched a man in the throat. She looked around for more threats, and her eyes settled on

Sophia.

Caelistra broke into a run. Sidestepping a pair of men fighting to get past the hydra, she scooped up a knife with a glowing blade as she moved. The godborn she'd been fighting moments before sprinted after her, until Sophia lifted her gun and put two bullets in the woman's chest.

The hydra lashed out, and Caelistra threw herself onto her knees, sliding across the floor. The serpent's fangs snapped shut just overhead, and she skidded to a stop next to Sophia as the snake whipped around to find easier prey. Caelistra's dress was torn up one side, the fabric smeared with blood, but she didn't seem hurt. She inspected the blade of the knife she'd found, glanced up once to make sure the hydra wasn't still intent on devouring her, and then settled on Sophia.

"Report."

"See the group of godborn guarding the door to Setesh's room? One of them went inside. I think it's the woman who kidnapped Rashmi at the docks."

The two of them leaned around the edges of the table to take another look. As they did, the door to Setesh's room slammed open, and the same masked woman ran through it. Clutched tightly in her hand was Rashmi Bhagvara's bomb. Moving with professional coordination, the squad of armed men and women who'd been watching the door formed up around the thief. Together, they retreated toward the nearest exit.

Sophia and Caelistra ducked back behind the table. "We can get the bomb," Sophia said. "You draw their attention. I'll grab it."

Caelistra was shaking her head before she'd even finished. "Too risky." An explosion rocked the balcony, tearing stones out of the wall and showering them with dust.

"We can't let them take it!" Sophia insisted, shouting back through the ringing in her ears. "I'm going. Cover me, or not." She stood up from behind the table.

And found the godborn who'd been pummeling Caelistra a moment ago, the one Sophia had shot, looming over her, teeth bared.

The woman seized Sophia by the shoulder before she could raise her gun, pivoted, and hurled her across the room.

For a brief moment she was flying above the action. The hydra had pressed itself to one side of the auction hall, its heads—eight of them, now—tearing at a doorjamb, trying to get at the people inside. A squad of Aztecs poured out of the private room, running to help their leader, a band of bloodied Celts on their heels.

Then she struck the ground. The gun went flying from her grip at the impact, and she slid across the slick tile and bumped into something. Legs.

It was one of the killers escorting the bomb. He turned in surprise, the muzzle of his gun dipping toward her.

Instinct and adrenaline drove Sophia's muscles. She snapped a hand up and seized the barrel of his weapon, forcing it away. Her foot lashed out, cracking into the killer's ankle.

His gun barked once, tearing into the tiled floor, and then he collapsed on top of her. She bucked, rolled, fought for the rifle. They slammed into something heavy and gold—one of the basins collecting sand from the ceiling. Sophia worked to put the basin between her and the rest of the man's squad. She had to buy time. She smashed his knuckles into the basin, but he didn't release his grip. He was stronger than her, which meant he had more divine power. Which meant...

He let go of the gun. She was still trying to push it away from her face, and the weapon went skittering away as she fell to one side, off balance.

A thin blade of ice crystalized in his hand and stabbed toward her neck.

Sophia twisted aside in the nick of time, and the blade screeched across the tile. She slammed a fist into his gut, his ribs, the side of his face. He grunted, baring his teeth—row after row of teeth, serrated like a shark's. He drew the blade back, and Sophia caught his wrist before he could stab again.

He muscled through her grip and stabbed the knife into the meat of her shoulder.

Frigid, bone-gnawing cold shot through her arm. There was a flash of pain, instantly swallowed by a paralyzing numbness.

He reared back to stab again, and she retained just enough focus to buck her hips at exactly the right moment. He lurched upward, and she wrenched herself to one side, managing to throw him off.

She scrambled away, but he was after her in an instant. The knife slashed through the air, and she felt the air chill as it passed less than an inch from her skin. She ducked his next swing and smashed her elbow into the killer's side, feeling something crack.

His foot crashed into her, and she slammed into the gilded basin with enough force to make her head spin. She raised her working hand, desperate, and blinked her vision free in time to see him lunging at her.

Until Caelistra stepped into view and caught him by the hair.

His head snapped back as his momentum tried to carry the rest of him forward. Caelistra laid the blade of her scavenged knife against the man's neck.

"I suggest you hold still," she growled.

Sophia put one hand on the basin and peered over the edge, her other arm still limp. "The bomb! You came for me instead of... Shit."

They were too late.

The thief and her escorts had reached a door, leaving corpses in their wake. A group of Celts charged after them, screaming war cries, but they were outmatched. Two members of the thief's team crouched in the doorway. One guarded the rear, taking aim at target after target and dropping them with precise, professional calm. The other summoned flames from the air, gathering them into a blinding sphere in her hands.

She dropped the sphere to the ground and ran.

Sophia barely saw. Her eyes were fixed on the face of the man who'd been covering their retreat with such murderous efficiency. The face of one of the people who were stealing Rashmi's bomb.

Her brother's face.

In a single moment of awful clarity, she watched her brother

124

scanning the room, carefully choosing and killing the nearest charging Celts. Then Gahiji ducked through the doorway after his compatriot and vanished. The instant they were gone, the ball of fire left in their wake exploded, tearing stone and concrete from the walls and ceiling and collapsing the tunnel behind them.

The man Caelistra held at knifepoint chuckled.

"Funny that they left you behind is it?" Caelistra said. "Sophia!" Sophia turned around, her mind as numb as her arm.

Gahiji? *Gahiji* was helping to steal the bomb? He'd been a petty thief for their childhood, a middling fence ever since, but a cold-blooded killer? It was so at odds with what she knew of her brother that Sophia wondered whether she'd taken a harder blow to the head than she'd thought.

"Sophia!" Caelistra kicked her. "Focus! It's gone. Time to go!"

Sophia shook herself. Caelistra was right, this time.

"There," she said. "The door we came in through." She glanced at the man under Caelistra's knife. "Bring him with us. He might be useful."

They skirted a handful of small battles that were still raging across the room. No one was left to stop them. There was a ragged hole where the hydra had torn apart a door and the surrounding wall, and a trail of bodies and blood leading deeper into the mountain after the monster.

"Keep an eye out for Setesh's guards," Sophia said. "Reinforcements might be coming."

"You take the lead. I'll worry about our friend here," Caelistra growled.

Her captive laughed. "You're dead, you know that? You don't know who you're screwing with."

"And I would be happy to hear all about it later," Caelistra said. "Just—"

She was interrupted by an earsplitting *crack*. Sophia turned in time to see the entire balcony tear free from the wall in a shower of dust and debris. It slammed into the ground, crushing people beneath its weight.

Impaled atop the ruined balcony by a spike of perfect glass was one of the Aztecs. He was writhing in place, trying in vain to get free, his terrified eyes fixed on something above.

Setesh floated through the hole in the wall and descended to hover in the air before the man. He *blazed* with power, and just glancing toward him left searing afterimages across Sophia's vision. If the air around him had rippled like a heat mirage before, now half the room swam with maddening curls of wind and sand.

When Setesh spoke, all other sound fled before the thunderous force of his voice. His words reverberated off the walls in an eerie chorus of disparate languages. **"Did you plan this betrayal with the Celts? With one of my enemies here in Memphis? Speak, worm, and your death shall be swift."**

Sophia hurried toward the exit. She could barely hear her own pulse beneath the awful echo of Setesh's words, but terror coursed through her, driving her onward. She shot one last look over her shoulder.

Another Aztec was slumped against the wall behind Setesh. He raised a gun in trembling hands and pulled the trigger.

Setesh didn't even turn around. The roar of gunfire was as faint and as brief as a whispered word. The bullets puffed into dust. The gun followed. The man who'd fired on Setesh opened his mouth to scream before transforming into sand and collapsing into a pile on the floor.

The Aztec pinned to the balcony whimpered, begged for his life, his words snatched away by the roar of Setesh's divine power.

"I will ask but once more: who is your master?" His voice was filled with such rage that the walls trembled.

Sophia, Caelistra, and their captive ducked through the door and hurried back toward the stairs that would take them back up to the nightclub. The screaming began a moment later, and it didn't stop until they were outside.

CHAPTER SIXTEEN

Setesh slowly cleaned the blood off his fingers with a handkerchief. He gazed into space, thoughtful, hardly seeing the ruined body of the Aztec man he'd been torturing or the carnage spread across the room. His keen nose could pick out every scent in the room, from the acrid reek of the severed hydra head to the delicate, flowery notes of the fine wine that had been spilled in one corner, but he noticed none of it.

Millions lost in goods and property damage. An even more valuable opportunity stolen. Important clients and business partners dead. Valuable employees, also dead.

But all of that paled before the embarrassment. He was *Setesh*, the lord of sand and storm, and some *maggot* had come into his house, stolen from him, and gotten away with it.

"You summoned me, your worship?"

Amretis, his assistant and most trusted employee, stopped a respectful distance away, carefully avoiding the gore. She held a pistol in one hand and a phone in the other—ready, as usual, for whatever he might require.

"Release a statement," he said. "There was a gas leak below the Sandstorm Club. Tragically, some of our employees lost their lives in the explosion, but we are relieved that no guests were hurt."

"Of course. I'll make sure the gas company backs up the claim. Also, you will be pleased to know that we have secured the hydra, with only limited loss of life."

Setesh nodded slowly, his mind already darting ahead. "Have the corpses of the Celts and the Aztecs returned to their respective governments."

Amretis looked surprised. "As a threat? Or a peace offering?"

"A bit of both." His hands clean, he tossed the bloody handkerchief aside and frowned down at the body of the Aztec leader. "I am confident now that neither nation planned this. It was my new 'rival.'" He spat the word as if it were poison. For three thousand years, he'd had no rival but his brother Osiris. Three millennia of dominance, and now this? It was past time he reasserted his control.

"Are you certain, your worship? We barely managed to question any of the Celts…"

"The Celts were caught off guard as much as anyone." He shook his head. "No. It's that *scum* trying to cut into my gunrunning business. Trying to muscle *me* out of Memphis. They are the only enemy unaccounted for."

He turned around and gazed up at the ragged hole where he'd torn the balcony free in his rage. His anger had cooled now, leaving him with the empty clarity of a moonlit desert. Cold, but no less deadly. "It is time to refocus our efforts."

"Your orders?" Amretis asked.

He considered the two Furies who'd had the guts to try to infiltrate his auction. No doubt they were already preparing to stage a raid in greater numbers. He had contingencies in place, plans to relocate illegal activities, call in favors with prosecutors and judges…

But there were more immediate threats than the Furies. "Recall Decimus and Itisen from Rome. Infiltrating the Roman Mob can wait. Have them start digging into this mystery organization. I want to know the name of my enemy."

First they'd stolen Rashmi Bhagvara at the docks, and now the bomb itself. He could feel the insults to his pride, like wounds in his chest.

"Your worship, we had been assuming that it was some upstart godborn cutting into your business, but…"

Setesh laughed. With the tapestries shredded and most of the walls bare, the sound echoed through the room. "No. Not after this. None but a god would dream of attacking me here. This reeks of some smug, ancient power, playing at crime to undermine what I've built. The only question is who. Loki? Eris?" He shook his head. "It won't matter, once we find them."

"As you say."

Setesh's eyes were drawn to one of the pillars of sand still pouring down from above. He had faced many, many enemies over the eons. All of them, all except Osiris, had been scattered at his feet like grains of sand. This enemy would be no different.

Cities came and went. Life flourished and faded.

But the desert always endured.

CHAPTER SEVENTEEN

The godborn operative they'd captured at the auction sat on the floor of the tiny cell, his legs crossed, his hands resting on his knees. His clothes were torn, but the wounds beneath were minor, nothing more serious than the bruise spreading from his cheek. He gazed at them pacifically, confidence unshaken by the cage he was in.

"'Worship is dead. The Great War killed it.'"

Sophia wasn't impressed. "Every schoolchild in the Conclave learns that quote."

He chuckled. "As they should."

Seeing the gods personally take sides in the Great War had been the first blow to all claims of divine superiority. Seeing Ares, the Mad God, turn on his own forces when they refused to fight had driven the knife deeper into worship's heart. Seeing soulfire, the first human-made, large-scale thaumatechnological weapon, devastate armies, regions, *cities*, at the command of a mortal… That had ended worship for good.

Ended worship, but not the fighting. *That* had taken hard work, and its own kind of heroism. In the beginning, the Babylon Conclave had been nothing more than a dream of a better world. A secret gathering of gods and mortals from numerous nations, all working behind their leaders' backs and at great personal risk to end the war. Many had died, executed before the peace was signed for "treasonously" building a future where gods and mortals lived as equals. Sophia had always been moved by their sacrifice, and it was fitting that the Babylon Conclave had lent the Intercontinental Treaty Coalition's its more colloquial name.

She was less impressed by the smug condescension of their prisoner. She leaned back against the desk opposite the cell, her arms crossed. It felt good to have changed back into normal clothes again, even if it had meant borrowing a T-shirt and some pants from a a similarly sized police officer. Her expensive clothes had been a total loss. Beneath the bandage, her shoulder still ached from the godborn's miracle, but at least she could move her arm again.

"Is there a point that you're making here?" she asked. "Because we didn't drag you all the way back here to talk philosophy."

The prisoner grinned at her, baring row upon row of shark's teeth. "That quote is everything, in this modern age. Those who recognize how the world has changed prosper. But those who fight progress are crushed beneath the weight of history. The Silver Court is now headless, because they believed mortals were beneath them. Setesh still thinks himself untouchable. Will he be next, I wonder?"

"What about you?" Sophia asked. "And whoever you work for? Where do you fall?"

"Why, on the side of progress and cooperation, of course. If you let me out of here, for example, I'm sure *your* cooperation would be rewarded."

"Funny."

Sophia turned away, stifling a frustrated sigh. They were at the police station for Memphis's Fifth Precinct. A bit of a drive from the Sandstorm Club, but it was worth it. Woven through the metal of the cell bars were hints of red and gold: aurichalcum, one of the rarest and most valuable metals in this or any world. Sophia had barely a trace of divine power in her, and zero experience working miracles, but even she could feel it deadening the air. Inside the cell, the suspect's divine power would be negated entirely.

Caelistra sat at a desk, the room's sole piece of furniture outside the cell, frowning as she typed away at a computer, clad in camo pants and a tank top. She made one last dramatic keystroke and then gave the screen a small, satisfied smile. "Got him. Hekema Masahar. Egyptian citizen. Quite the record here, ever since he murdered his parents when he was a teenager."

Hekema clicked his tongue. "Self-defense. You'd understand, if you'd known them."

"Who do you work for, Hekema?" Sophia asked.

"Myself, of course. We all do, even if we won't admit it. The only difference is how we clothe our naked self-interest. Behind necessity? Behind service to the community, like you? Behind ancient entitlement and a desperate belief in one's natural superiority, like the Silver Court? It's almost a mercy that they are dead."

Sophia raised an eyebrow. "Are you admitting to playing a part in their murder?"

He chuckled. "Of course not, Fury. But you must agree that they had no place in the modern world. Like every godborn who can't pass for human, I know exactly what it's like to feel humanity's envy. Their resentment. Their fear. And like most, I lack the power or the money to rise above it. It is easy to mistake the power we are born with for something we deserve. I have no such illusions."

Sophia tapped her fingers against her arm. "That should make it easy for you to answer our questions, then, if naked self-interest is all you have. Tell us who you work for, and I'll make sure some time is taken off your sentence."

Hekema threw back his head and guffawed. "I'm afraid I have more immediate concerns, at the moment. Bring me some water, and I'll be much more inclined to talk."

Sophia traded a look with Caelistra, shrugging. "I have a better idea: we leave you in there to think about how thirsty you are and come back later."

She saw his smile waver. "So cruel," he said. "The people of the Conclave would be disappointed to know how their representatives treated—"

132

Caelistra followed Sophia out of the room and out into the main lockup, shutting the door on him as she left.

"He'll talk," Sophia said. She looked around, but as promised, they were alone. This part of the station was empty, the suspects moved elsewhere, the police keeping a respectful distance.

Caelistra raised her eyebrows. "Getting him *talking* isn't the problem. You realize that you're not a police detective anymore, right? You don't need writs, or cause, or the rest of that red tape."

"I know, I know. We answer to the Conclave Assembly, and that's it," Sophia said, turning away. "Just because we're allowed to do something doesn't make it right. What do you want to do, go in there and start pulling fingernails? I can read people. This is going to work."

Caelistra smirked. "You're stalling. Distracted. Got something you want to share with the class?"

Because my brother was one of the people stealing Rashmi's bomb.

Sophia felt like she was teetering on a razor's edge, where her fraying nerves could send her into the precipice at any moment. She knew Gahiji. The worst thing he'd ever done was move stolen property. He was clever, and charming, when he wanted to be, but hardly a cold, professional killer. It was a preposterous idea.

But no matter how many times she tried to tell herself that it was a trick of the light, Sophia couldn't shake the certainty. She'd seen him gunning down Celt after Celt with ruthless, practiced precision.

"I have no idea what you're talking about." She shrugged as casually as she could. "I guess I could still be on edge from the auction."

"The auction? Or the disaster that followed? We should have left as soon as I realized something was wrong," Caelistra muttered.

"If we hadn't stayed for that 'disaster,' we wouldn't have Hekema. It was risky, but we made it through."

Caelistra shot her a sidelong glance. "You talk like everything was under control. You fight—"

"Like a brawler. I know. Can you blame me? I wasn't the one who decided new recruits should be thrown straight into cases without any training."

"No. You're just the one who decided to hurl herself into danger against my instructions, rather than keeping to the *safe* parts of the job like I asked."

Sophia ached to retort that she hadn't exactly had a choice at the auction, but she held herself back. She met Caelistra's glare for a good couple of seconds. Then she took a deep breath and said, "The case isn't going to wait for us to debate this." She pointed to the table strewn with Hekema's possessions. "Any idea what this stuff is?"

Caelistra watched her for just a moment longer before accepting the peace offering. She moved to Sophia's side and surveyed the table's contents. A burner phone with no numbers in it, some cash, and an expensive watch were the most unremarkable items. There was also a thin plastic disc, barely larger than a thumbnail, that trembled with divine power. Beside it lay some kind of thaumatech device, a tiny cube with blinking lights and a short power cable.

And, strangest of all, what looked like the last inch of a statue's finger, attached to a cord. Hekema had been wearing it around his neck, under his shirt.

"Some kind of thaumatech, I imagine," Caelistra said.

Sophia picked up the strangest of the objects. "Why did he have the tip of a statue's finger around his neck? Does that strike you as thaumatech too?"

"Could be. Godborn were slapping together protective amulets out of weirder things for far longer than corporations have been making thaumatech phones." Caelistra leaned against the bars of the nearest cell, shot an irritated glance at the smoke detector on the ceiling, and ended up tapping an unlit cigarette against her thigh. "Maybe we can get *you* a protective charm. You could use one."

Sophia rounded on her, incredulous. "Gods, Caelistra, will you leave it alone?"

"No. You almost died more than once back there, and we didn't even get the bomb. We should have left when I said."

"What, empty handed? We may not have the bomb, but we have a suspect who can tell us where it is. And we've personally seen Setesh selling stolen property, murdering people…"

Caelistra snorted. "There's a right way to do things, and there's a wrong way. A surgical strike with a squad of Furies is the right way. A single recruit going after the objective without even a trace of a plan? That's the wrong way. And Setesh wasn't our objective."

"So, what, he gets a pass?"

"He's a god. One of the Directors will put together a team of our best people and deal with the problem. That's not my job. Keeping you from getting yourself killed is."

"We didn't have a squad of Furies, Caelistra. I made do."

"And I suppose you want me to be impressed by your resourcefulness?" Caelistra sighed, waving a hand dismissively. "Forget it. I've had this conversation before. I know how it goes." She turned and started to walk away.

Sophia frowned after her, hands on her hips, Gahiji driven from her thoughts for the first time since she'd seen his face. "Hold on just a second." Caelistra turned, and Sophia stared her down. "I don't know who you're remembering, but I'm not those people. Give me some credit. *Work* with me."

Caelistra gave her a sympathetic look. "I did that, Sophia. I tried to give you advice, and you didn't listen. And it will happen again." She shook her head. "I already know how this ends. You just can't see it yet."

"Caelistra—"

Caelistra turned her back on Sophia. "We need an expert to look at Hekema's gear, and I don't want to wait on forensics. I'm going outside to call Dr. Tinaalto and have a smoke." She left the room without another word.

Sophia glared after her, growling frustratedly. She wanted to throw something, or hit someone. Instead, she forced herself to take a deep breath. She had another lead, one she didn't dare tell Caelistra about. Not until she'd verified it, at least. Maybe not even then, considering how

135

Caelistra saw her.

It was time to talk to her brother.

She gave Caelistra a minute's head start before following her out of the jail, and she was relieved to find her partner nowhere in sight. The only people in view were a pair of detectives huddled together outside the detention area, and a handful of other officers still at their desks.

The two detectives hushed the instant they saw her, and the starstruck look one of them gave her made her stomach lurch. He was struggling to seem composed, despite the blush spreading across his pale skin. The other, a godborn with huge muscles and pebbly skin—troll blood, maybe?—was staring intently at her own feet.

Sophia was overcome with a strange sense of vertigo, like she was in two places at once. If the Furies had come into her station and taken over the jail a month ago, she and Kofi would have stared and traded rumors behind their backs just like this. If she'd never been killed, she would be just like these two, focused on some smaller, more mundane problem.

They looked at her with awe, but the only thing that set her apart from them was a deadly miracle to the chest and a small investment of divine power. How was she any more qualified for this job than they were? She'd been operating on bluster and stubbornness ever since her death, afraid that if she admitted that she was out of her depth, everything would fall apart. She felt like a character in an old cartoon, able to keep running long past the cliff just as long as she didn't look down.

And she couldn't stop now. She wandered over to the duo, hands in her pockets. "Taking bets on how quickly we'll get him to talk?"

The light-skinned man stammered out a denial, but the godborn woman met Sophia's eyes. "Can you blame us, Fury?"

Sophia chuckled. "Not even slightly. And please, call me Sophia." They traded names as they shook her hand. The troll-blooded woman was Neferat, her partner, Eirik.

Eirik looked like he was slowly starting to relax. "City's been going crazy. Grapevine says you guys were at the docks when that shit went down? And now you've got that godborn locked up in the cell..."

"Wild couple of days," Sophia agreed. "You catching any of it, up here?"

Up here. As if I still worked in the Boneyard.

"Maybe," Neferat said. "Handful of bodies turned up under the highway... Three other people dead in a house fire in the north end." She shrugged. "Could be gang related. Could be random."

Eirik yawned, barely covering his mouth in time. "I just hope we can get some sleep tonight, or it's going to be a rough day tomorrow."

"Ah. Captain's got you here to keep an eye on us, huh?"

"We're your liaisons. Got to represent Memphis PD's best, in case you need anything from us."

Sophia didn't have to see the tension in their bodies or the nervousness in their eyes to know they were there. She'd felt the same, every time she had to work a case that would be handed over to the national police or the Furies. It was a thankless job, with full potential for blame and no chance of getting credit.

"Well, I appreciate your help. Maybe our friend in the cell will realize how thirsty he is and save us all some time, but either way, we'll try to be out of your hair as quickly as we can so you can get back to your caseload." An idea struck her, and she smiled. "Tell you what: you might be stuck here, but no one's stopping me from stepping out and grabbing some food while our friend stews in his cell. Can I get the two of you anything?"

Eirik blinked at her. "But... You're..."

"Dead. Yeah. Doesn't mean I have to leave behind comfort food. Going once..."

They took her up on her offer, and she left the police station and went straight to the bus stop. It would only be a short ride to Gahiji's. If she really had seen his face at the auction, he damn well owed her some answers. If not... Well...

If not, then she was about to make a horrible mistake.

CHAPTER EIGHTEEN

"'But aren't you dead?' Wow. Smooth, Eirik," Neferat said as soon as the Fury left.

Eirik snorted. "Right, like you wouldn't have put your foot in your mouth if she'd let you keep talking."

Neferat gave him a look of mock offense. "I am the pinnacle of grace and poise," she said in her best posh accent. "I would have done no such thing, sir!"

He'd known a lot of godborn who thought they were better than him, but Neferat always had his back. He was about to pull out his phone when his least favorite person in the station stood up from his desk. Eirik groaned, stopping to nudge Neferat. "Heads up. Remebi's coming this way."

They both put on smiles as the other officer joined them. "Heading out soon?" Eirik said. It was a challenge to keep a hint of hopefulness out of his voice.

"Gods no. You know how much work I've got?" Remebi grumbled.

Yeah, Eirik thought. *Same as the rest of us, asshole, and the captain doesn't have you on Fury duty.*

"What's up?" Neferat asked. She scratched lazily at the rocky skin of her neck, producing the soft sound of stone scraping across stone.

"I want in. Twenty denarii say that the Furies don't get any answers by morning."

"Wow. Pessimist."

Remebi shrugged. "I call 'em like I see 'em."

"Fair enough. All right, you're in," Neferat said. "Just keep it to yourself. The captain won't be happy if she finds out we're taking bets on the Furies."

"Yeah, 'unprofessional antics,'" Remebi said, snorting. "Don't worry about me." He didn't make any move to walk away.

Asshole.

"I need to take a piss," Eirik announced, pushing off the desk he'd been leaning on. "Hold down the fort for me?" As if the Furies needed their help to keep an eye on a single godborn. Especially one locked in a cell that made him powerless.

At least Remebi didn't follow him to the restroom. Thank all the gods for that.

Eirik preferred to have privacy when he betrayed the police force.

His throat felt painfully dry, his hands sweaty. No matter how many times he did this, it never got easier. The faint chatter of the police station faded as the door shut behind him, until all he could hear was his own heartbeat.

He went straight for one of the stalls, locked the door, and pulled out his phone. He felt like he was going to vomit.

Fuck. Keep it together, man.

He took a deep breath, staring at the picture of his sons gazing up at him from the lock screen of his phone. He had to do this, for their sake. He didn't have a choice.

That didn't stop his fingers from shaking as he tried to type out the text message: *Furies brought a suspect to the Fifth Precinct. He's on the list. Please advise.*

He pressed send before he could have second thoughts.

He waited. And waited. Finally, he stood up and actually did take a piss.

His phone buzzed while he was washing his hands. He looked himself in the mirror, swallowed, and pulled it out of his pocket.

The reply was short and simple: *Make sure he doesn't name names.*

Eirik grimaced, watching the messages delete themselves. He knew the drill. The Furies were a complication, but there were plans for complications. Gods damn it.

He looked in the mirror again and tried to rearrange his face into something presentable, into the cheerful features of the man who bantered with his colleagues and didn't disappear into the bathroom to conspire with murderers.

It took him several minutes before he could conceal his self-loathing.

CHAPTER NINETEEN

Sophia found her brother unloading groceries from the back of his car. He was wearing jeans and a stained T-shirt, instead of the earlier body armor. So mundane. So normal. As though he hadn't been infiltrating a black market auction and murdering people earlier that night.

Through one of the windows, she caught a glimpse of Teshan and Meret before the two disappeared deeper into the house.

Good. Better if they stayed out of this.

She watched Gahiji from the shadows beneath a broken streetlight. Years of familiar preconceptions warred with the rage burning in her heart. Gahiji might be a criminal, but he was a charmer, not a fighter. A fence, not a killer. She *knew* him.

Didn't she?

Gahiji carried two armfuls of groceries to the door and left them there. Sophia made her move while he was going back for the rest.

He walked back to the car, bending over with a grunt to pick up the remaining bags. When he turned around, Sophia was standing right in front of him, her arms crossed.

Gahiji jumped backward with a strangled cry. The bags slipped from his hands, sending fruit and cheese tumbling to the ground. Sophia waited while his mouth worked soundlessly. She could practically see his brain struggling through the options. Was she a ghost? A trick? A hallucination?

"I'm with the Furies, Gahiji."

"You… I don't… The Furies?"

"I didn't think you were the auction-going type."

She'd been catching her brother in lies since the day he'd learned to talk. She recognized the twitch in his cheek, the carefully calculated look of confusion he adopted.

It hadn't been a trick of her imagination. He'd really been there.

She wasn't prepared for the scale of the anger that roared to life inside her. She lunged forward, catching Gahiji by the shirt and trapping him against the car. "You're a *murderer*? You helped steal Rashmi's invention? Do you even know what it can do?"

She expected a weaselly smile and a clever deflection. Instead, Gahiji gazed back with something new, something she'd never seen before: fearless, unflinching defiance.

"Without admitting to any of that? I do what I have to, Sophia. For myself, and for Teshan."

Sophia pressed him against the bumper, snarling. "For Teshan? Really? You could have *died* today. And for what? Some cash? Styx, I should arrest you right now."

Gahiji's lip curled. "You could have arrested me years ago, but you're a coward. You didn't do it then, and you won't do it now."

"Don't push me. Back then I didn't know you were a murderer."

He shook his head. She had him pinned against his car, but for the first time she could remember, he looked strong, self-confident. "You have no idea what I am, Sophia."

"I bailed you out of jail! I came *every time* you asked me for help! And you know why I put up with all your shit? Because you're my brother. Because I wanted to believe you could be better. Osiris's blood, have I ever known the real you?"

"Have you ever tried to?"

Guilt stabbed into her heart, just as he'd intended. "Fuck you, Gahiji. You don't get to put this on me. I've tried to help. I've tried to be there for you. I *get* how hard it is, living in the Boneyard. But no matter what

I do, you refuse to change."

"You get it?" He scoffed, put his hands on her shoulders and tried to push her back. She didn't budge. "How could you get it? You haven't lived here since we were kids. You see Teshan when it suits you. I'm the one who puts food on the table. I'm the one who tells her stories before bed every night."

"Stories about the people you murdered? I'm trying to fix things. I want the Boneyard to be a safe place to live. You're actively making it worse."

"Is that what you tell yourself? You *left*, Sophia. You ran away. How many times have you come back here, *not* for Teshan? Gods above, you can't even be civil with Dad anymore."

Sophia threw him back against the car with a frustrated growl and turned away. She'd accused Gahiji of *murder*, and somehow he'd brought the fight back around to old, well-worn ground. If they just rehashed the same argument, they would shout at each other until they were hoarse, and then Sophia would leave, feeling guilty because he was her brother and some part of her still wanted to be on his side.

And feeling enraged because he'd done so much to make that impossible.

Behind her, Gahiji sighed heavily. "I don't mean to fight with you, Soph. None of that matters right now." His voice was quiet, subdued. Almost... sad.

She faced him again, eyes narrowed. "Tell me what you know."

He shook his head, still holding her gaze. "I'm not saying I know anything," he said carefully. "But whatever you're talking about sounds dangerous. Stay out of it. Please."

"This is my one shot, Gahiji. My one chance to be a Fury. I'm not giving it up on some vague hint from my criminal brother."

"You should. You fought long and hard, Sophia. I admire you for that, even if you don't see it. I... Your funeral..." He swallowed. "I was devastated when you died. I had to be strong for Teshan, but gods, Soph, you're my big sister. You're a preachy, self-righteous ass sometimes, but

I never imagined you *gone*. But you know what?"

Sophia shook her head. "What?"

"I was almost happy for you. I saw how hard you worked, and how frustrated it made you when nothing changed. You deserved a break. Imagining you in an afterlife, your fight finally over... It was all that got me through the last month."

"You should know me better than that."

He chuckled softly. "I guess so."

Sophia reached out a hand. Hesitated. Then she placed it on Gahiji's shoulder. "I don't know what you're involved with. I don't know how deep you are. But I can *help*. For you, and for Teshan."

There was no more defiance on his face, no more deception. Just sadness. "Do you really think it's that simple?"

"It can be. The Furies have resources. We can protect you."

"You can't."

"Gahiji, please. I'm asking, as your sister... Who are you working for? What are they planning? There are lives at stake..."

"And I'm asking you, as your brother: stay out of this case. Please."

"I can't do that. We've got one of your 'friends,' remember? We're going to get to the bottom of this one way or another." He shook his head. Sighing, Sophia let him go. She scribbled down her new phone number in her notebook, tore out the page, and offered it to him. "Call me if you change your mind. This is your last chance, Gahiji. Please take it. For Teshan's sake."

Gahiji gave her a sad look, but he took the slip of paper with her number and tucked it into his pocket. "I wish it was that easy."

"Gahiji..."

The door to his house swung open and light washed over the road.

"Dad? Are you okay?"

Sophia was behind the car and out of sight in an instant. The sound of Teshan's voice drove deeper the knives Gahiji had already buried in her heart.

She heard movement as Gahiji looked around. "Just fine,

144

sweetheart."

"I thought I heard you talking to someone."

Gahiji let out a laugh. "Just myself. Dropped the damn groceries."

"Oh. Let me help—"

Sophia's heart lurched. There was nowhere she could go, not with the light streaming past Teshan to illuminate the street. She could recall herself to Tartarus, but it would cost her precious time. Caelistra would wonder where she'd gone, if she wasn't already.

"No, no, it's okay. I've got it." She heard Gahiji scooping up the fallen groceries and stuffing them back into the bags. She heard his footsteps retreat, and Sophia slowly let out a breath.

The door closed behind him, and darkness fell over her again like a blanket. Safe. Comforting. And completely separating her from the people she loved.

Sophia sighed. The right thing to do would be to arrest Gahiji. He was a coward; he'd give up the people he worked for eventually. Wouldn't he?

Gods, I'm not even sure I know my own brother anymore.

But, right thing or not, Sophia couldn't bring herself to do it in front of Teshan.

CHAPTER TWENTY

Sophia still didn't feel comfortable showing her face in Kehinde's, the place she *actually* wanted to go for food, so she went for her second choice, which conveniently wasn't run by a family friend. She returned to the police station with gyros from the best Greek place in the city.

Neferat and Eirik were nowhere in sight, but one of the other officers sent her toward the lockup. "They're doing something for your partner, I think? Your thaumatech expert's here, though."

Sophia hurried past him, eager for answers. She was confident that she could crack Hekema with enough time, but it might help to know what he'd been carrying.

Ixtele stood over the table with his belongings, muttering to herself as she poked at a handheld thaumascanner. She'd changed into a pair of canvas pants, a white button-down shirt, and a light leather jacket. Faint silver lines still shone across her skin. "Fire, hmm? That's unexpected. Maybe just for ignition…"

Sophia cleared her throat as she crossed the room. "Dr. Tinaalto?"

"Call me Ixtele, please," she said absently, not looking up. "Only my students call me that."

"Sure. Have you seen Caelistra? Oh, and I've got a gyro for you, if you want one."

That brought her around, her eyes lighting up. "What kind?"

"Lamb gyro. Might not be up to Athenian standards, but it's the best in the city."

She'd barely held it out when Ixtele snatched it from her hand and held it like it was a priceless treasure. "First some interesting thaumatech, then food?" Ixtele flashed a grin. "What did I do to earn this?"

"You offered to help figure out what all that is," Sophia said, gesturing at the table. She leaned back against the bars of the cell opposite the table and pulled out a gyro of her own. When she looked up, she caught Ixtele holding the paper-wrapped gyro up to her face and breathing in deeply. "Smells like home?" she guessed.

Complicated emotions crossed Ixtele's face, too fast to follow, and she fiddled briefly with one of the moons on her necklace before she caught herself. "In more ways than one," she sighed. "My mother used to bring Greek food whenever she'd visit."

Sophia winced. "Sorry if I brought up bad memories. I swear I was just trying to keep our expert fed."

Ixtele stopped unwrapping her gyro for long enough to give Sophia a smile. Now that she was looking closer, Sophia realized that the glowing lines spiraling across Ixtele's skin shifted almost imperceptibly from moment to moment, like kelp tugged by the tides. "Only good memories. Mostly. I don't see my mother all that often, but that's not a surprise. You know, goddess business. Her visits were always fantastic, though. We'd go out into the jungle and just explore..." She laughed at herself. "And there I go, rambling straight through normal small talk and out the other side."

Sophia shook her head with a rueful chuckle. "I think this might be the first normal conversation I've had since my death. It's nice, actually."

Ixtele gave her a long, curious glance. Then she held up her gyro like she was proposing a toast. "To normal."

Sophia mirrored the gesture, and, with exaggerated solemnity, Ixtele bumped their pitas together like they were clinking glasses.

A deep, genuine laugh roiled out of Sophia before she could take a bite, and Ixtele let out a triumphant cry. "Ha! There it is! I knew you couldn't always be that serious."

Sophia looked at her incredulously, still smiling despite herself. "I'm not… I think you're mistaking me for Caelistra."

"I'm definitely not. She's the sarcastic one, who wants everyone to think she doesn't care. You're the serious one who wants to be a Fury so badly that you put up with all her shit. The difference is very clear."

Sophia shook her head, looking down. She knew she was wound too tight, but she was busy, focused on the case. No, it was more than that. She'd barely had a moment to herself, to draw, to think, to *process* her death, or joining the Furies, or being back in Memphis.

Ixtele nudged her. "We toasted; you have to take a bite now. It's the rules."

Sophia couldn't argue with that. She savored the crunch of the pita's buttery, toasted exterior, the mingling, explosive flavors of herbs and meat and tzatziki. She leaned her head back against the bars with a sigh. "I did not realize how much I needed this."

"Tough day?"

"You have no idea."

"Once, I got trapped in a canyon for a week while an angry chimera tried to get in and eat me."

"Okay, I will admit, that sounds pretty terrible."

Ixtele shrugged. "Could have been worse. For a thing with three heads, chimeras are really dumb. There was another way into the canyon. If it had stopped clawing at the rocks for a minute and just gone around, I would have been lunch."

Sophia laughed, and Ixtele looked pleased. "Seems like you lead an exciting life, for a professor."

"You sound like the dean. 'Ixtele, I wish you'd spend more time on campus, instead of gallivanting around the world after exotic beasts,'" she said in an exaggerated, gruff voice.

Chuckling, Sophia gave her a curious look. "Isn't that kind of the idea? Don't you have classes to teach?"

Ixtele waved a hand dismissively. "Nothing my grad students can't handle. Besides, the university can't really argue. My gallivanting produces the best papers and brings in grant money."

"Right. You're definitely not just doing it so you can see the world." Ixtele's grin answered for her, and Sophia felt her curiosity drive her on. "Is that how you picked up Egyptian? During your gallivanting? It's strange to meet a demigoddess who speaks more than one language."

Ixtele's eyes lit up. "Only because most people are boring. 'Divine power is universal,' and all that, but Immortal just gives you literal meaning. There's so much nuance lost that way!"

"How many languages do you know?" Sophia asked, curious despite herself.

"Fourteen. Not including Immortal." She looked proud, and Sophia could hardly fault her for that. Fourteen languages… "I want to pick up Nahuatl next," Ixtele continued, gesturing with her gyro. "Nobody does somber fatalism like Aztec writers. Totalitarianism will do that to you."

"You are a strange person."

Ixtele grinned at her. "What, because I find culture as interesting as thaumaturgy?"

That drew Sophia's gaze back to the table. She sighed, but she *did* need to get back to work. "Speaking of which, any luck with Hekema's gear?"

"Oh, yeah!" Ixtele wolfed down the last of her gyro and started talking with her mouth half full. "The disc is a kind of stun grenade or something. Crack the casing, and it will release enough light to blind you even through your eyelids. The design is ingenious: lots of divine power crammed into something so small, easy to hide from a pat down… Not much good if they've got a thaumascanner, but with the right storage method, maybe—"

"Woah, hang on," Sophia interrupted, holding up her hands. The use of the thing wasn't the priority, anymore. "Any way to tell where it came from, or who made it? From the way you're talking, I assume it's not mass produced."

"Oh no, definitely not. Well… Maybe not. I might be able to figure it out, if you give me some more time. It's probably a custom job, but sometimes there are distinctive features you could plug into a Fury database or something."

Sophia gave her a sidelong glance. "Which you know how?"

"Because even if thauma*tech* isn't my area of expertise, I try to stay on top of the literature." Ixtele grinned suddenly. "Why? Worried that I'm secretly a bad guy?"

"I worry about everyone." Ixtele frowned at that, and Sophia pointed at the cube with the cable. "What about that?"

Ixtele's enthusiasm was back in an instant. "Oh, that's…" She scratched at her head, fingers brushing the close-shaved hair just above her ear. "Okay, well, I'm not 100% sure yet, but the initial results are exciting! My first thought was some sort of sabotage device—plug it in, start a fire after a delay, that sort of thing—but there's not enough power in it to do much damage. It could be a transmitter of some sort, maybe. A lot of fire-attuned energy for that kind of thing, but I've seen weirder stuff. It could be—"

Sophia cut in before she could keep going. "Okay, not done yet. Got it. The finger tip?"

Ixtele opened her mouth, and then shut it as her eyes fell on the strange token. She shook her head. "Frankly? I have no idea." She bent down and peered at the finger tip from up close, as if that would make a difference. "There's only a trace of divine power inside it. So faint that my thaumascanner is barely able to get a read against the background levels. Is it some kind of earth power? Healing? A curse?" She shot Sophia an excited glance. "I can't wait to figure out what it is!"

"Let me know as soon as you do. Just don't curse the building, please."

"Oh, that's definitely not going to happen. Probably."

Sophia finished her gyro and pushed off the cell bars. "Let's hope. Thanks for your help, Ixtele. Let me know if you figure something out."

"Of course." Ixtele's eyes grew distant for a moment. "I hope Rashmi's okay."

"I thought you barely knew him."

"I wouldn't even go that far. But just hearing him talk... He wanted to make the world better." She looked at Sophia. "I really hope you get him back okay."

"So do I."

Sophia took the wrapper from Ixtele's gyro and headed for the trash can. She was just turning back around when Eirik and Neferat came inside.

Sophia waved them over. "Got some gyros here with your names on them." She sorted through the bag she'd brought back. "No tzatziki, that's for you, Eirik. Which means these two with extra meat..."

Something seemed off about Eirik's smile as he took the food, but Neferat pushed her way past him before Sophia had a chance to say anything. "This is amazing," Neferat said with a huge grin. She cradled the gyros in her rocky hands like they were made of glass. "What do we owe you?"

Sophia waved them away. "My treat. I know what a detective's salary is like."

Ixtele was already back at work, her thaumascanner in one hand as she mumbled around the stylus between her teeth. Sophia frowned, remembering a question from earlier, before she'd let Ixtele sidetrack her. "You seen Caelistra?" she asked the two detectives.

"No. We were just about to go find her. She had us digging through some old files for information on your suspect. Didn't find anything, unfortunately."

"Hmm. Ixtele, do you know where Caelistra is? Ixtele?"

"What? Oh. She's in there with the prisoner, I think. She said... Sophia?"

Sophia realized she was glaring at the door and muttering curses. She made herself take a deep breath. "Thanks Ixtele. Keep at the thaumatech."

She stalked toward the room with the aurichalcum cell. They'd *agreed* to give him some time to stew. But still... She kicked herself for not seeing this coming. Caelistra was all sarcasm and low expectations, right up until she decided that she had to do everything herself.

Eirik and Neferat traded a look and went with her. "Everything okay? Can we help?"

"Everything's fine. Just some miscommunication. Enjoy the gyros." Sophia unlocked the door that led to Hekema's cell.

And then she froze.

Hekema was huddled against the wall, his hands raised protectively. Caelistra stood just outside the bars, holding a gun on him.

Sophia rushed in immediately, Eirik on her heels, Neferat squeezing through the doorway after him. "Woah, Caelistra... What's going on?" She looked around for some kind of threat. Had someone gotten inside and attacked Caelistra? Had Hekema found a weapon?

She came up empty.

Caelistra didn't take her eyes off the suspect. "You left, and I got tired of waiting. You're still playing by detective's rules. Like you still need to get writs, and read people their rights, and all that. Seemed like it was time to show you how the Furies do things."

"Caelistra, we don't—"

Caelistra spoke over her. "Last chance, Hekema. Who do you work for? Who has the bomb?"

"Just hold on a minute," he said. "Listen to your partner. She—"

Caelistra shot him in the leg.

CHAPTER TWENTY-ONE

The gunshot roared through the room and was swallowed by the soundproofed walls. Hekema howled in pain, clutching at his thigh as blood spurted between his fingers. Eirik's and Neferat's shouts of alarm added to the din. The two detectives went for their weapons, but Sophia stepped between them and Caelistra, her hands raised.

"Everyone hang on a minute!" She lowered her voice and leaned closer to her partner. "Caelistra—"

Caelistra fended her off with her free hand. "We need answers. What are you worried about? He's obviously not an innocent."

Sophia hesitated. Legally, Caelistra was right: she wasn't a detective any longer. She didn't need to go to a judge for a writ just to perform a search, or read suspects their rights, or, Styx, even treat prisoners humanely. The Furies had the authority to do whatever they needed to do to keep the Conclave and its people safe, answering only to the Directors and the Assembly's Security Committee. She and Caelistra had personally witnessed Hekema murder multiple people in the process of stealing a bomb that could kill thousands more. The Assembly wouldn't bat an eye at this.

But none of that made this the *right* choice.

Caelistra pushed past her and glared down at Hekema. "The next one goes in your kneecap. Talk."

He was still trying to apply pressure to the wound, hissing through his teeth. Surrounded by aurichalcum, his body couldn't just heal the bullet wound. Before Sophia could object, he said, "What do you want to know?"

Caelistra gave Sophia a smug look. "See? Do things my way and you get results." To Hekema, she said, "You were stealing the bomb for someone. Who?"

Hekema smiled a shark's grin as laughter rolled out of him. "Leading with the hard questions, aren't we?"

Sophia grimaced as she watched him. Eirik and Neferat had taken their hands off their guns, but they both looked like they were going to be sick. She couldn't blame them. Knowing that the Furies had the authority to do something like this was one thing, but seeing it was another. Every instinct she had screamed at her to stop Caelistra.

And yet, it was too late to put the bullet back in the gun. If he could help them find the bomb before it was used again...

She walked to Caelistra's side and crossed her arms. "It doesn't seem like a hard question to me," Sophia said. "Just give us a name."

Hekema sighed and leaned back against the cell's cot. "Setesh has had his fingers in every criminal activity in this city since the last pharaoh. The police couldn't stop him. The Furies couldn't stop him. He's stronger than ever." He chuckled, shaking his head. "But the balance of power is shifting."

Comprehension dawned on Sophia. "Guns," she breathed. The day of her death, she and Kofi had assumed that the gun runner they'd caught had been about to give up Setesh. But they'd been assuming that Setesh still controlled all of the city's illegal weapons trade. "You're muscling Setesh out of arms dealing," she said.

Hekema held up a finger. "A point for the lady not holding a gun on me."

Sophia's head spun. This was the information she'd been about to learn before she died. This was the information she'd been *killed* over. Not the proof that Setesh was the criminal everyone knew he was, but rather, evidence that he was losing his chokehold on the city's crime.

Caelistra's pistol didn't waver. "What does any of this have to do with the auction?"

"Everything. Think of that auction as Setesh's last hurrah, before it all comes crumbling down around him."

Eirik cleared his throat. "This is your show, Furies, but... I know this city. If someone were threatening Setesh, wouldn't we know it? There'd be turf wars, murders in the streets..."

Sophia shook her head, still watching Hekema. "There have been. We just assumed it was minor players making moves, or more violence on the edges of the Silver Court-Dockyard Hounds war."

Despite all of Gahiji's bullshit warnings and angry judgment, despite how guilty the current situation made her feel, she was starting to think that she'd made the right choice. As a Fury, she might finally have a chance to cut out the cancer eating at the city's heart.

"Details," Sophia said. "You need to give us details."

Hekema chuckled ruefully. "And if I do? You'll protect me?"

"Sure. But if you give us the name of your boss, you won't need protecting from them for long," Caelistra said.

Hekema winced and adjusted the pressure he was putting on his leg. "You have no idea. I assume you had a look at the items you so rudely took from me. Remember the stone finger I was wearing around my neck?"

"What is it?"

"A warning."

Caelistra tapped a finger against the side of her gun. "See this? This is a warning about what happens if you refuse to talk. Your boss isn't here. I am."

Hekema gave her a weary smile. "Just trying to help you appreciate my position." He grunted in pain and lifted his hands from his leg. Both palms and most of his pant leg were stained red. He swayed, blinking dizzily. "I'm giving you what you need. Any chance I could get what *I* need, now?"

Caelistra cocked her head slightly. "Sure."

Sophia looked at her in surprise. She watched Caelistra take a look around the room before settling on the gyros and water bottles that Neferat and Eirik had brought with them, now long forgotten. Caelistra scooped up a water bottle.

"Fury, what—" Eirik protested.

"Shut up. He asked for water earlier. I'm giving him what he needs," Caelistra said. She tossed the bottle through the bars of the cell.

Hekema missed the catch and had to scramble after it before it rolled away. He took a long swig and then grimaced at her as he reapplied pressure to his wound. "Not exactly what I meant."

"Huh. Maybe you should have been clearer about your demands," Caelistra said unconcernedly.

Hekema laughed, still grinding his teeth against the pain. "I like you. You're ruthless. Practical. Have you ever considered a change in employment?"

"Not recently."

"Maybe you should. Let me out of this cell and my boss will be willing to overlook this troublesome incident. No? What about the rest of you?"

Neferat looked angry. Eirik kept glancing nervously toward the door.

Sophia shook her head with a sigh. "I would hurry, if I were you. I don't think you want to test my partner's patience. Maybe if you give us a name, we can do something about that wound."

Hekema took another pull from the water bottle. "I used to do jobs all over Egypt, you know. Freelance. And then I made the mistake of trying to steal from the boss." He chuckled ruefully. "Starting to wish I'd robbed someone else." His leg spasmed, and he hissed in pain, the water bottle tumbling from his fingers and spilling across the floor. "Shit. What—"

Caelistra muttered under her breath and raised her pistol. "Nice try, idiot."

Another spasm sent Hekema's head crashing back into the wall. He fell to the ground, twitching, his feet kicking at the bars. Neferat let out a cry of alarm.

Sophia pushed Caelistra's gun aside. "He's not faking it! Let me in there! Now!"

Caelistra looked at her in surprise, but at least she listened. She slapped the appropriate button on the desk, and the cell door swung open with a grating buzz. Sophia hurried inside.

She'd felt the aurichalcum's deadening influence from outside the bars. Inside, it was far worse. She could still breathe, but each breath felt dead, lifeless, left her gasping for another. The spark of divine power burning inside her faded until she could barely sense it.

She pushed forward anyway until she was at Hekema's side. Another spasm cracked his skull against the floor. Sophia took his head in her hands, trying to protect it. She could feel his muscles twitching wildly beneath his skin.

"Caelistra, put your gun away and get in here! I need your help! Someone call an ambulance!"

"I'll do it!" Neferat ran out of the room, the door slamming shut behind her.

Caelistra banished her gun into shadow and rushed into the cell. One of Hekema's legs snapped out and nearly kicked her feet out from under her, but Caelistra sidestepped just in time. "Help me move him away from the bars before he hurts himself!" Sophia called to her. Caelistra seized his legs, struggling to hold on.

Hekema reached a hand up and put it on Sophia's shoulder, fighting against the spasms. His eyes found hers. Amidst the erratic twitching and the agony there, there was a hint of urgency. Hekema opened his mouth and ended up snapping the end of his tongue off when his jaw jerked shut.

"Shh, it's okay," Sophia said, tensing as his neck tried to whip back again. "Help is coming."

He opened his mouth again, eyes still fixed on hers. "No... The... Boss." He swallowed, choking on the blood from his tongue. His mouth worked soundlessly for a moment before he found his voice again. "She

157

did this to me… Meret… Tanu."

Sophia's blood froze. It was impossible. Meret Tanu, the founder and manager of the largest shelter in the Boneyard? Meret Tanu, the kind, quiet, generous woman?

Meret Tanu, the mother of Sophia's niece?

Hekema wasn't done. "Meret… She—"

His next words were stolen by the roar of a gunshot. The front of Hekema's head crumpled, spraying blood across Sophia and Caelistra.

Eirik stood in the doorway of the cell, his pistol smoking in his hand.

Sophia and Caelistra lunged at exactly the same moment, but Eirik was closer. He slammed the cell door shut, muttering curses under his breath and stumbling backward as it locked automatically.

"You traitorous fucking scum!" Sophia growled. He was dirty. She knew that there was corruption in the Memphis Police Department, but this…

This had been right under her nose, and she hadn't even caught a whiff of it. Styx, she'd bought the man a gyro.

Eirik glanced at Hekema's corpse and winced, looking away. "This isn't my fault!" His eyes were wild, his skin flushed. "This wasn't supposed to happen!" He began pacing the length of the small room, shaking his head from side to side with his free hand clenched in his hair.

"You murdered him! How could this possibly not be your fault?" Sophia snarled.

Eirik swallowed, unable to meet her eyes. "He shouldn't have said her name."

CHAPTER TWENTY-TWO

Gahiji had personally chosen the meeting place. The Five Dragons Telecom Building was aiming to be one of the most impressive skyscrapers in downtown Memphis. If its owners lived up to their promises, they would bring thaumatech communications to the masses, revolutionizing the telephone in the same way that miracle-infused fertilizer had revolutionized agriculture.

At the moment, however, the building was a half-finished skeleton of concrete and steel. The twentieth floor was little more than a bare slab of empty grey, lit only by a single lightbulb that dangled down from its cable and swayed gently in the breeze. The small puddle of illumination it cast barely extended a few yards before being swallowed by the night.

Gahiji stood at the shadow's edge and gazed out across the city. Behind him, downtown Memphis still blazed with light, festive and healthy. Ahead, the Boneyard smoldered like the resentful, sickened remnants of a garbage fire. He'd picked this spot as much for the view as for the privacy. What better place to decide the fate of the neighborhood than from a vantage that commanded the entire district?

He checked his watch and nodded to himself. Their "guests" would be arriving any minute now. Gahiji stifled an exhausted yawn and rubbed his neck, trying to release some of the tension there.

He'd planned out tonight with careful precision, only for his sister to show up and throw the schedule into disarray. Now, after hours of scrambling, things were finally back on track. Teshan was home, hopefully asleep while he handled some last minute "business." Backup was waiting nearby in case it was needed. Teams were in place throughout the city, just waiting for his call. He always counted on something going wrong, but he hadn't expected Sophia returning from the dead. His back still ached from where she'd slammed him into the car.

He sighed down at the city. Sophia, a Fury. Of course the Furies had seen her potential. And of course she'd accepted the job. She'd always been too driven for her own good, too committed to her mad quest to fix the world. The fucked up thing was, he couldn't figure out whether he should be angry or proud of her.

Maybe both. Gods above, if she didn't stay away from this case, it was going to get her killed. Again.

He'd been stunned to learn that one of his own people had murdered his sister. What should have been a simple job—one trusted employee, one loose-lipped contractor who should have never been brought into the organization, one bullet—had left him holding his daughter while she sobbed herself hoarse. Not to mention the trouble Sophia was now in the position to cause *him*.

Gahiji shook his head at the nervous hammering of his heart. He'd spent years encouraging her blindness, so she wouldn't see the truth. Years hiding behind the mask of empty charm and cringing cowardice, behind the face of the man he used to be. It was a useful lie, but even pretending at the weakness he'd spent a lifetime trying to erase made it easy to slip back into old habits.

He wasn't that man anymore. For Teshan's sake, he couldn't afford to be.

The sound of footsteps echoing off bare concrete walls brought him around, and he forced himself back under control. He folded his hands behind his back, faced into the light, and waited. He'd been through this exact meeting before, with other groups. He knew how it would go, had planned for the slightest deviation from the script. There was no reason for the flutter of anxiety in his chest.

Three people came up the south stairs. Little more than starlit shadows, they paused when they saw Gahiji and put their heads together, talking softly. It took a few moments before they ventured into the light.

There were two men and a woman, all wearing jackets unsuited for the weather in a poor attempt to conceal guns. Gahiji knew their names and faces, of course. The woman, Sitre, was the new leader of the Dockyard Hounds. Her eyes were clever, calculating. Gahiji gave her better than even odds of seeing the next sunrise.

Sitre stopped just inside the light, flanked by her two bodyguards. She crossed her arms and watched Gahiji intently. "Who are you? And why am I here instead of somewhere with air conditioning?"

"I'm just a facilitator. You're here because you share an enemy with my employer."

Sitre narrowed her eyes. She was about to respond when more footsteps became audible from the stairwell on the other side of the floor. Sitre and her companions took cautious steps back, pulling their coats aside for easy access to their weapons.

Three new people stepped off the stairs, snarling and storming into the light as soon as they spotted the Hounds. The ornamentation on their clothes marked them as members of the Silver Court. At their head was a burly young man whose faintly blue skin rippled like wind-kissed water. Degi, the new Silver King.

He glared at Sitre, his breath misting in the air despite the heat, before rounding on Gahiji. "Why are *they* here?"

Gahiji looked from one group to the other, an expression of studied aloofness on his face. "To talk, the same as you. Perhaps to plot Setesh's death, if you will put aside your differences for just a minute."

There was still raw hate in their eyes as they glared at each other, but no one worked a miracle or drew a weapon. That was enough, for now.

Gahiji stepped forward, and six sets of murderous eyes turned on him. He ignored the jolt of panic that went through his heart.

"My employer wishes to make you all an offer. Whatever our past grudges, we all share an enemy. You," he said, nodding to Sitre and the Dockyard Hounds, "have been attacked on your own turf by the desert god. Your people were killed. Your property was taken. Your leader was murdered without provocation."

He turned to Degi and the Silver Courtiers. "And you. Your predecessor trusted Setesh's hospitality. And then he and his closest advisors were all slaughtered by Setesh's own guards." A bit of a lie, but none of the Hounds or the Courtiers had survived to contradict his story.

Sitre's lip curled. "And your mysterious 'employer?'"

"She has lost those closest to her, thanks to Setesh. Just as you have. Just as we all have." Gahiji shook his head slowly, meeting each of their eyes in turn. "No more. It is time for Setesh's control over this city to end."

Degi scoffed. "Is your employer Isis? Loki?"

"No."

Meret stepped out of the shadows and walked to Gahiji's side. Gahiji knew she wasn't what they'd expected. She was no mighty godborn, no burly crime boss. Just a short, reasonably fit woman wearing dark slacks, a cream-colored blouse, and a simple silver bracelet. She could have blended into any crowd in Egypt.

Sitre was the first to find her voice. "You?"

They all knew her. Everyone in the gangs knew her. They'd sent children to her for protection. They'd trusted husbands and wives to her, when the fighting had gotten particularly bad. They'd come to her with problems, and she'd solved them with gentleness and compassion.

Degi threw back his head and laughed. "*You* are going to take on Setesh? I could snap you like a twig."

Meret regarded him coolly. "Doubtful. But that attitude is why you have failed. Both of you, again, and again, and again. You see everything as a contest of muscle, of power. That is why your old leaders are dead. That is why you work for me now."

Sitre and the Hounds looked hesitant, but their counterparts seemed less impressed. Degi took a step toward Meret, cracking his knuckles one by one. "This is outrageous. The Silver Court—the Silver *King*—bows to no one." The air grew heavy with moisture, and the deep, ocean blue of Degi's irises rippled out to suffuse his eyes. An intentional display of power, or a sign he couldn't control himself? Gahiji couldn't decide.

The Hounds looked like they were one loud noise from going for their guns. Gahiji stayed where he was, stifling the fear swelling in his chest. Degi looked ready to spear him or Meret with a miracle, but that was the idea. Everything was going according to plan.

Meret watched Degi, unconcerned. "I'm not asking you to grovel. I'm asking you to fight." She looked each gangster in the eye, one by one. "There are very, very few people in this city who know to associate my face, my name, with anything but the Riverside Shelter. Honor the trust I've placed in you. Honor that anonymity. Work for me, and we will all profit. Work for me, and our enemies, even Setesh himself, will fall."

Gahiji could feel the *or else* hanging in the air, unspoken. They all could.

Just as they'd expected, Degi disregarded it.

Blind, proud rage turned his face into a snarl. "No." He spat, and the saliva froze on the concrete floor. "The Silver Court works for no one. Especially not some arrogant *mayfly*."

The Hounds all bristled at the slur, but their eyes went to Meret. They wanted to see how she would react.

Meret turned her full gaze on Degi, her hands still at her sides, her face still untroubled. "The Silver Court's antiquated bigotry has no place in the future I'm building for Memphis. It is time to set it aside."

"I have a better idea," Degi snarled.

A miracle shimmered to life around his fingers, a blade of focused, cutting water. He drew his hand back to throw.

Gahiji's heart hammered against his ribs. For a second, he thought Degi might actually release the miracle.

And then a hand appeared from the shadows and snatched Degi's wrist. With a single twist, Degi was pulled off balance, bending backward at the waist.

A figure stepped into view. She was dressed in black, a hood thrown over her head. Sunglasses and a balaclava hid her features, but Gahiji fixed his eyes firmly on the floor. It was safer that way.

Degi started to struggle. He shouted for help. The other Silver Courtiers shuffled nervously, halfheartedly gathering their power.

The woman holding Degi ignored them. She bent over until her face was inches from his, reached up with her free hand, and pulled the balaclava and the sunglasses from her face.

Degi screamed.

The petrification began at his fingers and toes. Veins of grey crawled across flesh and clothing like ink spreading through water. A mortal would have been dead in mere moments, but Degi's own divine power fought the curse.

Fought, and failed.

His thrashing slowed to agonized twitching as his limbs hardened into solid, dead stone. His screams choked off as his chest, his lungs, became rock. His face contorted until the very last moments, his eyes pleading.

Within seconds, the only sound was the eager, sibilant hissing of serpents.

"My lieutenant, the gorgon Euryale," Meret announced, striding past Gahiji to Euryale's side. "By her standards, that was a merciful death."

Euryale replaced her face mask, her sunglasses. At a gesture from Meret, she stepped back and released Degi's wrist.

Bent over backward, the statue toppled to the floor without her support. Stone cracked and shattered, and pieces of Degi's petrified body tumbled across the floor.

Meret bent over and picked up five of the pieces. Finger tips, mostly. She carried them into the center of the circle and dropped them beneath the lightbulb. "For each of you. Keep them with you, as a reminder that there are consequences for foolish choices. Such as speaking my name or questioning my authority." She glanced toward the two stunned, leaderless water spirits, who were eyeing both her and Euryale with abject terror. "Congratulations. One of you is the new Silver King. I leave it to you to decide."

She walked back to her place beside Gahiji. Euryale followed, standing on Meret's other side. Slowly, hesitantly, the survivors took pieces of Degi's body from the floor.

"I know what you're thinking," Meret said. "There are five of you, and only one gorgon in my employ. Once you are far away from here, you can begin making plans to destroy me."

She waited. No one said anything, but Gahiji knew she was right. They'd seen it before, time and again. And just like Meret's other lieutenants, these ones needed to know what was at stake.

"I suggest you think twice before you do something you will regret. I knew each of you, before today. You trusted me with the things that you value above all else. Your parents. Your siblings. Your children. I know where they go to school. I know where they live. I know where they are this very moment. Serve me loyally, and I will protect them as if they were my own. Betray me, breathe even a word of my identity to anyone, and I will make them suffer." She let that hang in the air for a moment. "Now, does anyone else have any objections to my authority?"

There was a long silence, broken only by the faint breeze brushing through the tower.

"Good," Meret said. "I don't care about your old loyalties. I don't care about your petty feuds. You work for me now, and you will work *together.*"

Sitre took a step forward, her spine straight, her eyes carefully avoiding the Silver Courtiers. "What do you need us to do?"

"There is a problem that would be well suited to your combined talents. I want a team of Dockyard Hound gunmen and the Silver Court's toughest fighter at the Fifth Precinct police station within the hour. I will relay further instructions once they are there."

The two groups traded dark looks, and Sitre said, "Just one

Courtier?"

"One godborn is worth more than your entire squad," one of the surviving water spirits scoffed.

Meret sighed. "If this is going to work, we need to be precise. Surgical. The more people involved, the more chance it will be traced back to me." She looked between Sitre and the Courtier who'd spoken up. "And of course, if there is any hint of infighting between your two groups, all of you will die. Is that understood?"

Gahiji barely saw the gangsters scamper off. The Fifth Precinct. He knew what was there. *Who* was there. If the gangs were being sent there, he'd been kept out of the loop. Were they backup? Or clean up?

"Thank you, Euryale. Go make sure that Rashmi is still hard at work on the second device, if you don't mind."

"Consider it done," Euryale rasped. Silent as a snake, she vanished into the gloom.

As soon as he was sure they were alone, Gahiji rounded on Meret and crossed his arms, unable to keep the anger from his face.

Meret pulled out her phone, not even glancing his way. "We need the police to turn a blind eye for as long as possible. Can you handle that? And tell Judge Ankilu and our people in the prosecutor's office to be ready to pull some strings." She paused when he didn't respond and turned to face him. "Gahiji?"

"You didn't tell me."

Her gaze softened, pain and sadness filling her eyes, mirroring his own. "Ever since your sister was given this case, we both knew it might come to this." She hesitated for just a moment before putting her phone away and walking to the skyscraper's edge.

He joined her. She was right. Still, even dogged as Sophia was, Gahiji had never imagined that she would actually get close enough to be a real danger. Meret was careful. She'd kept herself anonymous for years, pulling strings behind the scenes. The thought of actually ordering Sophia's death made his stomach churn.

Gods, maybe Meret had been right not to tell him.

He swallowed. Weighing his questions, trying to figure out which of them he actually wanted to know the answer to. "Are you going to have her killed?"

"That depends on her. The situation is still developing."

"If this were anyone else, I would be handling it," Gahiji said.

"True."

"You have more important things to worry about. Have I ever given you a reason to doubt me?" There it was. Even more than the thought of Sophia's death, that was the question that was clawing its way up his spine. If Meret didn't trust him...

Meret gazed out at the city for a long time before answering. "When I was a child, my mother would tell my brother and me stories, every night. Stories of ancient heroes and long-dead rulers. She had been a starving pickpocket for most of her life, and she wanted better for us. I think that's why she gave me a queen's name." There was a hint of something in her voice. Scorn? Regret?

Gahiji stood beside her and let the wind tug his clothes toward the drop.

"Her favorite stories were about the gods. She loved the tale of Isis and Osiris, because she thought Isis's devotion, piecing her husband back together after Setesh chopped him into bits, was the height of tragic romance."

Meret chuckled softly. "But that story always terrified me. Growing up in the Boneyard, there was never a day when I felt truly safe, but the idea that *family*, the people who were supposed to love and protect you, might chop you into pieces and scatter you across the desert... That frightened me more than a thousand gang wars."

Gahiji grimaced. He knew her well enough to know what she was thinking. "And then your father made all those nightmares come true."

Meret sighed, toying idly with her bracelet. "We are so close, Gahiji. Closer than we've ever been. I am not going to let anyone get in the way of that."

Gently, Gahiji stepped forward and took her hands in his. "I am not

Setesh. Or your father. I am not going to betray you, or our daughter. The two of you are everything to me."

Meret sighed. She looked up, gazing into his eyes. "Family first."

Gahiji touched his forehead to hers. "Family first."

CHAPTER TWENTY-THREE

Caelistra paced back and forth across the length of the aurichalcum cell, periodically shooting glares through the bars at Eirik. She'd dragged Hekema's corpse into the corner by his mud-crusted boots to free up room, but the cell was still too small for more than a couple of steps. A cigarette dangled from her lips, unlit because Eirik had taken her lighter.

Sophia ignored Caelistra's nervous motion and sat on the cot cross-legged, watching their captor. He'd been holding them at gunpoint for less than twenty minutes, and he'd been sweating the entire time like he was the one in the cell. He kept glancing at the door. Worried that Neferat would come back? Hoping that she would? Sophia still wasn't sure whether they were in this together.

Or, Styx, how many other officers in the station were dirty.

Meret. The question is, how many of them work for Meret? *Gods below, that's still hard to believe.*

The longer they were in this cell, the worse their chances were. Sophia's weapons were on a table behind Eirik, alongside their phones, and Caelistra couldn't summon hers inside the cell. Ixtele was on the other side of soundproofed walls, and besides, demigoddess or not, she was a professor, not a fighter.

They needed a plan. Which meant they needed a way to distract Eirik.

"Caelistra—" Sophia began.

Caelistra didn't even glance at her. "I'm thinking."

Of course she was. Now that things were serious, she was back to doing everything herself.

"Both of you shut up," Eirik growled. He glanced at his phone for what felt like the hundredth time, always nervously keeping the two of them in view.

Sophia narrowed her eyes at him. "What are you waiting for, Eirik? Backup?"

His gun hand twitched, sending a jolt through her heart. "I said, shut up." The weapon in his hand was just a standard police sidearm, no miracles involved, but with their power—including natural regeneration—suppressed by the aurichalcum, that was all the firepower he'd need.

But vulnerable or not, Sophia made herself keep going anyway. "You must be waiting for something, right? Why bother? You're a loyal foot soldier, right? You can do it yourself."

He raised the pistol until she was staring straight down the barrel. "You want that? Really?"

She looked him in the eye, ignoring the gun. "If you were just going to kill us, you would have done it already. So what's the plan? You waiting for backup? Or directions from *Mere*?"

Eirik flinched.

Sophia chuckled grimly. "Not used to hearing someone say her name? You going to shoot me too?"

"Don't have to. You're trapped in there. No one's getting word out." To her surprise, he almost sounded... disappointed.

That was something she could use.

Sophia stood up and walked past Caelistra to lean on the cell door. She lowered her voice and put as much sympathy as she could muster into it. "What's she got on you, Eirik?"

He controlled himself well, but not well enough. There was a slight twitch in his mouth, a momentary distance to his gaze, before he glared at her. "No. I'm the one asking the questions. Tell me about the case.

Everything you know, or I take a page from your partner's book and start putting bullets in you."

"Oh? I thought you were waiting for backup?" Sophia shook her head. "What is it? I can tell you're not doing this for money. Blackmail? Threats against someone you care about?" The raw pain in his eyes was impossible to hide. Sophia's heart sank. If he was betraying his oath to protect the people he loved, they were in more trouble than she'd thought. "I'm sorry," she said.

There was a part of her that still rebelled at the idea of Meret threatening *anyone*, let alone coercing the police to do her dirty work. She could be fierce—growing up in the Boneyard had seen to that—but threatening someone's family? That wasn't the Meret Sophia knew.

The gun pointed in her direction told her otherwise.

"It's not too late. If you let us out, we can protect your family. The Furies have resources all across the Conclave. Meret—"

Eirik was already shaking his head, but he winced again when she said the name. "You don't understand. You haven't seen…"

Sophia frowned at him as realization struck her. "You didn't know her name before, did you? You learned it the same moment we did." Eirik's expression answered for him. "You think she's going to let you live, knowing what you know?"

Eirik turned away with a snarl, pulling out his phone. "Where is she…" he muttered to himself. He began dialing.

Caelistra paced right up to Sophia's side and stopped, leaning in close. "Keep pissing him off," she breathed. "Try to get him close to the cell. You grab him, I'll go for the gun."

Eirik turned back around, and Caelistra resumed pacing just in time. The phone rang. And rang.

It finally picked up just when Eirik was starting to look nervous. "Neferat? Where the fuck are you?" Sophia couldn't hear the response. "Then get in here. And bring the others." Another soft reply. "Go to Hel. They're Furies. Of course I'm nervous."

Gods above and below, how much of this precinct does Meret own?

Eirik hung up the phone, shaking his head. Sophia caught his eye. "We can help you. You, and everyone you care about. It's not too late."

"It is for me," he said quietly. He glanced back at the sound of the door unlocking. "Make a noise, and I kill you both." For the first time, he looked deadly serious, all the doubt scrubbed from his face.

Three men entered the room, expressions grim. None of them were obviously godborn, but they could have been human-passing. *They're certainly passing as honest police officers*, Sophia thought grimly.

Neferat was the last one in. She turned to shut the door.

A silver-streaked hand caught the door and held it open. "Hey, so I figured out a couple things you guys might want to hear," Ixtele's voice said a moment later. "That stone finger? I think—" She stuck her head through the door, and her eyes went wide as she saw the two of them in the cell. Sophia's heart leapt into her throat.

Two of the corrupt officers went for their guns. Solid sheets of stone formed over Neferat's knuckles, cracking and grinding as her power drew them into place. Despite Eirik's threat, Sophia tried to shout a warning.

Ixtele didn't need one. She was inside the room in a flash, the door slamming shut behind her. She raised a hand, and a flare of silver light burned across Sophia's vision. Neferat and the other officers staggered, blinded, shots and miracles going wide.

Sophia tried to blink her vision clear. She saw Ixtele snatch something—Sophia's gun, hurriedly grabbed by the barrel—and throw it at someone's face. The officer fell back with a cry, his shot going wide.

Ixtele charged Eirik as he tried to get a bead on her. He panicked, fired, missed. She crashed into him and slammed him into the cell bars. His pistol tumbled free and skittered into the corner.

"Ixtele, button on the desk!" Sophia shouted.

Miracles flashed and gunfire rang, deafening, through the room, but Ixtele managed to dart toward the desk and slam her hand down on the button that unlocked the cell. Sophia forced the door open, muscling Eirik out of the way.

Stepping out of the cell was like taking the first sip of water after being stranded in the desert, but there was no time to savor it. Sophia dove for her gun. Caelistra followed her out, and every shadow in the room curled toward her.

Someone shouted, "Shit! Shoot her, shoot her!"

A hand caught Sophia's arm. She twisted, lashing out with her elbow. She felt something crunch, and the grip loosened. She pulled free, scooped her pistol off the floor, and kept going, putting her back to the wall.

When Caelistra stepped out of the darkness, she'd cast off her human form for a Fury's true, terrifying visage.

Her skin had gone from tan to dark, dried-blood red. A pair of feathered night-black wings stretched from her shoulders. Her fingers were tipped with razor-edged claws. Her hair was a nest of spitting, hissing vipers. A forked tongue lashed between a mouthful of teeth as jagged and irregular as broken glass. Her eyes, twin pits of utter darkness, wept trails of liquid shadow down her cheeks.

When she spoke, her voice was like metal grinding over concrete. "You chose the wrong side." With a single beat of her wings, Caelistra threw herself toward Neferat and the other officer by the door and vanished from view.

Sophia caught a glimpse of Ixtele grappling with Eirik on the far side of the room.

She was about to go help when a figure loomed in front of her, blocking the way. His nose was broken, his cheek bleeding. There was a gun in his hand, rising toward her.

Sophia put three rounds in his chest, and he dropped.

Ixtele was outnumbered. One man seized her by the shoulders, dragging her off Eirik. Eirik scrambled back, searching for his pistol. Ixtele backpedaled, struggling with the man who'd grabbed her.

Sophia stalked closer, trying to get a clear shot. Ixtele let out a grunt of frustration. She snatched the officer's hand from her arm, twisted her hips, and threw him. It was hurried, imprecise, but with a demigoddess's

173

strength, it didn't matter. He hurtled backwards, crashed into the open cell door, and crumpled to the ground.

There was a flash of movement, and Sophia jerked back just as a massive claw of solid gloom, conjured by Caelistra's will, seized Neferat and sent her flying past Sophia and into the bars of the cell. Neferat groaned, trying to push herself off the floor, and Sophia kicked her in the head. Pain shot up her shin as though she'd kicked a rock, but the fight went out of Neferat.

Toward the exit, Sophia caught a glimpse of Caelistra holding a thrashing officer against the door by the throat. She didn't need any help.

Sophia seized her sword from the table as she passed. Ixtele was leaning against the wall, breathing heavily as she stared at the man she'd thrown.

In the corner, where Ixtele couldn't see, Eirik had found his gun. He turned, clutching his chest with his other hand, his teeth clenched. He trained the gun on Ixtele.

Sophia rushed past her and drove her blade through his wrist.

The miracle-worked steel parted his flesh like tissue paper and punched into the concrete wall. Eirik howled in pain. Sophia ripped the gun from his fingers and tugged her sword free.

"You should have taken my offer," she said.

Eirik collapsed, gasping, and Sophia turned away to scan for other threats.

She didn't find any. Neferat was motionless beside the cell. Caelistra strode toward them from the door, an officer sprawled across the floor behind her. The man Ixtele had hurled into the cell door wasn't moving. The man Sophia had shot…

He had a cell phone in his hand, a bloodied finger tapping at the screen.

Sophia and Caelistra noticed at the same moment. Sophia lunged forward, hand outstretched.

Caelistra conjured her pistol from the shadows and shot him in the side of the head.

Sophia lurched back as the gunshot rang out. Her ears ringing, she picked her way past his body and snatched up the phone.

"Message sent" was all the blood-stained screen said. Even that was fading after a moment.

"Shit," Sophia said.

Eirik groaned from the corner. "You shouldn't have fought back."

Caelistra snorted. "You shouldn't have tried to murder us."

He shook his head, tears streaming down his face. He still cradled his wounded wrist to his chest. "You don't understand. She'll have a backup plan for this. If we'd handled it quietly, no one else would have gotten hurt. Now..." He shook his head, choking back a sob. "You shouldn't have fought back."

Sophia looked down at the phone, comprehension dawning. "Shit," she said again. "Call HQ," she said to Caelistra. "They have to know what we've learned." She rounded on Eirik. "What's the backup plan? What will she do?"

"What do you think? She—"

"No signal," Caelistra interrupted. "We're being jammed."

That settled it. Sophia offered Ixtele a hand and helped her up. "We need to move. First we go back out into the station and get everyone left in the building. Then we find a way out of here." Sophia pointed her bloodied sword at Eirik. "On your feet if you want to live."

He laughed despairingly. "You think there's going to be a way out?"

"I think I'm going to ask someone who didn't try to kill us. Let's go!"

Caelistra stalked to Sophia's side as soon as they were out of the room. "This is stupid," she hissed, her voice still harsh, like razors scraping bone. "We're close enough to the Deathgate. We can return to Tartarus. HQ has to know about Meret."

Sophia shook her head. "There's still time. We can get them out."

"What if they work for Meret?"

"What if they *don't?*"

She snatched the plastic disc—the flash bomb—from the table with Hekema's belongings. It might come in handy. Then she stormed across the room and slammed open the door from the lockup to the main office.

A handful of heads jerked up in surprise—twelve more people left in the station, all told. "Listen up!" Sophia shouted. "There are people coming here to kill us all *right now*. I need everyone in the armory. Grab body armor and the strongest thaumatech weapons you can find, and *hurry*. Whoever's been here longest, I want to know the best way out if we're surrounded. We're in this together. Do you understand?"

Most of them stared at her. One, the grouchy man she'd talked to earlier, stood up and saluted. "Yes ma'am!"

The window behind him shattered, and gore spattered his desk as a bullet tore through the back of his head and burst out of his face.

CHAPTER TWENTY-FOUR

"Sniper! Everyone down!" Sophia shouted.

She threw herself to the floor as more bullets tore into the building. Each gunshot had the loud, distinctive *crack* of a high-powered rifle. The misses shattered glass and sent tufts of insulation and bits of shredded paperwork into the air. The hits ended lives.

An officer across the room reacted too slowly and took a shot through her spine. Another tried to sprint across the room and was cut down the moment he left cover.

"Stay away from the windows!"

A man scrambled toward Sophia, bullets tearing past him. He stumbled as he reached them, and Sophia and Ixtele reached out and dragged him into cover.

An explosion rocked the building, and the power cut out.

One of the officers struggling toward them froze in a blind panic, and the next shot brought him down. Sophia had never been more grateful for her newfound ability to see in the dark. She scanned the room, picking out the handful of people left. "You, by the water cooler. Stay low and go straight ahead."

"I can make light," Ixtele offered, crouching by the corner and squinting into the darkness.

"Not yet! It'll just draw their fire." The scattered emergency lights illuminated patches of the station in harsh shades of orange, but shadows clung to most of the building. Anything that lit up the place would just make it easier for the snipers to see them. "Caelistra, we're the only ones who can see. Help me get them over here!"

Together, they managed to gather the survivors to her. All four of them, not counting Eirik. The officers huddled around them, clutching their guns and each other in the dim light that streamed through the ruined windows. The last one to reach them had a piece of glass lodged in her leg, blood pumping past it onto the floor.

Sophia knelt beside her. "Here, I can help—"

Caelistra put a clawed hand on Sophia's shoulder and dragged her back down the hall and away from the others. "We have to go."

Sophia stared at her. "And just leave them to die?"

"If *we* die helping these people, no one knows Meret has the bomb! That's what she wants. That's what she's *counting* on. How many more people will she kill if we stick around and try to be heroes?"

"So we'll find a way out."

"Meret wants us to try that. With our phones jammed, there's only one way for us to get word out about her identity. We have to go."

Sophia glanced over her shoulder, grimacing. Eirik lay against the wall, away from the others, holding his maimed hand to his chest, but the rest were all watching Sophia and Caelistra. Sophia could see the terror in their eyes, and the desperate hope. Two months ago, she would have been one of them, out of her depth and trusting the Furies to have an answer.

What had changed? Just a tiny spark of divine power? And yet, Ixtele was looking at her with quiet confidence and not a hint of doubt. They were all relying on the Furies, and she wasn't going to let them down.

Sophia turned back to Caelistra.

"You're right. HQ needs to know about Meret."

Some of the tension left Caelistra's frame, and her writhing snake hair settled back against her scalp. "You... You surprise me." She glanced back toward the others. "This is the right choice."

"I know," Sophia said grimly. She put a hand on Caelistra's shoulder.

"Go back to Tartarus. Tell them what we know. Then come back here and pull our asses out of the fire."

Caelistra bared her jagged teeth in a snarl. "I spoke too soon."

"You're right that we can't risk Meret's identity dying with us, but we can't just leave these people either. It's our job is to protect them."

Caelistra let out a frustrated growl. "Our job is to protect *everyone*, not just a handful of lives. And part of *my* job is to keep *you* out of danger!"

A gunshot split the night. Somewhere above them, on the second floor, there was a scream, cut off by another bullet a second later. Sophia looked Caelistra in the eye. "It has to be you. With your wings, you can go and still make it back here in time. I couldn't." Caelistra tried to reply, but Sophia didn't give her the chance. "I'm staying. You can argue, or you can go warn HQ and come back to help."

"Mars's battered shield..." Caelistra shook her head, jaw clenched, and then glared at Sophia. "If you live through this, I am going to kick your ass." But she gathered the shadows to her, and when they vanished, she was gone.

One of the officers was staring after Caelistra in horror when Sophia returned to the group. "Are you going to abandon us too? Oh gods—"

Sophia took him by the shoulder and forced him to look at her. "I'm not going anywhere. And *she's* going to get help."

There was a tremendous crash, and plaster rained down on them from the ceiling. It hadn't sounded like an explosion, but there was only one explanation Sophia could think of: their attackers were coming in.

The youngest officer let out a panicked cry and leapt to his feet. Ixtele caught him by the leg and yanked him back just before a bullet would have taken his head off.

"Get off me! We're fucked! Get—"

"Hey! Look at me!" Sophia crouched next to him. "You've got to stay calm. I'm right here with you, but I need you to focus. Where's the armory?" Any doubts she'd had about the loyalties of the remaining officers had faded when the gunmen outside had started shooting them

179

indiscriminately.

She watched him swallow, some of the terror subsiding in his face as she gave him something else to focus on. "That way. Around the corner and to the right."

"All right. Make a chain, since I'm the only one who can see. Ixtele, take my hand. And put Eirik in the fucking middle so he can't—"

There was another shuddering crash, closer this time.

"Give me a gun," Eirik said softly.

"What, so you can shoot us in the back?" Sophia scoffed.

He shook his head, even though no one but Sophia could see him. "You guessed right, earlier. They're threatening my family. I..." He choked, and had to swallow before he could keep going. "Give me a gun. I'll buy you time to get to the armory."

She swallowed. "Eirik, we can help—"

He shook his head. "It's the only way my family will be safe." He chuckled weakly. "No need for leverage on a dead man."

Sophia studied him for a moment. Then she took the sidearm from one of the other officers and handed it to him, along with a spare magazine. "Good luck."

"And you. I'm... I'm sorry."

They left him in the hall. Sophia led the rest of them through around the corner and down the hall to the armory. "A bit of light, Ixtele? Just enough for this room?"

A soft glow appeared in Ixtele's palm and floated up toward the ceiling, casting eerie shadows across racks of equipment. "Guns and body armor all around," Sophia ordered. "Hurry!"

She almost pulled on a vest herself before realizing it wouldn't do much good. Any bullet with enough divine power to do her lasting harm would cut right through the armor. She put a hand on Ixtele's arm, the meager light casting her features in sharp relief. "You all right?"

"Today was certainly full of surprises." Ixtele hid most of her panic behind a lopsided grin, but she was breathing quickly, and Sophia could see her hands trembling slightly with adrenaline.

"I'm sorry you got dragged into this," Sophia said, "but gods am I glad for your help."

"You can make it up to me by buying me more food if we survive."

Sophia squeezed Ixtele's arm before turning toward the most senior officer. "What's the most defensible spot in the building?"

"Um…"

The *bang, bang, bang* of distant gunshots reached their ears as Eirik stood his ground with nothing but a pistol. Distantly, someone let out a cry of pain.

Then the gunshots cut off, and there was only silence.

Valkyries guide you, Eirik, Sophia thought. He would probably do time in a prison afterlife for his betrayal, since Caelistra was getting the full story to the Furies, but she would put in a good word for him.

If she survived.

"Defensible spot?" she urged.

"Up the stairs, to the captain's office. Has good lines of sight, some decent cover."

Sophia clapped him on the shoulder. "Good." To the group, she called, "Time to go! Everyone stay together and make sure—"

The wall of the armory burst inward.

Debris showered the room, sending the nearest officer to her knees, and a huge godborn man came crashing through the rubble. He seized the dazed officer by the head as he charged past and smashed her skull into paste against the far wall.

Then he rounded on the rest of them, laughing savagely. He was easily eight feet tall, a giant of bulging muscle. In the dim light of Ixtele's miracle, Sophia could see tiny silver scales gleaming from his body in place of skin, and waves of water rippled around his huge hands like miracle-wrought knuckle dusters. Even without his finely-tailored clothes, Sophia would have recognized him as a Silver Court enforcer from his arrogant sneer.

She emptied her magazine into the godborn's chest, and the police officers didn't need any prompting to join in. Fabric tore and scales flew as the miracled bullets tore into him, but none of the shots drew blood.

Unflinching, the Courtier strode forward and backhanded the officer between him and Sophia, sending him flying into a rack of body armor.

Snarling, Sophia holstered her gun and drew her sword. The Courtier struck at her, but she ducked under his ponderous swings and plunged her blade into his side.

The stronger miracle bound into the steel worked where the bullets hadn't, punching through scale and flesh alike. He roared, flailing, trying to reach her. A burst of water caught her in the side just as she tore her blade free, sending her slamming into the wall.

Spots swam in front of her eyes. She tasted blood on her tongue, but if there was any pain, it was hidden beneath the pulsing adrenaline. Sophia righted herself with a groan.

The hulking enforcer had already stomped past her, going for easier targets. Ixtele stood by the door, concentrating as a miracle built in her hand. The woman with the glass shard in her leg stood her ground, reloading methodically and opening fire on the godborn again. The other officer backed out into the hall, firing wildly until he passed a window. A sniper's shot rang out, and he crumpled with a bullet in his chest.

Sophia pushed herself off the wall and stumbled forward, still dazed. She caught up, but not in time. The godborn reached the wounded officer and raised a clenched fist, chuckling throatily.

And then a flash of light painted the world white. Something crashed into Sophia and drove the air from her lungs. She scrambled blindly to the side, covering her head with one hand. There was a crash, followed by the clatter of guns spilling across the floor. She found the wall and stood unsteadily, her legs wavering.

Her vision slowly cleared. Through the afterimage, she saw the Courtier flailing blindly, pulverizing racks of equipment and taking chunks out of the walls. As she started toward him, his gaze settled on Ixtele, and he stomped forward. "Determined to protect these mayflies, cousin?" he roared. Ixtele sent a lance of power toward him, but he sidestepped it. The water around his hands bent into blades, the edges hissing with pressure. Ixtele scrambled back against the wall, gathering more energy, starting to look panicked. The Courtier stormed right past the injured officer, all his attention on Ixtele.

Which meant that he didn't notice Sophia closing in.

Just as he raised his hands, she lunged, swinging her sword with all her strength.

The steel sheared through his scales and tore into the muscle of his leg. He toppled forward, sending a tremor through the floor. His fist grazed Ixtele and sent her spinning back into the doorjamb. Roaring, he tried to right himself, but his leg wouldn't take his weight.

He twisted around and slashed at Sophia with a snarl. She caught his watery blade with her own and was surprised when his miracle collapsed, splashing her with liquid. While she tried to blink her eyes clear, his hand lashed out and seized her by the arm, yanking her closer.

Fighting the urge to flail, Sophia reversed her grip on her sword and stabbed it through his wrist.

He let go with a howl, sending her flying past Ixtele and out the door. She slid across the floor, scrambling for purchase. She came to a stop against the body of the officer who'd fled this way moments ago.

The instant she regained control, Sophia launched herself into a roll. A bullet ripped into the floor where she'd been, and she pulled herself upright, scrambling away as another shot grazed her thigh. She threw herself back into the armory.

The godborn was hammering at Ixtele with his fists, trying to land a blow as she ducked his punches. Each swing ripped out chunks of concrete and plaster, until one clipped Ixtele and sent her sprawling. He raised a hand to crush her.

Sophia leapt into the air and drove her sword through the side of his neck.

There was a slick grinding noise as her blade scraped across his spine, and the fight went out of him.

She wrenched the blade free as he slumped to the ground, and stumbled back to lean against what was left of the doorjamb.

Ixtele was breathing heavily, her eyes wide, bleeding from cuts across her face and arms. The woman with the glass through her leg sunk down to the ground, checking how many bullets she had left. The man who'd been thrown through into the wall was righting himself, a dazed look on his face.

"Everyone all right?" Sophia asked.

"Styx," Ixtele muttered. The Courtier's leg twitched, and she jerked back, a silver glow erupting from her palm. She shook her head and looked up at Sophia. "Gods above, I— Sophia, look out!"

Sophia ducked on instinct as soon as she heard her name. There was a rush of movement, a flare of pain across her arm as something struck her from behind. Then Ixtele raised her hands, and the world went silver.

Sophia staggered, her eyes burning. Her fingers found blood-slick concrete. Shattered glass. The edge of the doorframe. She dragged herself back to where she knew cover had to be and put the solid, reassuring weight of the wall against her back.

She blinked, tears streaming from her eyes, and vague shapes swam into view. She rubbed her arm across her face and felt something wet smear her cheek.

When she could see again, the first thing she found was Ixtele huddled in the opposite corner, staring past Sophia in horror, faint motes of light still drifting from her fingers.

The second was Neferat. Or what was left of her. Her head was gone, along with most of her arm and shoulder. The rocky pebbles that had coated her skin were white hot and molten around the wounds as she fell backward, twitching. She collapsed to the floor and fell still.

Sophia forced herself to breathe. The Courtier was down. Neferat would have killed her without Ixtele's warning, but she was dead now. Which just left the snipers outside.

Unfortunately, they might also be enough to finish the job.

"We need to move," she said. "The captain's office is our best bet. We hole up there and wait for reinforcements. Are you with me?"

There was a crackle of static before anyone could answer. Sophia flinched at the sound, her sword jerking into a guard, but it was just a radio.

The radio on the Courtier's belt.

A man's voice came from the speaker. "Djau? What the fuck is going on in there?" There was a pause. "Djau?" Another pause. "We're sending a team in. I swear by all the gods, if you try something, Courtier, I will end you."

Sophia grimaced. "Looks like we're going to have more company. Ixtele, I need you to watch this hallway. Ixtele?"

Ixtele was staring at Neferat's body in utter horror, her lips moving soundlessly.

Shit.

"Someone cover this hall. I'll take the one—"

It was too late. A booted foot crashed through a door farther down the corridor, and its owner followed it through. Sophia caught a glimpse of a tall man with a dog's snarling maw tattooed across his throat before she ducked back behind the doorframe.

"Take cover!" she hissed. As quietly as she could, she set her sword down and unholstered her pistol.

"I saw something," a man's voice echoed down the hall. "Watch my back."

Glass scraped as footsteps closed in on the armory. Sophia found herself weighing the situation in her head. The Hounds were mortals, but if there were enough of them to flank the armory, the odds weren't looking good. Her best chance was to strike now, before they could be surrounded.

It might get her shot, but at the very least, she could buy Ixtele and the two police officers some time.

She took a deep breath and curled her fingers around the grip of her gun. The footsteps grew closer, closer. There were two, maybe three people, she judged. Just a little longer...

There was another gunshot from outside. Then another, and a

panicked scream.

The footsteps in the hall paused. "Team one?" a voice whispered. "Team one, come in."

She wasn't going to get a better chance.

She pulled Hekema's flash bomb from her pocket, cracked it between her fingers, and hurled it through the doorway before squeezing her eyes shut.

Even around the corner, even with her eyes closed, she felt the blast stab into her retinas. She heard the Hounds cry out in alarm, and she ducked around the doorframe.

She caught a glimpse of three Hounds with rifles raised. She put a bullet in the chest of the nearest one and turned to fire on the second, expecting them, even blinded, to shoot back at any moment.

Twenty feet down the hall, just behind the Hounds, something exploded through the wall. Chunks of debris rattled to the floor, and plaster dust choked the air. Instead of firing on Sophia, the Hounds spun, shouting.

A huge, winged shape tore through the gap, crashing into one of the gunmen.

Caelistra.

She had a shield on one arm, an ax clutched in the other. Shadows coiled around her, shrouding her from the Hounds' sight. Gunshots rang out, but the only blood that fell belonged to the Hounds.

Sophia leaned back against the wall, finally letting exhaustion spill through her. The cavalry had arrived.

CHAPTER TWENTY-FIVE

Glass crunched underfoot as Sophia picked her way among the blood and bodies strewn across the floor. Red and white emergency lights spun on squad cars outside. They'd managed to get the power back on, not that it mattered: the sun was rising, and morning light was beginning to filter through the broken windows.

Happy birthday, Teshan, Sophia thought sadly.

Sophia felt sick to her stomach as she looked across the carnage. The giant, scaled godborn lay sprawled among a trio of humans with dogs tattooed on their throats. Hound snipers, providing covering fire for a Courtier... The two gangs had been out for each others' blood for as long as Sophia could remember. Now, their dead mingled peacefully.

"Message sent," Caelistra said from the far side of the hall. She held up a phone she'd taken from one of the attackers. Fortunately, it had been easy enough to disable the jammer once the attack had ended. "Let's hope Meret believes we're all dead. That'll buy us *some* time, at least..." By the end, she was muttering half to herself.

Sophia barely heard. *Memphis PD has been trying to end the gang war for decades, and Meret's done it in a handful of days.* She shifted, sending a twinge up her side. Some of the wounds the huge godborn had dished out were still healing.

"Sophia."

She looked up and found Caelistra leaning against the wall with her arms crossed, a surly expression on her face. Sophia could feel the challenge in the glare. Under the circumstances, she was surprised that Caelistra was even waiting for some provocation, rather than simply exploding at her for staying to fight.

Sophia wasn't eager to give her an opening, so she looked around at the bodies and broken windows and tried to focus on the job. "Are the Furies giving us more resources?"

Caelistra scrutinized her carefully before pulling out a cigarette and tucking it into the corner of her mouth, unlit. The movement would have looked casual, if not for the tight, angry tension coiled through her body. "Not as long as the person with the bomb is a mortal who runs a shelter. Unless you happen to know of any gods or dragons in her employ?"

"Until today, I didn't know she had anyone but *shelter volunteers* in her employ," Sophia muttered, still feeling the sting of Meret's betrayal.

"Oh really?"

A handful of angry retorts floated through Sophia's head, but after fighting for her life, fighting with Caelistra just didn't hold any appeal. "You can imply whatever you want, but it's not going to change anything. You know as much as I do."

"Hmm. So you don't know where to find her?"

Sophia sighed. "She's smart. Even if she thinks we're dead, she's not going to show her face at the shelter or her home until she's absolutely certain her anonymity's intact."

"Makes sense." Caelistra looked around thoughtfully, nudging one of the dead Hounds with her toe. "So we comb the station, see if anything here can lead us to her. Maybe track down some of these gangsters…"

"I have a better idea," Sophia said as the thought occurred to her. "We need to put the word out."

Caelistra scoffed. "Why? To show our hand? To tell her we're alive, and that we know her secret?"

"She's not going to stay convinced that we're dead for long."

"Not if we do that."

The curt dismissal in Caelistra's voice made Sophia seethe, but the more she thought about it, the more she was convinced this was the right play. An angry retort wasn't going to win her anything. The right argument might.

"I know you've got more experience than I do. You were right to bring Ixtele onboard here. Your plan for getting into the auction was perfect. Styx, maybe you were right and I should have stayed out of the fight at the docks. But this is different. Anonymity was Meret's greatest weapon. She was willing to assault a police station to keep it secure. If we put her face on every TV in Memphis, she won't be able to set foot outside without someone noticing."

Caelistra kept her arms crossed, but at least she gave the suggestion some thought, scrutinizing Sophia closely the whole time. "She has people who can do her dirty work for her. She doesn't *have* to set foot outside. If we do this, we give up our biggest advantage."

"It's not much of an advantage if we don't know where she is. The Furies don't have anyone to spare. There's no way to know how many police are corrupt. That leaves us with two sets of eyes. If she's lying low, we're not just going to stumble on her ourselves. If we put out an APB, at least—"

"No," Caelistra said with finality. She shook her head, decision made. "We've done things 'your way' long enough. I forbid it."

All of Sophia's frustration boiled up inside her. "If you're just being petty—"

"I'm being wise. I'm going to make some calls and see if I can get forensics down here any quicker. You go talk to Dr. Tinaalto and see if she's up for helping."

"Caelistra—"

"This is the job. Hard work and patience. Maybe you should think about learning that, *recruit.*"

There it was, the bitterness Sophia had been expecting. After fighting for her life for gods-only-knew how long, exhaustion clung to her body like lead weights. The dead didn't need to sleep, but if she focused, she could feel the spark of divine power in her belly flickering like a dying candle, so much of its power spent to keep her active and alive. It would need time to recover.

And now Caelistra was trying to pick a fight.

"I seem to recall you saying that this was my case to solve," Sophia said wearily.

Caelistra gave her an incredulous look. "When we were checking out a crime scene, or talking to witnesses. Not when snipers and water spirits are coming to murder us!"

"I made the right choice."

"You forced my hand so that you could stay here and risk your life! In direct violation of my orders!"

"Yes, it was risky! But it was still *right*."

Caelistra turned with a snarl and started to pace the short width of the hallway. "Do you care about your responsibilities? Your life?"

"What? Of course I do."

"Do you think the tiny piece of divine power you've got makes you invulnerable?"

Sophia laughed bitterly. "Considering I feel like I've been beaten half to death? I feel distinctly vulnerable."

"You're not acting like it."

Sophia started to turn away, too tired for this. Caelistra closed the distance between them in an instant, caught her by the shoulder, and whipped her around.

"No, look at me. What do you think you even accomplished here?"

Sophia could feel the dead all around her, even with her eyes on Caelistra. Police officers, scattered among the monsters who'd slaughtered them. But not *all* the officers. That was the thought she held onto. "I helped save lives."

"A few. You think that makes this a victory?"

"Fuck off, Caelistra. I know that Meret has more foot soldiers. Probably more police on her payroll." She threw up her hands. "There are always more guns. More drugs. More criminals." It was an old litany, and it brought with it the same familiar despair as ever.

"Yes. There are." Caelistra's jaw was clenched tight, genuinely angry for the first time since they'd met. "I wonder how many of them you know."

Sophia gave her an incredulous look. "What the Styx is that supposed to mean?"

"You're buddies with our primary suspect. Is that a coincidence?"

"Apparently not, if she controls as much of Memphis's crime as it sounds like. Seriously, Caelistra, don't you think I would have said something if I'd known?"

"I don't know. Depends who you're really working for."

Another time, from another person, the accusation might have rankled, but all Sophia could manage in response was a bitter laugh. "If I were working for Meret, I would have been on the other side of those aurichalcum bars, and we wouldn't be having this conversation. Styx, you're the one who picked an assignment in Memphis. We could have gone anywhere in the Conclave…"

Caelistra studied her silently for a few seconds before she said anything. "I'm trusting you, for now, but you are walking a very fine line. As far as I'm concerned, you're one wrong move away from ending your career."

Sophia snorted. "You've thought that from the very beginning."

"I've also thought you had *potential*, even if you insist on squandering it." Caelistra shook her head. "Slip up one more time, disobey one more order, and I will send you straight to an afterlife. Do you understand?"

Sophia rubbed her face, exhaustion seeping deeper into her bones. She'd spent an entire lifetime trying to do things the right way… and Meret could snap her fingers and make Dockyard Hounds and Silver Courtiers work together. What were a detective's tools in comparison to corruption and violence? She'd jumped at the chance to become a Fury, to finally do more than chip away at the edges of crime, but were a Fury's tools any better?

What if nothing had changed?

"I understand," Sophia said.

Caelistra glowered at her. "I hope so. Go talk to Dr. Tinaalto. We've got work to do."

She walked off before Sophia could get in another word.

Sophia watched her go, feeling just as drained and frustrated as she did after a fight with Gahiji. Time and time again, he would go off and do something stupid. Something that put himself first, secure in the knowledge that Sophia or their father would take care of Teshan while he vanished off to gods knew where, or spent a few days in jail.

Now Caelistra was doing the same thing, in her own way. She could complain all she liked, but she was the one putting her own personal hangups before the case. She was so convinced that Sophia didn't know what she was doing that she wasn't willing to take a risk.

And her caution was going to get people killed.

Sophia was moving before she even realized she'd made a decision. She had a responsibility to the Furies, to the Conclave. As hard as it was to believe that Meret was behind all of this, the pieces fit. She'd seen Gahiji's face at the auction, and she'd never known anyone but Meret to earn even an ounce of true loyalty from him. Meret had a bomb that would have been in a class of its own even compared with the Great War's deadliest thaumatech weapons. Sophia still had a card, and it was time to play it.

She went back downstairs and found a computer that had survived the firefight. The police around the room were busy moving rubble and trying to secure the station. She got to work as soon as she was satisfied that no one was paying her any attention.

She knew the Memphis police system like the back of her hand. It took her a minute to get logged in with a generic ID, another minute to find what she needed.

When she was done, every news outlet in the city had received a bulletin warning that Meret was armed and dangerous, wanted on suspicion of murder, and that anyone who saw her should contact the

Furies immediately.

Caelistra could threaten her and question her loyalty all she liked, but Sophia hadn't joined up to sit on her hands.

CHAPTER TWENTY-SIX

Meret's nightmare began the same way it always did, with a bell jangling through the halls. Meret was out of her seat while the teacher was still shouting the weekend's assignment after her. She hefted her backpack over one shoulder and jogged through the halls, beating the stampede. Hetefer met her with a grin on her face.

"You ready?"

"Yeah! Let's go!" Meret said, grinning back. She was bubbling with excitement, backpack bouncing as they sped away from the school.

There was dread as well, quiet and cold. But it was always there, the scaffolding around which everything else was built, and today, it was buried deep beneath her joy. She could always feel that joy in the dream, even as a distant part of her remembered that it wouldn't last.

"How do you know your mom has a surprise planned?" Meret asked.

"I overheard her and Dad talking."

The two girls giggled, and Hetefer tossed her braid over her shoulder like she always did when she was feeling mischievous.

Meret wondered what it would be like to have a real birthday, without having to watch her dad like he was a time bomb. It sounded nice.

"I wish Gahiji could be here," Hetefer said.

"No you don't. I saw him throw up all over the teacher."

"Which teacher? Please say it was—"

"Woah, hold on," Meret interrupted, her voice dropping to a

whisper. She stopped Hetefer before she could start across the street.

Two Silver Court godborn walked down the sidewalk, strutting like they owned the city. One of them was playing with a stream of water in one hand like some of the kids in Meret's class had learned to spin a pencil between their fingers. He was showing off, proud of his power.

They ducked into a storefront. "Do you think he dries out in the sun?" Hetefer giggled.

Meret didn't crack a smile this time. She leaned around the edge of the wall, watching until the two godborn were gone. They probably wouldn't hurt a pair of kids. Probably. But just like godborn children didn't go near Dockyard Hounds, two kids without a scrap of divine power between them didn't go near the Silver Court.

Stay back. Stay safe. Hetefer always tried to laugh it off. Meret had never been able to.

The two Silver Courtiers approached a group of construction workers on the job at the big lot by the drug store. One of the workers had skin like marble, and she was carving blocks of earth from the ground with her will and dragging them out of the way faster than a tractor could have managed. Her mortal companions backed away when they saw the Silver Courtiers, and the two gangsters moved to flank the godborn worker.

Only water spirits joined the Silver Court. They like to talk a lot of bullshit about godborn being entitled to respect from their "lessers," and they didn't just mean humans. Here in Egypt, at the heart of a great, hostile desert, water was life, and the Silver Court knew it. Meret had seen them thrashing humans on a whim, but any godborn who didn't pay them protection money got treated even worse.

Meret looked away, flinching, as one of the Silver Courtiers raised a miracle-sheathed hand. "Let's go," she whispered.

Her heart didn't stop pounding until they were two streets away.

"It's going to be okay," Hetefer said, taking her hand for a moment. "Just wait 'til you see what's at home."

A bit of Meret's excitement bubbled back to the surface, and by the time they reached Hetefer's apartment, the Silver Court was all but forgotten. They raced each other up the stairs, laughing.

Hetefer was grinning at some joke Meret had told when she put her key into the lock. Meret could never remember what the joke had been.

All she remembered, all that was ever clear in this awful dream, was the look on Hetefer's face as she opened the door.

"Mom? Dad?" Her voice cracked as she choked on the words, staring at her parents' corpses.

Everything after that was an awful blur.

Hetefer called the police, even though Meret begged her not to.

The first officer on the scene was in the Dockyard Hounds' pocket. Hetefer died a few feet from her parents' bodies. Meret ran before he could see her face.

She ran all the way home, too scared to cry. She pushed past her brother, ignoring his surprise, his questions.

No. No no no no no. Not this again.

But it was always the same.

She was halfway to her room, halfway to safety, when her dad caught her by the hair.

No no no no!

The crushing, merciless fear was finally enough to shatter the dream.

She jolted awake and lurched upright, gasping for breath. Her hands clenched tight around the arms of the chair. Frantically, she took in the safehouse around her. Bare, cracked walls. Extra locks on the door. Rashmi, bent over his workbench in the corner, studiously avoiding looking in her direction.

He's in the past. It's all in the past.

"Dreaming about your father again?"

Euryale's voice was rasping and horrible, a product of the same curse that had transformed her appearance into a weapon. She strode into view and leaned close enough that Meret could see the writhing, squirming movement of the snakes beneath her hood. As usual, her face was hidden by a mask and sunglasses. "Water?" Euryale offered, holding out a bottle.

Meret took it gratefully and drank a sip. "It's always him," she said, soft enough that Rashmi wouldn't be able to hear. "No matter what else is there, it's always him." She rubbed at the dark circles under her eyes. Her body ached. When was the last time she'd gotten a full night's sleep?

Euryale watched Rashmi work, hissing softly. "Vengeance will only stop eating away at you when you finally destroy the one who wronged you. Artemis stole my revenge from me when she killed Zeus. But we will be ready for your vengeance soon. Once Setesh is dead, we can hunt down your father. Once that is done, he will no longer haunt your dreams."

"Perhaps."

Euryale had never understood. Zeus had cursed Medusa for spurning him, and cursed her sisters out of sheer spite. That curse had made them terrible and deadly, but it was the bitter rage in Euryale's heart that had made her a monster. It was her rage that made her such an easily manipulated tool.

No, it wasn't vengeance Meret wanted.

She took another sip of water and stood up. It was time to get back to work. She glanced at Euryale. "You must have news for me, if you're back."

Euryale sighed heavily. "I checked out the police station. The message we received was a lie, just as you suspected. The Furies survived."

Damn it. There was only one question that mattered, then. "Have they gone public?"

"I checked. Your face is on the news. Wanted for murder and kidnapping."

Meret felt her precious anonymity, cultivated over years of hard work, shatter like a dropped glass. There was sorrow, and rage, at the realization, but she closed her eyes for a moment and let them go. She was still in control. When she was awake, she was always in control.

"This doesn't change what we have to do. It just moves up the timetable."

"Maybe…" Euryale hesitated.

"Are you worried?" Meret glanced toward Euryale, gazing straight into her sunglasses. She knew the terror that the gorgon exerted on the others, and she made a point of showing that she didn't share it. Fear was a weakness that she didn't tolerate.

"We should have sent more people after the Furies."

"That would have carried risks of its own." Meret waved a hand. This wasn't a defeat. Not yet. She'd planned for this eventuality. "It's in the past. Get the rest of our teams ready. We need to move on Setesh as soon as possible."

Setesh. The lord of sand and storm, and the last obstacle between her and true dominion over Memphis.

Euryale nodded slowly. "I may have something, if we're accelerating the plan. We caught some of Setesh's people trying to break into the warehouse on Eighteenth Street. Normally, they wouldn't be first priority, but under the circumstances…"

Meret nodded sharply. "Bring them here."

Euryale turned and stalked off without acknowledging the order. Meret wasn't concerned. She would do as she was told. There were people she wanted dead, people only Meret could help her find. Sadism and vengeance were such predictable desires.

Meret crossed the room. She could see Rashmi tense at the sound of her footsteps approaching, and she felt a pang of frustration. There had been a time when he'd been all raw enthusiasm, with nothing to occupy his thoughts but his obsession over his project.

Damn the Hounds for interfering. Things had been simpler when Rashmi had thought her nothing more than an eccentric, anonymous patron. A part of her regretted not sequestering him sooner, but she knew she'd made the right choice. He'd been more compliant before he'd seen the darker side of her work.

"Progress?" she asked.

"Slow," he said. "These tools aren't nearly as good as what I had before, and I still need more materials for the casing."

"I will see that you get them." She put a hand on his shoulder. "Time is of the essence, now, and your work is vital."

She could feel the tension in him, could see it release as she pulled away. Another problem she was going to have to address. She needed his trust, not his fear.

Meret turned away, suppressing a sigh. Her eyes fell on the glowing contraption resting on the table by the far wall.

At least they had recovered the prototype. She'd put too much money, too much effort, into its creation to see it stolen by some Hound thugs. And then taken by Setesh, of all people? Her gut churned. She was lucky that none of them had seen its true potential.

She approached the table, slowly turning her bracelet around her wrist. Setesh was starting to dig his way toward her, dogged as ever. The Furies were closing in, unrelenting as their motto claimed.

But there was no need for apprehension, not anymore. She ran a finger over the device's glass casing, watching the raw divine power swirl inside. Slowly, the sour feeling in her stomach began to retreat, and her next breath felt more invigorating, less empty than the last. No setback was too great to overcome. No enemy was too great.

Soon, no one would be in a position to threaten her or her family ever again.

CHAPTER TWENTY-SEVEN

Sophia was still sitting at the computer when Caelistra found her.

Caelistra stormed up to the desk, her fists clenched and face locked in a snarl. The shadows shuddered as she passed.

"You are done," she spat, thrusting a finger in Sophia's face. "I have been more than patient, but you never listen! A recruit who won't take advice and can't follow orders doesn't belong in the Furies."

Sophia had known this was coming as soon as she'd put Meret's face on the news. She set down the sketch she'd been working on to clear her mind, crossed her arms, and glared back at Caelistra. "Really? You tell me that it's my case, and then you refuse to listen when I try to solve it. I want results. I want the people of Memphis, and the Conclave, to be safe. What do you want, Caelistra?"

"I want you to *listen*!" Caelistra practically shouted. All around the room, police officers studiously pretended not to hear them. "I've been at this for forty-five years. I've seen how cases like this play out. And I know what happens when people like you take unnecessary risks!"

"It was a *calculated* risk."

Caelistra scoffed.

"What are you going to do? Drag me back to Tartarus and throw me out?"

"Yes." She looked down at the page Sophia had set down, the page where she'd been sketching the Furies' badge. "Good choice. Might be the last time you see it."

Sophia rolled her eyes. "You've been snide and condescending since the moment I died. Not *once* did you offer any help unless someone was shooting at us. What did you expect me to do?"

"Frankly, this is exactly what I expected." Caelistra's shoulders slumped. "Go back to Tartarus. I'll be along as soon as I finish cleaning up the mess you made, and we'll take this to the Directors. I wish... I wish it hadn't come to this." She gave Sophia a long, disappointed look and then walked away.

Sophia stared after her, stunned. She'd misread Caelistra. It hadn't been a bluff after all. She was done. Out of the Furies before the ink was dry on her contract.

It felt like taking a bullet to the chest.

I did the right thing. The only thing. Looking back, she couldn't find a moment where she would have made a different choice, but that did little to dull the sting. The idea of heading off to an afterlife, taking an endless vacation while someone else fought the good fight...

Her hands curled into fists. No. She wasn't going to take this lying down. Caelistra was wrong, and she still had a chance to make the Directors see that. And if she failed... She looked down at her sketch of the badge. If she failed, then at least for a short time, she'd been the Conclave's shield, breaking the swords of its enemies.

Riding that wave of fierce, righteous indignation, Sophia logged out of the computer and pushed herself to her feet. She would go back to Hades, as ordered, but first she wanted to talk to Ixtele. After everything she'd done to help, she deserved a goodbye, at least.

And after that, she would fight this with everything she had.

CHAPTER TWENTY-EIGHT

"They know, Gahiji."

Meret sounded calm, but Gahiji knew her well. He could hear the knives hidden behind the placid surface.

He cradled the phone against his shoulder and tried to free his keys from his pocket. "It didn't work?"

"The Furies survived. They know I attacked the auction. They know I have Rashmi, and his invention. The police will come for you, even if the Furies don't. You can't be there when they do."

Gahiji took a deep breath. Sophia was still alive. Alive, and ruining everything. Gods above and below, how had it come to this?

"Meret..."

"There's no time. We made an escape plan for a reason. You need to use it." There was a moment of silence. "You need to protect our daughter."

Gahiji froze with the key halfway to the door. Cold terror clawed its way across his bones. "She's just a kid. If she learns—"

"I know. But until I own this city, it's not safe to be my daughter."

"Has anyone threatened her? Specifically?"

"It doesn't matter. They will, sooner or later." There was a pause, and a muffled exchange from the other end. "I have to go. Our plan can still work, but I have to act *now*."

Another acceleration. Years of careful groundwork, scrapped in a single moment of desperation. Recovering Rashmi and the prototype had gone a long way toward stifling the deep, gnawing worry inside him, but now he could feel it again, chewing through his guts like a parasite.

He swallowed, casting about for other solutions. For an option that wouldn't reveal to Teshan the sort of life her parents led. One stood out from the rest. "We don't have to hit Setesh immediately. We can bide our time. Move our people, shore up our defenses, make sure the entire organization is airtight."

"It would just give Setesh time to regroup."

"But we could focus on keeping our daughter *safe*. If we attack now…"

"There's only one way for her to be safe, and I am not going to pass up our best opportunity. Get her out of the city, Gahiji." Her tone brooked no argument.

He hung his head in defeat. "I will."

Meret hung up.

Gahiji slowly returned his phone to his pocket. The morning sun was burning its way into the sky, beating down on his back like it was trying to push him through the door. How was he going to explain any of this to Teshan? *Grab your things, kid, we've got to flee the city. Happy birthday!* He had the terrible feeling that one more lie piled atop the tower would be enough to bring the whole thing down.

He forced himself to unlock the door and go inside. There wasn't time for planning, anymore. That was the problem.

"Dad?"

Her voice sounded high, panicked. He almost dropped his keys before he raced into the house.

He found Teshan in the kitchen. She was standing in front of the fridge in her pajamas, a takeout container of leftover Chinese food and a pair of chopsticks forgotten in her hands.

Meret's face was plastered across the TV, over the headline, "Local Shelter Manager wanted by Furies."

Teshan turned a devastated face on Gahiji. "Dad, what is going on?"

Gods help me, he thought, half-formed lies and obsolete plans dying on his tongue. He'd had nightmares about Teshan learning the truth since she'd been old enough to talk. They hadn't prepared him for the reality. "I don't... Teshan, I don't know."

"This is bullshit. It has to be."

"Teshan—"

"It said she's wanted for *murder*!" Teshan let out a strangled, hysterical laugh. "Mom's not a killer. Can you imagine?"

"Teshan, listen to me!" He hadn't meant to raise his voice. She jumped, almost dropping her food on the ground. Grimacing, she carefully set it down on the counter. Gahiji paused and took a deep breath. "You need to go upstairs and get dressed. Pack a bag. Essentials only."

She stared at him, and his heart broke as he saw the wheels turning in her head.

Quietly, she said, "Are we running from Mom? Or from the police?"

Gods, Meret would die if she heard you ask that.

"We're just taking a precaution. Your mother loves you, more than anything in the world. She would never do anything to hurt you."

"Why are they saying she's a murderer?" Teshan stifled a sob. "She's only ever tried to help people."

"I don't know. But the Boneyard is a dangerous place, especially right now. The important thing is that you're safe."

He could see the last shred of hope fading from her face as her shoulders drooped. She sniffled and rubbed the tears from her eyes. "Where are we going?"

"I don't know yet. Somewhere that's not here. Please, Teshan, we have to hurry. Go get ready."

Teshan glanced at the TV, anger mixing into the torrent of emotion on her face. "I don't believe it. Not about Mom." She went into her room and slammed the door.

Gahiji leaned on the counter and put his head in his hands. "Merciful gods..." he muttered. His head was spinning, weighing and discarding plan after plan before lurching back to Teshan's horrified face each time. The damage it had done to see her mother's face in the news like that… What a way to spend her birthday.

But everything could be patched up later. The right lies, carefully applied, made all the difference. Right now, all that mattered was living long enough to fix things, and that meant following the escape plan.

He pushed off the counter and went into his own bedroom. One backpack was all he allowed himself, the same as Teshan. He filled it distractedly, his mind already racing ahead, rehearsing the steps to a plan he'd hoped to never carry out. His hands moved automatically, shoving in a couple changes of clothes, a toothbrush, water. He opened up the air vent in the corner and added a miracle-forged knife and some extra ammunition for the gun in his waistband, just in case.

He went to the bedside table and opened the drawer. Inside was the colorful bracelet that Teshan had made him, years ago. He didn't wear it, most of the time. In the secret life he led, a sign of attachment was a sign of weakness. But now… He pulled the bracelet from the drawer and tied it around his wrist. He was doing this for her. Everything, for her.

He shouldered the backpack and went back out into the hall when he was done. "Teshan? Almost ready?"

There was no reply. Gahiji's heart lurched. *No no no…* "Teshan!" He pulled open her door.

The window was open, the screen set aside. Teshan was gone.

"Fuck!" Gahiji swore. He ran to the window and stuck his head out, but she was nowhere in sight.

This is bullshit. It has to be. That's what she'd said.

Gahiji's heart sank. He knew where she was going.

He dropped his backpack and sprinted out of the room, fumbling for his car keys. He had to get there first.

CHAPTER TWENTY-NINE

Sophia found Ixtele in the lockup, the most intact room in the station, being checked over by a police medic.

Or, as it turned out, fighting with a police medic.

"I realize that you're a demigoddess. But you also have two cracked ribs, a cut on your face that needs stitches, possibly a concussion—"

"They'll heal. Back off."

"I can't—"

They both looked up as Sophia entered the room, and the medic let out a huge sigh of relief. "Will you talk to her?"

To Sophia's surprise, the glowing lines across Ixtele's skin were completely gone, and for the first time since they'd met, Ixtele could have passed for human. She sat on a table next to one of the cells, her arms hugged tight around herself, her entire body tense and her eyes frozen in a thousand-yard stare.

Sophia recognized the look.

She gave the medic a tight smile. "Give us a minute?"

"Gladly." He left the room, shutting the door behind him.

Ixtele slowly let go of her sides. Her fingers twitched nervously for a moment before she knotted them together in her lap. She said nothing.

Sophia crossed the room and sat down next to Ixtele, careful not to touch her. Seeing her like this, guessing at what she was going through, made all of Sophia's problems seem small by comparison. "If you want to talk, I'm here to talk. If you don't, that's okay too."

Ixtele swallowed. "I think I want to talk." She didn't say anything else, but her hands were trembling slightly. There was dried blood on her fingers, her forearms.

Sophia nodded. Ixtele stayed quiet for a long time, and Sophia let her think. Eventually, Ixtele said, "I thought I was prepared for everything."

Sophia smiled gently. "No one is prepared for everything."

"You haven't met my mother."

"That's true. But even if she *were* prepared for everything, which I doubt, she's had a long, *long* time to figure things out. A lot longer than you and I've had."

"I'm sorry I froze," Ixtele said, shaking her head.

"What?"

"After… After I…"

"Ixtele, if you hadn't been here today, Caelistra and I would be dead. A bunch of police officers would be dead. We would have no idea who took Rashmi and the bomb."

Sophia had thought that that might spark Ixtele's curiosity, but Ixtele just shrugged, her blank stare not wavering. "Still." She shifted slightly. "I ki…" She took a deep breath, and a tear trickled down her cheek. "I killed a person."

"Yes. You did. A person who was about kill *me*. I know it's not easy, but I'm glad you did it." Sophia watched Ixtele look down at her hands and flinch when she saw the blood there. She ached at the pain on Ixtele's face. "Here. Let me help."

The medic had left a few supplies behind, including some water and a roll of bandages. Sophia tore off a strip and dabbed it into the water. She reached out a hand. Ixtele nodded faintly. Sophia took her arm and started gently washing the blood from her skin.

"I've been there, you know. I don't know if you feel the same way I did, but I've been there."

Ixtele made a skeptical noise.

"The first time I shot a suspect, he was threatening a kid. It was clear cut, absolutely no choice, and it still gave me nightmares for months. People think that putting yourself in danger is the hardest part of law enforcement, but it's not. Killing people is."

Ixtele had gone completely still. Sophia softly unknotted her fingers and scrubbed away some of the blood between them.

"You build up scar tissue, eventually. Emotional scar tissue," Sophia said. "But it never gets easy. Therapy helps. So does staying connected to people you care about."

She faltered slightly. The thought was like a punch in the stomach, even as she said it. People she cared about? Like her brother, secretly a trained killer? Her father, who could barely say a word to her without getting into a fight about why she couldn't forgive Gahiji? Meret, who'd been pulling the strings behind the city's gang war for gods only knew how long?

Compared to all of that, Teshan's everyday teenage angst was practically comforting.

Ixtele turned slightly, her eyes focusing for long enough to glance desperately at Sophia. "When I did it, I felt…" She fell silent.

"Exhilaration? A kind of triumphant, ecstatic thrill?" Ixtele not denying it was answer enough. "That's normal. I *still* feel it." Sophia shook her head, a bitter smile tugging at her lips. "And even though it's normal, I still feel guilty about it. Maybe that's necessary. Maybe that's what keeps us from becoming monsters."

Ixtele's gaze grew distant again. "When I was eight, my mom visited. We went into the jungle, just the two of us, for a week. She taught me to hunt. Everything we ate during that week I either foraged or killed myself."

"That's quite the vacation." Sophia cleaned the last of the blood from Ixtele's right hand and started on the left.

A smile touched Ixtele's lips for the briefest moment. "That was a pretty tame one, actually. Still, at the very beginning, I was *horrified* at the idea of killing an animal. By the last night, I could put an arrow through a deer at forty yards every time, skin it, and cook it for dinner."

Sophia laughed. "Ixtele, if you don't mind my asking, who is your mother?"

Ixtele chuckled slyly. "Artemis. Greek goddess of the hunt and the moon. My dad was stop number 178 on her world tour after Zeus's death meant no one was forcing her to be a 'virgin goddess' anymore. I mostly inherited the moon part." She held up her right hand, which lacked even a hint of silver tracery. "I only glow when the moon's above the horizon. Otherwise, I can pass for human." Every trace of cheer faded from her face a moment later. "I thought I'd be ready, if I had to kill someone. To save a life, you know."

"You *were* ready. You *did* save my life. Everything after that? All this? Completely normal."

Ixtele grimaced. "I threw up."

"Also completely normal." Sophia glanced at the empty water bottle at Ixtele's side. "Do you need more water? Food?"

"Oh my gods yes."

Sophia chuckled and set down the bloody rag. "Stay right here."

She came back with a bottle of water and two bags of crackers. "Looks like everything's currently on sale for the low, low price of, 'the glass on the front of the machine is completely broken.'" Ixtele managed a laugh before taking a swig of water. Sophia offered her the crackers. "Tomato and olive, or cheese crunches that for some reason are shaped like squids?"

"Both?"

Sophia chuckled and handed them over. "You earned them."

Ixtele tore into the crackers like she hadn't eaten in weeks. She winced and shifted her weight, holding her broken ribs.

"You all right?" Sophia asked.

"It's just pain. Not the first time some crazy adventure has left me with broken bones. Just the first time it's been other *people* breaking them." She gave Sophia a sidelong glance. "I'm glad you're okay."

"Ha. I'm glad you got us out of that cell." Sophia sat down next to her again. "I'm sorry if I was harsh with you. Before."

Ixtele blinked at her. "Harsh?"

"Before tonight. I wasn't entirely sold on the idea of bringing in an outside consultant. Especially one who was a witness. I'm..." She chuckled ruefully. Talking to Ixtele had let her focus on someone else's problems, but her own were still there, waiting for her. "I *was* still getting used to the way the Furies do things. Maybe I was a little too suspicious."

Ixtele was giving her a curious look. "I understand. When all you do is slog through the worst people have to offer, it can be hard to see anything else."

Sophia swallowed. She didn't know the half of it. "The point is, I'm sorry if I came across as rude. You clearly deserved better."

Ixtele threw back her head and guffawed. She slowed to a chuckle, holding her ribs. "Oof, that wasn't a good idea."

"I think I'm missing the funny part," Sophia said, studying her.

"Sophia, I'm from Maya, right? I was one of *two* godborn at my entire school. Most of the kids treated me like I was radioactive, because of the *kind* of person I was. So I moved to the Conclave, where gods and humans live side by side, right?"

"Sort of..."

Ixtele snorted. "Yeah. Most godborn live in communities with other godborn. Most humans live in communities with other humans. Except for a few human-passing godborn, everyone mostly keeps to themselves. And it shows. People treat the unknown with fear and curiosity. Some people try to touch the lines on my skin. Others cross to the other side of the street, or bow and scrape like they're afraid I'm going to smite them if they're not polite. None of them can look me in the eye."

"Fuck," Sophia muttered, shaking her head.

Ixtele gently took her arm, and Sophia met her gaze. "You are one of very few people I've met who has treated me like an individual," Ixtele said. "Promise you won't stop now."

"Ixtele, I..." Something in her open, earnest gaze made Sophia's heart dance and her cheeks grow hot, and then everything she'd been trying to forget came crashing back down around her. She cleaned the last of the blood from Ixtele's left hand and pulled back. "I actually came in here to say goodbye."

"What? Why?"

"I ignored a direct order because I thought there was no option. Caelistra was... not pleased. She's having me thrown out of the Furies."

Ixtele sat up straight, looking personally affronted. "That's insane! If you hadn't stayed here, everyone in the station would be dead."

Sophia shook her head. "I know. It doesn't matter. The point is, I thought I owed you a conversation before I went back to Tartarus."

"Sophia..." Ixtele put a hand on her arm. "Caelistra's wrong. You've been working on this case nonstop. You stepped up to defend these people." She shook her head. "If your bosses care for another opinion, tell them to ask me. You're a good person, Sophia. You would be a fantastic Fury."

Sophia had to blink away a tear. "Thank you, Ixtele." Ixtele smiled at her.

A good person... She'd always thought of herself as trying to be good. Her brother had always been part of the problem; she'd always tried to be part of the solution. But did that matter? If nothing ever changed, was she doing good? Or had she just picked one side of a meaningless stalemate?

Ixtele looked down at the bag of snacks in her hand as if surprised to find it empty. She let out a long sigh. "It sounds like Caelistra's going to try to do the rest of this on her own. I'm still curious about the stuff that guy was carrying when you brought him in, after the auction. I wish I could have asked him about that stone finger he wore. Now he's just some dead guy, as useless as the mud on his boots."

Sophia grunted in agreement, trying to push her doubts away. "We'll see. You think..." She trailed off, going completely still. She turned slowly toward Ixtele, her eyes widening. "Hold on. What did you just say? Mud on his boots?"

"Um... Yes?"

Sophia stared at her. "Ixtele, it rains here barely a handful of times a year. Ten to one odds that's river mud."

"Okay..."

"When we first met, you told me that you wrote a paper on the..." Sophia tried to recall the exact phrasing. "The thaumaturgical variance of Nile water?"

Ixtele laughed. "I can't believe you remembered that."

"Please, please tell me that you can figure out what part of the Nile the mud on his boots came from."

A slow grin spread across Ixtele's face. "I think I can."

Sophia shot to her feet. "I'll let you inside; I still have the key. How long will it take?"

"It's an old paper, but I should be able to find my data. If you can find me a working thaumascanner I can use on the mud, it should only take a couple of minutes."

"Then let's get to it. We need to have an answer before Caelistra comes looking for us."

CHAPTER THIRTY

Rashmi kept his head down and his eyes on his work. *Containment shielding looks good. Transmission coils aren't as stable as I'd like, but they'll have to do... Flow regulator—*

A cry of pain sent the pliers jerking out of his hand and his train of thought careening off the rails. Rashmi gritted his teeth as he fished the pliers out of the tray of scrap. *Focus on the work. Don't listen to the torture. My work is the only thing keeping me alive... Okay. The flow regulator isn't working yet. I'm going to have to—*

He winced as another agonized howl tore through the safehouse. Behind him, Meret clicked her tongue. "It's a simple question. I'm not taking any pleasure in this."

Euryale's laugh sent a chill down Rashmi's spine. "I am."

"There's no simple answer! The mountain under the Sandstorm Club is a fortress. There's no easy way in unless Setesh *lets* you in. Ahh!"

Euryale cackled softly as his cries of pain subsided into whimpers. "Wrong answer. Try again. Don't worry, you have a lot of fingers left."

Rashmi kept his eyes on the plans spread across his workbench. They were a diagram of his proudest accomplishment, his very soul distilled to its bare essentials. Glass and wires and thaumaturgical circuits, yes, but also a lifetime of striving despite the ridicule of his peers. The awe he felt whenever he looked at the plans was usually enough to drown out everything else.

It wasn't quite enough, today. The clever workarounds and hard-fought solutions were still there, but with the screams behind him, it was impossible to keep his mind on his task. Even for him, it took concentration to make sense of the plans.

Things would have been simpler if he hadn't worked layer after layer of shorthand, obscuring language, and misleading diagrams into the blueprints, but now more than ever, he was glad that he'd made himself indispensable. He'd been blind for so long. So eager to complete his work that he'd taken Meret's money without a second thought. Why doubt his mysterious benefactor, the first one who finally saw his potential?

Another scream ripped through the room. "I can call her off," Meret said. She sounded as calm and gentle as ever. It was the same voice she'd used to guide Rashmi through the darkest moments of failure and rejection. The same voice she'd used to tell him that she shared his dream of a bright, shining future, back before he'd known who she was. Probably the same voice she used to comfort the desperate at her shelter.

She'd fooled him, and now he was so tangled up in Meret's plans that he couldn't see a way out. She didn't want unlimited food and energy for the world, or commercial flights to the moon, or any of the other dreams he still yearned to achieve.

She just wanted a weapon.

A bone snapped. Rashmi kept his eyes down. The screams and the begging were automatic responses to painful stimuli. Nothing that required his attention. He had to keep going. He had to survive, and wait for an opportunity.

He wasn't sure how long it went on before the man they'd captured was a gibbering mess, spilling Setesh's secrets like blood from his trembling hands. Or, at least, spilling something. Time would tell whether he actually gave them anything useful. He'd seen enough to know that Euryale didn't care; for her, the torture was an end in itself. Meret would claim to detest such crude, unreliable methods, and then she would do the same awful things to their six other captives and see whether their answers lined up.

Rashmi's hands wanted to work automatically, but that was the only thing more dangerous than not working at all. He knew this project by heart, now. It wasn't perfect, but the crude contraption that Meret called a success was easy enough to reproduce.

After which he wouldn't be needed anymore. He was Penelope, alone and outmatched, surrounded by enemies, with only his hands and his mind between him and the abyss.

"That's better," Euryale was hissing, the snakes on her head joining in. "Tell me everything."

Rashmi bent over his task as footsteps crossed the floor. *Into the acid bath to strip the coating, no more than thirty seconds...* He carefully lowered the components into the acid with tweezers and activated the timer.

Meret placed a hand on his shoulder. He managed to suppress a flinch, but he was still glad he was nowhere near the acid.

"How much longer?" she asked.

"Not long. I need to finish treating the secondary conduits, and then install them, of course. Once that's done, there's just the external casing to finish. Oh, and I need to double check the transmission coils, since—"

"Rashmi." Meret's voice was gentle. Gentle and terrifying. "How long?"

"Two days? Maybe three? Just like before, I'll need someone to provide a small amount of divine power for the test run, since I obviously can't do that myself."

"That won't be a problem."

The timer went off, and Rashmi silenced it as he lifted the treated components from the acid.

Not for the first time, Rashmi imagined sabotaging the device so that it exploded during the test run. It would be a horrible way to die, but he was surrounded by horrible ways to die. It might be the best option. He could go out on his own terms. If he was honest with himself, the chance of actually escaping was vanishingly small. Even if he got out of the building, he had no idea where in the city they were.

It was the thought of his legacy that stopped him from killing them all. He was only human, and he felt the petty need to be remembered, the vindictive need to see his detractors silenced. But both were dwarfed by the desire to remake the world, free of scarcity and the suffering it brought about. If there was a chance, however small, to make that dream a reality, didn't he owe it to everyone not to take the easy way out?

Meret's hand tightened on his shoulder for a moment. "Keep up the good work. Soon, very soon, we won't have to hide here any longer. You can have a real lab again, with everything you need to do your work." She chuckled. "Maybe we can even get you a lab assistant or two. We can still save the world together."

He glanced at her, too taken aback to hide his surprise. "You want more? After the first one, I thought…"

Meret laughed. "Do you think Achilles went into battle with only one weapon? Did Rama carry only a single arrow in his quiver?" She patted his shoulder and left him alone.

Rashmi stared down at his work. Did Meret really think he still believed the lie that she shared his vision for the future? It hardly mattered, he supposed. He'd known nothing of Meret's plans until today, but the bigger picture was already coming into focus, and he was terrified by what he saw. The thought of Meret wielding only one of his inventions was utterly terrifying. With two, or ten, or *twenty*…

No.

The only weakness in those plans, the only piece that couldn't be replaced, was him. So long as no one could replicate his plans, he was indispensable.

Five minutes. A handful of modifications. That's all it would take to send us straight to the next life.

He didn't do it, though. If he waited just a little bit longer, he might have a chance to escape. A chance to live to see his work become a blessing instead of an abomination. He wasn't sure whether that made him a hero or a coward.

Almost thirty minutes passed before he was jarred out of his work again. This time, it was a phone ringing, not a scream. "A minute of quiet, if you don't mind," Meret said. The captive's cries became muted grunts as a gag was forced into his mouth. "Euryale, I think we're almost done with this one, unless he proves himself more useful than he's been so far. Why don't you get ready for disposal?"

Amid louder, pleading grunts, Euryale chuckled and walked to the front door. She fished the keys from her pocket and started on the locks.

Rashmi counted as each one was undone, picturing the door in his mind. *Three left. Two. One. How did I end up here?* he asked himself. *Locked inside a room with two murderers, working night and day on a device that will only be used to kill people?*

Euryale opened the last lock. Freedom was so close. All that stood in his way was a gorgon who could kill him with a glance.

Meret answered her phone. "Hey, Teshan." All Rashmi could hear of the voice on the other end was rapid jumble of noise. "Woah, woah, woah, slow down. What's going on?"

Rashmi turned around, frowning. He saw Euryale turn away from the door with one hand on the handle. Meret's brow furrowed as he watched. "Hold on. Why do you think something's wrong?" She held up a hand toward Euryale and beckoned her over. Together, they went into the next room.

Leaving Rashmi alone with the prisoner.

The man's eyes found Rashmi's immediately. His words were lost in the gag, but his pleading eyes spoke volumes. Rashmi looked at the door. For the first time since he'd arrived at this gods-blasted safehouse, the locks were all undone, and no one was watching him.

He didn't even have to pause to make his decision.

Rashmi turned back to his workbench, his heart thundering so loudly he was afraid Euryale would hear. With a series of deft movements, he uncoupled the flow regulator and damaged the primary circuit so it would short. He slid the power source into the housing and leapt backward.

Sparks cascaded out of the device as it fused into a useless wreck.

That device, at least, would never kill anyone.

The working prototype was in the other room with Meret and Euryale. As much as he longed to, there was nothing he could do about that. The plans he left on the table. They were the best trap he could leave for anyone who wanted to retrace his steps.

He turned his back on the smoking wreckage of his labors and ran for the door.

With each step, he expected a scaled hand to wrap around his wrist. The prisoner groaned, rocking the chair he was tied to. Rashmi ignored him. Heart in his throat, he pressed down on the handle.

It turned. Mercifully, it turned. The door creaked open, and he had to squint as he stepped out into the blinding Egyptian sun. He'd never been so happy to see it.

His eyes darted, desperate for a way out. Squat concrete buildings, faded signs, graffiti new and old, the enormous, snaking bulk of the Nile...

Behind him, there was a slam. "Rashmi!" Euryale shouted after him, her voice dripping with wrath.

He put his back to the river and ran.

CHAPTER THIRTY-ONE

Caelistra maintained a white-knuckled grip on the steering wheel the entire time they were on the highway. She was completely silent for most of the drive, before finally letting out a sigh and giving Sophia a brief, stern look. "This isn't a second chance."

Sophia regarded her coolly. "I understand. You're bringing me along because we need to move on Meret quickly and I'm all you've got."

Caelistra kept her eyes firmly on the road, taking an exit that would lead them to the river. And, hopefully, to Meret's hideout, if Ixtele's analysis was correct. "Just don't do anything rash. Stay with me, and follow my lead."

Sophia's eyebrows rose. "Really? You're not ordering me to stay in the car, this time?"

"Can't afford to. Remember, until the Directors say otherwise, you're still a recruit. I expect you to do your duty to the Conclave. Or to make your best attempt, at least."

"Your confidence is overwhelming." Sophia could read between the lines. She wasn't just the only backup available: now that Caelistra had decided she wasn't fit for service, she was expendable.

There was something else buried beneath Caelistra's usual condescension, but Caelistra spoke up before she could place it. "Are we close?"

Sophia consulted the map on her phone. "Almost there. It's got to be…" She craned her neck. "One of those buildings."

They were too far north to be in the docks district proper, but there were a handful of isolated wharfs and launches along the bank for less industrial applications. Sophia got a good look as Caelistra parked the car. From the signs, the buildings in question belonged to a river tour company, an advertising firm, and an independent printing press. None of them looked terribly busy, but Sophia was pleased to see patches of mud along the edge of the river. Mud that could have matched Hekema's boots.

Thank you, Ixtele. She had wanted to come along, but not being able to stand up without getting dizzy had made it hard for her to argue with the medic.

Considering what they might be walking into, Sophia couldn't decide whether she wished Ixtele was there to help or glad she was safe.

Caelistra lit a cigarette as she climbed out of the car. "We check the tour boat company first. If they're—"

"Hang on," Sophia interrupted. Caelistra shot her a glare, but Sophia barely noticed. There was someone sprinting toward them from between two of the buildings. "Is that… Styx, that's Rashmi Bhagvara!"

Caelistra didn't need to give an order. Both of them took off running.

A lithe, hooded figure rounded a corner and tore after Rashmi, moving too fast for a mortal. Rashmi must have heard the footsteps, because his face, already stricken with fear, became a mask of pure panic.

They weren't going to make it in time. Sophia slowed, drawing her gun. "Conclave Furies! Freeze!" She couldn't get a clear shot, not with Rashmi in the way. Just a little bit to one side…

Rashmi's pursuer lunged before Sophia could get a shot off.

Without slowing, Caelistra slashed her hand through the air. A mass of shadow wrenched itself free from the advertising office, twisted into a monstrous claw, and hammered the figure behind Rashmi.

Rashmi scrambled behind a concrete ramp as the figure pulled itself to its feet.

Sophia recognized the person, even with all her features hidden. It was the same woman who'd snatched Rashmi from the docks. The same woman who'd stolen the bomb from the auction.

"Keep your hands where we can see them! Lower your hood and get on your knees!"

A rasping laugh issued from beneath the mask. The woman raised her hands and reached for the edges of the hood.

"No!" Rashmi yelled. "That's Euryale! Don't look at her face!"

Euryale. A gorgon.

Sophia averted her gaze just as Euryale snatched her hood back and tore the sunglasses from her face.

Darkness swirled, and Caelistra stepped out transformed, with one wing curled around her, shielding her face. "Find a mirror!" she shouted. She thrust her claws toward Euryale, and a wave of shadow rolled across the ground, tearing at the concrete.

Euryale laughed, and the rasping sound sent a chill up Sophia's spine. The hissing of her snake hair clashed discordantly with the angry whispers of Caelistra's own serpentine tresses.

Sophia ran back toward the street. Every parked car along the curb had mirrors she could use. Once she could actually see her opponent…

"Shit!" Caelistra swore. "Sophia, look out!"

Something slammed into Sophia from behind.

The blow sent her tumbling to the ground, ears ringing. She spun on the ground, kicking wildly, and felt her shin catch something. There was a snarl, and then a hand smashed into her jaw, claws raking across her cheek. She tasted blood. She threw a punch, felt it connect. A hand closed around her gun, tearing it from her grasp, as a weight settled over her abdomen.

"Look at me, little Fury."

A blow sent her head slamming into the pavement. Spots swam across her vision, and a clawed hand closed around her jaw. She fought, but inch by inch, Euryale forced Sophia's face toward her.

Sophia squeezed her eyes shut, fighting to free her sword. Euryale laughed.

There was a rush of air—Caelistra's wings!—and then an impact, and the weight vanished from Sophia's chest. She heard Euryale let out a cry of rage, heard blows land as the gorgon turned on Caelistra.

Sophia pulled herself upright. Blood streamed down the side of her face, but the pain was muted beneath the hammering of her heart and the adrenalized panic of the fight. Her gun. Where was her gun? She started looking before realizing that it wasn't going to do her any good when she couldn't look at her target. She drew her sword instead.

And, on a sudden stroke of inspiration, her phone.

Perseus had needed a mirrored shield to fight Medusa, but Sophia didn't, not in 2772.

Ears straining for any warning, she fumbled the passcode into the phone, opened the camera, and held it up. With her head turned to one side, she could see the phone screen without seeing what was past it.

Sophia expected some awful monster, but Euryale's face was beautiful. Contorted into a sadistic snarl and surrounded by hissing vipers, but beautiful nevertheless. She pummeled Caelistra with her bare hands as Caelistra struggled blindly to keep her shield between them.

Sophia stepped forward and brought her sword slashing toward Euryale's neck. The gorgon twisted aside at the last moment and delivered a stunning kick to her gut, forcing her back.

So much for surprise. Euryale fought as if the snakes on her head could see attacks coming.

"Flank her!" Sophia called. "She can only fight one of us at a time!"

It was a meager advantage. Euryale slid out of Sophia's reach with every attack, laying into Caelistra. She tore the shield aside, raking her claws across Caelistra's chest, her face, her arms.

Finally, Sophia managed a successful feint. Euryale shifted, and Sophia's blade slashed across her upper back.

Euryale spun with a snarl, turning her back on Caelistra. Sophia kept her head averted, her eyes on her phone.

It wasn't enough. No part of her police training had ever covered fighting a murderous godborn without the ability to look directly at her. Even with the camera, it was almost impossible to keep up with Euryale's attacks. For each blow Sophia deflected, five more hissed past her blade, opening gashes on her arms, her abdomen, her other cheek.

Her thigh.

Sophia stumbled, and Euryale's hand shot out, going for her throat.

Caelistra slammed her shield into Euryale's side, blasting her to the ground.

Panting, blood streaming into one eye, Sophia fought to keep her footing. She could feel her meager divine power struggling against the wounds dealt by the gorgon's cursed claws. Caelistra was better off, but even she hadn't managed to land any serious blows.

Past Euryale, Rashmi still cowered where he'd taken cover.

Shit. He should have been long gone.

"Rashmi, don't just stand there! Run!"

Euryale's head whipped toward him, and Rashmi whimpered, shielding his eyes with one hand. Legs shaking, he bolted toward the street.

Euryale lunged for him, but Sophia grabbed her ankle and yanked her backward. The gorgon's other foot snapped into the side of her head. Sophia staggered back, crashing into a pair of trashcans outside the tour boat office. Caelistra nearly decapitated Euryale with her ax, but the gorgon jerked away from the blow, hissing. She landed a kick to the side of Caelistra's leg, staggering her, and then threw herself at Sophia.

Euryale wasn't focused on Rashmi any longer, but with the claws flashing toward her face, Sophia found it hard to celebrate. She backpedaled, each step bringing her closer and closer to the Nile. She was running out of room.

"Caelistra, if you have any brilliant ideas, now's the time!"

Caelistra made a frustrated growl as Euryale avoided another blow from her ax. "We need a better way to look at her face."

A better way. More mirrors?

Euryale scoffed as she darted past Sophia's sword and scored a hit on her shoulder. Sophia felt her wounds and exhaustion threatening to drag her weapon out of her hand.

"Furies," Euryale laughed bitterly, "trying to bring me to justice. As if there was any justice in Zeus cursing me and my sisters. Any justice in our own city, our own *family*, turning their backs on us. They called us *monsters*."

"So you decided to prove them right?" Sophia said. "Zeus is long dead." *Killed by Ixtele's mother.* "So is everyone else who wronged you, but you're still murdering their descendants."

Euryale ducked a blow from Caelistra's ax, twisted, and came up swinging. Sophia tried to block, but the weakness stealing through her limbs slowed her down. Euryale's claws slashed across her wrist and sent the phone tumbling from her fingers.

Sophia lurched back, swinging blindly with her sword. Euryale laughed. "Much better. I hate the modern world. Too many cameras. Too many mirrors."

None that were within reach, though. *A better way to see...*

Except, that was wrong. *Seeing* Euryale's face wasn't the goal.

"Caelistra! Shadows around her face! Now!"

Sophia *felt* the miracle build around her. Shadows curled away from their natural homes, coiling together in the air. She didn't look up until she heard Euryale snarling with rage.

Caelistra had gotten the idea. Darkness shrouded Euryale's entire head, soaked with such power that even a Fury's eyes couldn't pierce the gloom.

Now it was Euryale's turn to flail blindly. Caelistra caught her claws with her shield and slammed her ax into the gorgon's side with a crunch of grinding bone. Euryale howled, scrambling back. Power gathered around her scaled fingers, crackling in the air, but Sophia didn't let up. She ducked a blow, felt a claw rake her scalp, and plunged her sword into Euryale's chest.

Euryale fell back, gasping, and slid off the blade. She coughed, and a spray of blood emerged from the shadows around her face.

"Surrender," Caelistra ordered.

Euryale let out a wet laugh. "Never." She crouched, and Sophia and Caelistra both braced themselves for another attack.

Instead, Euryale darted to one side and threw herself into the Nile.

Caelistra started after her, teeth bared.

Sophia shook her head. She sagged, the tip of her sword scraping across the pavement. "Let her go. Rashmi and the bomb are more important."

They turned away from the river and limped back toward the road. "Rashmi?" Sophia called.

The top of his head appeared behind their car. He slumped against the hood when he saw that they were alone.

"Oh, thank all the gods! Thank *you*! I thought I was dead."

"We're glad you're not." Sophia looked around cautiously as they approached the car, sheathing her sword. She scooped up her phone and her gun as she passed them. "Meret and the bomb. Where are they?"

He pointed a shaky finger at the advertising office. "In there. You have to stop her! She's going after Setesh. Her plan—"

A pair of gunshots rang out across the empty street, and Rashmi staggered, crimson stains blooming across his chest. There was a third shot, and Rashmi dropped with a bullet in his head.

There was no time to respond. No time to save him.

Meret strode around the corner, a pistol smoking in her hand. She stopped behind the car and studied Rashmi briefly. Then she tossed aside the gun and turned toward Sophia and Caelistra.

She looked like she always did, a short, strong woman in plain slacks and a loose shirt. Her eyes held the same gentle sadness that Sophia was used to seeing there.

The only difference was the sword at her hip, which she unsheathed and pointed at them.

"Walk away, Sophia. I don't want to have to tell Gahiji that his sister has died a second time. For nothing."

Angry tears welled in Sophia's eyes. "Meret, *why*?"

225

"For Teshan. Memphis isn't safe."

Sophia let out a bitter, incredulous laugh. "You're making the city safe? With murders? Kidnappings? Bombs?"

Meret shook her head sadly. "You've fought for years to fix the Boneyard, but somehow you never learned its most important lesson. Nothing is safe as long as someone stronger can snatch it away."

She raised her other hand. Clutched in her fingers was Rashmi's invention. A maelstrom of raw divine power barely larger than a fist roiled inches from her knuckles, separated from her skin only by a thin barrier of treated glass.

"Walk away."

It was the same warning Gahiji had given Sophia. She'd refused him then because she'd believed that this was her one chance to finally change the city for the better.

She hadn't given up for her brother. She wasn't about to give up for Meret.

"No." She looked down the sights of her gun, silently begging Meret not to make her pull the trigger. Even seeing her standing over Rashmi's body with the bomb in her hand, it was impossible to forget the kindhearted, compassionate woman Sophia had come to know over the years. Surely not all of that had been a lie. "You don't stand a chance, Meret. Using the bomb would kill you too. Surrender. You're just one mortal, against two Furies."

Meret raised an eyebrow. "Oh?"

Without taking her eyes off them, she slowly reached the hand that held the battery across to her other arm. With a single, precise movement, she unfastened the thin silver bracelet around her wrist, the bracelet she'd worn for as long as Sophia had known her. She dropped it into a pocket.

Meret rolled her head from side to side, popping her neck. She let out a sigh, as though a great burden had been lifted from her shoulders.

When she looked up, red smoke poured from her eyes. Her sword rippled, crackling with the same energy, and the weapon grew until the blade was a good six inches wide and nearly as long as Meret was tall. A mortal shouldn't have been able to lift the thing, let alone wield it.

Meret hefted it easily and rested the point against the pavement. Her eyes followed the crimson power racing up and down the blade.

"This power is the only thing my father ever gave me. The cruel, violent tool of a cruel, violent man." She looked up, and when she met Sophia's gaze, there was no trace of compassion in her eyes. "But sometimes, simple problems require simple solutions."

CHAPTER THIRTY-TWO

Sophia opened fire. Her bullets tore through the air, the miracles embedded in the metal leaving shimmering, heat-mirage trails in their wake. She emptied the magazine, round after round punching into Meret and spraying blood across the pavement.

Blood that burned with crimson power. The blood of a godborn who'd hidden her nature for decades.

Energy poured from the device in Meret's hand, crackling across her skin. Her wounds knit themselves shut, bullets plinking against the ground, but the flow of power didn't stop. It gathered in her limbs, her eyes, her sword.

Sophia stared, even as she went to holster her gun, horror stealing through her body.

Rashmi's invention *worked.*

Meret didn't want a bomb. She wanted an actual divine battery, brimming with enough power to challenge the gods.

There was no time to wonder how Rashmi had done the impossible or to work through the implications. Meret slammed her foot into the side of the car, sending it skidding over the curb amidst screeching metal and shattering glass. It slammed into Sophia's chest.

The impact sent her tumbling backward. She saw Caelistra launch into the air at the last moment and throw herself at Meret. Grimacing, pain radiating from cracked ribs even as they began to seal themselves back together, Sophia drew her sword and used it to lever herself upright.

Caelistra tucked her wings and dove. She held her shield before her, her ax cocked back.

Meret turned, impossibly fast, and swung her sword in a mighty arc.

Caelistra's shield took the hit across its shining grey surface. The miracle-engraved bulwark, forged of adamant by Hephaestus himself, cracked down one side with a sound like a thunderclap.

The deafening boom echoed off the buildings, the force of the shockwave buffeting Sophia. Caelistra was launched backward. Her wings beat once in a desperate attempt to stabilize herself, and then she crashed through a window in a shower of glass.

Gods above and below. No godborn was this strong. But with Rashmi's battery in her hand, pumped full of divine power, it didn't matter how much strength Meret had been born with.

They had as much chance of stopping Meret as they had defeating a god.

Sophia turned and ran. She needed time. Time to figure out a new plan, or time to call in backup... Time she didn't have. She could hear Meret on her tail, and she knew this wasn't a race she could win. She turned up the stairs and crashed through the doors of the tour boat company.

To her relief, piles of life vests and poorly stacked crates of fishing gear filled the space. Sophia wound through the detritus and threw herself down.

Just in time.

Meret's kick blasted the doors off their hinges. She swept her sword through a heap of life vests, sending them tumbling.

"Hiding? This is what we've come to?"

Sophia pressed herself against the floor and held her breath, immensely glad that she didn't need oxygen.

"I'm sorry that this had to be you, Sophia. Your idealism, your dream of making the city better... It was sad, but I could tolerate all that, as long as you loved my daughter. When you died, Teshan and I mourned you together."

Another hiss, another clatter as her blade toppled another tower. Closer, this time. Scraps of paper fluttered through the air, a handful landing on Sophia's back, on her legs.

She clenched her teeth, her heart racing. Would Caelistra find her way back to the fight? Or, more likely, was she already gone, returned to Tartarus on her own? She wouldn't think twice about sacrificing Sophia.

"People will say you were blind, not seeing the truth about me after knowing me for years." Meret's sword trailed behind her, scraping across the floor as she spoke. "They will be wrong. You couldn't have known. Not when I've spent my whole life wearing this mask."

Styx, Caelistra would be right to leave her. This was too important to wait. Meret wasn't just a fanatic with a bomb. With the battery, Meret could kill anyone she liked. Mortal, godborn, or god. Sophia had to get back to the Furies.

She found the spark of power at her core. Bound to it, constantly tugging gently at her soul, was the tether tying her to Death. It had been easy to draw herself back when she'd done it before, but she hadn't had a murderous godborn stalking toward her then.

She focused on that connection, tried to draw herself along it. Meret's sword tore through a stack of crates.

"I thought I was human for the first eighteen years of my life," Meret said. "I learned to survive by my wits. Survive the streets. Survive my father. And then one day, after my father had left, my brother crossed the wrong people, and Setesh had him murdered."

Sophia remembered, distantly, when Meret's brother had died. Gahiji had been torn up about it, but she'd barely known the Tanu family at the time. She'd had her own friends, her own problems.

"It was like having my heart ripped from my chest. And that was when I learned what I really was. When the divine power ripped its way out of me for the first time, and I almost destroyed the house."

Meret's shoes scraped against the concrete. Edging ever closer.

"That's when my mother finally decided to tell me the truth. That's when I learned that my father wasn't some failed businessman with an anger problem. He was Ares. The Mad God." She laughed bitterly. "He spent sixteen years here, despite being the most wanted criminal in the Conclave, all because he was amused when my mother picked his pocket on the street."

The daughter of the Mad God. Styx, how did I never notice?

Sophia tried to tune her out. She focused on her tether to the Memphis Deathgate, driving everything else away until it was all she could feel, and willed herself back.

Power gathered along the tether, and the shadows all across the room bent toward her.

Shit.

Meret whirled. Her sword flashed, parting bottles of water like they were smoke. Liquid splashed across Sophia's back an instant before Meret stomped through the wreckage and kicked Sophia in the ribs.

Sophia slammed into the wall. The impact, and the agony shooting up her side, shattered her concentration, and her tether to Death slipped through her grasp. Through the haze of pain, she saw movement, and she raised her sword in a desperate attempt to parry.

Meret's massive blade crashed into Sophia's, driving her to the ground. Before she could move, before she could do anything but groan, Meret loomed over her. Slowly, Meret pressed down on her sword.

Sophia's own miracled blade, trapped between her chest and Meret's weapon, began to bite into her flesh. Sophia pressed her other palm against the flat of the blade, pushing back with all her strength.

It wasn't anywhere near enough.

The edge of Meret's sword, burning with power, cut through Sophia's jacket. Sophia's arms shook, but she couldn't keep the weapon back. It dipped lower, lower, slicing into the skin of her shoulder. Agony spread through Sophia's body, and a strangled scream escaped between her clenched teeth. A simple cut would have healed, but she could feel Meret's divine power soaking into her flesh, overwhelming her own as it ate into her body.

"You should have backed off when Gahiji gave you the chance," Meret said.

Sophia could barely hear her through the pounding of her pulse. She pushed on her sword with every bit of force she could muster, heedless of the gash she was carving into her palm, but Meret overpowered her. Slowly, inexorably, Meret's sword sank deeper and deeper into the muscle of her shoulder. Blood poured down her chest, down her back, soaking into her clothes.

Sophia cast about for options with what little rational thought she could manage. She couldn't let up. The angle was all wrong for a kick. She had no training with miracles. The best she could hope for was somehow dislodging the battery from Meret's hand, but it was too far away.

Desperation gave way to dread. She'd only felt so powerless once before, when she'd been falling to her death. There was nothing she could do to save herself. Nothing she could do to stop Meret. That helplessness was worse than any pain.

Sophia's strength faltered, and her grip slipped. Her own sword sliced the flesh from her palm and fell away.

Meret's blade, unopposed, cut into her collarbone. Sophia screamed. There was a moment of resistance, and then she felt the bone splinter.

The divine power in her soul flared, fighting back on sheer instinct, and the force of its last, desperate attempt was the only reason Sophia didn't black out.

The only reason she saw when a shadow detached itself from the ceiling and tore Meret away from her.

Caelistra stepped into the room, shadows curling around one hand, her cracked shield held in the other. "Sophia, move!" she shouted.

Sophia blinked. The pressure was gone, the sword wrenched from her shoulder, but the wound still blazed with pain. Her body was leaden with weakness. The idea of moving was laughable.

Her eyelids started to droop.

Meret banished the darkness clawing at her with a swipe of her sword. She lunged at Sophia, blade extended.

Caelistra threw herself across the room, interposing herself between them.

Meret's sword crashed into Caelistra's shield, and the crack on the shield's face split apart completely.

The shield detonated.

The explosion struck Sophia like a god's fist. She was distantly aware of Caelistra slamming into her. She had a vague sense of motion, of air rushing past, and then she struck something hard and sensation vanished for a moment.

The next thing she knew, she was plunging into water. She sucked in a breath before she knew what was happening, and panic raced through her as water flooded her lungs.

Her eyes, piercing the gloom, found Caelistra below her, sinking toward the bottom amidst a stream of bubbles. She was unconscious, her eyes closed, her wings limp. A jagged piece of metal—a fragment of her shield—was buried deep in the side of her neck, surrounded by a growing cloud of blood. That snapped Sophia back to herself.

Forget the water. I don't need air.

The only sensation from her left arm was pure agony, but she reached out with her right and snatched Caelistra's hand. Straining, fighting through the pain, she dragged Caelistra to her and shut her eyes.

The divine power inside her soul was guttering like a spent candle. Where was her connection to the underworld?

Sophia bared her teeth, felt the Nile washing blood from her mouth. They knew about the battery. Meret needed them dead. Water wasn't going to stop her.

Focus.

Sophia forced herself to remember the sensation of dying. Of lying broken on the pavement as her life slipped away. She thought she'd forgotten the moment itself, but she'd just hidden from the horror of it. It was still there.

And with it, her tether back to the underworld.

She seized that connection with the little strength she had left. She had no idea whether it would work, but she tried to extend her consciousness to envelop Caelistra.

Something splashed into the river behind her. Meret was coming.

Focus.

Shadows gathered, shrouding the world. Even with her eyes closed, Sophia could *feel* them. The darkness coiled inward, and for a split second, she was nowhere at all.

Then she landed with a jolt on the floor of the Valkyries' Tower, water splashing from her clothes.

She clung to Caelistra's prone form, struggling just to lift her head. The world began to spin around her, but she could make out indistinct figures backing away from them. The vibrant red of the blood gushing from Caelistra's throat stood out from the black floor.

Sophia tried to speak, but her lungs were full of water. She managed to twist onto her side and cough it up. The pain from her shoulder was almost enough to drive consciousness from her. Distant murmurs and cries of alarm reached her ears.

"Help," she croaked. She collapsed against the floor as the last of her strength left her. "Someone, help."

CHAPTER THIRTY-THREE

Gahiji was on the edge of panic when he reached the shelter. This was a bad time to be out in public, what with Meret's face on every news station in the city. This was a *particularly* bad time to be at the shelter. People knew him. They knew Teshan. If someone wanted to hurt Meret...

He barely paused to turn off the engine before leaping out of the car. He gave the parking lot a hurried scan—nothing—before heading toward the building. In a brief moment of panic, he almost called Meret before he caught himself. If she found out that he'd lost their daughter, *now* of all times...

He pushed through the front doors with his pulse pounding.

"Hey, Gahiji!" A bedraggled man limped toward him with a huge grin on his face, expertly riffling a deck of cards between his hands. "Long time!"

Gahiji tried to find a smile for his face and came up empty. "Hey Ademe. Have you seen Teshan?"

"Not today. Why? You—"

Gahiji left him behind. His heart beat a steady, insistent rhythm beneath the chatter of the shelter. He pushed through the crowd, eyes darting from face to face.

The shelter was unusually crowded for midday; it was normally all but empty after people cleared out in the morning. Another time, he might have wondered if something had happened. Now, he didn't have the energy. A couple volunteers and a handful of regulars waved at him and tried to say hi, but he didn't stop.

He checked Meret's office first, but Teshan wasn't there. *Where's the next place she'd go to look for her mother? Think!*

His head felt like it was stuffed full of lint. No clear answer presented itself.

So he started in the southwest corner and worked his way around the building, room by room.

Most of the activity rooms were empty. A pair of volunteers were having an argument in one. A different pair helped clean up the second, which looked like someone had trashed it. The third had been converted into a makeshift clinic, where a tall godborn with iridescent skin was pouring healing energy into a wan old woman.

Damn it, Teshan, where are you?

Meret would kill him if something happened to Teshan on his watch. Actually, literally kill him. She was calm, gentle, and patient, right up until the moment she lost her temper, and picturing the raging firestorm of her anger was enough to quicken his steps.

He caught a glimpse of a figure that sent his heart soaring with hope, but it wasn't Teshan, just a young woman with the right kind of clothes. She glared at him when she caught him looking.

He wandered through the shelter in a daze. He almost ran into a man leaning against one of the pillars. "Woah, sorry," Gahiji said. The man pulled away in a hurry, clutching his coat around him.

Strange... But there was no time to waste figuring out what had tripped his instincts.

Gahiji passed a volunteer—an ancient earth spirit who'd worked there since the shelter had opened—trying to console a sobbing man. He slipped between two people having a quiet conversation, and their grumbled complaints followed him through the room.

He finished with the entire first floor. No luck.

Gods, Teshan, if you're not here...

He strode out into the middle of the floor, heading for the back stairwell. And froze.

Teshan stood at the railing of the second-floor walkway, frowning down at the crowd, turning her phone over and over in one hand. She must have changed before leaving the house, because she was wearing torn jeans and a shirt from one of her favorite bands. She saw him standing there, glared, and turned to walk away.

Just as a man in a heavy coat—the same man Gahiji had run into earlier—stepped up behind her and pressed something to her neck. She spasmed, struggling for a bare instant, and then collapsed into his waiting arms.

"No!" Gahiji shouted. "Teshan!"

Gunfire and screams swallowed his words.

All around the shelter, men and women drew automatic weapons from beneath heavy coats. Everything Gahiji had been ignoring in his haste clicked into position in a moment of complete, horrible clarity. The tactical part of his brain recognized their spacing, designed to maximize the killzone without the risk of friendly fire. The part of him that had organized Meret's operations for years recognized their equipment, their professional bearing. *They work for Setesh.*

The rest of him howled in fear and anguish as his daughter disappeared from view.

Bullets tore across the room, cutting down everyone in sight. The people closest to the doors ran for the exits, only to find them locked. The shelter, neutral ground for more than a decade, filled with cries of pain and terror.

Gahiji was moving without conscious thought. He ignored the gunfire, ignored the screams. There was no trace of fear in him, not for himself. He had his gun in his hand, though he didn't remember drawing it, and desperation in his heart. He had to reach Teshan.

He was halfway to the stairs when the first bullet struck him in the back.

CHAPTER THIRTY-FOUR

Someone helped Sophia up. She had no idea who, just a vague awareness of a presence by her side lifting her to her feet and taking some of her weight.

"Caelistra," she groaned.

"Shh," a voice said near her ear. "We've got her. Don't worry."

"Have to get back to Fury HQ," Sophia said.

If her savior said something in response, it was lost in the pain cascading through her body. Walking, even with assistance, was absolute torture. Her back ached like she'd been pummeled with bricks. Her collarbone was shattered, her left shoulder sawed through. She felt every inch of movement like Meret's sword was tearing into her all over again. The clearest thing she could feel through the pain was the constant flow of blood down her skin. Blood was the only thing she could smell, the only thing she could taste.

She tried to turn her head, and she caught a glimpse of Caelistra, carried between two unfamiliar people. Was she breathing? Sophia's vision wasn't clear enough to tell. How was she supposed to tell whether a person who didn't need air was still alive? What did it look like when a Fury died?

She didn't remember crossing the bridge from the Tower to Hades, but they were passing through bare stone, now. She was lying on her back, still moving. A vehicle? A stretcher? How long was the walk to

Fury HQ? She couldn't remember. Sometimes, she blinked and only a moment passed. Other times, she was in a completely different place.

She was losing time. That didn't seem like a good thing.

"Doctor," she croaked.

That got her a bitter laugh. "That's where we're going. Not a lot of demand for doctors in Hades, outside the Furies."

Sophia got a glimpse of the people helping them as a turn jostled her head to the side. A man and a woman in formal clothes sat by her side. "Valkyries?" she said groggily.

"That's right."

It made sense. The only other people around would have been the newly arrived dead, who probably weren't in any shape to help.

"Just..." Sophia broke off as coughs racked her body, and she almost passed out from the pain.

"Hold on," said the valkyrie helping her. The tunnel opened up around them, and heat buffeted Sophia from all sides. "Tartarus. See? We're almost there."

Sophia let out a relieved sob when she finally saw the stalactite that housed Fury HQ looming before her. "Badge," Sophia managed. "On my belt." She didn't have a spare hand to grab it.

One of the valkyries used the badge to open the door. "Need some help here!" he shouted. "Got two very wounded Furies in need of medical attention!"

Sophia was lowered into a chair in the lobby and almost passed out as the movement jostled her wounded arm. When she could see clearly again, Caelistra was on the ground, a folded coat placed under her head. The shard of adamant still protruded from her neck. The flow of blood had slowed, but that didn't seem like a good thing. Would a doctor even be able to help?

A Fury jogged into the room and knelt at Caelistra's side, setting down a medical kit. A handful of people followed, swarming around Caelistra with practiced coordination as the valkyries backed away.

Good. That was good.

Sophia had lost all sensation in her arm, but her shoulder and chest still burned with agony. Exhaustion gripped her with leaden claws, trying to drag her away from the pain. She could rest now. It would be so easy to just let herself slip away.

Someone sat down next to her. Another doctor, probably. The woman asked Sophia a question, but it didn't register.

There was blood dripping from Sophia's left arm. Styx, there was probably more coating her back, though it was hard to tell. "Sorry I'm staining the seats," Sophia slurred. As she watched, though, the blood began to boil away into nothing once it had been apart from her for a time. Did it always do that?

Her eyelids began to sink. She had fought. She had done her duty. That was all anyone could ask of her.

One of the valkyries gasped, and then the room went completely silent.

Sophia's eyes shot open. The HQ's front doors slid aside, and a woman strode through. She was radiant, her olive skin shedding a gentle light amidst the gloom of the underworld. A cloud of auburn hair billowed behind her, tugged by the same unseen breeze that toyed with the hem of her elegant green dress. Interlacing streams of leaves spun around her body, and the scent of a riverbank, rich and vibrant with life, finally swept the reek of blood from Sophia's nose.

Sophia had never seen her before, but she recognized her all the same.

"Persephone," she mumbled.

One of the doctors let out a relieved sigh. "Your worship, we were just about to call you. Their wounds…"

"Are serious indeed," Persephone finished. She gave Caelistra a worried look before turning a gentle smile on Sophia. "Hades told me you'd arrived. My husband can't help you, but like you, I am of two worlds. Life, and death. I can heal you, if you will allow it."

Hope forced aside the languorous, creeping complacency that had been spreading through Sophia's body. "Please."

Persephone lifted a hand, and the Fury doctors withdrew. A gust of wind brushed through the room, and then a soft glow bloomed from her palm. Warmth trickled through Sophia's skin, spreading through her flesh to suffuse her whole body. It washed away minor aches and howling agony alike, until nothing but the soothing sensation remained.

The world returned slowly. The first thing Sophia noticed was the lack of pain. It had been so constant, so immense, that being able to feel anything else was like taking off a blindfold. Her store of divine power was still pitifully low, but at least she was whole again.

She saw Persephone standing over Caelistra, one hand extended, that same pleasant glow bathing Caelistra in light. Before Sophia's eyes, Caelistra's wounds healed. Bones knit, flesh mended, the sickly grey tint to her skin faded back into a healthy crimson. The shard of adamant clattered to the floor beside her unblemished neck.

Caelistra's eyes fluttered open and then went wide at the sight of Persephone.

Caelistra shifted on the floor, grunted, and then gathered the power to banish her wings and return to human form.

"Thank you, Persephone."

Persephone smiled. "This is the third time I've dragged you back from the brink of oblivion. You have a knack for getting into trouble."

Caelistra grimaced. "Not by choice." She looked around, her gaze pausing briefly on Sophia before settling on one of the other Furies. "Are the Directors here?"

"No," he said, after a moment's hesitation. "The Celts launched a major attack on the border, and some of their dragon riders got through. The Directors took everyone we could spare to help hunt them down."

"What?" Caelistra sat up straight. "When?"

"A little over an hour ago."

Sophia leaned back, stunned. The border hadn't been secure since Sirideán's Wars had unified the Celts, but there hadn't been dragon riders in Conclave territory in years. "Where's the battle?" she asked.

"Aosta, near the edge of Roman territory, I think," the Fury said.

Caelistra was frowning intently as she pulled out her phone. There was blood smeared across the screen, but it turned on. "The Directors need to know what we've learned. Unless the entire border's falling, they'll send us reinforcements. They have to, for this."

Sophia wondered whether she was as confident as she sounded.

Relief spread across Caelistra's face as soon as the phone stopped ringing. "Director Alecto? It's Caelistra Horatia. I have something to report."

Meret was a godborn with a working divine battery.

Sophia's heart sank as everything from the last few hours came crashing back into place, filling the space left by injury and pain. The bracelet Meret had always worn must have had an aurichalcum core, designed to contain her powers so she could pass for human. Sophia had felt the smothering weight of the awful metal when they'd been trapped in the aurichalcum cell, and Meret had *chosen* to endure that for years on end?

Despair's icy tendrils crept through Sophia. They'd failed to stop her. Styx, even Caelistra had been hard pressed just to survive. The only good news was that they'd made it back to spread the word and get help.

Which might end up being the last thing Sophia did for the Furies. Her shoulders slumped, and she closed her eyes for a moment, but under the circumstances, it was hard to worry about herself. With Rashmi's invention in hand, there was nothing Meret couldn't do. No one she couldn't destroy.

Persephone drifted closer to Sophia and settled into the seat beside her while Caelistra talked on the phone. "Thank you, your worship," Sophia said. Her voice seemed dull, distant, even to her own ears.

Persephone laughed, and the sound was like sunlight dancing through falling rain. "Please, just Persephone. I'm just glad I arrived in time to help." She frowned and gestured toward Caelistra, who was giving Alecto a hurried summary of what they knew. "Did you truly encounter Euryale?"

"Unfortunately."

Sorrow swept across the goddess's features. "One could say that the gorgons' entire lives have been tales of misfortune."

Sophia looked at her in surprise. "You feel sorry for her?"

"Of course. I was there, on Olympus, when Zeus cursed them, over all of our protests. I saw them flee, cast out of their homes, for deaths that were the curse's fault, not theirs."

"Lots of people face horrible injustices, and not all of them turn to indiscriminate murder as a way of getting even. They could have tried to make things better, instead of worse."

Persephone studied her with a gaze as piercing as summer sunlight, and Sophia's stomach fluttered. Could the goddess know, somehow, that she was thinking about her brother as much as about Euryale? About her own choices?

"True," Persephone said finally. "Stheno, Euryale's surviving sister, for example. She makes some of the most exquisite sculptures I have ever seen. She takes inspiration from her suffering, rather than reflecting it upon others. It is easy to look at the two of them and pass judgment, but I wonder which path most of us would take, in the gorgons' position. Sometimes, not giving into hate and despair is the hardest challenge of all. But you know this." She nodded toward Caelistra without taking her gaze off Sophia, a challenge in her eyes. "The situation she's describing sounds... dire."

Dire. That was one way to put it. Only a few hours ago, Sophia had thought that the case was narrowing to its end. She'd been right. Just not in the way she'd hoped. Now, Rashmi was dead, and Meret had a working battery, brimming with energy.

A burst of inspiration struck, hope flaring like a candle in the dark. "Could you help? I don't know whether the other Furies can make it in time, but with a goddess's aid..."

Persephone shook her head sadly. "Athena or Artemis could, if I had any idea where they were, but I'm no warrior. If this Meret is as strong as she sounds, I would do worse than get in the way: I would just be another danger, another bomb waiting to go off."

Sophia clung desperately to that shred of hope. "But with your power—"

Persephone smiled and put her hand on Sophia's shoulder. Her intact, fully mended shoulder. The goddess's touch was like a warm spring day. "Power, alone, isn't enough."

Sophia sighed, and Persephone gave her a mysterious smile. Sophia looked down at her hands. Power might not be enough, but when Meret had all of it and they had none, nothing else mattered.

Caelistra hung up the phone and walked back to Sophia. She hesitated.

Persephone rose, giving Sophia one last, knowing look. "Come along, valkyries. I believe the Furies have plans to make." A breeze stirred the room as she turned toward the door.

Sophia dreaded what Caelistra was about to say, but she had the wherewithal to catch one of the valkyries' arms as they followed Persephone out. "Thank you. If it weren't for you, we wouldn't have made it."

"Don't mention it." He grinned. "You were a little... bloodier than most, but guiding the dead is what we do." The others chuckled and slapped him on the back as they went out into Tartarus, proud of a job well done.

Sophia felt a surge of envy. The valkyries knew their duty. It was an unending cycle, but it was a cycle that kept the world functioning. She was no longer sure she could say the same.

The other Furies gave them space at a glance from Caelistra. She spun her phone between her fingers and scrutinized Sophia.

"Just spit it out," Sophia said. She'd had enough of the slow, building dread.

Caelistra watched as her blood evaporated from her phone before slipping it back into her pocket. She sat down next to Sophia with a sigh, stretched out, and crossed her legs at the ankle.

"We're being pulled off the case."

Sophia looked at her in surprise. "What? Both of us?"

Caelistra nodded. "Director Tisiphone is returning from the border. She's going to personally lead a team to capture Meret. Now that we know Rashmi's invention works, they don't want to take any chances."

That made sense. Would it matter, though? Meret had godborn on her payroll, and enough power in Rashmi's battery to personally take on an army. She'd had been undermining Setesh's empire before; now, she had the opportunity to *destroy* him. What would a handful of Furies do, even with a director on their side?

The pain had faded along with her injuries, melting away before a goddess's miracle, but she almost wished it back. Now that she was fully conscious of their situation, a bone-deep weariness settled into her in its place.

Sophia looked at Caelistra. "How long?"

"They're at the border, a long way from the nearest Deathgate. They'll have to fly back before they can recall themselves to the underworld." She shrugged. "At the earliest, by nightfall in Memphis."

And while the Furies flew home, Meret had time to plan, to act.

Sophia shook her head. It would have to do. Their earlier encounter had conclusively shown that they couldn't fight Meret without serious backup.

If there even was a "they" still...

Sophia opened her mouth, but Caelistra spoke first. "She's going after Setesh. If she kills him..."

"The city's gone." It was bizarre to be rooting for Setesh, but the thought of Memphis under Meret's control—or, worse, reduced to a crackling wasteland of malice and thaumaturgy—made all the difference.

"Would she do that? Risk herself, her family, the empire she's built?"

Normally, Sophia would have said no. But now... "Setesh had her brother murdered, it turns out. I'm not sure she's completely rational about this."

Caelistra grunted, looking away.

The question caught in Sophia's throat finally forced its way free.

"Do I need to give you my badge?"

Caelistra scoffed. "Kind of a selfish question right now, isn't it?" She waved a hand at Sophia before she could protest. "It doesn't matter anyway. We're off the case. What happens to you isn't exactly pressing anymore."

Sophia sat back, feeling dazed. It was just a stay of execution, but a part of her was relieved even at the slight delay.

Caelistra got to her feet with a sigh. "I'm going outside for a smoke."

Sophia rested her elbows on her knees and listened to Caelistra's retreating footsteps. Meret was someone else's problem now. There was nothing she could do but sit in Tartarus and wait. Wait for the Directors to render their judgment. Wait for word that her home, her family, had been saved or annihilated.

Every afterlife offered the option of memory erasure for those who wanted to truly leave their lives behind. A sip from the river Lethe in Hades, a cup of specially concocted wine in the Duat... She'd never felt tempted before, but considering the feeling of utter helplessness swelling inside her, it might be the only way for her afterlife to be anything but misery.

CHAPTER THIRTY-FIVE

Sophia stayed where she was for a long time. The far wall had a window that looked out on Tartarus, and it was easy to lose herself in the view. Magma poured from cracks in the cavern walls, plummeting down to join the lake below. Strange, fluttering creatures chased each other around the ceiling or darted among the buildings, too far away to make out any details. A handful of people walked the thin, winding bridges, probably Hades employees going about their business. The incandescent glow of the magma played across dark stone, giving the entire chamber an eerie cast.

Even knowing they were off the case, even knowing that she was one conversation from being shipped off to an afterlife, Sophia couldn't stop herself from worrying about Meret. The case was a puzzle to solve, and she'd never been able to let go of a puzzle. She considered ways to find Meret before she made her move, weighed strategies to defeat her despite Rashmi's battery.

But no matter what she came up with, it never felt like enough. Her mind kept dragging her back to the boathouse, reliving the awful moments, stretched out in her memory, as she fought to keep Meret's blade away from her flesh. Fought, and lost. Even now, safe and whole again, the feeling of helplessness was overwhelming.

Despair was finally enough to bring her feverish planning to a halt. She'd been a fool to think that joining the Furies would change anything.

Even with a full investment, Caelistra had been like a flailing child, compared to Meret.

Nothing is safe as long as someone stronger can snatch it away.

That's what Meret had said, and in a way, she was right. Sophia had fought her entire life to change the Boneyard. To stop the people trying to claim the neighborhood for themselves, and protect the people just trying to live their lives. To root out corruption, to make communities safe again.

She'd been trying to plug a cracked dam with her fingers. And here she was, trying to do it again.

If there was one thing she'd learned from Gahiji, it was that people never changed. *Looks like I'm no exception.* Maybe Caelistra was right. Maybe it would be better if she didn't join the Furies.

Sophia stood up. Her jacket clung to the chair for a moment. All the blood had boiled away into nothing, but her clothes were still shredded and dirty. Maybe after this she'd go change.

Caelistra was just outside, standing at the edge of the platform and gazing down into the magma. She had her hands in her pockets, and a cloud of a smoke hung around her head. As Sophia watched, she flicked the last of her cigarette down into the magma and lit another.

Sophia watched her in silence for a moment.

"You were right, Caelistra," she said finally.

Caelistra let out a short, grunting laugh. "Glad to hear it. About what?"

"I don't belong in the Furies."

Caelistra turned to face her, frowning. "What?"

"I grew up in the Boneyard, right? Just like Meret. My whole neighborhood was a battleground between the Dockyard Hounds and the Silver Court. The front lines shifted every day, but the war was always there, even when there weren't any bullets or miracles flying. My mom died in a bombing when I was five. I barely remember her. My dad and my brother were all I had." She joined Caelistra at the edge of the platform, sighing. "And I left them. Do you know why?"

Caelistra shook her head.

"Because I wanted to come back and help fix things. My whole childhood, I'd heard about other places that had it better. Places where children didn't have to worry about what would happen if they took the wrong street home from school. It wasn't long before I realized that they weren't all exotic, far off lands: the rest of my own city wasn't like this. Which meant that the Boneyard didn't have to be either." She sighed. "It sounds cheesy, but I left to become a police officer so I'd have a chance to make a difference."

"It's not cheesy," Caelistra said quietly.

Sophia laughed bitterly. "My dad never understood. He wanted us to stay together, no matter what. My brother hated me for leaving, like I was doing it to spite him. And I didn't care. It was so easy to write them off, because I was doing the right thing."

"You were."

Sophia scoffed. "I accomplished *nothing*. I had the highest conviction record of every detective in the station, but what difference did it make? The Boneyard is the same, just with a handful of new faces in old roles. I thought being a Fury would be different, that I could make a difference *somewhere*, at least. But I was wrong. It's like trying to fight the night with a flashlight. As soon as you turn around, the dark comes right back."

Caelistra sighed. Her hand twitched up like she might try to touch Sophia before she stopped, shaking her head. "That's not why we fight."

"It's why *I* fought. And I think I'm done. I'm tired, Caelistra."

"You're setting your sights too high. You are one person. If the only way for you to succeed is to change the world forever, then you're setting yourself up for failure."

Sophia crossed her arms. "Why, then?"

"Someone has to step up. Someone has to fight the fight, even if it's just to keep things from getting *worse*." She gestured emphatically with her cigarette. "Sometimes, it's not about pushing the darkness back, it's about carving out a space in the darkness where people can live."

"And that's enough? Fighting tooth and nail and never seeing things get any better?"

Caelistra put the cigarette back between her lips and turned to look down into the magma again. "It's enough for me."

"Not for me."

Sophia knew what it was like to live in fear. And not in some dangerous backwater, not on a war-torn border or a monster-filled frontier, but in the capital city of one of the largest and most prosperous nations in the Conclave. Because for every person like her fighting to make things better, there was another person with more power and influence who was committed to keeping things the way they were, out of ignorance or prejudice or corruption.

The thought of an endless, hopeless battle was too much to bear. She had kept herself going for so long, but now, at last, she had run out of fuel.

Sophia sighed. "Thank you for saving my life."

Caelistra grunted. "We're even. I would have died if you hadn't brought me back here."

"Fair enough." Sophia looked around at Tartarus. In the three short days since she'd been recruited, she'd barely spent any time here, but Caelistra had been right. It had started to grow on her. "I'm going back inside," she said, turning around. "You can come find me when it's time to turn in my badge."

She'd barely taken a step when Caelistra said, "You fought well."

Sophia turned around, feeling like her eyebrows were trying to climb off her face. "Is this where I'm supposed to check to make sure you're not an imposter pretending to be Caelistra?"

The barest hint of a smile touched Caelistra's lips. "I'm serious. We fought a gorgon, and we did it as a *team*. For once, you were brave, but not reckless. And the idea to wrap her head in shadow was ingenious. Ever since Perseus, all anyone's been able to think of is mirrors."

Sophia swallowed, unsure what to think. "Thank you?"

Caelistra met her gaze earnestly. "You have a lot to learn, but you have the potential to be a great fighter. The more aggressive person wins most fights, true, but if you just had a bit more patience, if you *studied* your opponent instead of just throwing yourself at every opening... Wait for your moment, *then* commit yourself completely."

Sophia looked down at her hands, her stomach churning as a hundred different emotions fought their way through her. "You picked a strange time to decide to actually be a mentor. I'm not sure any of this matters anymore."

Silence. She glanced at Caelistra and found a look on her face like she'd eaten something rotten.

"If you felt like I was trying to sabotage you..." Caelistra began. "Well... I'm sorry."

Sophia stared at her in surprise. "Caelistra—"

She was interrupted by a shake of Caelistra's head. "That wasn't my goal. I don't... I'm not good at this. Mentoring. Or..." She waved a hand through the air in frustration. "Do you know what scared me the most, from the moment I read your file? You reminded me of myself."

Sophia laughed, which earned her an irritated look. "You're joking."

"Why do you think I worked so hard to stop your crazy heroics?" Caelistra reached up and scratched absently at one of the scars across her face. "I've seen the results firsthand."

"I've lost friends too. I know—"

"You *don't*. It's different, for the Furies. The things we're up against, either monsters or people? They're stronger than we are. Better equipped. Unconcerned with collateral damage. And ultimately, there will always be more of *them* than there are of *us*."

Caelistra took a long pull from her cigarette before continuing. "You had this much right, before. We arrest one criminal, and another takes their place. We take down one crime ring, and another fills the power vacuum. We kill one monster, and its children are burning towns and sinking ships a few years later. But lose one Fury... Even at the best of times, we're shorthanded. Every casualty costs the Conclave hundreds of lives."

"What are you saying? That we can't take *any* risks?"

"I'm saying that your brand of rash heroism gets people killed. I know. I've seen it. I've *done* it. It's luck, pure and simple, that I'm even standing here talking to you."

"Sometimes, there's no choice," Sophia insisted. As exhausted as she felt, she recognized in Caelistra's cynicism the same bitter despair that had threatened to overwhelm her for years. For some reason, hearing it from someone else's lips was too much to bear. "We're not just fighting a battle of attrition. I can't accept that. Sometimes, you have to make a stand."

Caelistra shook her head. "I used to think that. The world taught me otherwise."

Sophia was about to reply when her phone rang. She stopped, frowning, and looked at it.

Gahiji.

Heart in her throat, she answered the phone.

"Tell me where you are, and I will come arrest you."

The choking, wet laughter on the other end of the line stole the next words from her tongue. "I'm at the shelter, Soph. Setesh's people were here. Killed everyone. Took Teshan."

Sophia felt like she'd been dropped into a tank of ice water. Her head swam, and she had to grab the door for support. When she could speak again, she said, "Why should I believe anything you say?"

"Because I'm the only one who can help you save the city. I know where Meret's going. I can help you stop her before…"

Sophia's free hand slowly balled into a fist. This was her fault. She'd been the one who announced Meret's guilt to the world. She was the reason Setesh knew his enemy's name.

But even as the guilt swelled within her, all of her doubt, all of her despair, bled away into perfect clarity as she pictured Teshan in Setesh's clutches. Once she learned that her daughter had been taken, Meret would destroy everything in her path to retrieve her. And with the working battery, an advantage Setesh didn't know she possessed, even a god wouldn't be enough to stop her.

If anything happened to her daughter, Meret would kill Setesh, and reduce all of Memphis to a cursed, smoldering ruin.

Maybe it was the conversation she'd just had with Caelistra. Maybe it was the desperate conviction that there had to be a better way, that something better than stasis *had* to be achievable. But for the first time in as long as she could remember, all of Sophia's doubts faded away.

"Hang on." She muted the phone without ending the call. "Caelistra, that was my brother. Setesh attacked Meret's shelter and took her daughter." Caelistra's eyes widened. She opened her mouth, but Sophia cut her off. "Save the I-told-you-so. We have to go."

Caelistra crossed her arm, cigarette still burning. "Absolutely not. Director Tisiphone is on her way—"

"She won't get there in time. We can. And if we go save my brother, we'll have an advantage that she wouldn't. He can take us to Meret."

"Who will kill us."

"Caelistra… I know how you feel. I know you've lost hope. But if Meret thinks her daughter's been killed, she will *destroy* Setesh, Memphis be damned. We can stop that. One of these is all it would take," she said, holding up her badge. "There are *millions* of people in the city. Even if you're right overall, *this* has to be worth any sacrifice."

Caelistra's jaw was clenched tight, her muscles tense as her fingers clutched at her arms. Sophia could see the war raging behind her eyes.

Finally, Caelistra let out a frustrated snarl. "You'd just run off without me if I said no, wouldn't you?" Sophia smiled, and Caelistra made a disgusted noise, flicking her cigarette over her shoulder into the lake of magma. "Fine. Lead the way."

Sophia brought the phone back to her ear, heart in her throat.

"I'm coming, Gahiji."

CHAPTER THIRTY-SIX

First responders beat Sophia and Caelistra to the shelter, since they didn't have to make the trip all the way from Tartarus. When the two of them pulled up outside, a godborn with the fire department was drawing water from a hydrant and precisely dousing the last of the flames. EMTs carried people out of the building on stretchers.

Only a handful of people. Not nearly enough.

Sophia didn't remember crossing the street. Caelistra must have flashed her badge at the police, or they wouldn't have been allowed inside, but she didn't remember that either. She was fixed on the doors. Her brother was inside. He was still alive. He had to be.

Gods, what's wrong with me? I've been angry at Gahiji for years, and now I can barely breathe?

He could help them stop Meret and save Teshan. He was useful. That had to be it.

The shelter's doors had been fused shut by a miracle. Judging by the way they'd been torn off their hinges, it had taken another to get them open when the police had arrived.

Inside the shelter...

Sophia had seen more than her share of awful crime scenes. A serial killer's murder room, the aftermath of gang shootouts, a bombing that had brought down an occupied apartment building.

But for all that, even through the dazed panic as she looked for her brother, the sight of the shelter's main room was enough to make her gag.

This wasn't a battle between armed killers, like the auction beneath the Sandstorm Club. This was a wholesale massacre, one-sided, without a chance for the victims to defend themselves. Bodies carpeted the floor, torn by bullets and trampled in panic, and gore filled the space between them. The charnel reek hit her as soon as she got close, like a faceful of blood and ash and shit, making her wish she'd remembered to stop breathing a moment sooner.

"Gahiji!" Sophia called out. She gulped in a breath so she could shout again, and the smell almost made her vomit. "Gahiji!"

He'd said he was on the right side of the room before ending the call. The right side from which direction? He'd always been bad with that. She turned from the door and started picking her way through the bodies.

She was only distantly aware of Caelistra at her back, of the EMTs struggling to find anyone still alive. All of her attention was on the faces of the people she passed. Faces twisted with fear and agony. Faces of people who shouldn't have been caught up in this: the old, the sick, the young. Which was worse: the people who'd died clutching loved ones to their chests, or those who'd died alone?

This was all my fault. Try as she might to keep it at bay, that same thought had been bubbling back to the surface all through their hurried trip back to Memphis, an infection that would never completely go away.

Caelistra was right. I shouldn't have told the world about Meret. It's my fault Setesh knew where to attack, whose daughter to take.

She recognized some of these people—volunteers she'd met before, longtime residents of the neighborhood, a couple of gangsters now permanently out of the fight. Two men she'd gone to high school with, curled up together in a pool of their own blood.

This is a crime scene. Don't throw up and contaminate the scene. Gods, she hadn't needed to recite that litany to herself for years.

"He might be outside already. The EMTs might have found him,"

Caelistra said.

Sophia shook her head. She had a fierce, irrational certainty that Gahiji was still here, that if she didn't save him herself, he was going to die in this slaughterhouse. This was her fault, and if she didn't fix it…

When she found Gahiji, she almost moved on without recognizing him. He was half-buried beneath a corpse, groaning so faintly she almost missed it. It was his arm that she recognized: around his wrist was the bracelet Teshan had made when she was seven, a twin to the one Sophia wore.

He never wore that bracelet, but Sophia knew it instantly.

"Gahiji!" She almost tripped as she ran to him, heedless of everything in her way. She checked the body on top of him—definitely dead—and heaved it off.

He lay on his belly, bullet holes in his back, his leg. Blood began to pump freely from the wounds now that the pressure was off them.

His eyes found hers, and a beleaguered smile appeared on his blood-stained face. "Soph…" Shudders wracked his body, and his face twisted in pain.

Sophia choked. It was Caelistra who shouted, "Medic! We've got a man down over here! He needs help, fast!"

Someone gently nudged Sophia aside. EMTs helped Gahiji onto a stretcher. She could barely hear through the resounding thunder of her pulse, but she caught snatches of what they said. "Blood loss—" "Multiple gunshot wounds—" "Needs a healer, get him outside!"

She was back in the parking lot before she realized what was happening. An exhausted godborn with the Rod of Asklepios on her uniform bent over Gahiji, concentrating.

Sophia sobbed when light began to stream from the woman's palm, flowing into Gahiji's wounds.

Styx, please work. Even miraculous healing wasn't perfectly reliable, and if it went just slightly wrong, the side effects could be disastrous if they did anything beyond accelerating the body's natural recovery. *Gods, if this works, I'll never fight with him again.*

The glow faded, and Gahiji began coughing, tears streaming from his eyes. He blinked, trying to focus, until he found Sophia's face. "Teshan!" was the first thing he said.

The healer sat back, wiping sweat from her forehead. "He's going to live."

Gahiji looked himself over, his expression grim. "My leg."

The healer glanced at the wound. "A bullet shattered his tibia. If I try to fix it now, it's not going to reform right. Safer if we—"

Gahiji snatched at her hand. "Please," he said. "My daughter... I need to be able to walk."

"You don't understand," the healer protested. "It could permanently cripple you if I try to heal it now.

"Will I be able to walk?"

"With a limp, maybe. But if we just wait—"

Gahiji met Sophia's eyes, pleading. She'd doubted him for as long as she could remember, but in that moment, she could see that there was nothing on his mind but saving his daughter.

"Do it," Sophia said. "Fury's orders."

The healer grumbled to herself, but she did it.

Gahiji didn't spare a second glance for his leg. He pulled himself upright as soon as she was done. "We have to... Woah." He swayed and would have toppled over if Sophia hadn't caught him.

"You've been through a lot," the healer said, scowling. "You need fluids and calories, or you won't be walking anywhere."

"On the way," Gahiji said. "Soph?"

Sophia got an arm around him and helped him to his feet. Even with her substantial strength, he was wobbly enough that Caelistra had to take his other side.

"Thanks." He blinked at Caelistra. "Who are you?"

"Your sister's partner. Caelistra Horatia."

Gahiji grunted as they helped him toward the car. "Thank you for watching her back."

Sophia shot him a sidelong look, surprised, but then they were there and there was no time for talking. "Help him in. I'll grab him something to eat so he doesn't collapse on us."

She jogged over to the store on the corner. They had a "Closed" sign firmly planted on the door—no doubt thanks to the massacre across the street—but Sophia pounded on the door anyway. She was about to kick the damn thing in when a man hurried out of the back to shout at her. "Can't you see the sign? We're—"

Sophia slammed her badge against the glass. "Conclave Furies! Open the damn door! I just need to buy some food."

Stunned, wide-eyed, the man stumbled toward the door and unlocked it for her. She pushed past him, grabbed a sports drink, some candy bars and a bag of chips—the second time in as many days that she'd given someone junk food after they were nearly killed—and slapped a bill on the counter that more than covered what she'd taken. "Keep the change."

Caelistra intercepted her outside the car, where they could talk without Gahiji. "Director Tisiphone is still on her way," Caelistra said, crossing her arms. "She's got a full squad—"

"And waiting for her was a good plan before we knew the full situation. We have to do this." Sophia watched her partner grimace, saw the doubt crossing her face. "If I'm wrong, and Meret's not trying to murder Setesh when we get there, we can always hang back and wait for the Director."

Caelistra sighed, but she nodded and got into the car.

Sophia tossed the armful of calories into the back with Gahiji and then climbed into the passenger seat. Caelistra peeled out of the parking spot and headed north.

"Eat and talk," Sophia said to Gahiji. "Tell us everything. No holding back. No trying to protect Meret."

Gahiji looked sick. "That ship has sailed." He sighed, staring into space like he didn't know where to begin. "Setesh attacked the shelter. If he didn't know Meret... If he didn't know we were trying to take over his operation before, he knew once the news broke about Meret."

Caelistra gave Sophia a long, pointed look. As if it were possible to feel more guilty about that.

"And you saw him take Teshan?"

"His people, not him. I heard them talking, before they left. He's going to use Teshan to draw Meret out, make her angry, and kill her." He let out a short, bitter laugh. "It would work, too, except for the battery. Do you know…"

"We know about the battery. She almost killed us with it."

"I'm sorry—"

Sophia bit her tongue before she could snap at him. Gahiji grimaced.

"I don't expect your forgiveness. Just…" His voice cracked. "Help me save my daughter. After that, you can arrest me, do whatever you want. As long as Teshan's alive."

"If Meret kills Setesh, Teshan isn't going to be the only one in trouble." Sophia twisted around to look him in the eye. "You know how to get into Setesh's mountain?"

"Even better, a secret way in. We… Um…" He cleared his throat. "*Spoke* to a bunch of Setesh's people. They proved to be unusually cooperative."

Caelistra glared daggers at him, and Gahiji shifted uncomfortably.

"This had better work," Sophia said.

"It will. Getting in isn't the problem. Setesh is the problem. And…" He sighed heavily. "And Meret."

"Your lover. The mother of your child, who's going to blow up the city," Sophia said flatly.

"Fuck you, Sophia," Gahiji said through a mouthful of chocolate. "You think I had a choice? By the time I knew what kind of person she *really* was, it was too late. Teshan was born. What was I supposed to do, take her and run? Meret would do *anything* for her daughter. She would hunt us down anywhere in the world and make sure I died screaming."

"So why help us now?" Caelistra snapped.

"Because I know what's going to happen if she gets there and finds Teshan dead."

That was what Sophia was most afraid of too.

She got out her phone and started dialing. "What are you doing?" Caelistra asked.

"Calling Ixtele. Hoping for a technical solution."

The phone picked up after the second ring. "Dr. Tinaalto speaking."

"Hey Ixtele. It's Sophia."

"Oh no you don't, I'm about to get on a plane back to Greece. One of my grad students found a nest of Stymphalian birds. If you're going to drag me back to Memphis, it had better be life and death—"

"It is, but I just need you to answer a few questions. Have you been watching the news?"

"No…"

"Those people who came to kill us at the police station? They were sent by a demigoddess named Meret Tanu. She's the daughter of Ares."

"Shit." Ixele let out a worried laugh. "You're saying my own cousin sent people to murder us?"

"That's not the bad news. Rashmi's invention works, Ixtele. It's not a bomb. Meret has a working divine battery, full of power."

There was a long pause. "You're kidding me."

"'Fraid not. She almost killed me with it."

"Styx! Are you okay—"

"More or less. Listen, I need to know everything you can tell me about the battery."

"I mean, besides the fact that it should be impossible?"

"I'll take anything you've got, honestly."

Ixtele hummed thoughtfully for a moment. "Imagine you've got a bucket underneath a faucet, filling up with water. The water's divine power. The size of the bucket is your capacity for that power. And the flow rate through the faucet is how quickly your power regenerates if it's spent. With me so far?"

"I think so." Sophia's own store of divine power felt fully recharged by now, probably because her "bucket" was tiny.

"A working divine battery would be like a second bucket. In theory.

260

I think Rashmi wanted to make the battery's capacity at least five or six Taxmals, but I can't tell what he managed without checking out the battery. Which, by the way, would be *amazing*, if—"

"So if she had enough power, she could kill a god with it," Sophia said, her heart sinking. "That's what I was afraid of."

"Exactly! Sort of. There's more to a fight than just power, of course. Plus, she wouldn't have the same *type* of power as a god. Gods' power is different, which is why they can do different *kinds* of things from the rest of us. It's really interesting, actually; we think it has to do with a sort of internal pull, sort of like gravity, that condenses a god's power—"

"Ixtele, I appreciate that you're fascinated by this, and if I survive, I'd love to hear about it another time. But right now, I'm on my way to fight Meret."

"Right. Sorry. Um… Basically, if she's been storing up power since she got the battery, she might not *be* a god, but she might be able to *kill* a god."

"Wouldn't it weaken her to put all her power into the battery?"

"Sure. And then she'd recharge, and have all of her natural power, plus what was in the battery. Styx, if she had someone else fill it, she wouldn't even have to wait for that. If I remember Rashmi's talks, then theoretically, anyone with divine power should be able to store energy in the battery, and anyone else can use it. He was pretty convinced that stored divine power reverted to a raw state."

Sophia groaned. "Wonderful. What about any weaknesses? Is there an easy way to stop her?"

"Well… No."

"Shit."

"Definitely don't try to shoot the battery. It can't be unstable all the time, or she wouldn't be able to safely draw power from it, but if you mess with the containment, it could explode. Like at the convention center, but probably bigger. Especially if she has more power in it."

"We will try our best to avoid that."

"Hmm. She has to be touching one of the conductive handles to make it work, right? So your best shot is probably to get the battery away from her."

"Right. If only she weren't an expert fighter."

"Oh, right. I think that's something all of Ares's children are born with, like my bond with animals. Sorry."

Sophia sighed. "Okay. I appreciate your help. We wouldn't have gotten this far without you."

There was silence on the other end, and for a minute, Sophia thought the connection had gone dead.

Finally, Ixtele said, "Do me a favor, Sophia?"

"What's that?"

"Live through this. Give me a call, once it's over."

Sophia had to swallow before she could reply. "I'll do my best."

They left the city behind. Ahead of them, Khufu's Pyramid, capped with gold, shone in the afternoon sun. Looming behind it was Setesh's mountain, topped with the Sandstorm Club. And, unusual in the middle of the day, a spiraling cyclone of dust.

"Setesh is still alive," Gahiji said, breathing a sigh of relief.

"We'd know if he weren't," Caelistra grumbled.

Sophia drew her gun and gave it a quick inspection. "I can't believe I'm saying this, but… let's try to keep him that way."

CHAPTER THIRTY-SEVEN

Gahiji had his head pressed against the car window, squinting out at the roadside. "There," he said. "See that barricade around the bend up there? Turn off the road right after that and head toward the mountain."

"If you're fucking with us..." Caelistra grumbled.

"Then Setesh's people will kill me, and there won't be anyone left to save my daughter. Does that seem like a smart plan?"

Caelistra just grunted and pulled off the road. The car shuddered across the uneven terrain, sending up a cloud of dust behind them.

Gods grant that everyone's too busy to see us coming.

Gahiji had spent the entire drive telling them everything he knew about Meret's organization. The only good news was that Euryale hadn't made any attempt to report back to him after her encounter with Sophia and Caelistra. The rest...

Even after everything she'd seen, Sophia was horrified by how far Meret's corruption had spread. She didn't just control street gangs and gun runners; she owned police, judges, politicians... Not all of them, by any means, but enough to pluck at their strings and watch the city dance.

Sophia had her elbows on the dashboard so she could look up at the top of the mountain. Every time the cyclone shifted, every time there was the slightest glimpse of light from within, her heart seized in her chest. Was that a wayward miracle? A break in Setesh's control over the storm? A sign that he was dying? It would have been so much easier if

Caelistra could just fly up there, but even if she avoided being shredded by the storm, she'd be all alone, without any backup.

Gahiji shifted in the back seat and put a hand on Sophia's shoulder. "We're going to make it in time."

She forced her jaw to unclench, made herself lean back and stop staring at the sandstorm. "Teshan should never have been involved in this. The same with the poor people at the shelter." A bitter laugh escaped her lips. "And now, the only way to rescue her is to save Setesh's life."

"Doesn't mean we can't arrest him once we're done," Caelistra said. That was some comfort, at least.

"What about Meret?" Gahiji asked.

Sophia could hear the pain in his voice. She forced herself to swallow the sharp retort on her tongue—he was helping, for once. "We have to stop her, Gahiji. We've seen how powerful she is. We can't hold back."

Gahiji just sighed.

The searing, molten rage that had kindled inside her at Meret's betrayal made her feel like she was in a furnace, despite the AC. She'd wanted so badly to believe that there was another person who'd emerged from the Boneyard uncorrupted. Someone else who wanted to make the city a better place. But Meret was just another monster, hiding beneath a mask of compassion and charity.

"That's the entrance," Gahiji said. "That rock face, between those bushes."

He climbed out of the car as soon as Caelistra put it in park. Caelistra caught Sophia's arm before she could follow, gazing after Gahiji with her eyes narrowed. "How far can we trust him?"

Sophia watched Gahiji feverishly pacing back and forth before the entrance, scrutinizing the rock as he searched for something. He was limping, heavily favoring the leg that would never completely heal right. A sacrifice he'd made for his daughter. And yet... *People don't change. Gahiji is still Gahiji.* "We can trust him to protect Teshan."

Caelistra grunted and opened her door. Sophia followed a moment later, after checking to make sure her armor was buckled on tight. They'd raided the Fury armory before leaving Tartarus. Sophia wished she had adamant equipment like Caelistra's, but military-grade weaponry and a miracle-forged breastplate would have to be enough. Meret could probably cut through it like it wasn't there, but it would come in handy if any of Setesh's minions tried to stop them.

Gahiji was already in motion when they joined him by the entrance. "Just like they said," he was muttering. "Clever bastards…"

He moved back and forth, pressing his hand to the stone here and there. Sophia couldn't see any markings beyond subtle irregularities in the rock. She half expected the whole thing to be booby-trapped, but when Gahiji pressed the final spot, a doorway-sized section of the mountain slid aside with barely a sound.

"Not even hidden with a miracle," Gahiji said. "Just good, old-fashioned camouflage."

"Thaumaturgy could be detected," Sophia said.

Gahiji stepped back and motioned at the door. "Well, I can barely walk. After you?"

Caelistra took the lead. Gloom gathered around her, solidifying into her ax, a breastplate, and a pair of greaves to protect her legs, all of the finest adamant. She stayed in human form for now. As Gahiji had put it earlier, "Snake hair pretty much guarantees that Setesh's guards won't ask any questions."

Assuming there were any guards left. Even with only a fragment of a Fury's full investment, the scent from inside was unmistakable. "I smell blood," Sophia said for Gahiji's benefit. "Stay alert."

Here in the mountain's lowest reaches, there were no opulent decorations or strobing lights. Just stark, industrial corridors.

And bodies.

The first corpse was an armed guard. His submachine gun had been sliced clean in half. So had his chest. The next body belonged to a godborn in the same uniform. She'd put up more of a fight, judging by the ragged tears in the walls around her, but it hadn't done her any good.

"Wounds all match Meret's sword," Caelistra said.

"Makes sense." Gahiji kept his voice low, eyes darting from shadow to shadow. "We were still trying to get our people together when Teshan was kidnapped. She didn't have time to raise an army." He pointed down one of the twisting passages. "This way. Should be an elevator just ahead that'll take us all the way up."

Sophia hardly needed his directions; all they had to do was follow the trail of gore in Meret's wake. They passed another body, then an intersection where a full squad of guards had tried to make a stand. They lay in pieces amidst a blast of hissing steam from a damaged pipe on the ceiling.

A string of bloody footprints led past the group to an elevator.

They'd barely passed the bodies when the floor bucked under them and a rumble spread through the mountain. Sophia grabbed Gahiji's arm to keep him from falling, and they traded a grim look.

The head of Caelistra's ax bobbed as she flexed her grip. "We need to hurry."

"Could be worse," Gahiji said nervously. "At least the elevator works…"

He cut off as Caelistra hissed at him, motioning for them to get back. Sophia grabbed Gahiji as soon as she caught the sound of hurried footsteps from up ahead, but his limp slowed them down. Before she could get him out of sight, seven people rounded the corner between them and the elevator.

One of them let a shout of alarm as soon as they spotted Sophia's group, and an instant later she was staring down the barrels of multiple guns.

"Woah, hold on!" Sophia said, stepping forward with her hands raised. She focused all her attention on the woman at the head of the group. The rest all looked like guards, but she wore formal business attire, stark and black, and she carried herself with authority. "We're here to help."

The woman snorted, still sighting down the pistol in her hand. "I know everyone who works for Setesh, and you're not among them. You have two seconds to tell me who—"

"Furies," Sophia said. "We're with the Furies." This earned her a single raised eyebrow. "The woman who cut her way through here to get to your boss? We think she's here to kill him. And if she does, you and I die along with everyone in Memphis. We can't let that happen."

Setesh's lackey scrutinized them with cold, calculating eyes. Her gaze settled on Gahiji. "He's not a Fury."

Gahiji shook his head, his fists clenched with anger. "I'm not. I'm the father of the girl your people kidnapped."

Sophia flinched as seven fingers tightened on triggers, but no one fired. She fought the impulse to edge in front of Gahiji.

"You are not helping your case," the woman said. The mountain shook around them again. No one flinched.

"Believe me, I want nothing more than to kill every one of you," Gahiji said. Once, Sophia would have laughed at the idea of her bumbling, petty crook of a brother making a threat like that. Not anymore. "But not at the cost of the city," Gahiji continued. "That price is too high."

There was a long, tense silence.

The woman at the head of the guards lowered her weapon.

"I'm Amretis, Setesh's second-in-command. Setesh is at the top of the mountain, fighting Meret inside the nightclub. I can offer—"

She never had the chance to offer anything. Sophia saw two of Setesh's guards exchange a look. One of them nodded.

The other raised his gun and shot Amretis in the back of the head.

CHAPTER THIRTY-EIGHT

Sophia grabbed her brother around the waist and dragged him around the corner just as gunfire erupted. She saw Caelistra sweep forward, shadows rising around her to intercept bullets. Sophia drew her pistol, sparing a glance for Gahiji, who looked more angry than scared. She edged around her cover as soon as the gunfire slowed.

All but two of the guards were already down. Caelistra seized one by the wrist and sent him slamming, face first, into the concrete wall. The last of them lunged at Caelistra, and Sophia shot him in the chest.

Gahiji limped around her while her shell casings were still clinking against the floor. "Stay down!" she hissed, scanning the hall, but there was no one left to make a threatening move. Caelistra had cut through the guards without taking a scratch.

"They were working for Meret," Gahiji said dully, looking around at the bodies. "And I didn't know it. She's been keeping secrets from me."

"Are you surprised?" Sophia asked.

He hesitated. "I just thought... Gods, I'm such an idiot." He paused next to one of the bodies and reached down to take the man's sidearm.

Caelistra seized his wrist. "Not a chance."

"If I'm going to help free Teshan—"

"No weapons, Gahiji," Sophia cut in. "You haven't earned nearly that much trust."

"Sophia, I'm not here to help Meret! When will you—"

The mountain rocked, and cracks spread through the ceiling, raining dust down around them.

Sophia pointed at the elevator. "No time. Go."

Gahiji glared at her, but he turned and hobbled into the elevator. Caelistra gave Sophia a brief nod before following.

They punched the button for the top floor, labeled "Sandstorm" in golden hieroglyphs. Sophia found herself holding her breath, grimacing each time a miracle shook the mountain. She knew that an elevator wasn't the safest choice, under the circumstances, but they didn't have time to take the stairs.

Caelistra took out a packet of cigarettes and lit one, gazing defiantly at Gahiji as if daring him to object. He didn't even seem to notice. "This was too easy," Caelistra said. "If she had people in Setesh's organization, why aren't there whole armies standing in our way?"

Gahiji shook his head. "We only had a handful of infiltrators."

"That you knew about."

"If there'd been more, she wouldn't have needed to wait this long to make her move."

"Hmm. Maybe."

Caelistra popped her neck from side to side. As the number above the door began to tick up, every shadow in the elevator bent toward her, taking on volume as they clouded the air. When they returned to their natural positions, Caelistra had crimson skin and snakes for hair. She positioned herself in front of the door, keeping her wings furled in the cramped space.

"Sophia, once we're up there, you and I need to split up." Caelistra's voice was as harsh as the alarming grinding of the storm-battered mountain. "Better chances of getting close that way."

"Right. As we wade through the full-on god battle," Sophia said dryly. She was already taking slow, conscious breaths as she holstered her gun. She had no doubts about what they'd find at the top of the mountain. Just surviving long enough to intervene was going to be a challenge. She wanted to be ready.

Caelistra's snake hair hissed and lashed at the air, betraying the tension she was otherwise hiding well. "With any luck, we can turn the tide in Setesh's favor. If not... We use the badges to contain the explosion."

Sophia touched the badge at her belt. It felt like everyday metal, not a world-changing piece of thaumatechnology. "Anything I need to know about these? I didn't exactly have time for thorough training."

Gahiji looked worried, but Caelistra just shook her head. "If Setesh dies, just hold up the badge. The closer the better. Gahiji..." Caelistra gave him a brief glance. "You find your daughter and get her as far from the fighting as you can."

Gahiji nodded, his jaw clenched.

Caelistra pointed at the floor counter. Two to go. "Get ready."

They didn't make it that far. The next miracle hit with one floor to go, and it didn't just blast the mountain. It tore the elevator out of alignment, throwing all three of them to the floor. The lights shattered overhead, showering them with glass and plunging them into darkness. One of the doors was ripped aside in a cascade of sparks and screeching metal.

And then, with gut-churning finality, cables snapped and the elevator lurched downward.

Caelistra lunged toward the door, hands outstretched, and the darkness writhed. Through the ruined door, Sophia caught a glimpse of huge, shadowy claws wrapping around the elevator, just before it ground to a halt.

Her jagged teeth clenched together so tightly she couldn't speak, Caelistra jerked her head toward the opening.

Gahiji was pressed up against one wall, blinking uselessly in the dark. Sophia took his hand, and he tried to jerk away. "Gahiji! It's me!"

"What—"

"Come on!" She didn't know how long Caelistra's miracle would last, but from the strain on her face, it wouldn't be long.

Sophia half-led, half-dragged him to the door. She stuck her head through and traced back the thin trickle of light that streamed down. The elevator was askew in the shaft, enough to put the roof at a shallow angle. And sure enough, there was an opening above. Not an open door, by any means, but a tear in the wall large enough for a person to crawl through.

Since the nearest actual door was a bent wreck crammed with rubble, it was the best they could do.

"Caelistra, hold on."

Caelistra grunted, sweat streaming down her face.

"Gahiji, can you see the opening up there?"

"Yeah. Barely."

"I'm going to give you a boost out the door. Ready?"

Her stores of divine power had had time to recharge, and his weight was trivial for her now. She lifted him up to the roof and pulled herself up after him, ignoring his offered hand. "Time for one more boost. Be careful."

The elevator slid a fraction of an inch downward. "And hurry!" Caelistra growled from below.

Sophia lifted Gahiji up to the gap. He caught the edge with his fingers and grunted something at her, but she couldn't get him any higher. He scrambled up enough to get his broken arm over the lip. He let out a muffled scream as he put his weight on it, but he clambered inside. As soon as his feet had disappeared, Sophia leapt up after him.

Caelistra's miracle faded, and the elevator plummeted.

Sophia's heart froze with alarm.

And then Caelistra launched herself out of the door, wings tucked to her sides. She unfurled them the instant she was clear, hovering in place. "Go!" she called to Sophia.

Sophia crawled through the hole in the wall after Gahiji. She had to duck past jagged bits of metal and climb over patches of broken glass, but it wasn't too far to Gahiji's anxious face waiting on the other side.

To her surprise, she knew where they were. One wall was a cracked, straining ruin, and one of the doorways was choked with rubble, but they'd come through here before on their way to Setesh's auction.

Caelistra emerged from the hole a moment later. The crawlspace wouldn't have fit her wings, but she returned to her true form as soon as she was free and re-summoned her weapons and armor.

"Up those stairs and down the hall, and we should get to the nightclub," Sophia began. "If we—"

A thunderous crack echoed down the stairs, followed by the ringing clash of weapons. The three of them traded a look. "Hurry," Gahiji said grimly. "I'll catch up."

Sophia and Caelistra ran, taking the stairs two at a time as they climbed into the ruined skeleton of the club.

There was no hallway to head down once they reached the top. In fact, there was barely a building at all. The nightclub had been torn away, reduced to sand-blasted pillars and a handful of cracked walls at the summit of the mountain. The cyclone was still spinning wildly around them, shrouding the rest of the world from sight. Some of the projectors that decorated the wall of dust and sand had somehow escaped destruction, and mad images of ethereal light danced across the whirlwind's surface as if nothing were amiss.

Sophia's eyes scoured the rooftop, and her heart stopped when she found what she was looking for.

Teshan.

She was locked in a metal cage, resting on the crumbling remnants of what had once been a balcony. She had her hands wrapped around the bars, and she was gazing down at the battle raging outside Sophia's line of sight with a heartrending mixture of rage and terror.

The only relief was that she didn't appear hurt.

Caelistra looked at Teshan, then paused and caught Sophia's arm. "Sophia…"

Teshan was right there, scared and alone. They didn't have time to stand around. "I know, I know. Don't be a hero, no unnecessary risks…"

"No." Confused, Sophia met Caelistra's eyes, and for once, she didn't find any hint of sarcasm or scorn there. "Do what has to be done,"

Caelistra said. "Whatever it takes."

The mountain rocked beneath them. They traded nods and broke apart, circling toward the fight from opposite sides. Sophia caught a glimpse of Gahiji following them out onto the rooftop and saw him sag with relief when he saw Teshan.

Steel rang, and a wave of sand rolled out from the other side of the cracked wall where Teshan was looking.

A low, booming chuckle followed, spreading through the summit like an earthquake. **"You've made a grave mistake, child. It doesn't matter how much power you have in that toy. I have been fighting foes stronger than you for eons."**

When Meret replied, her voice dripped with scorn. "Fighting? When have you fought anyone? You didn't participate in the Great War. You stabbed Osiris in the back. I could blame you for my brother's death, but you didn't even do that yourself."

"He must not have merited my personal attention," Setesh said with a grim laugh. His words should have stretched out into the atmosphere, with no walls to rebound off of, but they reverberated off the cyclone in thousands of different languages. **"Is that why you're here? For vengeance?"**

"No. I'm here for my daughter."

Sophia reached the edge of the wall. Slowly, she leaned around it, and a blast of wind and sand almost took her face off.

Watching Meret and Setesh fight was like watching two avalanches collide. Setesh stood tall, his snout wrinkled with rage, needle teeth bared, triangular ears buffeted by the force of their conflict. Muscles rippled across his chest and arms every time he condescended to sidestep an attack. His hands were clasped behind him, as he fought with miracles rather than steel. Heat, wind, and sand roared to life at his command. His power melted sand into razor-edged glass, or sent ribbons of flensing dust to thunder against Meret's defenses.

And yet, he was losing. Sophia almost didn't realize it at first, but the signs were there. Golden ichor, the blood of the gods, leaked from nicks

273

and cuts across Setesh's torso. One of Meret's sleeves was burned away, displaying the corded muscles of her arm, but every time she took a wound, more power streamed from the battery in her other hand to heal it. She hurled no miracles of her own, but her impossibly huge sword moved so fast it seemed to be everywhere at once. Setesh's attacks burst when they struck her blade, sending crackling energy arcing across what remained of the nightclub's trappings, and with every miracle she deflected, she dealt another blow to Setesh.

Sophia hesitated at the corner. She was fifteen feet away, but each echoing collision of their power tore at her skin like a hurricane. Could she survive to get any closer? Even if she did, what could she possibly do to help Setesh?

Before she could decide, Meret sidestepped an attack, and one of Setesh's miracles slammed into the wall where Sophia hid. Stone shattered, spraying molten shrapnel, and Sophia fell back, stifling a cry of surprise.

Meret's eyes locked on Sophia.

It was a tiny opening, but it was all Setesh needed. He lunged forward, hands raised, and sand spiraled out of the storm, melting and resolidifying into a hundred glass blades that burned with divine wrath. His lip curled, and his eyes flashed with triumph as he moved in for the kill.

Meret's distraction was a feint. Sophia saw it in Meret's stance, in the casual, almost lazy way she shifted her feet, raised her sword.

"Setesh! Look out!" Sophia shouted.

It was too late. The knives of glass descended, and Meret rose to meet them. They tore into her flesh, shredding meat from bone, but even under the full force of a god's attack, power blazed from the battery and repaired her wounds.

Her sword, unconcerned with deflecting the deadly miracles, slammed into Setesh's side in a spatter of golden gore. Meret wrenched the blade free, and Setesh staggered back, clutching his ribs, a snarl on his face. Gleaming strands crisscrossed the huge wound, struggling to knit it back together as the miracle left by Meret's blade burned into his flesh.

Sophia expected him to flee, to disperse into a cloud of sand and cast himself from the mountain, to stride continents in his desperation the same way that Zeus had in his flight from Olympus. Meret had the power to match him, but surely anyone in his position, even a god, would want to buy time.

But even now, even with his incandescent life force pouring from his side, it wasn't fear that wrinkled Setesh's snout. The desert god raised his right hand and crooked a finger. Behind him, sand rose from the floor of the balcony around Teshan's cage. Helpless, Sophia watched her niece's eyes go wide with fear as the sand melted into spikes of deadly glass.

Setesh glared at Meret with his teeth bared. **"This has gone on long enough. One more step and your daughter dies—"**

Meret didn't need to take a step. With a cry of rage and a single, fluid motion, she hurled her sword. The blade hissed through the air, leaving a smear of scarlet in its wake like the streak of paint across the world.

Before Setesh could move aside, before his miracle could do more than twitch toward Teshan, the crackling, crimson-sheathed blade plunged through his heart and erupted from his back in a spray of ichor.

CHAPTER THIRTY-NINE

Meret crossed the floor in a flash, closing her hand around the hilt of her sword before Setesh could free it from his chest. Energy roared out of the battery, arced across her body, and then blazed through her sword into the desert god. It tore at his flesh. It obliterated his defenses and burned away his miracles.

Setesh staggered, fingers fumbling at the blade. His mouth worked soundlessly, his eyes huge and staring. Power gathered around his hands, sputtered, and failed. The glass spikes floating around Teshan clattered to the ground.

A ripple spread outward from his body, an awful, shuddering tremor through the fabric of reality that left Sophia's head swimming. The churning vortex of the sandstorm cut out like a helicopter losing engine power. Grit and dust hung in the air for a moment and then plummeted toward the earth. All sound faded, as if existence held its breath for the death of a god.

Burning golden light burst from the wound in Setesh's chest, blazing past the sword. It flared outward, eating away at him. He threw back his head, howling, but the smothering silence devoured the sound before it reached Sophia's ears.

She cast about, scanning the top of the mountain, but Caelistra was nowhere in sight.

Shit.

Gritting her teeth, squinting through the blaze, Sophia snatched the badge from her belt and ran toward Setesh. Meret saw her coming, and Sophia braced for an attack she knew she couldn't avoid.

Instead, with a small smile on her lips, Meret released her sword and took a step back.

She wanted this. She needed the Furies there to contain the explosion, to save the city. That was why there hadn't been more resistance on their way into the mountain.

Sophia could see it in her eyes: everything was going exactly as she'd planned. Was Teshan's kidnapping part of the plan too? Gahiji's confession?

It didn't matter. She didn't have a choice.

She tore her eyes from Meret's smug expression. With the Fury badge extended before her, Sophia closed the last few steps toward Setesh.

He exploded just as she reached him.

The golden light shining from Setesh's core brightened for the tiniest fraction of a moment before bursting into a white so stark and violent that it devoured all color, all shadow. A great, roaring *sound*, its every other characteristic overwhelmed by the sheer volume, shattered the silence. It reverberated through Sophia's skin, her ribcage, her skull, until she was aware of nothing but the awful force of the explosion.

She was certain that she was dying. She was certain that she'd failed, and Setesh's death throes were laying waste to Memphis.

And then, slowly, her awareness of time returned. With it came bits of the world.

There was no longer even a hint of normal matter left in Setesh's form. All that remained was a burning nimbus of raw divine energy writhing in the vague shape of a person, impaled on Meret's sword. Through the blinding light, Sophia saw the huddled suggestion of Teshan's body, Meret's proud, victorious form, and a shape that might have been Caelistra swooping in for the kill.

Sophia fought to make out more detail, but she could barely focus through the pain. Power streamed from Setesh's silhouette and into her fist in shuddering, crackling tendrils. The flesh of her left palm burned like she was clutching a handful of molten lead.

And not all of the power was contained. Bits of divine energy arced away to shatter pillars or melt parts of the floor. The air around Setesh roiled as if the very atmosphere would ignite, melting flecks of dust into beads of glass and boiling the sweat from Sophia's face. Waves of force rippled outward from Setesh's core, one of them catching Meret and Caelistra and blasting them across the rooftop.

With each wave, the light radiating from the dying god became a fraction less blinding. Sophia saw Caelistra and Meret slide to a stop beneath the crumbling balcony where Teshan's cage rested. Caelistra righted herself instantly and attacked. Even without her sword, Meret held her off easily.

Teshan!

Sophia squinted, trying to find her niece through the veil of blinding white that lay across her vision. Her thundering heart eased a bit when she saw Teshan pressed against the back of the cage, alive and unhurt. More relief spread through her when she saw Gahiji limp into view and stop beside the cage to fiddle with the lock.

It was working. She was containing the explosion. Most of it, at least.

She longed to leave the badge and help Caelistra and Gahiji, but her muscles were locked in place as surely as if she'd gazed into Euryale's eyes. Pain clawed up her arm, and she could smell the flesh of her hand burning.

Was the badge going to be enough? It was untested technology. No god had been killed since Artemis slew Zeus, before the Conclave's founding. What if it couldn't hold the entirety of Setesh's being?

She stood, frozen, as Gahiji wrestled with the lock of Teshan's cage. Below, Caelistra fought just to stay alive, but she wasn't a match for Meret's power. Helpless, Sophia watched Meret lunge inside Caelistra's reach, smash an elbow into her face, and seize her left wing.

With an almost contemptuous ease, Meret ripped the wing from

Caelistra's back in a spray of blood. Caelistra threw back her head to scream, but all Sophia could hear was the roar of Setesh's death. Immediately, the wing's black feathers began to boil away into flecks of shadow.

Sophia tried to cry out, but her lungs were as frozen as the rest of her. All of her strength wasn't enough to set her limbs in motion. Her sword waited, useless, in her right hand. Tears streamed partway down her cheeks before evaporating in the loose shreds of Setesh's power. Caelistra staggered, maimed and bleeding.

Meret turned her back and walked toward Sophia.

With a low, thunderous rumble, the roar of the explosion cut out. The last of Setesh's power poured into Sophia's badge. The god's blazing silhouette faded until it was nothing more than an afterimage across her retinas, freeing Meret's sword to clatter onto the ground.

Sophia staggered back, suddenly able to move again. Fighting through the agony, she managed to unclench her fingers, and the badge tumbled to the floor, burning white hot and trailing sparks and smoke.

She felt as though she'd spent an eternity containing the explosion, but it couldn't have been more than a few moments. All around the mountain, the last of the sand that had been caught in the cyclone fell from the air to scatter across the slopes. The crimson glare of the sinking sun engulfed the summit, painting it with the same bloody shades it cast across the desert. The pyramids below and the shining city of Memphis beyond were all intact, for the moment.

Sophia fell to one knee, exhaustion leeching into her limbs. Meret was still striding toward her, pausing only to slide the toe of her shoe beneath the blade of her sword, kick it up, and snatch the hilt from the air. She barely gave Sophia a glance before turning and stalking back beneath the balcony to finish Caelistra.

Sophia forced herself to her feet. Gahiji had taken up one of the glass spikes Setesh had created and was using it to pry at the lock. Sophia silently urged him to hurry, to get Teshan free and as far from the battle as possible. Then she focused all her attention on Meret.

She still had a job to do. Memphis was intact, but she'd be damned if she let Meret rule the city she'd just saved. She met Caelistra's eyes over Meret's shoulder. Even missing one wing, Caelistra tightened her grip on her ax and nodded with grim determination.

Together, Sophia and Caelistra closed on Meret and attacked.

Meret shook her head. At the last instant, her sword rose to meet their blades.

It was like trying to fight a tornado. Time after time, Sophia's sword caught nothing but air. Meret forced her back with deadly counterattacks now and then, but most of the demigoddess's attention was fixed on Caelistra. Sophia was just a nuisance to keep at bay while she dealt with the greater threat.

Meret's sword moved like a bolt of crimson lightning. Straps on Caelistra's breastplate parted. Scrapes appeared in its adamant surface. Steel and miracle bit into her flesh, spraying blood. Caelistra fought with barely a hint of self-preservation, throwing herself at Meret to create openings.

And Sophia found one. Meret's weight was on her front foot, her sword extended toward Caelistra. The battery, clutched in her left hand, was as close as it had ever been.

Sophia lunged, swinging her sword with both hands.

Meret turned her head just in time. The tip of the blade just barely grazed Meret's wrist as she snatched the battery out of reach. Moving so fast she was a blur, she kicked Caelistra in the side, forcing her back, and then pivoted to swing her sword in a deadly arc. Sophia brought her weapon up on instinct alone.

The impact rang across the rooftop and blasted her to the ground. The sword was torn from her hand, clattering to the ground a few feet away. Caelistra attacked Meret with a howl before she could finish Sophia.

And at the edge of the ruined dance floor, Teshan, finally freed, hurried down the stairs from the balcony with one of Gahiji's arms wrapped protectively around her.

Sophia saw the moment Teshan turned and took in the fight, nearly all of which had been hidden from her by the balcony. She saw Teshan's eyes go wide as she found Sophia, bloodied and unarmed. She saw Teshan's mouth open in surprise as she saw a monstrous stranger hacking at her mother with an ax.

And then she saw the divine power kindle in Teshan's soul. Crimson flames ignited behind the girl's eyes. Power burned beneath her skin, and a scream of absolute wrath tore itself from her lungs.

She pulled herself free from Gahiji's grip like he was a child. She scooped up a jagged, razor-edged shard of glass, heedless of the blood that coursed down her palm.

Sophia shouted, panic driving all words from her mind, but Caelistra and Meret were both too focused on each other to hear.

Teshan approached unseen, unheard. Sophia scrambled to her feet, but she was too far away, too late. Burning with divine power of her own, Teshan plunged the miracle-sheathed spike through a rent in Caelistra's armor and deep into her back.

CHAPTER FORTY

Caelistra staggered, choking on her own blood. Teshan's enraged howl petered out into panting sobs as she fell back, the power in her eyes fading away. Sophia stumbled forward, numb with horror.

Meret stared at her daughter, the fight forgotten. "Teshan..."

Gahiji wrapped his arm around Teshan and pulled her away from Meret as the girl quivered and shrank in on herself.

Meret gave Gahiji a warning glare before turning a gentle smile toward her daughter, heedless of the blood that marred the expression. "It's okay. It's safe." She edged forward, moving past Caelistra's kneeling form like it was nothing. "I'm here to protect you."

The torrent of emotion flooding Teshan's features solidified into anger, and a hint of fire flared back to life in her eyes. "Protect me?" She pulled free of Gahiji's grip effortlessly and planted her hands on her hips. "You *lied* to me! You told me you were human!"

Step by cautious step, like she was approaching a wounded animal, Meret moved closer. Gahiji, looking frantic, kept trying to drag Teshan back, but Teshan barely moved, her glare fixed on her mother.

"I wanted you to be safe. I have enemies... *We* have enemies."

"Enemies? We..." Teshan looked down at her bloodstained hands, as if the truth of what she'd done had just caught up to her.

Sophia ached for her, but Meret would only be distracted for so long. As soon as she'd moved away, Sophia raced to Caelistra's side. She reached her partner just in time to catch her when she toppled over.

The glass spike extended all the way through Caelistra's chest to scrape against the inside of her breastplate. Blood bubbled around the edges of the wound, but it was the wisps of shadow leaking through that really worried Sophia.

"Caelistra, hold on. You're going to be okay."

"Doubt... it." Caelistra's voice was thick and ragged, and her eyelids were beginning to droop.

Sophia winced. They were well within the radius of the Memphis Deathgate. "Can you get back to the Tower?" Caelistra shook her head, baring a mouthful of jagged teeth as she grimaced against the pain. Sophia could see the strain on her face: even the slight effort of pulling herself back to the underworld might kill her.

Sophia hesitated. She could recall them both to Tartarus. A valkyrie might be able to get help in time.

And Meret would go free, taking Teshan with her, whether she wanted to go or not.

Caelistra's eyelids fluttered and then flew open. She reached up with a shaking hand and gripped Sophia's arm, her snake hair falling limp against her head.

"Make this count," Caelistra growled. "Be..." She drew in a slow, rattling breath. "Be a better Fury than I was."

Sophia felt like a glass spike had been driven into *her* heart. "Caelistra, I swear—"

Caelistra's head fell to the side, her muscles going slack. The darkness streaming from her eyes faded to nothing. She became lighter and lighter in Sophia's arms as her flesh boiled away into darkness. In moments, Sophia was holding nothing but bloodstained clothing and armor.

Caelistra was gone. Not dead, not departed for an afterlife, but *destroyed*.

A shout brought Sophia's head up. Numbly, she watched Gahiji back toward the stairs, still trying to shield Teshan with his body. "Meret, you've won. Setesh is dead. The city is yours."

Meret snarled at him. "Stop trying to placate me like I'm a danger to her, Gahiji! She's my *daughter*! Everything I've done has been to keep her safe!" Her control was slipping, but Teshan didn't seem to notice. All the fight had gone out of her, and she was staring at her mother with the same bewildered expression Ixtele had worn when she'd killed a person for the first time.

Sophia's fingers closed around the empty clothing she held in her hands. She had lost friends in combat twice before. Each time, a superior officer had given her a job. A purpose, to force the grief to the back until later. This time, without anyone else there to do it for her, she had to find that purpose herself.

She found it on Gahiji's face. He was looking at his lover, the mother of his child, and yet the only emotion she could see in his features was fear. Fear for himself. Fear for his daughter.

Slowly, Sophia straightened, fingers closing around the hilt of her sword as shock and loss gave way to clarity. Clarity, and a deep, consuming anger.

Make this count, Caelistra had said.

Sophia stalked toward Meret. She'd been going about this all wrong. The battery was Meret's strength, but it was also her weakness. Not just because it could be taken from her, but because she had to protect it at all costs. Sophia could use that. She crept forward, sword clutched in her hand.

"Teshan, your dad's not thinking straight. Come to me. I'll keep you safe." Meret drove her sword into the floor and extended her hand to her daughter. Teshan kept staring at her hands without looking up. "Teshan! Listen to me!"

Sophia was almost there. Just a little closer…

Gahiji drew Teshan back. "Don't you see that she deserves a better life than we had? How are we supposed to give that to her with the number of enemies we've made?"

"There are no enemies left that matter. Not anymore."

"I wanted to keep her safe. You wanted Setesh dead. You were so focused on your plans that we almost lost everything." He shook his head. "She's not going with you."

Meret snarled, and power rolled up her arm from the battery. She closed her hand around the grip of her sword. "Yes, Gahiji. She is."

Sophia's heart pounded against her ribs. Meret held the battery to one side, vulnerable, but Sophia wasn't close enough. She watched Meret pivot, setting her feet as she prepared to lunge.

Gods damn it!

"Meret!" she cried.

Sophia's shout brought Meret's head around. The battery jerked back, away from Sophia, but it was too late to worry about that. In the moment she'd bought by drawing Meret's attention, she planted herself between Teshan's parents.

"Run, Gahiji."

Sophia's eyes were fixed on Meret, but she could hear Gahiji's feet shuffle as he hesitated. "Sophia…"

"Go! Take Teshan and run!"

She heard Gahiji run, dragging Teshan with him.

And then Meret let out a cry of rage, ripping her blade from the floor, and Sophia didn't have time to think about anything else.

Through all her years of sword training with the police, in the handful of actual sword fights she'd been in, she had never felt the stark, crystalline clarity that she felt now. Even with grief and rage and guilt howling through her mind, it was as though she could predict every move Meret made. Even without the battery, Meret would have been stronger, faster, but Sophia knew how to put her off balance. One desperate move to protect the battery, and Sophia would have the advantage she needed.

"I trusted you!" Sophia snarled between blows. "I admired you! I thought you cared about the Boneyard and its people. And then you let Setesh *slaughter* them!"

Meret shook her head. She wasn't even sweating. "They died because I didn't have the power I needed. Because Setesh still stood in my way.

And because *you* announced my name to the city. *You* caused the massacre at the shelter, not me."

Each accusation echoed Sophia's own doubts. She snarled with rage, forcing the guilt from her mind. Her sword flashed and blurred as she leaned into the attack. She dodged one strike, then another, then another, scoring hits of her own in return. She saw surprise flash across Meret's face as she landed a single, shallow cut across Meret's left wrist.

And then Meret's sword caught Sophia's a foot above the hilt.

The miracled steel snapped. A sound like a roaring wildfire mingled with the shattering of metal. The blade clanged against the concrete. Meret pivoted and slashed low, and her sword sliced through the meat of Sophia's thigh, dropping her to one knee. Her cry of pain was cut short as Meret kicked her square in the chest, driving her to the ground.

She held the tip of her sword against Sophia's throat, drawing a tiny drop of blood.

Sophia froze. She'd lost.

Meret shook her head sadly. "You learned the wrong lesson from the Boneyard, Sophia. You spent so long trying to fix *everything* that you lost sight of everyone around you. Family is *all* that matters." Without moving her sword, she kicked the broken, useless hilt from Sophia's fingers.

"Your family is terrified of you," Sophia spat. "You're no better than your father."

Glaring, her jaw clenched tight, Meret lifted the sword. Sophia tensed to spring aside, but she had no illusions that it would be anything more than one final act of defiance. She prepared herself for oblivion.

"Wait!"

Meret froze.

Gahiiji stood a few feet away, his uninjured hand spread wide, his face pleading. Teshan crouched behind him, sheltered behind a pillar.

No! You were supposed to run! Sophia thought desperately, despair crashing through her. If she'd bought them time, everything would have been worth it. Now...

"Please, Meret," Gahiji begged. "You've won. You don't have to kill her."

Meret looked at him coldly. "We've been over this. Family first."

"She *is* my family."

A snarl twisted across Meret's face. "She abandoned you, and your father! She flits in and out of Teshan's life as though family is a part-time job! She treats you with nothing but scorn!"

"She's still my sister."

Every one of Sophia's instincts shouted at her to attack. Meret had turned so that she could keep an eye on both of them, but she was talking to Gahiji. It might be enough of an opening.

Wait for your moment, then commit yourself completely.

Caelistra's words held her back. Sophia had seen how fast Meret was. This wasn't her moment.

"Please," Gahiji begged. "Don't do this."

Meret looked down at Sophia, her eyes cold. "As always, I will do what you don't have the strength to."

She brought the blade down.

"No!"

Gahiji lunged. He caught Meret's arm just as Sophia rolled aside. Together, it was enough. A line of fire traced down Sophia's neck, but there was no blaze of agony, no enervating gush of blood.

Meret twisted with a snarl and backhanded Gahiji across the face. He tumbled backward, his hurriedly healed leg twisting under him, and he collapsed to the ground with a cry.

Something inside Sophia broke. She had given up on her brother a long, long time ago. Even before she knew the full truth about him, she'd condemned him as a thief. A man who'd seen two paths clearly ahead of him and chosen the wrong one, not out of ignorance or desperation, but out of sheer selfishness.

Yet here he was, defending her. Defending his sister, who had given up on him.

And in the split second while Meret's back was to her, Sophia saw her moment. She seized the hilt of her broken sword and threw herself to the side. She saw alarm spread through Meret's body with impossible speed, but Sophia's eyes were fixed on her target. The foot-long length of ruined metal that remained of the blade hissed through the air.

And severed Meret's hand at the wrist.

The battery, still swirling with power, tumbled free.

Sophia dropped the broken sword, stretched out her burned left hand, and caught the handle.

Meret's howl of rage and pain was lost in the immediate, buzzing awareness of the power held within Rashmi's invention. The energy battered at its bonds, fighting to break free. It *wanted* to explode across the mountaintop, it *wanted* to melt the landscape to glass. Not out of malice, but in the same way that a thrown object wanted to fall. Sophia knew immediately that the battery was only a quarter full, but there was still so much power, so much raw potential, that it was like having a tsunami in her hand.

She was still struggling to understand what she held when Meret turned and drove her sword through Sophia's chest.

The blade tore through her armor like it was made of paper. There was a moment of dull pressure and surprise.

Then, snarling, Meret sent a crackling crimson miracle down the length of the blade, and pain devoured Sophia's consciousness.

She could feel her skin burning. Her blood boiled from her veins. Her flesh dissolved, crumbling into dust and shadow. She had to be screaming, but agony stole away every other sensation. The divine power within her soul guttered like a dying candle.

Oblivion pressed in around her, and the pain began to fade. It felt comfortable. It felt right. She could go out fighting, and leave the fight behind. No more saving one person just to watch another die. No more seeing people succumb to death and corruption despite her best efforts. No more desperate clawing just to maintain the stalemate.

It would be so easy to just let go.

But Gahiji and Teshan were still in danger. The thought opened cracks in her complacency, and pain swept through them. *No no no!* But it was too late. She pictured Meret cutting down Gahiji, seizing Teshan and raising her to be a monster.

Another thought, somehow just as painful as the rest, floated to the surface: she'd promised Ixtele she would do her best to live through this.

Sophia tore through the smothering weight of death and emerged back into pain. Her body was dissolving, her divine power flickering in its last moments, but through it all, she could still feel an insistent buzz through her hand.

The battery.

Power placed inside would revert to its raw form, Ixtele had said. It could be channeled by any god, any godborn.

Any Fury.

Sophia reached out with the last, dissolute fragments of her consciousness. Even without any training with miracles, without any idea what she was doing, she found the battery not with her hand, but with her mind. The energy trapped within called to her, begged to be used.

She let it free.

Agony coursed through her with the first spark of energy, but she was a Fury, and Furies were unrelenting. Power crackled through her blood like lightning. It flooded into her core, filling it to bursting and then beyond, overflowing through her body.

At first, the power was raw, typeless. Useless. But as soon as it flowed through the spark of divinity burning at her core, it transformed. Acting on pure instinct, driven by something deep inside that she hadn't even been aware of, Sophia remade herself.

Shadows engulfed her, pressing against her skin like a lover's embrace, driving away pain and injury where they touched.

Meret's sword pushed free of her chest and clattered to the ground.

When the shadows fell away, Sophia was not a mutilated husk. She was also no longer a dark-skinned, black-haired human woman.

She was a Fury.

She could feel the night-feathered wings that spread from her back, the forked tongue and jagged teeth in her mouth, the vipers forming a hissing cloud around her head. Her hand, clasped around the battery's handle, was red as blood, each finger ending in a deadly claw. Her eyes wept trails of liquid shadow down her cheeks.

The first thing she saw was Meret, sword back in her hand, slashing at her with a cry of desperate rage.

Sophia moved, but the tip of the blade sliced down her chest. Her power flooded into the wound, smothering pain and knitting flesh.

The blood spraying through the air called to her.

Sophia held out her hand and *pulled*. Before it could boil away into nothing, her blood ribboned through the air and gathered in her hand, coalescing into a double-edged, crystalline sword.

Meret struck again. Primed with power, all it took was a twitch of Sophia's weapon, and Meret's attack was off target. A flick of the blade, and a deep gash opened on Meret's arm.

The shadows cast by the sinking sun called to her with the same familiar voice as the blood. She reached out with her mind, and darkness gathered around her, bending to her will. She sent spikes of darkness lashing at Meret's flanks whenever she attacked, sent snares twisting around her ankles whenever she moved.

She'd never had to balance with a pair of wings on her back before, but it was as simple and natural as if she'd been born with them. Her body, her sword, and the shadows were all one, moving in perfect, effortless harmony. Her blood *sang* with power, every drop she expended replaced from the battery.

This was what she'd always wanted. The power to change things. The power to make a real difference, no matter the strength or influence of the people who stood in her way.

Meret fought with cornered desperation, but without the battery, she was just a one-handed demigoddess. Sophia forced her back, past Gahiji's scrambling form, past the column where Teshan crouched, to the very edge of the mountaintop. Setesh's last stand had torn away the guardrails, leaving a precipitous drop down a cliff face.

Meret lashed out, desperate to cut the battery from Sophia's hand.

Sophia sidestepped and struck in the same motion. The tip of her blade punched through Meret's palm and tore out the other side, carving through muscle and bone as it sliced down the length of her forearm. Meret let out a cry of pain, and her sword tumbled from her fingers and spun out into the air, dropping toward the sand below.

Sophia drew her blade free, and Meret fell to her knees with a ragged whimper. Sophia leveled the sword at her.

She yearned for Meret's blood. It was the only payment that could make up for her betrayal, for what she'd done to the city, what she'd been *about* to do. Wings unfurled, shadows swarming in the air around her, sword of blood in her hand, Sophia was the very picture of the Furies' inescapable justice.

But justice was blind, and Sophia was not. She could see Teshan crouching to the side, her eyes flitting from her aunt to her mother, her mouth moving with silent pleas.

When all you do is slog through the worst people have to offer, Ixtele had said, *it can be hard to see anything else.* Sophia had been wrong about Gahiji. She'd been wrong to think that people couldn't improve. Even when fighting to change the world, maybe the biggest difference lay in changing a single life.

"Surrender." Sophia's voice was harsh and grating, full of a Fury's terrible authority.

A harsh, coughing laugh racked Meret's body, blood leaking from the corner of her mouth as she tipped her head back to look at Sophia.

"It's a little late... for that."

Sophia's eyes narrowed. The wound she'd dealt was serious, but not fatal to a demigoddess, not with proper medical attention. She knew how much power she'd put into the blow.

But Meret's skin was ashen, her breath short. The gash in her arm was widening, tearing its way up her arm as though being cut by an invisible blade. In its wake, the torn flesh began to crumble into dust.

Meret wasn't healing. "I put everything I had into killing you.

Nothing left to fight the miracle spreading through my blood." A bitter, bleeding smile twisted across her face. "Unless you want to hand me the battery?"

When Sophia didn't respond, Meret sank back, her eyes losing focus. All the fight had leeched out of her.

Sophia let her sword drop to her side. "I respected you," she said softly. "Your compassion, your drive. I loved you like a sister."

Meret just shook her head. "Still blind as ever." She looked down at the decay spreading up her arm. "Maybe someday, you'll realize that you'll never win."

"Why—"

But Meret had turned away, her eyes struggling to focus as they searched for Teshan. She grimaced, teeth clenched against the pain, until her gaze settled on her daughter. Tears glistened in her eyes.

"Remember this, Teshan. Anything you cannot protect is not truly yours. Decide—" Meret coughed, choking, and spat a gob of blood to the side. She was trembling, as if it took all of her strength to hold herself upright. "Decide carefully who to love, and protect them with everything you have. Choose… more carefully than I did."

Meret collapsed.

Teshan ran forward, sobbing, and fell to her knees beside her mother. She looked up at Sophia, grief twisting her face. "Do something!"

There was nothing Sophia could do. Meret clutched Teshan's hand, her mouth working soundlessly. Then one long, last breath escaped her lips, and she fell slack in Teshan's arms.

Teshan threw back her head and wailed.

And then power flared in her eyes. She set Meret down and threw herself at Sophia, rage and divine power giving her strength. "You did this! You killed her! I *hate* you!"

Her fists pounded against Sophia's flesh like hammer blows, but she let them fall. She dismissed the miracle holding her sword together, letting the blade dissolve. When she tried to put an arm around Teshan, the girl shoved her away.

"Teshan, your mother—"

Teshan drowned her out with a howl and attacked her again.

Sophia barely noticed. Because in the distance, rising out of Memphis, were a handful of winged figures.

Director Tisiphone and her reinforcements.

Sophia wrapped her arms around Teshan. She struggled, but Sophia was stronger. "You need to go," Sophia said.

Teshan tilted back her head to glare. "You want me to leave her? You—"

"I want you to *live*. Somewhere safe, away from all this. Gahiji?" He limped over to them, blood streaming from his cheek, his eyes red and swollen. "Gahiji, I need you to take her. Take the car, and get out of here. Meret has enemies in Memphis. Go somewhere else, anywhere else." She released Teshan and found the car keys among Caelistra's clothes.

Gahiji caught them with a pained, mirthless smile. "You're not going to arrest me?"

Earlier that day, before all of this, Sophia would have. But Gahiji deserved a chance to change, and Teshan had already lost one parent today.

"Not this time," Sophia said. "Go, before it's too late. Leave this life behind."

Gahiji looked at Meret's corpse and nodded.

Teshan stumbled back, her knees wobbling, tears coursing down her face, sobs racking her body. She looked down at her hands, power flaring erratically across her skin. She'd looked so mighty when her power had first erupted, but now, she looked like a sixteen-year-old girl again.

No. Seventeen, as of today. *Gods...*

Teshan closed her hands, but the energy still crackled between her fingers. "I don't even know what this is. I didn't even know she was... How am I going to learn to control it?"

"We'll find an answer," Gahiji said. "Together. But only if we leave

293

before the Furies come to arrest me."

Teshan gave Meret's corpse one last tearful look. Then she followed Gahiji.

"Goodbye, Whirlwind," Sophia said. "Goodbye, Gahiji. I'll make sure they don't follow you."

Teshan didn't look at her, but Gahiji glanced back one last time. "Goodbye, Soph."

They vanished around a wall, heading for what had once been the front of the nightclub. They could take the road down the mountain while Sophia handled the Furies.

The winged figures were closer, but they were still a few minutes out.

Sophia turned her back on Meret's body and walked to the jumble of gear that marked Caelistra's final moments.

She set the battery on the floor beside her and sat down cross-legged.

"I'm sorry," she said softly.

The only response was the rush of wind over the mountaintop, tugging at Caelistra's shirt.

A glint of metal caught Sophia's eye. Frowning, she pulled free a set of military ID tags. One of them bore Caelistra's name, military branch—Roman navy—and blood type. The other...

The other belonged to someone else. Someone named Priscus. Half of that tag was illegible, melted beyond recognition.

Sophia laughed softly. "Looks like I wasn't the only one who reconnected with her past."

She leaned back with a sigh, letting the wind stream through her feathers. When Tisiphone and the other Furies arrived, they found her still sitting there, Caelistra's tags draped over one knee, gazing out over the city they'd saved.

CHAPTER FORTY-ONE

Caelistra's funeral brought together more Furies than Sophia had ever seen in one place, but she barely registered any of their faces. She barely heard their murmured condolences, their promises of support, their congratulations for saving Memphis.

Be a better Fury than I was.

The Memorial Wall stood in central Babylon, forming a triangle with the Monument of the Great War and the statue of the Founders. It was impossible to walk through the front doors of the Conclave Assembly without passing it.

The Wall was a six-foot tall solid piece of black marble. Etched into its surface in stark white were hundreds of names. The newest name on the list, still freshly carved, was *Caelistra Livia Horatia.* Along the top was a simple inscription: "That we might never forget their sacrifice."

The woman ahead of Sophia moved, the line shuffling forward. The older Fury placed a single, well-worn playing card—the six of hammers—beneath Caelistra's name. The card joined a growing pile of tokens. The woman said some words that slipped out of Sophia's head as quickly as they'd entered.

And then it was her turn. She could feel everyone's eyes on her as she approached the wall.

Be a better Fury.

Caelistra had been forged by failure, cynicism, and loss, and she'd wanted better for Sophia. But despite everything that had happened in the ruins of the Sandstorm Club, a bitter seed of doubt remained in Sophia's heart.

Sophia had been convinced that joining the Furies had been a mistake, that they were no more able to make a difference than the police. She'd been ready to embrace an eternity in an afterlife. She'd been ready to give up.

In the end, out of sheer stubborn desperation, she'd convinced Caelistra to abandon her grim pessimism and risk everything for the chance of a better future, but that had been a choice of moments. The prospect of trying to live up to that ideal every hour, every day… That was infinitely more daunting.

She uncurled her fingers, revealing the two Roman Navy ID tags Caelistra had been wearing. The soft grinding of the metal chain seemed painfully loud in the still, silent air. She set the tags next to the playing card, straightened, and bowed her head.

"Caelistra didn't want to be a hero. She thought that heroism was for idiots who couldn't just keep their heads down and do their duty. But in the end, when it counted, she made the ultimate sacrifice to protect the Conclave and its people. The Furies are poorer for her absence."

The words felt insufficient, shallow before the presence of so many people who knew Caelistra as a person, and not just as a partner. But all Sophia saw as she faded back into the crowd were nods and somber agreement.

Sophia kept her pace slow, and not just out of respect for the solemnity of the occasion. Sudden movements made her feel dizzy, and every time she turned her head too quickly, she felt like she was going to pass out. The Furies' doctors said it was probably a side effect of absorbing more power than she should have been able to contain, but they didn't know for sure. No one had ever done what she'd done before.

She was halfway back to her spot when she saw Ixtele's face among the crowd. She headed that way, unable to keep a slight smile from her face. "You made it," Sophia whispered.

"Barely, considering how late my flight was. Makes me miss the Tempest Rail in Maya. Are you all right?"

Sophia shrugged. She'd never been sure how to answer that question, in situations like these. Ixtele put her hand on Sophia's shoulder for just a moment, and then they stood together as the last people in the line left trinkets and said a few words.

The Directors approached the wall last, looking for all the world like three normal, human women who'd lost a friend. Tisiphone was the one who spoke. "Caelistra would have scoffed at the idea of a bunch of her friends shedding tears on her behalf. She would have grumbled something snide and told everyone that there was still work to do, that our enemies don't take breaks just because one of our number has fallen. And she'd be right."

More than a few of the Furies in the crowd bore visible wounds, tangible reminders that the Celts were never that far away, and this wasn't the only funeral since Meret's defeat. The border was quiet now, but who knew how long it would stay that way?

"But in moments of relative calm, it is important that we grieve. That we remember those we have lost. Because we have no chance at an afterlife. When we die a second death, memories are all that remain of us." She bowed her head, and her sisters followed suit. "We remember you, Caelistra Livia Horatia. We remember your service. And we remember your sacrifice."

The crowd bowed their heads, and silence stretched over the plaza, broken only by the flapping of the two flags above the memorial. One, silver on black, bore the Furies' seal. The Conclave flag stood beside it, slightly higher: a circle of interlocked golden rings on a field of green and blue divided by a diagonal white stripe. The flags Caelistra had fought and died for.

The Directors looked up, and the moment ended. Murmurs spread through the crowd, and people began to disperse. Shadows bent across the plaza, swallowing Furies who needed to return to Hades on business, but many stayed, talking quietly to one another.

Sophia found herself lingering by the Monument Wall.

Until Ixtele moved around to her front. "I see refreshments. Come on."

"I don't need food," Sophia said dully.

"Wrong." Ixtele prodded her in the chest with a finger. "You don't need nutrients. There's a difference." A pair of Furies with somber expressions tried to approach Sophia, but Ixtele warded them off. "Sorry, coming through. Gotta get some food in her first. Come back later!"

Sophia was inexpressibly grateful. She wasn't sure she could manage to make grieving small talk with people she didn't know right now.

Ixtele took over one of the tables before anyone else could try to stand around it, nabbing some food along the way. It was mostly Roman fare, to honor Caelistra. Ixtele seemed particularly thrilled by the sweet buns, but she took some bread and olives, pear slices, and cheese as well.

"Eat," she commanded.

Sophia ate. She felt numb, a familiar sensation from losing friends in the past. But even more than that, she kept returning to Caelistra's final words. She felt an overwhelming need to plan something, to *do* something, but every time she tried to think something through, the cogs in her head got all jammed up.

Ixtele watched her eat. "I am sorry about Caelistra. But I'm really, really glad that you came back alive. Or, sort of alive. You know."

An almost involuntary chuckle escaped Sophia's lips, cutting through some of the haze. "I do know. It was…" The memory of Meret's sword protruding from her chest, of deadly miracles ripping her to pieces, made her shudder. If she'd still needed sleep, she was certain she would have had nightmares about that. "It was close," she finished.

"You stopped a god from exploding and destroying Memphis," Ixtele said.

"Yes."

There were so many implications to think through that she felt like she was drowning in them. The corrupting tendrils of Meret's influence would have to be rooted out of the city. Gahiji and Teshan would have gone somewhere safe, hopefully somewhere far away. She had no idea how to get in touch with them, but that was probably for the best. Styx, her father was alive. She couldn't exactly forgive Gahiji, offer him a second chance, without doing the same for their father. Should she go see him? She'd be breaking the rule against reconnecting again, and this time for purely personal reasons.

Ixtele cut through her thoughts. "You realize that you are an idiot."

Sophia blinked at her. "What?"

"You heard me. You had a Fury badge chock-full of a god's power, and you didn't even look at it? Study it? *Smuggle it back so I could take a look at it?* It's one of a kind, you know. The first time the badges have ever been used to contain a god's death. And now it's going to get locked in a Fury vault somewhere in Tartarus."

Sophia looked down at her left hand, where her superheated badge had burned itself into her palm. The Furies' seal stood out against her skin: three feathers around a broken sword, over a mirror image of the word "Unrelenting." According to the doctors, the stiffness would go away, but the scar itself would be with her forever.

"I think I have had enough of that particular badge for the moment." She touched the one at her belt. "Already got a replacement."

Ixtele tapped a finger against her lips, a sly smile sliding onto her face. "Sure, but that one's empty and boring. You could have at least brought me the battery. You realize that it's literally the most important thing in the realms right now? More than Odin's throne, my mother's bow, Amaterasu's mirror…"

"What was I supposed to do? Fight Director Tisiphone for it?"

"Yes!"

Sophia snorted. "Apparently there's going to be a series of international summits to decide what to do with it. And with the plans we recovered from Meret's safehouse," Sophia said. "You could probably attend. You're an expert, after all."

"Oh, that is happening without a doubt. I'm just mad I've got to jump through hoops to see it, when you could have just shown it to me. I'm sure no one would have minded."

Sophia chuckled, and Ixtele looked triumphant.

Her curiosity was back an instant later, and she cocked her head slightly. "What was it like, holding that kind of power?"

It felt like a glimpse of what it would be like to be a god.

"Sophia?" Ixtele asked. She sounded concerned.

Sophia shook her head slowly. She wouldn't have shared this with anyone else, but Ixtele's earnest curiosity made it easy to open up.

"It changed me. Permanently. I only had a recruit's investment before, right? Now I'm a full Fury, at least in terms of divine power. All without going through the training or receiving the full investment from a Director."

Ixtele's eyes practically shone with excitement. "You have *exactly* the standard amount of power? Not more? Not less?"

"That's what the doctors said. I'm less thrilled with the splitting headaches and the dizziness. Their best theory is that I 'forcibly burned new thaumaturgical pathways into my soul,' or something like that. But they're just guessing, because no one's ever used a working divine battery like that before."

"Fascinating," Ixtele breathed. "The affinities of your initial investment must have determined..." She blinked and cleared her throat. "I'm sorry about the side effects, though. They'll go away?"

"Hopefully."

"I'm sure they will. Mostly sure." Ixtele's gaze grew distant. "This is incredible! The implications for affinity theory, not to mention the fact that it actually expanded your capacity..."

Sophia chuckled and cut in before she could get carried away. "Let me guess. You want to study me, now?"

Ixtele raised an eyebrow slightly, and Sophia realized what that sounded like. "Well, now that you mention it..."

Someone cleared their throat behind Sophia. She turned and found Director Tisiphone standing with her hands folded behind her back.

Even with the gentle smile on her face, her eyes had a piercing intensity.

"Director."

"Sophia. I apologize for interrupting. May I have a moment of your time?"

"Of course. Ixtele—"

"Oh, don't worry about me. I'm going to find more food."

Tisiphone took Ixtele's place at the table.

"I left my report on your desk, Director," Sophia said. "Nothing in there the debriefing didn't cover."

Of course, there were things she hadn't mentioned in either. Like that "Meret's lieutenant," who turned on her and helped them reach Meret in time at the Sandstorm Club, was Sophia's brother. Or that he hadn't just "disappeared" during the fighting. As far as anyone had to know, Gahiji and Teshan had simply never been found.

"I look forward to going through it, but that's not what I wanted to talk about." Tisiphone sighed and folded her hands on the table. "I know Caelistra can't have been the easiest mentor. I read her reports."

Panic tried to wrap its claws around Sophia's heart. "What did she say?"

"She was harsh. Condemnatory, even. And then, on her last day… I don't know whether she ever said anything to you directly. I suspect not. But Caelistra's final report was different from the rest. You did something to change her mind. Before the two of you were assigned together, I believed that Caelistra needed a chance to mentor another recruit. And despite the way that things turned out, I think perhaps I was right. You made a powerful impression on her, and I hope she did the same for you. She believed that you had a bright future in the Furies, by the end. And so do I."

A bright future? Caelistra had scoffed at her for risking the mission to save individuals, but individuals mattered. Individuals were *all* that mattered. The Conclave itself was only worth protecting because of the people who made it up. People like Gahiji. People like Caelistra. People who could change.

Be a better Fury than I was.

"Thank you, Director," Sophia said aloud. "I will try my best to make her proud."

Tisiphone nodded. "Good. Now, how are the headaches? Getting any better?"

Sophia hesitated. "Not that I can tell," she admitted.

"Well, I'm doing my best to keep our doctors from climbing over one another to examine you, but remember that they're here to help."

"Of course. Weekly checkups, and a visit as soon as anything changes. I know the drill."

Tisiphone spotted Ixtele coming back toward the table with a heaping plate. She chuckled. "I will leave you alone, then. I'm afraid you have a good deal more training ahead of you before you receive your next assignment, but I suspect you will be so exhausted that the time will pass quickly. I imagine you'll be on the Islands for your final test before long. Do the Furies proud."

"Yes, Director."

Ixtele hurried back over as soon as she was gone.

As if nothing had interrupted, she held up a piece of cheese toward Sophia. "You have to try this." Sophia took it obligingly, and Ixtele gave her a thoughtful look. "You know, this is good and all, but you know where I found the best saganaki I've ever had?"

"I probably don't," Sophia said, wondering where this was going.

"This place in Athens. Two blocks from the university."

"Okay…"

Ixtele rolled her eyes. "Sophia Akerele, I'm asking you out on a date. This weekend, in Athens. What do you say?"

Something in Sophia's brain short-circuited. She felt her face grow hot, realized her mouth was hanging open. Even with everything else on her mind, how had she not seen this coming? How had she not thought of it herself? How did Ixtele always catch her off guard like this?

Ixtele's hopeful smile was starting to fade. *Shit! Say something!*

"This is just an opportunity to study me, isn't it?" Sophia said, finally recovering.

Ixtele's grin was blinding when it flared back to life. She took a step closer. "Well, I certainly wouldn't say no to an opportunity to… examine you in more detail." She smelled like a moonlit forest.

A sudden, desperate need struck Sophia, leaving her breathless. "Let's go now."

Ixtele stared at her. "To Athens?"

"I don't care. Anywhere but here. With all the training ahead of me, I doubt I'm going to have a lot of free time. Let's go somewhere now. Just the two of us."

She held out her hand, and Ixtele took it with a sly smile. "I've been to Babylon before, once or twice," Ixtele said. "I might know a fun place."

EPILOGUE

"You are dripping on the tile."

Euryale came to a limping stop. Slowly, she turned her face up so she could gaze at the man through her mirrored sunglasses.

He looked right back, unimpressed. "You can wait over there. Please do not sit in the chairs."

Euryale let out a hissing breath through her teeth. "He's expecting me."

The man—the mortal, *human* man—sniffed at her. "I am aware. You can wait."

Euryale glared at him. It would be simple to leap over the desk and pin him to the wall. He probably had a weapon on his person or in the desk somewhere, but he wouldn't have time to go for it. She imagined peeling the skin off his sneering lips. With his low, melodic voice, his screams would be exquisite.

Instead, she turned away, walked past the spotless chairs, and found a place to wait by the window.

Babylon was beautiful. From this high up, with the setting sun playing across the Hanging Gardens, the whole city was like a sculpture of burnished bronze. There were tiny cars down below, winged godborn flying about their business, and figures atop the ring of weather control towers, but if she squinted, it was almost possible to forget that it was a seething hive of vermin.

Making her wait was a sign of displeasure. She'd never had to wait before. But she had nothing to worry about. She had never failed before.

No one threw away a useful tool because of a single mistake.

The man behind her cleared his throat. "He will see you now."

Euryale turned her back on the city. She kept her gait slow and measured, as if she was in no hurry at all. Even with the blood dripping down her leg, she did her best to hide her limp. She wasn't about to show weakness to a mortal.

She was almost blinded the instant she opened the door. The sun *blazed* through the westward-facing windows, washing the grand office into vague suggestions of furniture and decoration.

A man stood beside the floor-to-ceiling windows, gazing out without any concern for the glare.

Euryale cleared her throat. "Meret is dead."

The burning light framed a tall figure, broad shouldered, with his hands clasped behind his back. When he spoke his voice was soft but commanding. "I am not concerned with Meret. She was an unwitting tool, nothing more."

"The Furies have the battery."

"Disappointing." There was no change in his inflection, but Euryale had to suppress a shiver.

"They'll probably file it in the Lethe Archive and forget about it, but—"

"No. It's too late for them to sweep this under the rug. The Conclave is convening conferences to discuss the future of the so-called 'Bhagvara Device.' The first will be held in Maya, as a gesture of international cooperation. And I intend to be ready for it."

The fear rooted in Euryale's chest loosened its coils just a bit. "Of course. You always have contingencies in place. If you tell me what's next—"

"Are you still committed to the cause, Euryale?" Even soft as it was, his voice cut through her rasping tones like a knife.

She didn't know his name. She didn't have even the slightest clue to his identity. But she didn't need either to know that there was only one safe answer to that question.

She bowed her head. "I am. More than ever." The memory of her defeat, at the hands of a single Fury and a *recruit*, was like a bone stuck in her throat. The Furies were everything that was wrong with the world, fighting to protect the vermin from change. If she had her way, they would be the first to die.

There was the slightest pause, just long enough for her to doubt whether he believed her. Then he said, "Good. First, I will provide you with an appropriately discreet healer. After that, I have a new task in mind."

Euryale perked up, the snakes that framed her face hissing eagerly. "Yes?"

"If we are to guide the future, there are strings that must be pulled before this conference in Maya."

Euryale chuckled softly. "Pulled? Or cut?"

"Both. You leave tomorrow morning. Another of my agents will accompany you."

Anger kindled inside her at the suggestion she couldn't handle her task alone, but she knew better than to let it show. "I understand."

"I can hear the wrath in your voice. The bloodlust." Euryale flinched. "I am aware of your past. I am aware of the *rage* that drives you. But this is not about personal vendettas. We destroy only what we must to set things right. The intact cogs of a broken clock cannot be blamed when it tells the wrong time."

EXTRAS AND ACKNOWLEDGMENTS

APPENDIX

Thaumaturgy 111A: Fundamentals of Thaumaturgy
Dr. Ixtele Tinaalto
The University of Attica, Athens

Lesson 1
(Transcript)

Good morning everyone! I'm Dr. Tinaalto, and this is Thaumaturgy 111A. I can see that a bunch of you aren't thrilled about being awake this early. But I've got good news! The university has generously provided coffee and breakfast right over there!

Okay, so that was a lie.

[Laughter.]

But at least I've got your attention. This course is going to cover the laws of thaumadynamics, with particular attention paid to the first and second. We will address the heredity of divine power, with as much precision as is technically possible (not very much). We'll give you the tools to mathematically describe what's happening during the working of a miracle. After that, we'll go into detail on the nature of affinities, which are my particular specialty. And finally, we'll briefly discuss some theories on the nature of the divine.

This was probably clear already, but just in case, I want to remind you that this is a class about theory. If you were hoping for something more applied, you probably want to be in Professor Nevrakis's Introductory Thaumatechnology Lab. If you're a godborn and want something more hands-on, you can take Basics of Miracle Working for a PE credit. But if you want to understand the mysteries of the universe, you're in the right place!

Today, we're going to be talking about the very basics of divine power. Not the Laws of Thaumadynamics themselves. Those are going to get put off until our next meeting, once you've had a chance to do some preliminary work, since they're extremely complicated. Sort of like Greek laws, except that when you mess with them, you might spontaneously explode. For today, we'll discuss the core characteristics of divine power as it presents in individuals, with some extra detail on the nature of affinities.

This should be easy, right? Divine power is an invisible, omnipresent energy that pervades this and every other realm of existence. Gods and godborn naturally gather it within themselves, and can use it to change the world in certain ways, which we call working miracles. There. Done! Any questions?

[Laughter.]

Okay, so it's actually a bit more complicated than that. Thaumaturgically speaking, there are three characteristics that distinguish divine powered individuals: capacity, affinities, and recovery rate. Which calls for the first demonstration of the day! Hopefully most of you can see this, but for the people in the back, I've got two buckets here. The blue one is pretty normal. The red one has a bunch of holes cut in it. The buckets represent different godborn. Now, with the help of my wonderful TAs…

When you look at a bucket, one of the first things you notice is its capacity. For gods and godborn, **capacity is power**. It determines how many miracles you can work, the maximum scale of those miracles, fuels your ability to recover from injuries… When we talk about one godborn being more powerful than another, we are almost always talking about capacity. In this case, if the stuff we put in the buckets represents divine power, then the volume of the buckets is the godborn's capacity. Of course, again, imperfect analogy—it's possible to expand one's capacity through training and practice, but not to a huge degree. Anyway…

[Water running.]

See? One blue bucket, full of water.

But you guys are clever university students. You know that the red bucket isn't going to hold water. It's just going to pour out the holes, right? That's not a difference in capacity, but rather in **affinity**. It won't hold water… but it will hold rocks.

[Rocks clattering.]

There. It's not a perfect analogy, but divine power basically works the same way. Affinity is just a fancy word for the types of matter or energy that a god or godborn can manipulate. Poseidon's not called the god of the sea because he has exclusive and universal control over the oceans, or because he's the source of all seawater, but rather because he has an *affinity* for seawater and can control it. Have you ever heard of Jupiter working a miracle with sunlight? Or Anubis using his power to foster life and fertility? You haven't, because they can't. Even for the gods, their inborn nature determines their affinities.

Finally, this faucet is going to fill up the blue bucket at a certain rate, right? That's the divine power's **recovery rate**. It varies a bit, but generally speaking, most gods and godborn return to full capacity over the course of two to three days. Faster if they're near things they've got an affinity for, which is actually a deeply complicated subject that requires a lot of math to explain.

Everyone with me so far on the basics? Capacity, affinities, recovery rate.

Excellent. That means we get to move on to demonstration number two, which is much more exciting, I promise. Argyro, would you do the honors?

Oh, whoops, I didn't do introductions earlier. This is Argyro, everyone, and that's Kleitos. They're going to be your TAs, and you'll be seeing a lot of them, no doubt, as you pester them with questions. But right now, it's time to see if Argyro's artistic talents have improved since last year.

[*Laughter.*]

Argyro's part river nymph. If we give her this bucket full of fresh water that we conveniently have on hand—thanks, Kleitos—she can manipulate it. She can, for example, sculpt it into a little dancing image of… Argyro, who is that?

[*Reply indistinct.*]

Really? Ares? Is that supposed to be a sword?

[*Laughter.*]

I should probably stop giving her crap about her sculpting skills, because they put mine to shame.

[*Laughter.*]

Now she's mocking me behind my back, isn't she? I thought so. Okay, that's our cue to move on. Let's try exactly the same demonstration, but without supplying the water. Kleitos, can you remove the bucket, please?

Great. Argyro, if you don't mind?

This time, she has to actually create the water out of her own divine power. And in case you don't trust the face she's making, believe me: it's taking a lot more effort. In fact, any moment now…

[*Water splashes.*]

Oops! And there it goes. No, it's okay. Argyro, sit down. You've done enough for now.

She's exhausted, right? What principle did we just demonstrate? Well, two principles, come to think of it. How about… You in the Spartan pitz jersey. Gutsy choice, wearing that around here.

[*Reply indistinct.*]

That's right. A miracle worker can impose their will on the world, but **the natural state of a substance always prevails**. We've all heard stories about Furies stopping bullets with nothing more than bits of shadow, but those shadows go back to being insubstantial as soon as the miracle is done. Argyro can make statues out of water, but the instant she stops putting power into the miracle, the water will go back to filling its container.

"But what about Ismene's famous water sculpture in Heraklion?" I can see some of you thinking. *That* is a question for a couple months from now, when we cover miracles worked into objects. For now, just remember that the substance makes a difference. Water wants to act like water, but a godborn who makes a wall of stone can expect it to stay intact.

What about the second principle we just saw?

[Reply indistinct.]

Exactly! Well, almost. The way your textbook puts it is that **creation is more taxing than manipulation**. It takes three to five times more divine power to create something from scratch than it does to work with matter or energy that's already there. That's why the 17th Amphibious Division had the advantage at the Battle of Ikaria—you should try to avoid fighting ocean spirits on the ocean. It's also why the weather manipulation towers you see around major cities try to just *nudge* the weather, rather than change it entirely, or why Hephaestus does his best work in volcanoes. Oh, we've got a question. Yes?

[Indistinct.]

Did everyone hear that? He asked whether godborn also *heal* faster near the elements they've got an affinity for. The simple answer is yes. The more complicated answer involves a great deal of math, and I don't want to spoil the punchline of Professor Licinius's class on miraculous healing. So, in the hopes of encouraging you all to stay in the department, I'll just leave you with a puzzle: the vast majority of godborn are flesh and blood, right? So why is it that they can all recover from wounds, even if they have power over fire, or water, or plants instead of flesh?

This next principle is harder to demonstrate than the first, but that doesn't mean you're not familiar with it: **affinities and capacity are correlated**.

You probably all realize this, even if you haven't thought about it specifically. There are gods with power over life itself, but the vast majority of godborn can only affect a single type of simple matter. Those most distantly related to the gods might have power over plants, or seawater, or sand. Those more closely related to the gods often have not just *more* power, but control over grander, more cosmic forces. A desert spirit has an affinity for sand. Hades has an affinity for *death*.

Which brings us to the next, closely related principle: **Gods are a different category of being**. To use a vastly simplified analogy from physics: there's a limit to the size of a star. In essence, if a star is too massive, the normal physical forces that keep matter from collapsing in on itself simply can't keep up. Cram enough mass together, and it collapses into an entirely new form of matter. That's how you get neutron stars or black holes.

Cram enough divine power together... and you get gods. According to our best theories, a god's divine power is fundamentally different from any godborn's because it has been compressed into a different type of thing. That's why there are gods of sunlight, and war, and fertility— grand, conceptual things—while we godborn handle base matter and simple energy.

And one of the reasons that gods are different is the last principle: **divine power is heritable, but unpredictably so**. When two gods have children, their child is a god as well. But in every other case, the only thing that is consistent is that the amount of divine power passed down *always* reduces as one gets further away from the divine ancestor.

[Indistinct question.]

Yes, exactly: the child's *capacity* will always be lower. Even if two demigods have countless children, they'll never produce a single child who gets both "god halves," as it were, and ends up as strong as a god. In fact, while their children will inherit varying amounts of power, none of them will ever be quite as powerful as either demigod parent.

So. Unless there are any more questions...

Today, we covered the most basic ideas underpinning the entire study of thaumaturgy, in a broad, conceptual way. We talked about the three characteristics of gods and godborn: capacity, affinity, and recovery rate. We discussed the challenge of creation over manipulation, the unusual nature of gods, and the heritability of divine power. Next time, we're going to introduce math, and dive into the Laws of Thaumadynamics.

But for now, I'll let you go. I for one didn't eat breakfast, and lunch is calling my name. Before next class, please read pages 5-26 in *Principles of Thaumaturgy*. Feel free to skip it, as long as you're okay with being called on and embarrassed in front of the class. See you all tomorrow!

GLOSSARY

A Note on Names: Naming many things, especially the cities and nations of this world, was a constant balancing act between authenticity and readability. Because of the specific paths our own history happened to take and the phonemes familiar to English speakers, the most accessible names for nearly every culture or location are not the names locals would use. (In technical terms, we have English exonyms that we use in place of the local endonym.) Worse still, some are colonial impositions, resulting from events that occurred in our world, but not Sophia's.

This means, to one degree or another, that there are authenticity problems with everything from "China" and "Japan" to "Maya" and "Aztec" to "Egypt" and "Greece." But as much as I would prefer to avoid those problems, doing so would come at a cost. Even readers relatively familiar with, say, ancient Egypt might be put off by a barrage of ancient Egyptian, and I didn't want you to be constantly dragged out of the story by unfamiliar words when "Egypt" and "Nile" are so accessible. Unfortunate, perhaps, but this may be an unavoidable consequence of the rich diversity of language. In any case, the truth is that everything you read here is a translation: if Isis herself told you tales of the pharaohs in Immortal, a native English speaker would hear "Egypt" and "Memphis" and "Nile."

Aaru: One of the most popular realms of the dead, with historical ties to Egypt. Also called the Field of Reeds. Ruled by Osiris.

Ab urbe condita: Literally, "from the founding of the city." A Roman dating system that counts years from the founding of Rome. Adopted by the Conclave upon its foundation to fill the need for a unified calendar system.

Adamant: An extremely rare lustrous grey metal of peerless strength and durability. Much of the greatest armor and weaponry in all the realms is made of adamant that has been painstakingly infused with miracles.

Alecto: One of the original Furies, and a Director of the modern-day agency.

Amaterasu: A Japanese goddess, with power over nature and the sun.

Amazonia: The most widely-used name for the large continent east of Asia and west of Europe and Africa. Named for the Amazons, the local people first encountered by travelers from other continents.

Amretis: Setesh's assistant.

Anhur: An Egyptian god, with power over warfare. Has a lion's head.

Apollo: A Greek god, with power over sunlight, music, and healing. Twin brother to Artemis.

Ares: A Greek god, with power over blood and warfare. Called the Mad God. He was seen as bloodthirsty and dangerous even before the Great War, when his actions lead to his international condemnation as a war criminal.

Artemis: A Greek goddess, with power over nature, the hunt, and the moon. Twin sister to Apollo. Famously killed their father, Zeus.

Asgard: A realm of existence, home to many of the Norse gods. Location of Valhalla, where a select number of dead souls reside.

Asklepios: An ancient Greek demigod, son of Apollo with renowned powers of healing. The Rod of Asklepios, depicted as a staff with a snake coiled around it, has become a nearly universal symbol of miraculous healers.

Asphodel Meadows, The: One of the three regions of Hades. Once the destination of "average" souls, now it is simply one of the many options of the afterlife, no more or less exclusive than Elysium.

Athena: Greek Goddess, with power over warfare and artifice.

Athens: The capital city of Greece.

Atlantis: Once a prosperous island city state, until a cataclysm—the cause of which is disputed—sunk the entire island beneath the ocean. Now the underwater capital city of the Merfolk Federation, a member-nation of the Conclave.

Aurichalcum: An extremely rare red and gold metal that deadens divine power in the area around it. Used to contain godborn criminals.

Aztec League: A non-Conclave nation. A literal theocracy, in which the gods personally rule. Condemned by its neighbors and much of the international community for wars of conquest and numerous natural rights abuses. Controls much of central Amazonia and is intent on expanding further, though its southward expansion has historically been checked by the Maya and its northward expansion is blocked by the North Amazonia Defense Alliance.

Babylon (city): The capital city of the nation of Babylon. Also the capital of the Conclave itself, and the seat of the Executive Council, the Assembly, and the High Court.

Babylon (nation): A member-nation of the Conclave.

Babylon Conclave: A secret meeting, held in 2662, of gods, government officials, and military officers from all sides of the Great War. They worked in secret—and usually behind the backs of their own governments and superiors—to end the conflict. Their efforts brought about the end of the war and laid the foundation for the Intercontinental Treaty Coalition. The attendees came to be known as the Founders, and the name of their secret meeting came to refer, metonymically, to the organization as a whole.

Bekenre Djemi: A drug dealer and a thief. Also an informant of Sophia's.

Boneyard, The: A neighborhood in Memphis, poor and underserved since the Great War. Constantly fought over by the Silver Court and the Dockyard Hounds, the two gangs that control neighboring parts of the city.

Caelistra Livia Horatia: A Fury. Former sailor in the Roman Navy.

Celtic Union: A non-Conclave nation, founded in 2527 following the unification of the Celtic clans in Sirideán's Wars. Condemned by its neighbors, including the Conclave, for wars of conquest and numerous natural rights abuses. Controls most of western Europe, and is intent on expanding further, though the Conclave has historically checked its eastward expansion.

Centaur: A type of godborn, common in Greece and surrounding regions. Human from the waist up and horse from the waist down.

Cerberus: A huge, three-headed dog belonging to Persephone and Hades, tasked with guarding the entrance to their realms. A very good boy.

Chimera: A creature with the body of a lion, a goat's head protruding from its back, and a tail ending in a snake's head.

Conclave: Technically, the Intercontinental Treaty Coalition. An alliance of numerous sovereign nations founded in 2663 on the premise that all people, from gods to mortals, should be subject to the same laws. Member nations retain significant autonomy but are subject to the executive authority of the ITC Executive Council and its President, the legislative authority of the ITC Assembly, and the High Court of the Coalition. As with the international body itself, these bodies are almost always referred to by their informal name—Conclave Assembly, for example—except in the most official circumstances.

Crucible Thaumatechnologies: A multinational thaumatechnology corporation, one of the largest in the Conclave. Headquartered in Memphis.

Cyclops: A type of godborn, common in Greece and the surrounding regions. Human shaped but somewhat larger, with a single large eye in place of the two a human would have. Often have an affinity for earth or metal, and many were legendary smiths.

Deathgate: One of many hidden passages between the Valkyries' Tower and Earth. Located primarily in major cities. Travel to Earth requires stepping through the actual gate. For most, the same is true for travel in the other direction, but for a Fury, returning to the Valkyries' Tower requires only proximity to a Deathgate and an act of will.

Degi: A Silver Courtier.

Demigod: A type of godborn. Most commonly the child of a god and a mortal, but the term can apply to the offspring of a god and a godborn as well. Though the word is often used in a gender-neutral fashion, it sometimes refers specifically to male demigods, as distinct from female demigoddesses.

Denarius: A Roman currency, originally minted as a silver coin, though replaced by fiat currency in 2648. Adopted in its modern, paper form by the Conclave upon its foundation to fill the need for a unified currency system.

Divine power: A type of energy naturally generated and utilized by gods and godborn.

Dockyard Hounds: A gang in Memphis, primarily human.

Dragon: Can refer to one of two types of creature. The European dragon is a family of huge, winged lizards with a variety of subspecies. Some breathe fire, and all are fiercely territorial and extremely dangerous. They are roughly as intelligent as a smart dog. Despite the similar name, the Asian dragon is about as closely related to the European dragon as it is to the marmot. Asian dragons are sinuous, wingless creatures with—in most cases—power over wind and water and vast intelligence. While European dragons are deadly predatory animals, Asian dragons are honored members of their communities.

Duat, The: A realm of the dead, with historical ties to Egypt. Mostly serves as a gateway or antechamber to Aaru. Ruled by Osiris.

Egypt: A member nation of the Conclave.

Eirik: A detective with the Memphis Police Department.

Èkó: The capital of the Yoruba Nation, a member-nation of the Conclave.

Elysium: One of the three regions of Hades. Once offered as a reward for the souls judged most virtuous, now it is simply one of many options for the afterlife, no more or less exclusive than the Asphodel Meadows.

Eris: A Greek goddess, with power over strife, illusion, and chaos. Blamed for starting the Trojan War with a carefully placed golden apple.

Euryale: A gorgon, sister to Stheno and Medusa. Due to a curse inflicted on the gorgons by Zeus, anyone who sees her face is turned to stone.

Furies: Originally, three vengeance goddesses tasked with punishing those who transgressed against the gods. Now, a Conclave agency directed by those same three and staffed by dead mortals imbued with a fragment of the Directors' divine power. Tasked with protecting the Conclave's people from rampaging monsters, dangerous thaumatechnology, and criminal gods and godborn. Headquartered in Tartarus.

Gahiji Akerele: Sophia's brother. Teshan's father. Meret's lover.

Giant: A type of godborn, common in Norden but originating in other realms of existence. More accurately called a jötunn (plural jötnar), as the vast majority are basically human-sized. Jötnar come in many varieties, with a number of different affinities, most commonly fire and frost.

God: One of a number of divine entities with greater individual power than any other category of being. Gods have divine power that enables them to work miracles within one or more specific domains. Though the word is often used in a gender-neutral fashion, it sometimes refers specifically to male gods, as distinct from female goddesses.

Godborn: An individual whose ancestry can be traced back to a god and a non-god. Godborn come in innumerable varieties, but all have some amount of divine power that enables them to work miracles within one or more specific domains.

Gorgon: Three sisters, originally minor godborn, who were cursed by Zeus after Medusa refused his advances. The curse causes any who look upon their faces to die horribly as they are turned to stone. According to historical accounts, the gorgons were ostracized by their community, and Medusa terrorized the local populace until she was killed by Perseus. Her sisters, Euryale and Stheno, are still alive.

Greece: A member-nation of the Conclave.

Great War, The: The largest conflict in Earth's history, drawing in nations from across the continents on multiple sides of the war. The direct, visible involvement of numerous gods, as well as the deployment of soulfire and other thaumatechnological weapons, caused social and political change on an unprecedented scale. Began in 2659 with the Battle of Cyprus and ended in 2662 with the Truce of Babylon. No one side as a clear victor.

Gryphon: A creature with the body, tail, and hind legs of a lion and the head, wings, and front legs of an (oversized) eagle.

Hades (god): A Greek god, with power over death. Along with his wife,

Persephone, rules the realm that shares his name. Called Orcus or Pluto by the Romans.

Hades (location): A realm of the dead, with historical ties to Greece and Rome. Divided into three major regions: Tartarus, Elysium, and the Asphodel Meadows. Ruled by Persephone and Hades.

Hathor: An Egyptian goddess, with power over the sky, fertility, and death.

Hekema Masahar: A suspect. A godborn with an affinity for ice and water.

Hel: A realm of the dead, with historical ties to Norden. Ruled by the goddess of the same name, a daughter of Loki.

Hephaestus: A Greek god, with power over fire and metal. A master smith and engineer, credited with many of the Olympians' greatest feats of craftsmanship. Called Vulcan by the Romans.

Heracles: A historical figure, famous for the Twelve Labors he performed as an act of repentance after killing his family.

Hetefer: A friend of Meret's in school.

Hydra: A huge snake with immense regenerative properties. Famously, each time a head is severed, two more grow in its place. Defeating a hydra was one of Heracles's Labors.

Idunn: A Norse goddess, with power over fertility and nature. Famous for tending an orchard in Asgard that produces golden apples with the power to restore health and youth.

Imhotep: An ancient Egyptian architect, physician, and polymath. Namesake of Sophia's cat.

Immortal: A language innately spoken by anyone with divine power. A speaker of Immortal can understand any language, spoken or written, and can be understood by anyone as if they were speaking the listener's native tongue.

India: A member nation of the Conclave. Located in south-central Asia.

Intercontinental Treaty Coalition: See "Conclave."

Irkalla: A realm of the dead, with historical ties to Babylon and the surrounding regions. Ruled by Ereshkigal.

Isis: An Egyptian goddess, with power over healing, fate, and the sky. Repaired her husband, Osiris, after he was dismembered by Setesh.

Ixtele Tinaalto: A professor of thaumaturgy at the University of Attica, Athens, specialized in affinity analysis. A demigoddess.

Juno: A Roman goddess, with power over life, fertility, and war. Once called Hera by the Greeks, though she abandoned that name as soon as Olympus was freed of Zeus's tyranny. Responsible for working with Jupiter to reunify Olympus after the power vacuum that followed Zeus's death. Eventually elected one of the leaders of the Olympians, alongside Jupiter.

Jupiter: A Roman god, with power over the sky, lightning, and storms. Once a minor Etruscan deity, joined the Olympians after Zeus's death and was eventually elected one of their leaders, alongside Juno.

Kehinde's: A Yoruba restaurant in Memphis.

Khufu's Pyramid: The largest and oldest of the pyramids at Giza.

Kofi Asena: A homicide detective with the Memphis Police Department. Sophia Akerele's partner. Part nymph.

Kumasi: The capital of the Akan Federation, a member-nation of the Conclave.

Kyoto: The capital of Japan, a member-nation of the Conclave.

Lakota Alliance: A member-nation of the Conclave. Located in eastern Amazonia.

Lethe: One of the major rivers in Hades. Drinking its water causes permanent memory loss, to a degree that depends upon the amount consumed. Every soul who comes to dwell in Hades is given the option of drinking from the Lethe.

Loki: A Norse god, with power over illusions and transformation. Famous trickster, often helping the other gods one day and hindering them the next.

Manticore: A creature with a lion's body, a human head, and a tail tipped with venomous barbs.

Mars: A Roman god, with power over warfare. Celebrated for his steadfast and honorable defense of the Roman people after his ascent to Olympus.

Maya: A non-Conclave nation. Stretches across much of southern Amazonia. Historically at odds with the neighboring Aztec League.

Mazu: A Chinese goddess, with power over the seas.

Megaera: One of the original Furies, and a Director of the modern-day agency.

Memphis: The capital city of Egypt, a member-nation of the Conclave.

Meret Tanu: Runs the Riverside Shelter in the Boneyard neighborhood of Memphis. Gahiji's lover. Named for the mortal woman who married the god of the Nile's cyclical floods in the days before even the first pharaohs.

Merfolk Federation: A member-nation of the Conclave. Its territory is almost exclusively located on the sea floor in the Atlantic.

Midgard: The Norse name for the realm of existence in which Earth resides.

Midgard Serpent, The: Also known as Jormungandr, literally "huge monster," the Midgard Serpent is a great beast that coils through all of Earth's oceans. One of Loki's monstrous sons.

Miracle: A specific instance of divine power usage. When a godborn conjures a ball of fire or a god hurls a thunderbolt, they are working a miracle.

Mumbai: The capital of India, a member-nation of the Conclave.

Nahuatl: The language of the Aztecs.

Neferat: A detective with the Memphis Police Department. Part troll.

Nile: The longest river in the world, running through Memphis, Egypt. Source of much of Egypt's wealth and food.

Norden: A member-nation of the Conclave, home to the Norse.

Nymph: A type of godborn common to Greece and the surrounding regions, usually wielding power over some minor aspect of nature.

Odin: A Norse god, with power over death, warfare, and healing.

Olympus: A realm of existence, home to the Greek gods, at first, and later to the Roman gods as well. Many of these, such as Poseidon and Neptune, are the same deities, simply given new names by the Romans. A few, such as Zeus and Jupiter, are wholly different people. The realm is also known as Mount Olympus, though it should not be confused with the mountain in Greece by the same name.

Osiris: An Egyptian god, with power over fertility and death. Lord of Aaru and the Duat, after his dismemberment by Setesh and his repair by Isis.

Oslo: The capital city of Norden, a member-nation of the Conclave.

Persephone: A Greek god, with power over fertility, life, nature, and, death. Along with her husband, Hades, rules the realm of the dead that shares his name. Called Proserpina by the Romans.

Pitz: A sport invented by the Maya, involving two teams, a rubber ball, and a long court. Now one of the most popular sports worldwide.

Poseidon: A Greek god, with power over the seas. Called Neptune by the Romans.

Ra: An Egyptian god, with power over the sun.

Rashmi Bhagvara: A thaumatechnician and inventor.

Riverside Shelter: A multipurpose shelter in the Boneyard, founded and managed by Meret Tanu.

Roman Republic: A member-nation of the Conclave, usually referred to simply as Rome. Despite controlling relatively little territory, Rome was one of the few nations to weather the Silver Panic of 2573. As a result of its outsized financial influence and status as the banking capital of the region, its money and calendar were adopted by the Conclave upon its founding. The use of Roman currency and the Roman calendar have continued despite Rome's fading influence in recent years.

Rome: Capital city of the nation of the Roman Republic.

Sabu Inheru: A detective with the Memphis Police Department.

Satyr: A type of godborn common in Greece and surrounding regions. Human from the waist up—apart from the horns—with the legs of (usually) a goat.

Serqet: An Egyptian goddess, with power over animals, venom, and healing. Strongly associated with scorpions.

Setesh: An Egyptian god, with power over chaos, storms, and the desert. Famously, attempted to kill his brother Osiris and seize leadership of the Egyptian pantheon more than two millennia ago. Now runs a nightclub outside Memphis and insists that he is a law-abiding citizen of the Conclave. Has the head of a sha, an extinct animal.

Silver Court: A gang in Memphis, primarily river spirits.

Sirideán's Wars: A series of conquests waged by the demigod Sirideán in the 2520s. He began by subjugating competing clans, unifying the Celts and forming the foundation for the modern Celtic Union. Before his death, he led his armies southeast and managed to seize most of western Europe. Much of that territory remains in Celtic hands to this day.

Sitre: A Dockyard Hound.

Sophia Akerele: A homicide detective with the Memphis Police Department.

Soulfire: A weapon of mass destruction created with thaumatechnology.

SPQR: Stands for *Senatus Populusque Romanus*. Literally, "The Roman Senate and People." An ancient slogan carried into modern times, it has served many purposes and political agendas over the years. It is now used to reflect loyalty and devotion to the pillars of Roman society: its expansive and diverse population and the legislative body chosen to represent that population.

Stheno: A gorgon, sister to Euryale and Medusa. Due to a curse inflicted on the gorgons by Zeus, anyone who sees her face is turned to stone. These days, a famous sculptor.

Stymphalian Birds: A species of creature with bronze beaks and sharp, metallic feathers that can be hurled as projectiles. A flock was famously slain by Heracles as his sixth labor.

Styx: One of the major rivers of Hades. Often used as a curse in the Conclave.

Tartarus: One of the three regions of Hades. Once a place of eternal torment, now—after Conclave reforms—a prison afterlife for criminals who die without serving out their sentence. It is also the place of imprisonment of the Titans and the location of Fury Headquarters.

Taxmal: The unit of measure for divine power, named after the Maya scientist whose pioneering work on the laws of thaumadynamics enabled modern thaumatechnology.

Teshan Akerele: Gahiji and Meret's daughter. Sophia's niece.

Thaumascanner: A device that can scan an item or area for divine power and identify its type(s). Recently, handheld versions have become available, but they are not as reliable or precise as larger versions.

Thaumatechnology: The modern term for the integration of thaumaturgy with technology. Abbreviated "thaumatech" in casual conversation. The creation of thaumatechnology involves working a miracle or miracles into a device or object. However, unlike thaumaturgy, which is available only to those born with divine power, a completed thaumatechnological device can usually be used by humans without any power of their own. One who studies or practices thaumatechnology is called a thaumatechnician (also abbreviated "thaumatech").

Thaumaturgy: The formal name for a god or godborn's use of divine power.

Thoth: An Egyptian god, with power over artifice and healing. Director of Research and Development at Crucible Thaumatechnologies.

Tisiphone: One of the original Furies, and a Director of the modern-day agency.

Titans: Ancient gods, nearly forgotten by history. Remembered mostly for their brutal tyranny over gods and mortals alike. Following a massive war known as the Titanomachy, they were overthrown by the Olympians and imprisoned in Tartarus for all time.

Valhalla: Odin's hall, the seat of his power in Asgard, where the slain warriors chosen by the valkyries fight each day and feast each night in preparation for the prophesied final battle. Because of this unique, highly focused purpose, it has strict requirements for entry, unlike most afterlife options.

Valkyrie: Literally, "chooser of the slain." Once, they were dead souls, exclusively women, responsible for choosing the strongest and bravest of the Norse who died in battle to join Odin in Valhalla. Now, no longer gender-restricted, they have been outsourced to serve the entire Conclave by guiding the dead to their chosen afterlives.

Valkyries' Tower, The: A great tower located in a liminal realm between life and death. Serves as the hub of the realms of the dead.

Waset: A city in Egypt. Called Thebes by the Greeks.

Xi'an: The capital city of China, a member-nation of the Conclave.

Yomi: A realm of the dead, historically associated with Japan. Ruled by Izanami.

Zeus: A Greek god, with power over the sky, lightning, and storms. Former king of the Olympians, now deceased.

Zeus's Grave: A large section of eastern Europe rendered uninhabitable by the thaumaturgical backlash unleashed by Zeus's death.

ACKNOWLEDGMENTS

Alone, I never would have made it this far.

It takes a well-coordinated team of skilled adventurers to slay a dragon, and without the heroic support of my own party, this book would probably never have seen the light of day. Certainly not a version approaching this one.

My incomparable wife, Meg, deserves more credit than words can convey. She has been an invaluable brainstorming partner, an incisive and clever problem-solver, and a merciless cutter of my characteristic verbosity. Even beyond such direct assistance, however, she has been an unceasing source of encouragement and support as I pursue this mad dream of a career. May our adventures never end.

Also deserving of special mention is A. A. Woods, who has puzzled out more tricky solutions and read more drafts than I had any right to expect. Our writing group has been a stalwart fortress against the onslaught of frustrations and flawed scenes that every writer faces, and I owe her a great deal for standing at my side on the battlements. Pay a visit to aawoodsbooks.com to see what she's up to.

I suspect that the third member of the writing group, Christine, is secretly a Fury or a robot, since I can't imagine she gets any sleep. Somehow, while working full-time as a doctor, she still manages to show up to offer insightful writing advice *and* to work on novels of her own. Christine, I am honored that you thought it was worth spending any of your extraordinarily precious time reading or talking about nonsense that I've made up.

My cover artist, Jeff Brown, helped bring this book to life with astounding skill and attention to detail. For crafting such an excellent cover and for putting up with my barrage of feedback and ignorant questions, thank you.

I am immensely grateful to the numerous beta readers who took time out of their busy lives to read drafts that were often far less a source of entertainment than a workout for the comment button or the red pen. Their feedback has been ridiculously helpful, from the very earliest stages to the final round of edits.

A huge thank you to Rob, Amelie, Peter, Greg, Isaac, Dan, Taimoor (who raced through the manuscript with speed that would astound Hermes), Debbie, Carolyn, Charlotte, Lara (whose skill at hunting typos would impress Artemis herself), Audra, and my parents (who probably never imagined that my reading books of mythology over breakfast before school would lead to something like this).

Friends, I salute you.

And finally, reader, you deserve my thanks as well. It is no exaggeration to say that you are the reason this book exists. If even one person comes to love this world and these characters as I do, it will all be worth it.

The future holds more exciting projects, ranging from the continuation of Sophia's story to completely unrelated books. If you want to stay up to date, you can visit fowlerbrown.com and sign up for my newsletter.